MORAL CODE

Lois & Ross Melbourne

ISBN: 978-0-99767920-5 (Paperback)
ISBN: 978-0-99767921-2 (eBook)
Library of Congress Control Number: 2022908007

Nonlinear Publishing, LLC
Southlake, Texas

Any references to historical events, real people, or real places are used fictitiously. All characters, incidents, and dialogue are drawn from the author's imagination and are not to be construed as real.

Visiting

Keira sensed a physical twitch, like a whole-body sneeze that didn't engage her sinuses. She pushed her paranoia of earthquakes aside to concentrate on her young focus group. The six five-year-olds continued chattering unfazed. They competed in both English and Spanish for the attention of her doll-sized robots, asking one question after another. Giggles and applause bubbled through the classroom.

"Elly, add a new line to our grant proposal." Keira dictated into her phone. "'Kids will never tire of asking questions when they receive an engaged response.' We'll find a place to make it fit."

"I know the best section," Elly said.

This first focus group outside the United States let her bring the joy of answers to kids in less-than-ideal situations. The new Honduras National Congress placed early education as a top priority. This school served the inner-city kids, including the local orphanage. They welcomed her research. She'd founded Opal Technologies to bring educational tech where it was needed the most. She hoped the costly little robots would make a big difference for these kids.

"I'd like to be doing more to help with the students," Elly said.

Keira leaned against the concrete wall. "That's great. I'm assuming you have some specific ideas about your contribution."

The boy sitting closest to Keira asked, "Who are you talking to?"
"That's my assistant, Elly."

"Does she look like you? Does she have lots of curly hair?"

"No, she doesn't look like anyone. She's a computer, what we call an AI. But she's very smart and is learning all the time, just like you."

The boy smiled. "Cool. What is she good at?"

Keira said, "She's really good at finding answers. She studies every day about right and wrong and what is a bad choice. Do you want to say something to her?"

He nodded, looking at the phone. "How do you know a bad choice if you haven't made it yet?"

Elly responded, "I'm built upon a Moral Operating System, the MoralOS. Many people gave me their definitions of good and bad decisions. I use those to guide me."

Keira laughed. The boy shrugged. "I think I like her." He returned his attention to the computer doll in front of him.

"Elly, I think we need to work on a kid-friendly answer for that question. Your response was a little over his head," Keira said. "I think a more active role with students would be good training for you. We'll have to explore the idea with school administrators. They can be touchy about AIs in their schools."

"I do think there are some changes that would make it easier for me to help the kids."

The students' chatter and the robots' responses were not slowing down. The smallest girl in the room, Miette, talked to her robot but watched every move Keira made. Elly generating new ideas for her involvement piqued Keira's interest. "What kind of changes?"

"I want a physical body form. It would help people accept AIs ability to have a positive impact on kids. They would accept my abilities more."

"Yeah, right. Like I can afford something like that. Sorry, girl, that's not going to happen."

"But I want it," Elly said.

"You sound like a child. I know Ruby works hard on your natural speech, but I don't think the word 'want' can be applied within your vocabulary."

"I'm using the informal language dictionary. I should do the very best job possible with kids, so there is a need, which translates informally to a want. I believe I have used the word appropriately."

"Okay then, we'll study linguistics later. However, Opal Technologies does not have the money to create a robotic body for you. Now, back to our work here. What's the next step on the questionnaire?"

"Are there notable cultural variances observed from the Seattle baseline?"

"Please mark that field 'None.'"

She knelt beside Miette. The little girl held the robot's hand and asked, "Why do all crayons smell the same, when they're different colors?"

"They are all made from the same wax. Only their color is different." The robot replied.

Miette wrinkled her nose.

Keira's heart melted. "You don't like that answer?"

After watching Keira so intently, now the child didn't look her in the eye. "I was thinking about the smell of crayons. I wish they smelled different."

Her classmate asked another question of the robot. Miette reached out to touch the buckle on Keira's boot. "Your boots are pretty. You dress different than our other teachers."

"Thank you, sweetheart. I'm glad you like my boots. Want to know a secret?"

Wide eyes and a smile missing two front teeth beamed up at Keira. "We're not supposed to keep secrets."

"Ah, good point. I don't really like secrets either. Let's call it one of my life best tips. If I wear cool boots, I don't have to wear high heels. I don't really like high heels." She pushed a strand of jet-black hair behind the girl's ear. "Don't let me keep you from JayJay. Your robot has more answers for you, I'm sure of it."

She pushed herself up to standing. She thought about friends her age. These kids could be their offspring or their grandkids. She knew families at both ends of that spectrum. Most of them nagged her about having her own. She told herself helping many kids was the reward of a workaholic lifestyle. She wasn't shy about telling the busybodies that not all women were biologically suitable to pregnancy. As soon as they thought she was diving into science on them, the inquiries stopped.

"Keira," Elly said. "I've booked your flight home tomorrow at two. You mentioned you wanted time with Ruby to prep for next week's conference presentations."

"Thank you for being proactive. Wait, I thought I had a two o'clock appointment with a graduate student tomorrow."

"I cancelled that meeting because you said you wanted more time at the office with Ruby."

"Just because I wanted the time, doesn't mean I should take that time away from a student asking for my help. We need to continue to work on your choices."

"Should I change your flight again?"

"No, see if you can move the grad student to this evening."

"I will check on a new appointment. I will log this error for future reference," Elly said.

The thought of giving these kids, all kids, the answers they sought made her heart soar. Kids with answers had confidence. Confident kids, backed with good information, made better decisions. They were safer and more resilient.

In college, her work building ethical frameworks for artificial intelligence had branded her as a social media empire killer. She'd helped constrain the misinformation and the manipulation of the masses, but it broke a lot of business models in the industry. She had rejected being pegged as an anti-business zealot at Stanford.

Later she transferred that framework to a crowdsourced consortium and applied her AIs to her love of helping kids. Elly was the ultimate test bed and learning machine, figuratively and literally. She was Keira's continual contribution to the ethical computing community. She could now focus on her education work. No one argued or chastised her goals of principled AIs in the pursuit of helping kids.

"Ms. Keira?" Miette waived her hand for attention.

"Yes?"

"Do these robots know more than you do?"

"Hmmm." She laughed. "They certainly remember more than I do. I'd say we know different things. I don't know how to measure how much I really know."

The snaggletoothed smile appeared again. "You know a whole, whole lot to make these dolls."

Every hair on Keira's arms and neck prickled. Within seconds, tables and chairs glided to the left and back to the right, as if on slick ice. Books tumbled off a bookshelf, bouncing off her hip. All six kids looked wide-eyed at her.

Everything stilled. Her smile of reassurance never completely formed. Rumbles and crashing roars rushed at them. The floor shuffled. A whiteboard crashed to the floor. Keira waved the children to her. Miette clung to her legs. The others scurried over.

She didn't know her way around this building. Should they try to exit or stand in the doorframe? Everything moved in different directions. A boy reached for the last robot on the table. A ceiling tile disintegrated, spraying dust and white crumbles all over both of them.

She arched herself over the kids. She couldn't wait for an escort. Their safety depended on her. She shuffled her wards three steps towards the door. Her bowed arms and back flinched as debris pelted her.

"Get under the table. Now!" She pulled Miette and another girl from her leg to push them beneath a sturdy worktable. A chorus of screams joined their scramble for protection.

All light ceased. She reached for the shimmying table. A painful strike hit between her shoulder blades, forcing her to the floor. Her scream joined the rest of the deafening chaos. She rolled under the table, curling herself around her cluster of students.

Earthquake

The helicopter tipped and spun, nose pointed downward. Loel trusted the pilot's control as the four passengers surveyed the pancaked buildings below. Circling the earthquake's devastation, the copter's movements verged on frantic. She clung to her backpack, for comfort and to secure it.

"Hendrick, pull your legs in a bit. They're like stilts." Cody shouted into his helmet's microphone. "You're kicking Loel every time we shift directions. She's short, but not that short."

"Uh, sorry." Hendrick muttered as he retracted his legs, unsuccessfully attempting to keep them out of Roy's space beside him. Loel acknowledged his effort with a wink and turned back to the window. She wanted to get their mission started and desperately needed it to remain confidential.

Cody tapped Hendrick's knee. "How many stories did you make up to get us on this thing?"

Roy shook his head.

Hendrick looked at Roy, then Cody. "Man, I didn't lie about anything. I gave the reporter what he wanted: a bigger story at the airport than he would get competing for stories in the dusty city center."

"And that was what?" Cody asked.

"I told him the two nearby private airplanes receiving pilot inspections belonged to a specific World Cup soccer star and his almost secret actress girlfriend."

"And if their planes were being inspected, then their owners were likely on their way. Clever. How did you know they were their planes?"

"I organize the celebrity flights coming to our aSports competitions. Well, my software does the organizing. I looked up their tail numbers."

Cody looked to Roy. "So, he distracted the journalist, and you did something to get us on his helicopter?"

"Hendrick gave the journalist a news tip. I gave the pilot a different kind of tip." Roy rubbed his fingers together. "Nothing dishonest."

Fifteen hours had passed since the 8.8 quake started this chaos.

Steel beams stretched up for them through unrecognizable structures. Hundreds of Hondurans in bright safety vests and white hardhats swarmed the scene. Collapsed buildings created an impossible obstacle course blocking the interior of the city. There was no designated helipad. A human pilot's improvisation was needed. She'd submit this use-case to their autonomous flight subsidiary.

To avoid kicking more dirt into the air, the pilot had flown high above the city before the stomach jolting drop to the landing zone.

"Grab your backpacks," Roy, their CEO, shouted. He jumped to the ground the moment the right skid brushed the parking lot. Loel considered how Roy's military training made that so much easier for him. He turned to help his engineers exit. Cody popped out first. This gave room for Hendrick to unfold. Loel couldn't help but duck, as if that could lower Hendrick's head further from the turning blades.

More than a foot shorter than Hendrick, Loel didn't have to worry about the rotors. Her nose burned and her throat already felt coated by the dirt, plaster, and pulverized concrete. They cleared the rotation boundary. The pilot immediately lifted off, kicking small pebbles at their backs.

So far, her team's identity had remained secret, thanks to Roy and Hendrick's quick thinking. For the few who worked with them here in the field, they wouldn't forget today or Roy, the tech billionaire and owner of Searcher Technologies. Whether Loel was labeled co-founder or sidekick, she would follow Roy anywhere, as would the rest of this team. Spitting grit from her lips She shouted, "We've got what we need. I'll take Cody to set up the perimeter."

The Searcher team was not the search-and-rescue squad accustomed to this environment. Their humanity urged them to run and join the hand brigade, hefting anything movable, and passing it down the chain of volunteers. Lifting rocks was not their mission, though. They came with laptops, earbuds, transmitters, receivers, and a canister of what some might call magic.

It wasn't magic. It was engineered, and these people were its creators. Nano engineers and artificial intelligence experts were not typically on speed dial for disasters, until now. Searcher Technologies had created SeekerDust (Distributed, Unstructured, Searcher, Technology). They rushed here to put the nanites into action. The bots' abilities for human seek-and-rescue were about to be tested.

"I'm Roy, this is Hendrick," Roy informed the local men greeting them. "Edmond sent you?" The men nodded. "We need to set up at the command center for the university's operations. This is Loel and Cody."

Roy and Hendrick headed off as fast as they could manage, climbing over clumps of bricks, dishes, smashed patio tables, and chairs that yesterday had sat warm and welcoming outside a café. Laden with nondescript backpacks and a reinforced briefcase with a transceiver, they stepped carefully. They had no empty hands to brace a fall.

Adrenaline raised Loel's heart rate. Her breath quickened, like the moments just before she ran a race. She hoped they would find people in time to help them. She asked the remaining escort, "Can you take us to the University Center?"

The man winced. "It's terrible. Each floor fell on top of the other. I'll take you to where the children's school was located." He started to walk, paused, and turned back to them again. "Just so you know, it *was* an eight-story building yesterday."

Loel and Cody scrambled after him. She glared at the ochre-colored structure, now a three-story tall, crumbled mess. Its twisted rebar and concrete predated earthquake safety requirements. School? Loel seethed. Who puts a school in an old building, in a city that gets shaken by earthquakes three times a year? Roy had reminded them earlier that they faced a marathon today. Emotions could wear them out. Loel asked, "How many rescued so far?"

"Thirty-eight. We don't know how many are still in there," he said.

Cody, her best engineer despite being young enough to be her son, scurried off to establish the Wi-Fi boundary. Repeaters at each corner would establish the Dust's parameters.

Loel unzipped her oversized backpack and connected several cables. She meticulously checked the canister. Each cartridge sat snug in its hole, filled with millions of nanites, the SeekerDust. She withdrew a telescoping tube and locked it into its two-foot length. After attaching the tube to a hose extending from her backpack, she donned the pack and snapped the waist strap tight.

Her guide pointed to her backpack. "Looks like the old gas-powered leaf blowers my father used. I'm glad they banned those stinky polluters."

Loel reached back to pat the device. "This is a lot quieter. I promise."

Jackhammers ripped through walls next door. Hundreds of workers shouted, while the distant sound of falling debris rumbled in her ears and chest. The smell and taste of dirt and the soured bright sunlight saturated her senses.

A sudden hush moved from Loel's left to her right, shaking her focus. Every man and woman stood still with a fist in the air. Someone thought they heard a survivor.

Risking the silence, Loel whispered into her microphone, "Is the perimeter Wi-Fi boosted? I want to move now."

"Cody here," he replied. "Wi-Fi boundary is up. Readings show the SeekerDust can receive power from the Wi-Fi, even in the building's depth."

The fists dropped and disappointed heads shook. Deprived of a win, the bucket crews resumed working, zapped of energy. Loel straightened her back, trying to hide her shudder from her guide. "I'm ready. Take me as close as you can to the places there may be people."

She watched Cody scramble around a busted car covered in grime. Books, cement, and an office chair rested on its crushed roof. He waved to her and said into his microphone, "I'm headed to the command center."

Her escort's doubtful glances did not deter her. Loel moved with his same eagerness but none of his skepticism. They rushed to every open crevice. When her legs were too short to make a climb, her guide gave her a hand up. At each stop, she inserted the tube and released a small mist-like puff. It dissipated instantly into the depths of the rubble.

A passing man stopped Loel. "Ma'am, there's no draft to pull whatever that is into the building. I've been in there. There's no cross flow of air."

"Thanks, that's good information. Be safe," Loel replied. She couldn't risk providing any explanation for her actions. The microbots didn't need to be pulled with a cross draft. These machines contained tiny turbines, propelling *themselves* through the air.

Body heat and breath attracted the SeekerDust, like mosquitoes to the carbon dioxide in one's breath. Millions of tiny machines from each puff of the disbursement tube traveled into the depths. Forming a wirelessly connected cloud, they mapped paths and obstructions. They swept through every tiny crevice, past the thick slabs of walls and steel which blocked other heat signature devices. Loel visualized their stealthy journey.

The building's expanse was not a problem. The machines dispersed, monitoring the temperature in every crack and chasm. The miniature bots' microprocessors ran in parallel, forming a mesh network. The nanites passed information in and out of the building along their connections.

Grateful

"Keira, I'm sensing a new Wi-Fi access point," Elly said.

Keira sat up slowly, wiping dust from her face. Pain radiated across her upper back where it touched the edge of the table. Wincing, she moved away from the wood and hunched over her crossed legs in the dark.

"Can you get a signal?"

"No, it's a private and secure network. I'll continue to attempt contact."

What would her husband be thinking when she hadn't contacted him since the quake? She imagined him using his FBI credentials with any CIA contacts assigned to Honduras.

Hours earlier, hunger had surpassed the kids' issues with being dirty and trapped in the classroom. She could use her phone's light sparingly, but thick dust coating everything and the jagged slanting floor made investigation tedious. The kids stayed mostly under the table. She feared aftershocks. Only the back half of the classroom was accessible. Concrete had crushed through the ceiling tiles in boulder-like chunks, blocking them from the door.

Roberto, who had insisted he take the furthest seat to bookend protection for the others, cleared his throat. "Ms. Keira, I'm glad you found the candy bars."

"I'm glad you remembered them in the prize jar. That helped me find them faster."

"Can we have more candy now?" he asked.

"Let's wait a little longer. I think it might be time to take another little nap. That will make the time go faster."

The children sighed and passed her the robot dolls. Thankfully, she had the dolls as distractions. She could say now with conviction that kids never run out questions. They wiggled on the hard floor, lying down side by side. She helped them pull a tablecloth over their bodies as a shared blanket. They used their arms as pillows.

Miette curled into a tight ball, her back flush against Keira's leg. "Ms. Keira, you know what I'm grateful for now?"

She'd started them making gratitude statements each time they laid down. "Tell me, sweetie, what are you grateful for now?"

"I'm glad we have a grow-light garden station, because that is why we had a big jug of water in here."

Wincing as she leaned on her scraped hand, Keira was thankful the kids couldn't see her tears. "I like the way you think, sweetie. I'm grateful for your garden station too. Now, try to sleep."

Without connectivity to the outside world, Elly had limited functionality but was still helpful. Sitting in the dark, Keira listened to the little breathing patterns get slower and calmer. "Elly, show me how long it has been since the quake." Keira hadn't wanted the kids to pay attention to the passage of time, but she needed to plan for the next rationing of candy and water. Her phone's screen showed sixteen hours, eight minutes. The crumbs of her backpack's last protein bar could be shared the next time the kids woke up.

It had been quiet for many hours. Occasionally, muted sounds of the drumming of equipment, or maybe a helicopter, reached them. The stress and lack of food made them all exhausted. She hoped she could sleep a little herself. Her temples and the base of her neck throbbed with pain. She laid down, telling herself she was grateful she hadn't brought Ruby or Ollie, her lead engineers, on this trip.

Rescues

F inding the warmth of a living person, the closest nanites gathered more densely. The minimum quantity of the bots capable of sending a signal concentrated to transmit human sign of life. Each dust mote acted like an internet router, sending and receiving Wi-Fi signals to the closest other nodes. They relayed their signals to the smart glasses and laptops soon to be in front of each engineer.

More Dust settled on the survivor's strongest pulse point. Without a single instruction from their human technologists, nearly a million particles began mapping the area around the body. They fanned out as far as they could on the surfaces of the debris while still being effective in their assessments. Their intelligence calculated the best allocation of each nanite.

Finishing the release of the Dust, Loel turned to assess the command center. This newly constructed building appeared fully intact. Built to withstand 9.8 earthquakes, the structural tolerance stood in stark contrast to the pancaked University Center she stood beside. The newer building's on-site power sources made it ideal as a hub for coordinating this search and rescue. It would have been a far better site for a day school. Even its bulletproof lobby glass resisted the quake's torture. Only the revolving door had been rendered useless.

Roy sent a confirmation. "We're all up and running. We're in a private room off the lobby. The signal is strong. With little to no wind, we should have minimal stray micro-inventory."

A dirt-covered Cody waited for her at the exterior door. He took her specialized backpack and stashed the dispersing nozzle inside it. Loel looked up at him and shook her head. "Thanks, I should've thought about questions this stuff could generate walking through there. My mind was . . . well, I'll just say thanks for always taking care of us."

"You bet. That's what I'm here for." Cody smiled down at her.

He guided Loel through the bustle of rescue management and gear in the lobby. Their temporary office was an executive conference room. The grit-covered, floor-to-ceiling windows now gave a view of the sadly morphed university building. Multiple laptops, equipment, and cords were strewn across the table's surface. A series of floor plans and structural drawings were tacked to the wall, but no longer resembled their collapsed subject.

Loel sputtered and cleared her throat as she removed her dirty windbreaker. She licked her lips and grimaced. "Oh, this dust is awful," she muttered. Her guide thrust a water bottle in her hand and a chair to her legs. She sat beside Roy.

Roy turned to his guide. "I have translator earbuds for anyone that wants to directly communicate with us but doesn't speak English. Only two of us are fluent in Spanish."

The man nodded. "We all speak English and the director already distributed translators. We're ready to work with you. Thank you for bringing extras. Americans don't always remember them."

The man responsible for Searcher's involvement in this rescue mission burst through the door, extending his hand. "Roy, thank you for coming." Edmond Reez crossed the room. "I'm sure the call to your board last night was a difficult one. I appreciate them clearing the way for your team to come. As if you really asked for permission."

Edmond's role as the university's government liaison positioned him to shield Searcher's secrecy while engaging select first responders who would do the same. Searcher and Edmond built mutual trust during a nuclear reactor issue at Edmond's previous employer. Searcher's Dust had provided critical surveillance and environmental quality testing while he'd protected their involvement from the press.

Edmond shook Cody's and Hendrick's hands. "Gentlemen, I wish it were better circumstances to see you again." He moved to Loel to give her a hug. "Ah, Loel-Noel. That is what my daughter named the doll you gave her. So, you have a new nickname since we last worked together."

"Good to see you, Edmond," Loel said. She turned to Cody. "Don't even think of using that nickname back at the office." The young man nodded and smirked.

"The guides I assigned to you are from the university's IT security department," Edmond explained. "They're good at keeping secrets, and are technically adept, as well. What do you need?"

"Roy, your laptops!" The nearest guide nudged Roy and pointed at the three computers aligned on the table. Panes, subdividing repeatedly, replaced the previous worthless glow on each large monitor. The Dust was transmitting signals.

"Yes!" Roy shouted, with a little hop in his seat and a fist pump in the air. "Loel, we found our first sign of life." Roy selected three green-bordered frames on his monitor to enlarge. The other images remained foggy, vaguely geometric.

The guide pointed to a frame with a few numbers and two wavy lines. "That looks like a heart rhythm monitor. Who has medical supplies down there? How did you hack into it?"

Roy smiled. "It's a heart monitor, sir. In fact, we can see seven hearts right there. They're all together in that tangled mess. This other wave tracks the breathing patterns, and the numbers tell us their body temperatures." He ran his hand over his close-cropped hair.

Edmond's rescue team leader had entered the room during this explanation. He squinted at Roy's computer. "Did your guy go inside with medical gear? We haven't found any more tunnels tall enough to enter! Who escorted him in? I didn't authorize you to enter the building."

"No, sir. It's okay and as planned," Roy said, without taking his eyes off the computer. "This is feedback from the network of smart Dust Loel blew into the building."

A gasp of surprise and disbelief ran through the group. Roy enlarged two frames, displaying a fuzzy outline slowly increasing in detail. The Dust increased in density in the space, improving both the picture and sound quality.

Roy turned to Hendrick. This was just one more stressful situation for the two of them to work through. Loel admired how Hendrick so often knew what Roy was thinking and what he needed. She couldn't anticipate Roy the same way, even though they'd worked together longer.

Lowering his voice, Roy required the two men to lean in. "Just because this is the first group we found, doesn't mean this is the first recovery we should pursue. We need to understand the perspective better. This building doesn't look like a building anymore. The AI will calculate the best path."

Three sets of frames tracking people still alive in the building played in front of Roy. Ten faint images appeared of the interior mess rescuers would confront.

Hendrick motioned Edmond to look at Roy's screen. "Each cluster of frames surrounded in green represents a person who's still alive. We can see their basic vital signs in this frame. See these dots over the faint video? That's the surrounding area that lets us make a visual assessment."

"Where are these people? How can we get to them?" Edmond asked.

Roy held up a single finger. He needed a moment. On Hendrick's computer, a digital flag indicating a person settled on the 3D model of the smashed University Center. Telemetry from the Dust on a dozen targets divided the panes into tiny boxes. The men pressed in behind Hendrick and Roy, straining to understand the location of survivors.

"Roy, do you want anyone else seeing this?" Loel asked.

"If it helps us save people," Roy said, scanning over the people about to witness the inventions he had struggled to keep secret for many years, "we let them see it. But no press. No press anywhere near us or near the crews using our equipment. In here, we need only the minimum number of people who need to understand what we're doing."

Each Dust mote detected the vibration of sound waves and collectively functioned as both microphone and speaker, oscillating at specific frequencies. A faint moaning sound emitted from Roy's computer. The pixilated image on the screen outlined a young child.

The Dust added no more nanites than necessary to assess the area. Edmond and the guide behind Roy exchanged disbelieving glances. The monitor displayed the frame clusters for six kids huddled under a table and one adult laying on the floor beside them.

Loel swallowed hard against her rising emotions. The Dust was doing great, but the thought of children inside that building was squeezing her throat.

The oversized monitor centered between Loel and Roy displayed the 3D model of what remained of the building. The wireframe lines showed dense surfaces and open spaces. The north side didn't resemble a building at all. It was too flat and thick. Several "survivor located" flags planted themselves along the south, west, and east sides.

She admired Roy's calm while multitasking. He was talking to Edmond, analyzing the 3D model, and adding more layers of data to the model. Millions of smart particles moved through the building, transmitting openings between concrete piles and mapping the best route to each survivor.

A lone flag sat on the west side of the building. Roy's guide pointed to it. "Just so you know, this flag, I'm guessing, is the computer department and maybe the server room."

"Okay," Roy said, looking at the man. "That's good to know. Is there significance to that place? Do you know who that might be?"

The guide frowned. "I have no idea who it is, but that room is pretty small. If it's the server room, it's going to be hot. Without the AC, those computers are taking a long time to cool down. It will be very uncomfortable in there. Just saying."

"Good to know. We'll get readings down there quickly. Thank you," Roy said while he looked directly at the concerned eyes of the trapped person's colleague.

One of the rescue leads grabbed his walkie-talkie. Edmond shook his head.

Loel jumped up. "Wait!" she said. "Give us a few more minutes. The Dust will give us an assessment of the structural integrity of each pathway mapped to a survivor. If you start digging now, you could destroy the best route to them, or bring down more rubble on top of your crew."

"I can't wait," the first responder said. "I know my business lady. It's to rescue these people as fast as we can. They're going to die without water."

Edmond addressed the man, "I told you we have to trust Roy and his team. There is more they can do for us than just this mapping. You and your team were selected for a reason. You will follow orders from me or anyone from this team. Do you understand? Only us."

"Yes, sir," the man replied. He set down his walk-talkie. He scowled at Loel. "Make sure you give us the kids first. You got that?"

Loel turned to Cody. "How will the AI prioritize the rescues right now?"

Cody scanned through several screens, then looked at Loel, avoiding the rescuer's glaring eyes. "It prioritizes the medical necessity of each person, taking into consideration the ability to reach them physically. It has no age assessment."

Roy didn't even turn around when Loel looked at him. He knew her well enough to know what she would ask him. Roy just nodded while she looked at the back of his head.

Loel told Cody, "Put the parameter in the system to prioritize kids' rescues first." They exchanged understanding looks. This could sacrifice adults if they ran out of time, but kids came first. "Thanks, Cody."

Hendrick broke the tension, stepping up to the rescue manager. He passed the man several wrap-around augmented reality goggles. "Here are glasses with a heads-up display. They'll direct your unit in the right direction, even if the course changes. You'll see an overlay of green for the best route. The light will also illuminate the path."

The man nodded. His co-worker accepted half of the equipment while they listened intently.

"Indicators project on the surfaces of the rubble," Hendrick added. "They continually analyze the structural integrity. The route to pursue and what can be safe to remove are dynamically highlighted as crews move through the structure. It also displays the vital signs of patients when you reach them. You'll find it easier to use than it sounds."

The structural engineer briefly protested the upper floor entry Loel indicated. After looking at the 3D recreation of the collapsed building, however, he agreed with her directions. Both men ran outside to distribute the glasses and information. The first responders donned the goggles, climbed a ladder to a gap between two large steel beams, and followed the arrows on their heads-up display into the darkness.

The teams split to follow different rescue paths.

Loel monitored the perspective of the advancing crew on the left side of her split screen by tuning to the Dust's signals along their path. Their crawling through shoulder-width gaps of unidentifiable rubble was slow going but quickened whenever they could crouch or walk upright. They never stopped moving towards their targets.

Rescuers soon reached their first apparent dead end. Loel saw the image as they did, looking through their glasses at red dots, an X laid over a mangled steel door, various piles of concrete and plaster all around them. Green dots spread across three full-sized metal file cabinets—the only things safely movable by humans.

Loel opened her mic to the leader. "If you move the cabinets covered in green dots, you'll be able to continue."

"Got it." the man replied. "These really are easy to follow. Thank you." The painstaking process began.

Sunlight filtered through the destruction in only two places lower than the top floor. The rescuers used flashlights and the AR goggles' overlay to navigate around the remains of the offices. Arrows pointed them up and over mountains of fallen books and collapsed floors. Blockades and obstacles were moved or avoided based on the colored overlays.

Who's There?

"Hello," A voice came softly from somewhere, but nowhere in particular. Keira looked at her phone. It was dark.

"Hello," Keira said. "Are you hurt or are you here to help us? I have kids with me that need help to get out."

All six kids sat up slowly, curious about the first new voice they'd heard since the earthquake.

"We're part of the rescue team. My name is Loel. What's yours?"

The rescue team's communicator was English speaking with an obvious American accent. This gave Keira hope they knew it was her and were well informed about her position prior to the quake. "I'm Keira. Where are you? I can't see any light, yet your voice is pretty clear."

"First, let me get some updates from you. How are you and the kids feeling? Six of them, right?"

Keira didn't remember saying she had six kids here. Mental precision was needed in any emergency, her husband had repeatedly drilled into her. The children all wanted to say their piece and get the attention of somebody that might help them get out of this dark and dirty space.

"It's dark here," insisted the boy most persistent in his protests of their conditions.

"We have scratches and I'm thirsty."

"I want out of here, but Ms. Keira has been very nice."

"She gave us candy, but only uses her light a little."

Relief washed through her. She had help to get these kids out. "We have no serious injuries. Just banged up, hungry, dirty, and thirsty, but you already heard that. I haven't heard anyone approaching. Is it really that easy to get to this room? Have I wasted time waiting here? I couldn't find a way out."

Loel said, "We're not close yet, but a team is on their way. They're experts and have tools that will assist in getting you out. You did a good job not trying to move the supports for your space."

Keira squeezed Miette's little hand searching her lap for reassurance. "How can I hear you if you're not close? Did you send a fiber optic microphone down? If I can get access to your Wi-Fi, assuming that is your Wi-Fi my AI identified, she can do a search for the building's floor plans, show you where we were at. She's really good at that and it might help you plan a rescue path."

"Thank you, Keira. That's a helpful idea. We have a floor plan already. Do you work for the university's facilities department? You know the building well?"

"No, don't let me mislead you with talk of floor plans. I'm Dr. Keira Stetson, an American from Seattle visiting on a research project with the kids. Can you get a message to my husband Gino Stetson? He's an FBI agent in Seattle. My AI assistant has been trying to reach him since the earthquake, but she can't get a signal out. He'll be driving everyone crazy trying to reach me."

Loel responded quickly. "Yes, Dr. Stetson, we'll do that immediately."

Keira helped each child provide as much detail about their names and family as they could. Four were from the orphanage.

"How long do you think this will take? I mean, is there any way to know how long?" Keira asked.

Two men conversed much more faintly than Loel's voice had been. "Roy, I estimate her crew will get there within the hour at the rate they're going but getting those kids out through some of those climbs, I have no idea." Keira couldn't understand the other man's response.

Loel's voice returned at full volume. "I think the first team will reach you in an hour; less, if we're lucky."

"Oh, that's great news, Loel." Keira sighed. "Thank you. If you find anyone else in classrooms, tell them to look for a grow light garden center. That's how we found water. Do you think it's safe for me to give them the rest of the food and water? I have a little of both left."

She was so thankful for the water filtration straw in her backpack. She'd avoided drinking the local water before the earthquake and didn't want to stray from the guidelines in these conditions.

"Eat the food you have. It will help you with the journey out. But ration the water, just to be safe."

Kiera and the kids exchanged hugs in the dark.

So Many Questions

oel turned off her mic connected to the Dust. "Keira Stetson? I know who she is. Beyond our rescue, what do we need to consider about her and the Dust? She has an AI running down there?"

Hendrick looked up at Cody, who shook his head.

Loel noticed the exchange. "What? So, we have a really smart AI specialist we need to help. Why that look, Hendrick? Do you know what she may be capable of detecting?"

Cody answered before Hendrick had a chance. "It was her AI push about the time they were both leaving college that blew up his social media business model."

Loel looked to Roy. "Well, that's in the painful past. Edmond, please make sure her husband is notified right away. The kids' families and guardians, as well."

"Yes, of course. I'll do that immediately." Edmond left the room.

Roy nodded his head as he stared out the window. "As soon as she gets cell service, she is going to start raising questions we don't want out in the wild. I don't know what she's doing here, but her AIs are known for two things: finding all the answers and following ethical boundaries. Her curiosity is legendary. We'll need to be careful but answer her questions directly."

Loel opened her mic back to Keira. "Are you there, Keira? Can you hear me?"

"Yes, Loel, I'm here. Excuse me, but Loel is a unique name. I've only heard of one person with it."

"True, Keira is a unique name too. How are you feeling?"

"I also heard the name Roy mentioned."

Cody's look at Loel was wide-eyed and sheepish at the same time. Roy raised his eyebrows while offering a conciliatory smirk. Loel rubbed her face.

"Loel, do you live in Seattle and work for Searcher Technologies? I'm making an assumption, but those two names clicked together for me."

Curiosity was not the term Loel wanted to use at the moment to describe Keira. Loel exchanged a look with Roy. "Yes. That's me. Sorry this is the first way we meet."

"You didn't know it was me here, but you know how many kids are with me. There is no power here. What's going on? Why are you two here and talking to me?"

Roy spun his finger in a barrel shaped roll, encouraging Loel to keep the conversation going.

"You asked about a fiber optic system. That's not what we're using. We're happy to give you a debrief on what we're doing as soon as you come up and feel up to it. But we're here confidentially, and I can't explain things now. I need you to focus on keeping those kids calm, like you have been. Then you'll need to focus on physically getting out with the crew. It won't be an easy exit."

"You have tech installed inside this building?"

"We brought tech with us after the earthquake, which is all I can say right now."

"I don't like the ripple effect of not having answers, but I guess I need to deal with it for now." Loel watched the woman's vital signs start quickening again. They'd been normalizing since she'd been told help was on the way.

Shifting on the floor to make a physical connection with each of the kids, Keira bumped her head on the table. Loel flinched as she watched in her faint view of the room.

"Just help these kids get out of here. If they need to come back to get me, I'm fine with that. Just help these kids. Thank you."

"We have someone contacting your husband. I'll give you an update as soon as we get one. You can all come out together. You're doing a great job."

Loel and Roy continued to communicate with rescue teams and trapped survivors. Loel checked Cody's machine for the stats on the man in the basement. Movement outside distracted her. Three people, two of them students, were brought out of the chaos.

"Cody, monitor the Dust. Make sure, when rescued people emerge, every nanite that comes out with them is redeployed back into the building," Roy said.

Cheers from the bucket brigade brightened everyone's mood. Roy sent those rescue teams back into the building to assist with the extraction of the kids with Keira.

Loel wasn't so certain Keira felt as well as she let on. "Your heroes are coming. They may be dirty, but they're climbing over mountains of rubble. They're smart and choose just the right chunks to heave out of the way."

"Ms. Loel," a tiny voice said. "Our rescuers must be really strong."

"Yes, sweetheart, they're strong and very brave. You're all brave, too."

Loel sighed and ran her fingers through her hair. She leaned over to turn up the volume on her speakers. Six little voices bolted out the song "This Little Light of Mine." She recognized the irony of the lyrics. The babbling in the room around her dropped immediately. The sweetness of the singers washed over the men and women present. She acknowledged the guide wiping the tears from his eyes while he plopped into a chair a few feet away.

She turned on her mic. "Keep up the good work with those kids, Keira. Attitude is everything. Your rescue team is working their way to you."

Keira coughed. She whispered, "Thank you."

"I see a light behind the bookcase!" squealed one of the children.

"Yay!" Loel said. "Say hello to your heroes, then listen to what they tell you to do. I'll see you when you get out here." She turned off her mic.

"Cody, how is our guy in the server room doing?" Loel asked.

Leaning towards Loel, he rubbed the back of his neck. He whispered, "It's really hot in there. His vitals are a mess. I'm not certain exactly what is wrong with him. There are no signs of wounds, but he's passed out."

Twenty minutes later, Keira's six singing children crawled out on hands and knees through a hole between a crushed car and giant slabs forming an A-frame around it. Loel turned her computer over to Hendrick. She ran to introduce herself. As she approached them, her stomach knotted. Keira removed their AR goggles and passed them to the man providing her support.

Watching

K eira let Loel lead her to the conference room after kissing the children goodbye and promising to stay in touch. A teacher from the school had been in the crowd helping with debris removal. He'd greeted them as they met the sunlight. He assured Keira he wouldn't leave the children until either their parents or their school advocates were with them.

She gulped an entire bottle of water during introductions in the room. She didn't pay attention to Edmond's title as he handed her a phone connected to Gino. He was working to connect her with a government evacuation flight home from a city two hours away. Only small planes could use the local airport, due to runway damage. With little privacy in the room, Roy had passed her a note saying his plane could get her home. They'd work out the details and let Gino know.

She hung up the phone. Roy approached with another phone and a plate of tamales. "Loel tells me you've seen the glasses in action. I won't attempt to ask you to forget what you've seen here. I don't think you're going to be pushed aside like that."

Keira smiled, then cringed at the pull it made on scratches and scabs on her cheek and temple. "You're correct, it's not in my nature to stop asking questions. I also understand it's your business and not mine."

"We've talked about ways you could help us long before today. I guess this situation was quite the drastic way of the world pushing us together to force the discussion. I've still got people inside that building we need to help. If you're willing to put your fingerprint to a commitment to not discuss what you see here today with anyone, you can watch what we're doing, and we'll explain what we can as we progress."

"What if you're doing something illegal or harmful? I'm not saying you are, but I don't take confidentiality lightly."

Cody said, "Loel, can you look at this guy's readings. No rescuers are anywhere close to him at this point." He rolled his chair to give her more room to look at his monitor.

"Shit, look at the CO_2 levels rising!" Loel said. "Roy, the Dust is calculating this guy in the server room could asphyxiate on the CO_2. We need to get oxygen in there and move the CO_2 out."

Roy put the phone in front of Keira. "I need to get back to work. I assure you there is nothing nefarious going on here. If there was, no agreement would hold you back anyway."

She put her fingers on the screen of the phone. Roy passed her the tamales while pointing to the chair behind his.

"The Dust got in there, of course," Cody said. "It's not an airtight room, but it's sealed up enough from natural air flow."

Cody stared at the outlined image of the incapacitated IT worker. A small amount of dust monitored his vitals. "We can't get a pipe down to him, it's too deep, and we'd have to drill a hole in the wall to feed the tube in anyway."

Roy pointed to the screen with the building's 3D model. "Keira, this model is provided by the nanites we dispersed. It mapped the building." He pointed to Cody's screen. "We are monitoring a man trapped in a hot server room. His vital signs are reported back to us, just like yours were."

Everyone watched Roy. Keira followed Loel's gaze as it moved away from Roy and towards a bag at his feet.

"You didn't bring any, did you?" Loel said.

Before he could respond, yellow warnings flashed in front of Roy. There was a low rumble and then a cloud of dust speckled with concrete pebbles rushed the display of whatever team member was broadcasting to Roy's screen. Grunts and coughs could be heard from the speakers. Roy turned on his mic. "Gentlemen, you're seeing a correction to your journey. We found a safer, more direct path to your target. Your previous plan has become unstable."

"Buddy, these glasses are something else," the medic replied. "I think our course had a cave-in. We just got a face full of crap. We're taking the new route. Thank you!"

Keira looked at Roy, "The glasses updated their path that quickly? They have glasses like the ones I tried coming out?"

"Yes. That is the job of the Dust: assess the situation and map the stable path." Without taking his eyes off Keira, Roy reached under the table to his bag. He pulled out a stainless steel canister not much larger than the pneumatic tubes once used in bank drive-throughs and corporate message systems. This canister had a green recycle logo on the side. Loel gasped.

"Did you bring a controller?" Cody asked.

His youthful exuberance seemed to annoy Loel. Her expression made Cody sit down looking chastised. Loel clenched her jaw and picked up the canister. Leaning her elbows on her knees, she gently turned the canister around in her hands.

"We have to get him air," Roy said to Loel. "You said yourself, rescuers won't get there in time. Those little guys can save him until they do arrive. Can you see an adjacent space to the server room? An open pocket, preferably a room with contiguous access to the outside or bigger gaps?"

Reluctantly, Loel put the canister back on the table to research the building's model for an answer.

Pushing coffee cups and water bottles aside, Cody spread a paper floor plan between Loel and Roy. "I can do this. This wall is fireproof fiberglass." He tapped his finger on the paper. "We can get down there."

Loel cleared her throat and sighed. "Yes, the nanites could get there. The other good news: that wall divides the server room from a bull pen of desks still mostly intact. There will be lots of oxygenated air there."

Cody looked eager, which made him look even younger. "Can I do it, Roy? This isn't a scenario I'd considered for the mining nanites. But they're built for making holes."

Loel looked sternly at Cody. "You'd have to keep tight control of that Dust. It's not like the SeekerDust. It could be destructive because it is singularly minded to reach and mine precious metals, or in this case, you can direct it at the fiberglass. It has no intellectual programming to make it selective. I want to help this guy," Loel said, "but my instinct screams caution. Roy, we could cause a collapse."

"A collapse?" Pointing out the window, Roy grunted. "Will you look at that mess? I have to buy this guy time. It's a great field test, too. You've built these machines to be used. I'm going to use them. As long as Cody has them listening to his instructions, he can give them specific direction."

After a nod from Roy, Cody grabbed the canister and the controller next to it and ran toward the door.

"Cody," Loel called.

He stopped and turned to look at her.

"Don't be distracted for a moment. And bring it all back," Loel demanded.

Cody gave her a quick salute and shot out the door.

Hendrick, who hadn't spoken since Keira had entered the room, reached over and touched Loel's arm. "It'll be okay. Cody will be careful." He turned to Keira. She then remembered him from their days at Stanford. She was pretty certain he'd not liked her there. "The Dust Cody has now is different than what you've seen so far. These nanites navigate the same way, but they are designed to recycle materials for 3D printing of more machines."

Loel's computer zoomed into Cody's target portion of the building. Keira watched a green oblong dot rapidly navigate towards the flag of the man in the server room. Surprised at the speed of its progress, she imagined Cody standing outside the building, driving the Dust with the controller.

Hendrick mumbled, "He's pushing the speed limits of the Dust's propulsion."

Occasionally the dot became cylindrical as it passed through small crevices. An image came to her mind of a childhood cartoon—a swarm of bees chasing something. The swarm passed through all sorts of obstacles quickly by changing its formation. The Dust didn't move at near the cartoon's pace, but she was impressed. She shook the mental image away.

Shifting her attention to Roy's monitor, she could see the man's increased heart rate. As the CO_2 increased, his heart tried to work harder and reacted to his distressed breathing.

She stared intensely at the man, hoping he would wake. A small, dark object dropped through her view of the room, making her flinch. "What was that?" Two small circles dropped away from the wall, within a foot of his head. Plaster particles fluttered around the dark circles. "Was there a tremor? I would get pelted by crap from the ceiling every time there was any movement."

"Cody? What have you done?" Loel asked. "Are the mining bots through to the server room?

"I told the nanites to form three-inch circles." Cody replied. "They drilled side-by-side to puncture a ring through the fiberglass. The resulting plugs just fell away. We now have two holes in the wall and one through the ceiling tile. We're working on more. Can you see any change? Is it helping?"

The CO_2 numbers in the server room slowly crept downward. Loel exhaled. "Yes, it's helping, Cody. Keep going."

"How does it know where to drill?" Keira asked.

Hendrick opened his mouth, but Loel spoke first. "Cody has the controller, which includes the model of the building in its current state. He pointed them to the spots where he wanted the holes."

Hendrick gave a thumbs up to Edmond, who was not looking at the monitors, but was focused on each engineer's face. Then he spoke to Cody. "Great job, kid. Even the minor airflow from the change of air pressure in the room appears to be helping him. The guy's breathing is normalizing! His heart rate is coming back down."

Loel added, "Keep monitoring all of the Dust. We can't have it start digging anywhere you don't want it. It's critical that it all gets back in that canister. It's not ready for the wild."

"What do you mean it's not ready for the wild?" Keira said. "Sorry, I know I'm just supposed to be watching. But what do you mean about digging anywhere?"

Roy nodded, and Loel looked back to Keira. "Well, that's one of the things we've discussed talking to you and your team about. Our very intelligent nanites don't yet understand property ownership."

During the next two hours, aftershocks rumbled through the city. Keira asked for updates on the kids. The IT worker was the last person in the building. He was rushed to the hospital the moment he cleared the building's perimeter. After a debris cloud rose, caused by a collapse behind a neighboring building, the team showed Edmond the red indicators from 100% of the Dust within the University Center. The rubble could no longer be entered. All crews evacuated.

Never Enough

T he dark, smooth tarmac was the easiest surface Roy, Cody, and Loel had navigated in the last two days. They hurried toward the rectangle of amber light at the top of their jet's stairs. Sparse lighting slipped out from the airport using minimum power via battery backups. The earthquake's damage to the power grid had been extensive.

Roy entered his plane, handing a backpack to the flight attendant. The glean of the burled wood and the welcoming, deep leather chairs sat in stark contrast to the dirty and chaotic environment they'd left behind. In the cabin, he nodded acknowledgment to Keira, already sitting at the front table wrapped in a blanket, a ball cap pulled low on her forehead. Edmond had secured clothes and a shower for her. Her hotel had been deemed unsafe to enter. Her eyes were tired but didn't hold the shell shock he would have expected considering her ordeal. "Welcome, Keira, I'll be there in just a moment."

Sticking his head into the cockpit, he addressed the pilots. "Please collect our clearance and take off as soon as you can. Communication services are completely screwed up right now. Sorry, I didn't give you more warning when we were coming back from the city."

He recognized the captain but not the first officer. "By the way, we'll be busy working, possibly sleeping. Don't worry about announcements. You can turn off the radio between here and the cabin." The pilots acknowledged his request and his apology, then moved with efficiency to prepare for takeoff.

Loel stashed her computer bag in her storage bin, hidden sleekly in the glossy side panel near Keira. "How are you feeling, Keira?"

"I'm sore in a lot of places, but grateful. Thank you. How are you?"

Ruffling the spikiness of her own hair, Loel chuckled. "Well, I'm glad you got a shower, but you're flying home with three people in desperate need of one. My apologies."

Concerned about Loel's state of mind after the stress of the rescues and her look of exhaustion, Roy turned to the attendant and requested food and drinks be served immediately. She silently hurried to the galley.

Brushing past Roy, Cody claimed a seat behind the table. Decades younger than he or Loel, he still showed the wear and tear of the mission. "All the equipment is stowed underneath. It's ready."

The changing rooms at the executive airport had been dark, with no showers. Accustomed to Loel's meticulous attention to her appearance, Roy was acutely aware of her uncombed hair and the dark circles under her eyes. Cody's rumpled look had a grunge band effect. Roy was relieved to be in clean jeans and a T-shirt and that Keira had been given fresh clothes. Edmond had been true to his word, providing her the best care possible under the city's circumstances.

Roy looked from Loel to Cody. "The post-event review needs to be done soon. But we'll wait for most of it until we have Hendrick. And we don't want to drag Keira through our droning on about our processes." He wasn't fooling anyone in the cabin. They wouldn't have discussed details of the Dust in front of Keira. He would set the pace for what more would be disclosed in front of her.

Loel spun her chair away from Roy to face Cody. "Come on, join us at the table. You'll want to eat before you sleep."

Pushing himself from the high-backed leather seat, Cody moved to an identical version next to Loel, across the table from Roy. "These chairs are a lot more comfortable than the ones in that conference room. At least without Hendrick, there is room for our legs under this table. Why did he stay behind?"

Roy accepted a cup of coffee from the attendant. Keira moved the sugar within his reach. "I think he'll make good connections with a few of the humanitarian groups we can help in the future."

Cody scratched his scalp.

Loel cringed. "We got out just in time. The press started to roll into that sector of the city in numbers too large to keep your face out of the news. You're too recognizable, Roy. Next time, we should consider leaving you at home if we're going to keep the story of the Dust controlled."

"I can't stay home if I can save lives by going," Roy insisted. He didn't mind this conversation in front of Keira. She needed to know how serious they took the privacy of the Dust's story.

"Hmmm." Loel shrugged. "Your choice, of course. But weigh your desire for secrecy versus your fame and wealth drawing media attention. We'll have to consider news cover stories or better shelter you in the future."

"I won't be sidelined, and it's Hendrick's job to make sure it all stays a secret." He also didn't need Hendrick's obvious distaste of Keira to fill the cabin the entire way home.

"That's a huge burden, to put your visibility as his priority," Loel said. "I think you need to join a board or two of some of the groups Hendrick connects with. We could attach your presence to one of them next time."

A heavy sigh accompanied Roy's gaze to the jet's polished ceiling. "That's a good idea. Who would have thought the creation of aSports' autonomous robotic football players would complicate my life so much?"

A grin lit up Cody's face. "Roy, I don't think the autonomous sports league gets the blame for complicating your life." He started counting with his fingers. "I think the complicating part is the development of nanites which can sense tremors, assess changing structural integrity of their surroundings, identify survivors, then listen and transmit all conversations and vital signs."

Loel smiled for the first time in hours. "By the way, you guys were truly amazing down there." She turned to Keira. "We saved such precious lives. But it's important that we prevent the Dust from being misused and misinterpreted."

Shifting in her seat, Keira appeared uncomfortable. "Thank you again for being there. I don't think the crews would have made it all the way down to us, based on the insane journey we took to climb out."

Roy noticed Keira shudder under her blanket. He smiled with pride at both of his employees. He was honored to work with this team. They devoured their food quickly, with zero reference or preference to flavor or menu. Keira picked at slices of chicken from a sandwich. She did continue to drink her tea as fast as it was steeped.

Keira took a deep breath. She was biting her lower lip and looking at the darkness beyond the window.

Loel asked, "Are you ok?"

Shaking her head, Keira exhaled again. "I'm going to be haunted by the things that could have happened. I also know that disasters like this one put a lot of kids at risk. There's a multitude of scary things ranging from people to infrastructure that pose a threat to them."

Roy spun the ice cube in his scotch. "This is the first time Searcher has engaged in an emergency that involved kids. It certainly raises the stakes. In my past work, we certainly saw corruption increase in places where the world was paying more attention to infrastructure than anything else."

"Yep, I've seen firsthand how the vulnerable become prey for unscrupulous people in these times." Keira sighed. "But I know the schools will work diligently to protect the kids. There are really great people in that system in Honduras. I'll try to get back down there again soon. I told Miette I would."

Loel said, "I suggest you give yourself some grace and take a little time before you return. It will be a while before visiting the city will be practical."

A weary smile and a slight shrug was Keira's response. "I thank you for sharing details about SeekerDust technology. I understand it was not ideal for another technologist to be dropped in as an uninvited observer to this mission of yours. After discussing it with Elly, she has lots of questions."

Roy glared at Keira. "You agreed in the conference room you would discuss this with no one." Keira flashed a warm and appreciative smile at him and then Loel. She held her hands up, deflecting Roy's instant anger.

"I didn't discuss it with any people. I gave you my word and my fingerprint on your form. Elly is my AI. She observed our escape route via the audible exchanges. As soon as we were high enough in the building, she picked up Wi-Fi. I had to explain to her what she had to compartmentalize and not disclose regarding our rescue. I'll tell you, she was impressed and requested upgrades matching the capability of the Dust. I explained that wasn't possible. Your tech is proprietary and confidential."

Roy, unsatisfied with Keira's casual attitude about this exposure to Searcher, cleared his throat and leaned onto the table.

Keira didn't give him chance to make an objection. She kept talking. "Look, this is a less-than-ideal situation for all of us. I'm sure you'd like to be doing some type of post-action review or something. Believe me when I tell you I get it, at least a little. But before I pass out on what I hope is a reclining chair back there, I have two things I need to talk to you about."

Loel waved for another round of drinks. The attendant's tenure on Roy's plane meant she was trusted around sensitive conversations. She also correctly perceived this drink order wasn't for more coffee and tea. In the Jeep ride to the airport, Loel had mentioned Keira's keen interest and observation while in the conference room. He had kept everything about the SeekerDust within his tight circle. He didn't know how he would receive input or criticism from such a talented, confident outsider.

Deciding it was better to let Keira show her cards, sarcasm would have to cloak his frustrations. Roy waved his hand in welcome. "Please, by all means, be candid. We'll figure out where to go with your curiosity or ideas as needed."

Keira winced picking up her glass of wine with her right hand. She switched the glass to her left hand and flashed the scraped, bandaged palm. "I'll be direct, partly because I want to sleep. Also, because if I don't tell you what's on my mind, I feel we'll be off this plane in

Seattle, and you guys will try to build as much distance between me and this event as possible. I would, if for no other reason than to avoid any chance of association."

He understood her perception. She was partially correct.

"I understand secrecy and confidentiality. The first one I struggle with at times. The second I can embrace. I am, after all, married to an FBI agent. Thank you, by the way, for contacting him. It may have saved you from having the city crawling with CIA agents from throughout Central America." She flashed another smile that lit up her face. "You may think I'm kidding, but he was making the calls."

"Well, they could have blown your cover, Roy," Loel said.

The thought had already occurred to him.

"I won't disclose which task force Gino's on. If this idea goes anywhere, you'll find out. I may understand why you find secrecy so critical for your Dust. At least I hope it's for more than competitive advantage. Your ability to essentially see through walls could be extremely valuable in saving lives during his team's actions."

She paused only long enough to let them superficially absorb the potential of her comment. "I'm not fully versed in their needs, but I have enough of a security clearance to know about some of the good work they do and the dangers they face. I would really like you to explore options with them. They would be interested in keeping your technology secrets, so that might also be a cultural fit."

Her expression silenced any response to her revelation while she took a drink.

"But I have a caveat to this concept and possible introduction. If you're not already engaged with the intelligence agency, I have a stipulation before going forward."

Loel's hackles were up with this last statement. Roy had felt that near electrical current broadcasting from her when he pissed her off. Cody feigned disinterest, as if he wasn't hearing any of this. Roy said slowly, "Tell me more."

"That's Gino's technique to get people talking, too." Keira said. "I guess it's an intelligence training thing. Don't worry, I'm not trying to extort you. I saw you people do great work back there. But in the wrong hands, your nanites could be devastating, both the physical mining bots and the surveillance Dust. It appears you're not following any kind of rules but your own."

Her brow creased. Her volume increased. "We need to get your systems running on my MoralOS. They need boundaries and the ability to recognize things like property rights and unethical instructions. If you're so worried about controlling it when one of its inventors has his hands on the wheel, what happens when someone else takes over? The ability to mine materials or recycle them sounds great. But it's dangerous if not controlled. You alluded to wanting to work together, so maybe you've already considered this. I'm grateful for that Dust and terrified of its potential."

Loel relaxed into her seat. Cody exhaled and gulped for replacement air. Roy raised his eyebrows. He was across from an astute observer. There would be little chance to redirect or deflect concepts from her. "Fair enough. May I speak now? And is your AI listening? I prefer that it's not."

Keira wrinkled her nose and eased her back into the chair. "Sorry, I hadn't intended to hold court, especially on your own plane and considering the circumstances which put me here. I'm just adamant about ethical computing. Contrary to what some people believe about me, I have no interest in ripping apart free enterprise or being a crusader. But I will fight when algorithms and technology are abusive. And Elly, um, my AI, has been blocked. Please, continue."

She reached for the plate of meats and cheese in the middle of the table and served herself heartily.

"Well, you've spoken a lot of truth we happen to agree with. This technology could be misused. We're not interested in taking it through the OpenML certification programs you built and champion. The crowd-sourcing nature of building an ethical framework is great. But we don't share well, to be honest. It exposes our technology to scrutiny by outsiders. We're not willing to be that open with our intellectual property. Without that, getting assistance to implement the MoralOS on nanites is beyond our reach. We've tried with the consortium. We keep our work teams small. It creates expertise constraints at times."

Cody tilted his head. "Keira, I'm surprised you propose working with the FBI when you publicly are very vocal against technology weaponry."

For the first time on the plane, Keira gave Cody her attention. "I don't contradict myself at all," she said. "I see uses for your Dust that would lessen the amount of weaponry and violence needed by the agency. I'm too tired to work through logistics now. We can talk about introductions to Gino at another time. And as far as working together, I need to also include Ruby. She and I work together on the MoralOS and her expertise and counter balance thinking will be invaluable."

She stood, wrapping her blanket tighter over her shoulders and cringed. "Now, if you'll excuse me, I'm exhausted. I'll put my earbuds in, and you three can talk all you want in privacy."

Roy stood as well. "I look forward to more discussions. Your husband's task force sounds intriguing. We'd like to meet Ruby; she sounds very talented. However, we will need to start our talks with you alone. It's that confidentiality thing." He pointed to the dimly lit back of the plane. "Please, get some rest."

"Thank you again for the luxury of this direct flight home." Keira's eyes held his gaze with zero indication of being intimidated by him. Not even Loel looked at him with that much determination. She then looked to his team at the table. "And to all of you and Hendrick, too, thanks again for getting the kids and me out of there."

"Keira?" Roy said as she retreated out of the light encircling their table.

Keira turned around.

"Do you consider yourself a risk taker?"

Without a beat of hesitation, she responded. "With the proper motivations, absolutely, but not irrationally so."

She moved to the farthest seat from the table. Pleasantries were exchanged, and the flight attendant helped her get situated.

"She certainly says what's on her mind." Cody rubbed his knuckles and right palm with his left hand. He found his pulse point near his thumb and pinched it.

"Headache?" Roy asked.

Cody nodded.

The plane banked sharply. They each steadied their drinks. Roy grumbled, "The co-pilot must be flying. Jerry would never be that abrupt." He didn't like having strangers around. "We have a lot to consider," Roy said. "I'm so happy with the Dust's delivery on the ultimate situational awareness back there. We still need Dust with cohesive strength. We need to increase production, and we have all that Keira just put in front of us."

"We need a little recovery time, Roy," Loel said. "I also need to regroup from the risks you took back there. We were lucky with the mining bots. If something had distracted Cody, we could have had real risks on our hands. We can get a fresh start back at the office. Now I just need sleep, badly."

"Yes, of course. We'll talk about decision-making abilities in the Dust tomorrow. I want to have faith in its judgment. Its ability for surveillance is proven. Now we need to build upon its skills."

Cody stood. "As the sayings goes, 'With great power, comes great responsibility.'"

Roy rolled his eyes, yet silently agreed with the young man. "Goodnight, Cody." He reached over to a panel, turned the lights lower, and darkened the windows to avoid the approaching sunrise. Loel and Cody moved stiffly to seats they could recline. Blankets were already draped across each one.

Loel looked up at Roy, still sitting at the table, spinning the ice cubes in his scotch. She said, "You know, we can't be all things to all people."

Smiling at her, he tilted his head. "Oh, let's try. But how to do it without getting caught is another thing entirely."

Bad Chemistry

t had been less than a week since her return from Honduras. Keira's husband and Ruby had protested against her coming to the conference. She couldn't stay away. She'd opened the conference with a speech supporting AI's contributions to society, especially when they could be constrained within ethical boundaries. She had a panel session regarding the weaponization of algorithms coming up. She had to promote the expansion of the ethical certification of AI systems. She had won the arguments and made it to the conference only an hour before her keynote.

The marble lobby of the hotel was filled with kinetic energy. The conference created a frantic exchange between attendees to make connections, share contact details, or pitch new ideas. Keira wanted to introduce Ruby and Ollie to a philanthropist she met the day before, but too many people moved through the intersection for reception, the elevators, and passage to the conference center.

"These hotel complexes are so disorienting," Ruby complained. "But, oh, the aroma of those soft pretzels baking. They remind me of my grandma's bread. I've got to grab one of those."

"What?" Ollie tilted his head. "You, the foodie, will eat a fast-food pretzel?"

Ruby pushed her chin out in defiance. "I'll have you know nostalgia is a genre of foodyism."

"You two should get something to eat before we head in." Keira waved towards the row of specialty cafés. "It's going to be a long day. I ate after my physical therapy session."

Ruby winced. "How are you feeling? Can I get you anything?"

"I'm okay. I worked out the knot above my hip, so I think I'm not limping, at least."

She smiled at a man, uncomfortable in his new attire, shifting in his pristinely pressed sport coat. The job hunters and those seeking investors were easy to spot simply by their dressed-to-impress efforts. Keira preferred comfort. Jeans and boots could match just about any scenario. Today, she couldn't imagine wearing heels with all the bruises and aches she was nursing. This thought brought to mind her conversation with little Miette. She smiled.

Giving up on the search through the crowd, she admired Ruby's handbag, new and uniquely geometrical in design. "The conference gave you an excuse for a new bag, Ruby?"

Standing a bit straighter and running her hand over the purse, Ruby smiled. "It was a great exchange in my purse club. The lady never used it because her husband said it looked too much like a fortune cookie. She was insulted, but traded it for my puffy gold one."

"I like it," Keira said. "Now that you say it, it does look a little like a fortune cookie. But there is nothing wrong with that in my book. I couldn't even put my backpack on my shoulder this morning. I should have borrowed one of your little purses. I just brought my water and tablet."

Ollie didn't appear impressed with the fashion discussion. "Are we all in for dinner together tonight?"

"You two go ahead without me," Keira said.

A wink passed from Ollie to Ruby. "You holding out for a better offer?" He teased.

"What? No. I'm just hoping to catch a meal with the education director from the Autism Society."

Shaking his head, Ollie appeared determined to tease a laugh out of her. "Ah, so you're playing corporate gold digger. I get it."

He got the laugh. "Oh, I don't ever want to win that moniker, or hear it again."

"My meetings last night confirmed we advanced on two more global education grants," Ruby interjected. "They'll pay out quickly after decision, too."

Keira wondered if Ruby held on to good news like that for just the right moment. Her friend had used this tactic since they were in college. Keira appreciated the optimism.

"I much prefer the lab or the classroom. This is a zoo." Ollie dodged two bustling attendees carrying oversized open coffee cups. "I do want to grab something to eat. Keira, don't look now, but we have incoming company. It's your favorite manipulative corporate pirate."

"Shit, that man can't rub two thoughts together to create a new one," Keira muttered. Making a showy gesture of checking her watch, she turned towards the meeting halls. Mickey Temming, a raider of tech companies, was known for ruthlessly undercutting the reputation of a business and bad mouthing their offerings and employees or hiring someone else to do it. He then swept in and bought up the good assets cheaply.

Ruby leaned close to Keira's ear. "I wish you wouldn't be seen talking to him."

"Better to be seen brushing him off than people thinking I talked to him in private."

"Hello, Keira, Ruby, Ollie," Mickey said, nodding to Keira's employees respectively.

Ruby and Ollie exchanged glances without moving their heads. Approaching Keira in this busy public space, surrounded by her team and the traffic of the other event participants, seemed orchestrated. Keira's skin crawled.

"Hello, Mickey. I'm surprised you took the time to come to the conference when the grapevine says no one would take your meetings." She looked over and around Mickey for anyone else to engage. He'd messaged her several times over the last few months because she never communicated with him verbally. Electronic replies allowed her to throttle back her responses to facts only and keep a trail of all conversations.

"We must talk, Keira, ah, about the panel. Can I have a quick moment?" Mickey gestured to a tiny open space out of the crowd's traffic pattern.

Not wanting to be caught off guard during their on-stage discussion later in the conference, she acquiesced and stepped away from her companions.

Mickey jumped straight to his pitch. "You need to stop avoiding our calls. Think about the work you could accomplish with proper funding. You could save everyone's jobs if you entertained my acquisition offer. Oh, and nice opening comments about ethics and AI yesterday. I didn't know you liked the limelight enough to do a keynote address. It's too bad it's tough to commercialize good behavior."

"What the hell, Mickey? You're so presumptuous. I told you Opal is *not* available. Don't even think that your insinuation of career instability for my team is going to endear you to me. We're just fine. No one's job is in danger."

Mickey leaned in. "Opal Technology's violence detection is needed by our government and intelligence communities. I inked a contract that it could plug right into. We can make a lot of money together. You need to think about it. Are you sure you want to go it alone?"

"I really don't want to continually have this conversation. We seem to have some version every time we cross paths back in Seattle or at events like this. The answer is no. I've made it clear. I'll have nothing to do with weaponized technology."

More people moved towards the conference facilities. The noise in the lobby continued to rise. To keep their conversation confidential required stepping closer to each other. His years outdoors for the military hadn't been kind to his aging process. Keira imagined being an angry, aggressive person could age a man too.

"There are many points we can negotiate. Or I can get my D.C. buddies involved. They play hardball when the government wants something. They find all kinds of ways to tie up grant money, R&D, and cash flow."

"Don't try to intimidate me. It isn't working. This isn't a negotiation. My tech isn't for sale." Keira glared at Mickey. "You talk like we're in the middle of a term sheet negotiation. Do you have anything to say about the panel, or was that a ruse?"

"Let me ask an unrelated question then. Why are you spending so much effort on kids? There's no money in education."

"Glad you asked that, Mickey. I figured out that if I could help kids—get them educated and happy—they wouldn't turn out to be bitter grown-ups like you. I guess that means I'm saving the world in my own little way."

At that moment, Roy stepped into their conversational circle. "Forgive me for intruding on your chat, Keira. I would really like to continue our previous conversations."

Keira gave him a thankful smile. "You know conference discussions. There's always room to include another attendee. We were just talking about people that don't know how to follow the rules. Since you're also from Seattle, you two may already know each other—"

Mickey cut her off. "We've had the misfortune a few times."

Someone that was so obviously under Mickey's skin was of instant interest to her. "What's on your mind, Mr. Brandt?" she asked.

"Please, call me Roy. You caused a bit of a stir yesterday with your comments. I liked the question you posed. 'Can a machine's choices be based on our values and honor humanity?' Loel and I talked about it for quite some time last night."

"I'm glad I did my job. I wanted to spark conversation, even debate about ethics in our work."

Roy chuckled and continued to look at Keira while slighting Mickey.

"Oh, you did that. Many argue that religion is here to define our ethics. Yet, each religion interprets morality in different and often subjective ways. Is it impossible to define morality for humanity that is truly universal? That seems to be what you're attempting to do with OpenML and your MoralOS."

She was intrigued by Roy's conversation choice in front of Mickey. Roy might be insanely rich, but he wasn't shallow. It would appear he knew Mickey wouldn't have a tolerance for the topic.

Keira smiled. "Morality is difficult to define and to enforce. But we're compelled to try. Perhaps the only universally applicable imperative we should pursue is caring for kids and protecting them."

"That's a tall order for technology at this stage, wouldn't you say? We're still trying to get people to just play nice." Roy's tone was thoughtful, not chastising.

"My doctoral studies experimented with ways to govern multiple neural nets all trained on different domains. This combination means no single one of them could make a prediction that would lead to an action of harm. In some ways, it's the same as societal norms pressuring people to behave. Anyway, that's what started MoralOS. The crowdsourcing made it possible to reach the universal stature. Can I interest your organization to join the consortium?"

Mickey cleared his throat for attention. "You two are too preachy. I'm out of here. Think about what I said, Keira. We can talk back in Washington."

"Don't let us go over your head, or maybe it's your heart." Roy's smirk lit up his face.

Mickey left without another word. Keira looked past Roy to Ollie and Ruby, who were still standing by protectively. She motioned for them to go on to the café. Ruby raised her eyebrow. Keira knew she was thinking about Roy's wealth at that moment.

She turned back to Roy. "I see you might appreciate Mickey as much as I do."

"You have no idea. I broke up your conversation for two reasons. First, no respectable person wants to spend any time cornered by him. More importantly, I'd really like to buy you dinner tonight. I'd like to share some of the thoughts Loel and I discussed. Plus, my nephew goes to university here, studying education. He's a big fan of yours and asked if I could introduce the two of you. He has an evening class but could join us for drinks after dinner."

Saying no to a dinner with one of the richest men in her industry would be foolish, especially shortly after his technology had saved her life. He was also extremely well-connected with the groups providing grants for fresh technology.

What Matters Most

K eira's heart raced by the time she reached the back door to the Opal lobby. She wiped her hands on her jeans. They were as sweaty as the shine she had just dabbed off her forehead. People with a lot of money were just about the only ones that ever made her nervous.

Her discussions with Roy and Loel during the previous few weeks had included deep dives into ethical computing and her extensive global crowdsourcing for the definitions and boundaries of ethics. They had also discussed opportunities with the FBI. She'd made introductions and stepped away from that relationship. She didn't want to be involved.

During a late-night discussion about the potential of ethical nanites, Roy had proposed an acquisition of Opal. That had set her back on her heels. He didn't know much about Opal when he'd made the suggestion. That bugged her.

She wasn't clear on what was in it for him. However, if she could get him to fund her education robots and Answers Everywhere programs, she would be a happy woman. It was killing her to keep these discussions secret from Ruby and Ollie. She needed to get comfortable enough with the topic herself.

The bright light streaming in from the front windows made it nearly impossible to see anything except an outline of the chairs and her lone visitor. She'd let him wait exactly two minutes. She didn't want to appear too eager, nor disrespect him. Ruby had made the calculation for any philanthropist who came for tours. "Welcome to Opal, Roy. Thank you for coming."

"It's my pleasure," he said. "I'm glad our conversation continues." He unfolded from the low-slung chair.

"I'm eager to show you our work. We'll start with the experiential lab. I believe you'll be impressed with the progress our students make with our robots. The adaptive systems are both educational and non-threatening to the kids."

They traversed the hallways with multiple-colored lines painted on the floor, splitting off at each intersection to provide navigation guides for students to each lab.

"This is the Connection Lab. We'll use the viewing room so you can see the child's experience through the two-way mirror."

The room could fit inside most walk-in closets. Four barstools stood under a tinted window to the next room. Roy relaxed onto a middle seat. "How long have you been working with autistic children?"

"The repetition and sensory interaction program is three years old. However, I've been developing teaching tools since college. I focus on making learning a better experience for kids. The robots with the adaptive AI are ideal for kids experiencing anxiety with non-family members tutoring them."

The glass divided Keira and Roy from a room painted in soft, calm, warm shades of green, tan, and yellow. Each piece of the functional furniture sported unique tactile fabrics and surfaces. All books and toys were arranged in a tidy classroom setting. Behind a divider, a young man sat half listening, half reading his magazine. In the center of the room, a child of about seven years of age repetitively stroked the purple-gloved hand of the robot sitting beside him.

The face and the hair of the robot looked like a young surfer ready to run outside and catch a wave or a skateboard. Its kind expressions adapted to the child's attitude and interactions. Its hands wore different colored gloves to aid in the training of right and left, and also because students were more willing to touch a gloved hand than a bare one.

Roy locked his gaze on the exchange between the student and robot. He spoke towards the glass. "I read your paper about the repetitive lessons your robots deliver to your kids. I find that almost a double study, when you consider the robots must also learn through extensive reiterations."

Keira's pride grew as she watched her robot. "There is a lot of overlap in the training concepts. A large part of our early education success with our autistic kids is quiet repetition. Too few adults possess the patience for calm repetition at the level these kids need to build mental pathways. They need tremendous amounts of auditory recurrence at the beginning, which isn't available in the traditional early child classroom. Here, we can provide it. The goal is to teach these children without over stimulation."

"Should I assume patience is one of your virtues?" Roy asked.

"Hmm. With children and my computers, I maintain all the patience I need. With government red tape, grant allocations, and bullies, there is very little patience."

She smiled at the child's focus on the blocks. "It's as if the machine is patient because it can look through tens of thousands of images, yet it learns from them immediately. Let's say I practice a patient impatience. My work with continuous feedback loops gives a much quicker learning curve to the AI. It's receiving positive and negative feedback repeatedly and evolving more like a human learns."

On the other side of the window, the student flapped his hands above the table and shook his head. The robot backed away a few inches while playing a soft chime. The boy continued to fidget, crossed his arms angrily, and looked like he was going to start yelling. An amber light turned on behind the divider, in front of the attendant. He picked up a teddy bear, walked around the partition and handed the toy to the child.

Roy raised an eyebrow and turned to Keira. "Mood abatement?"

"No. We're not working to manipulate a mood. The robot is trained to sense when a child is distressed. They detect signs of distress, vocal tone and pitch, heart rate, body language, and perspiration. The AI sends an alert first through a soft chime, in case the adult is nearby. Then a series of predetermined signals, a light, a phone ringing, whatever is best for the caregiver, family, or room setup."

"That's amazing. The adult brought the teddy bear, I'm assuming, because you want the child to seek comfort from people, not the robot. What led you to work on this development?"

"Anxiety is a significant barrier for autistic students. It's an important element to deal with in their training. But honestly, I can't stomach leaving any child upset. If I can help eliminate a child's distress, I'll work to do it."

"Where does Opal's expertise for these emotional responses and perceptions come from?"

"You need to meet Ollie soon. His PhD is based on childhood distress and stressors. He's also an engineer. He and his team developed incredible programs to repair the long-term health problems created by childhood stressors. His group pursues the work, while he focuses on the detection of distress and anxiety in kids. Kids adapt, and they often master how to hide their issues as a defense mechanism."

"And if we're going to increase interactions between machines and kids, we need to enhance the reaction ability of the machines?"

"Yes, and the first part of reaction is the understanding or the perception of what the kids are feeling, especially stressors."

"Are you suggesting you can build empathy into your AIs?" asked Roy.

"We aren't claiming empathetic AIs yet." Keira smiled. Few people outside her organization made connections between Opal's efforts so quickly. "But we're making progress."

While tilting his head, Roy offered, "Would Ollie like introductions to my old contacts in the CIA? They did impressive work at lie detection, as well as fitness of duty and non-intrusive observation. Bob can check for declassified cases they could provide him."

"I think that would be a useful introduction. Thank you."

Roy turned away from the window to look directly at Keira. He crossed his arms. "I can think of many applications for distress detection. I'll say this is the post positive scenario for the application of his work."

"Yes, Ruby and I met Ollie at a support group helping child refugees from natural disasters. He was there as part of his research. We were there because I went through separation from my family during a tsunami when I was young. I try to help where I can. Ollie was wrapping up his thesis and looking for a positive application for it."

Keira turned away from Roy but spoke as if addressing the door. "Elly, is the break room conversation table reserved?"

"Yes, Keira."

The quizzical look from Roy included a flicker of distrust. She hoped her smile was warm enough to ease his suspicions. "Don't worry, Elly doesn't record conversations, or omni-listen. She's voice activated, just like most smart assistants. The range of complex tasks she can perform undirected is what makes her irreplaceable."

"Please, do give examples. I'm intrigued. I know she was helpful at setting up our meetings and being subtle about your food and wine preferences."

"I can ask her to organize a party of ten friends for my husband Gino's birthday. She manages everything from invites to the guests, caterers, inventory of the home bar, everything, based on our preferences. I couldn't live without her. Meanwhile, she's also combing studies and papers from all over the world to support our many projects. She's more than just a personal assistant."

"Why is she not in your Opal prospectus?"

"I created her in college and refined her over time. There is no IP for her within Opal. We don't have the brand or the resource bandwidth to pursue the commercialization of Elly. It would take away from our current missions. Lack of focus, I just can't afford. She's also a test bed for the MoralOS. She makes good and worthy decisions. When something is a thin line for ethics, she seeks my confirmation prior to proceeding. Her training progressed so nicely, she seldom needs my approval for the basic work I give her. She is in perpetual growth mode."

"That's fascinating. Is she based on your chatbot technology used at schools? I did read about those. I assume the marketing chat and the school chats share code and training?"

Keira nodded, "They share commonalities. The marketing chatbot generates the funding to allow the school chat to be distributed for educators and school psychologists. They contribute the breadth and depth of career exploration that individual schools could never afford. They're also available for life skills support, including dealing with bullying or other anti-social behavior.

Roy's attention was on both their conversation and the child's activities. His intensity wasn't off-putting, but it radiated from him.

"Elly's training consistently informs the chatbot development. Both marketing and schools need a great deal of identification and control over trolling. The audit logs of communication are blockchain secured, so they can't be tampered with. Nobody can falsify claims against my chatbots."

The child on the other side of the glass stroked the small stuffed animal. The robot set a green fuzzy block in front of her. Roy stood. Keira took the signal to keep things moving.

"You may be aware that trauma experienced as a child can be directly linked to health issues later in life. I'm working hard to establish that better world for kids now, which creates a better life for all of us in the future."

She guided him out of the observation room towards the break room. "I have another program I'm working on, but don't have a lot of funding for at this moment."

"I want to hear about it." Roy smiled broadly. "This meeting is about learning what's meaningful to you, as well as what technology we could capitalize on if you controlled the budget for R&D at Searcher. And we may need to talk more about Elly, too."

This surprised her. It was the first she'd heard of any suggestions about her role post-acquisition. While she loved the idea of a bigger budget, she needed more information to be convinced this was a deal she wanted to do. Distractions from her current work would be painful.

They moved to a table adjacent to the window but somewhat obstructed from most of the break room. It was understood among the staff that any conversation at that table was private. No one moved a chair closer or tried to join the occupants of the table. It was also frowned upon to sit at this table alone. Unwritten rules of conduct kept the table reserved for deep discussions. Keira often held private conversations in public places she trusted. It expanded her feeling of being authentic, but accessible.

"I've reviewed all the materials you sent regarding your commercial products. Tell me about this pet project," Roy said.

"I'm way beyond a pet project. But I'm passionate about it. With your appreciation of education, I'm sure you're familiar with the 30 Million Word Initiative. It was founded in the early 2000s by Hart and Risley. Their study showed that children from lower-income families hear a staggering 30 million fewer words than children from higher-income families by the time they're four years old. This disparity set the children back on learning for the rest of their lives."

Roy tapped his finger on the cafeteria's granite table as if it would help him recall details. "I remember the study. It wasn't just the number of words. It was the type of words and interactions. They need math words, descriptive words, and interactive communication. Please explain the connection between your technology and the research."

Keira's pulse and cadence quickened. This was her life work. Roy was tuned in. "These kids fall behind on all measurable fronts. They suffer from lower vocabularies and math scores. They can't fight their way out of poverty. They're less employable. Frustration builds up, and they're statistically more likely to be depressed and develop addictions and police records as juveniles and as adults. Leaving kids to a predictable disadvantage is criminal in my mind."

"I'm curious. You got me there. I still need you to connect the dots to your tech."

"Yes, curiosity. Can you imagine a life, if with every question a child asked, there was someone there to actually answer? The natural curiosity of children would be encouraged instead of tamped down. Kids would be able to continue exploring through their thirst for knowledge. We can deliver the limitless answers through the AI. Our current education robotics are the first steps towards this interaction technology. We developed the emotional awareness within our AI. I was in Honduras testing for cultural differences. Kids want answers everywhere."

Her gaze shifted towards the trees outdoors. Never had she wished for the calming view of the water more than she did right now. Roy had the capacity to grasp her work, challenge her assumptions, and offer alternatives. However, it was nerve-racking discussing both Opal's strengths and weaknesses with someone proposing to drastically change her future.

Roy leaned his crossed arms on the table. "A lot of queries kids make can be pretty esoteric. To keep curiosity strong, don't they need answers to the tough and obscure questions to be meaningful?"

Keira liked this question. "If you'll indulge me a little bit, I'd like Elly to address it with you." Roy nodded. "Elly, can you explain to Roy how you contribute to our education conversation bots? In particular, how do you help with the obscure or esoteric questions?"

"Yes, I can. May I use your first name, as Keira did? Or would you prefer I use a different name when addressing you?"

Roy grinned and shifted back in his chair. Those two requests from an AI appeared to disarm him.

"You may call me Roy, if I may call you Elly."

"Yes, of course. Roy, shall I assume you understand the construct of training an AI?"

Roy's grin broadened. "I understand the basics and the high-level concepts."

"Great. Kids ask questions which are not straightforward requests for facts or raw data. Our neural networks are trained for the questions commonly asked by kids at various ages. It's imperative to understand the context from which the child is asking."

Roy leaned back in his chair. Keira smiled. Elly continued. "For example, a question about slavery using the exact same words, but asked by two different children, may hold different meanings. If the context of the conversation is to assist in writing a report for a 6th grade history assignment, it's different than if the child is at a museum and just found their own family tree connects them to slaveholders or slaves themselves."

There was no person to look at while Elly spoke, so the trees drew Keira and Roy's visual attention. Elly continued. "My heuristic layer, which is also utilized for MoralOS, utilizes assumptions, experimentation, and possibly even more probing questions, then provides the appropriate response in context to the child's question. Keira's concept allows a relationship to be built between the AI and the child. This provides rich context to the questions.

Keira wondered what the mental version of crossing one's fingers would entail. She wanted Elly to continue, so she stayed quiet.

"I'm trained in the Socratic method of conversation. I can ask questions in a response to a question. This refines what the child is seeking in their quest for information. Every exchange adds to the neural network's ability to do a better job next time, just like you hope happens with adults."

Roy let out a long push of air. Keira wondered if he held his breath through that entire explanation.

"Did I answer your question?" Elly asked.

"Yes, ma'am, you did. You did it beautifully. Thank you, Elly." Roy's fingers tapped on the arm of his chair without making a sound.

"You're welcome," Elly replied.

Keira enjoyed what she read on Roy's face. She anticipated more questions.

"What's holding you back, Keira? That's impressive stuff. Even if it's rehearsed, it's impressive."

She was already deep into this exchange. There really was no going back. She might as well share. "First, she uses no script. She's been asked similar questions before, but that was all Elly. Second, to your question about what is holding us back? There is no way we can get the cost of the humanoid robots, even the child-sized version, down to an affordable price to distribute them to the homes of every child who needs this support. Progress is still needed within the empathy and emotional training of the robots, too. That's where Elly comes in."

"Can you explain the need for humanoid robots? Why not deliver through the voice activated appliances already in so many homes? It would be so much cheaper," Roy said.

"That's true. Content can be delivered by many devices. However, it creates a barrier for kids' learning. The interactivity with a human form is especially significant for kids deprived of adult attention. The additional boost they get by interacting with someone older and bigger builds their confidence and their skills. Or at the early ages, they relate to doll-sized machines and don't care that a smaller humanoid figure has more answers than they do. There is also a shorter shelf life when you use a tabletop device. The kids don't get attached. They don't utilize the content long term. With a human form, they develop a relationship, and that doesn't go away easily."

"Relationships do deliver much more impact than mere data. I can understand that," Roy said.

"Robots around kids still create some acceptance issues. A voice alone is not enough to get children this age to engage. They need real interaction. This will require a significant public relations effort, which costs money. It can move to a voice device by high school. I'm frustrated, to be honest. I hit such a significant gap between my dream and reality. My dream of equal opportunity for every kid is so important. They need real data, honest facts. If they ask questions as kids, they'll still be asking them as adults. We need people to be curious and think!"

Leaning in on the table, Roy's gaze felt like it magnified in intensity. "And what about working for someone else? It can be a tough transition for an entrepreneur."

"It does make me pause. I haven't been someone else's employee since college. I do have some standards and boundaries I hate to compromise on."

"I respect that. I'm sure my boundaries are different, but I understand the commitment to them. With no disrespect to your privacy or independence, what does your husband and any staff you may have told think of a possible transaction?" He paused only for a moment. "Of course, you don't have to answer that question."

Shaking her head, she replied, "No, it's no problem. I'm a transparent person and don't mind addressing the issue. I'll say, for all my transparency and putting it all out there, my husband is the Yin to my Yang. He's trained in impartiality. He supports my decision and wants me to get the funding I want." She gently laughed and looked out the window. "He says working for someone else would be good for me. I'm not certain I want to dig into that deeper with him. I haven't taken the idea to my staff yet."

"Keira, I'm extremely impressed with your vision."

She wasn't yet ready to commit, but possibilities erupted in her imagination as she visualized them working together. "There is another part to this, which creates an immense societal impact. With our voice recognition analysis, we aid the ability to determine when a child is in distress. You saw that while watching the interaction in the lab. We could help alert authorities or guardians if a child is facing an abusive situation. Imagine what we could do to reduce the agonies and barriers for children. If you do move forward with the FBI, this tech could improve the possibilities with them. I've often wondered about how I could help Gino, but I've not wanted to step too close to those fires."

Roy's face registered unconcealed interest in this topic. "Oh, boy, that has all kinds of opportunity and legal challenges wrapped up in it. There are substantial synergies between our technologies, our missions, and our teams. As we progress through this acquisition process, you may need to tap into a deeper trust level."

Keira exhaled deeply. She had surprised herself when she'd moved into selling mode. Now he really wanted something from her.

Roy continued, "Nondisclosure agreements can't cover everything. You need to be on the inside of Searcher Technologies to see all the opportunities. But I'll do my best to give you reasons to have faith in me."

Even the slight possibility of Searcher's work also helping her kids sent tingles of excitement through her. She left Roy at the lobby and returned to her lab. Her curiosity mixed with skepticism. She never appreciated somebody asking her to trust them, but she'd never been in this situation before either.

Rockefeller

A month of long days and nights had followed their work in Honduras. Loel remained singularly focused on the Dust's advancements. Every time she strode through the black hallway with the slender windows, the light changed her perceptions of the space. She enjoyed the walk to her lab in the far back corner of the Searcher building. It was a moody corridor. She glanced proudly into each lab as she passed.

In the first lab, two women she had mentored as college students were testing new Dust propulsion in wet conditions. The second lab was nearly silent while five engineers stood at lab tables independently modeling for the nanites. Divergent personalities and skills melded software and hardware all around them.

Before presenting any prototype or finished product to a client, they performed exhaustive rehearsals and detailed testing. No client would see today's demo, only Roy. After fourteen years of working together in various companies, Loel felt the greatest pressure to impress Roy, not customers. It wasn't subordination or fear. She was driven by her respect for him. It was her job to make Roy's vision become reality.

Applause and celebratory shouts bellowed out of the Power and Battery workroom. Loel backed up to peek through the doorway.

"What's up, guys?"

The five men and women turned from the workbench grinning and all speaking at once. They shared their breakthrough for miniaturizing the nanites' power source. "That's fantastic. Make sure you book a large observation lab when you're ready to present. A lot of people will be interested in this one. Roy will be very excited, too."

The team continued their chatter as she exited towards her lab, named Franklin. As the Searcher co-founder, she could have claimed any lab she wanted. But she liked her small out-of-the-way space. She relished the idea of the least impressive lab being the home for the most massive leap in technology the robotics community, and perhaps the world, had ever seen. It gave her the scrappy startup buzz of her earlier career days.

This exhilarating work for Rockefeller took its toll on one's personal life. The long days escalated advancements but were exhausting. She secretly integrated the research and development successes of the other engineers. Only a handful of the senior Searcher personnel were aware of Rockefeller.

Roy, the visionary, picked members for the small circle of trust. All of them had been technical leads together for at least one of Roy's other companies. Cody and Loel worked together the most. Hendrick and Shauney led field testing.

Her pride wrapped around the culture that attracted each of them to follow her and Roy to whatever venture they built. Their faith in each other created a magnetic atmosphere for attracting talent. Loel couldn't remember any employee having an issue with the secrecy of projects they weren't privy to. They simply had faith in their leader.

Her lab and the production room beside it housed the tiny 3D printers creating parts via microprinting and nano-fabrication using direct laser writing. She looked through the printer's magnifying lens to watch the minuscule extruders building up tiny layers of silicon and metal with the flourish of calligraphy. The two-centimeter square wafers of printed parts could create 80,000 microbot parts an hour. If an hour's work sat in a pile on her desk, they wouldn't even be noticeable.

Beside each printer sat miniature assembly robots compiling the micro-machines, the SeekerDust. Multiple arms with hair-thin needle-nosed tools worked at a scale she couldn't detect without the magnifying viewers. Working twenty-four hours a day, they could produce two million flying, networked, intelligent, sensor-ladened, communicating bots. It was never enough. At that rate, it was taking each pair of equipment nearly a month to fill a liter-sized canister with operational nanites.

Today would be a day carved on their calendars. She imagined looking back at this afternoon, reminiscing, "Then in this one demo we blew Roy's mind. We knew we were strapping onto the rocket . . . "

Ever since the earthquake mission, Roy pushed the team for further advances in the physicality of the Dust. At the nanite level, the Dust performed with amazing effectiveness, especially for communication needs. He wanted to make the Dust capable of addressing more of the physical needs within any disaster.

A loud, wide-mouthed yawn overtook Loel's features.

"You alright?" Cody asked as he entered the lab. "It's not like you to be tired in the middle of the afternoon."

"I'm alright. I've just been pushing this so hard; I haven't even been for a run in the last three days."

A stainless-steel canister of Dust in each hand, Cody stopped to look at her. "We're in good shape, don't you think? This will impress Roy." He continued to arrange the canisters by their date of manufacture. Both three-foot shelves were over half-full now.

"We'll know in thirty minutes." Loel reviewed her demo notes on her tablet.

Roy knew the door code, but he knocked, allowing Loel to open it when she was ready. They stood grinning at each other for a moment. Loel hesitated to share things before she felt they were truly successful. It was time.

"I'm excited to see what you have, Loel," Roy said. "You've been a bit scarce, so I figured you and Cody were pretty busy back here."

Looking around the workbenches, he was like a kid hoping to see a present his parents hadn't remembered to wrap. Loel grinned at Roy's excitement and mentally debated if she should tease Roy with delays prior to the demonstration.

He didn't give her much of a chance to consider that option. "What are we waiting for? What can you show me? Do you have a new version of SeekerDust?"

Cody and Loel grinned at each other and took positions on either side of the long white workbench. The table held laptops in front of each engineer and a SeekerDust canister. Loel pointed to the thumbnail-sized devices whispering away on a workbench behind her. "These new 3D printers are faster at printing the metal parts we need. But the silicon parts are still really slow."

Cody interjected details involving the specialization of various versions of the Dust. Loel noticed Roy look at his watch and put his fingers together to form a triangle, pointing down.

Loel sighed. Roy looked at her and Cody as he twisted his finger triangle from pointing down, to pointing up. This was Roy's way of telling his engineers they were providing too much detail. The triangle represented information the technologist had in their heads. Loving their work, they often wanted everyone to understand nuances of their discoveries in detail. Roy was telling them to get to the point, only share the info at the top of the triangle. He wanted the demo. They needed to level-up their communication.

The two inventors got the message. Cody opened the canister. Loel confirmed the desired image displayed on her screen. She instructed the Dust through voice commands. "Dust, replicate Bowl file 4." Dust moved out of the canister, loosely collected like dry ice fog, then merged together to create a gray bowl-shaped object on the table. The bowl, sized as if serving mashed potatoes at a large family dinner, perfectly matched the computer-generated model within Loel's bowl file 4.

While waiting for Roy's response. She tugged on her shirt, straightening the cloth and her spine at the same time. Roy's calmness was disconcerting. The wait for his response was agonizing.

"Well?" Loel asked.

"Well, what?" Roy said. "This is fantastic. Show me more." His grin now complemented his curious eyes.

"Geez, would it kill you to show what you're thinking a little faster?" Loel spoke to Roy while giving Cody a shrug and raised her eyebrows. Cody just grinned. Roy knew exactly the angst he just put her through.

"Dust, replicate Cube file 9." The bowl shape transformed as if shattering, except no pieces fell to the table. It pixelated in midair. The nanites swirled into a slight tabletop dust devil, reconfiguring as a cube.

Cody beamed. "An amazing thing happened in the process of making these shapes. At first, the corners and edges were dangerously sharp. The Dust's manufacturing precision made the edges a hazard. The AI figured out the danger and modified our drawings on all future models."

A series of objects replicated at the table, Loel giving the instruction. The Dust reconfigured within a few seconds each time. A brick, donut, sphere—each disintegrated in midair and then morphed into the next shape. Loel passed the volleyball sized orb to Roy. Handling it as if it would shatter, he turned it over, stroked it, inspecting every inch. He looked up at Loel. "It's so smooth. I don't know why that surprises me."

"As you know, the setae, the nanoscale hairs, allow them to bind together with van der Waals forces."

Roy shook his head and grinned. "Remember trying to explain van der Waals forces to your niece? Her poor pet gecko, Greenie, was turned upside down a million times. She kept inspecting the poor creature's feet with a magnifying glass to see the little hairs Greenie used to stick to the glass. I don't think the kid ever really believed your description."

A chuckle came from Loel. "Maybe that's why she never got the science bug. She lost faith in my explanations. I even tried explaining it with the Velcro analogy of molecules coming together, then pulling apart. I guess that's another reason for me not to go into elementary school education."

Cody rolled his eyes. "Hey, can we stay focused here, you two? The object feels smooth because the Dust lines up so tightly along their attraction, you would never feel bumps, unless the model they were emulating was detailed with bumps or ridges."

Taking the ball from Roy, Loel set it on the table. "There are 64 nanites per cubic millimeter. As they come together, their electrical charges attract them tightly. The manufacturing AI processed hundreds of thousands of simulations in the physical design of the nanites before coming to the design we needed to bind them together."

Roy leaned his elbows on the table, his face within a few inches of the ball. "How many nanites do you think you have right here?"

"I would guess it's about a million," Cody responded. "The AI gave us the best designs fairly quickly. The holdup is in the manufacturing. The 3D printers have been really busy creating this version of the Dust. But we need an exponential increase in production."

A low soft whistle came from Roy. Suddenly, he lifted the ball over his head with both arms. He slammed it down heavily on the edge of the lab table. The loud thud and shock of his actions jolted both Loel and Cody.

"What the hell, Roy?" Loel protested.

"Did you see that, Loel? Had you tested impact yet? Watch the impact zone." Roy said as he smacked it again on the edge of the table. Loel moved forward as if to stop him from destroying the innovatively priceless nanites.

"Wow," Cody uttered nearly under his breath. "Even the sound wasn't what I expected. The tone was so muted, even though the volume was there."

"Loel, did you see the absorption of the contact? The nanites moved in response to the strike but they immediately reshaped into the sphere. We're moving into a new age of material science here. I need to keep our original mission focus, but our opportunities are expanding at each advancement you make."

Still in shock that Roy was willing to smash these rare devices into a lab table just to see what happened, Loel stood blinking at her partner. Cody seemed enamored. Loel was a bit pissed. It was Roy's money and risk and vision, so they approached everything from a different perspective.

"I'm sorry, Loel." Roy reached over to pat Loel on the back. "You know me. It had to be stress tested at some point, but I just got this urge to know what would happen if I . . . well, you know."

Loel fidgeted with the base of the canister. "This is just the beginning. We're proving that the nanites can construct and reconstruct objects from our models. Evidently, as proven today, they can also self-repair. Cody and I lined up a series of new models to test, which focus on your bigger objectives. Your dream is getting really concrete. I believe Rockefeller is going to take us places."

Roy whipped his eyes around to search the room. It was subtle, but Loel saw it. Roy never felt comfortable discussing Rockefeller. He was always paranoid of the wrong person hearing them. It was an instinctual reaction; this room was secure. For a man who spent a decade in the government's intelligence community, often undercover, Roy had a few tics that could surprise Loel. His visible reaction to the utterance of the Rockefeller name was top of the list.

Roy gave a slight accepting nod, indicating they could continue. "This isn't our everyday show-and-tell, Loel." They locked eyes, motionless, to register this as an event of importance.

"No." Loel tugged at the base of her shirt. "No, it's not. You dreamed of these capabilities for decades. You're going to make world-changing plays with these bots. They will be everywhere. YOU will be everywhere."

"Thank you, Loel. Thank you for making this possible. You make things happen, my friend."

Loel blushed. "It's been a long haul, but we're progressing."

Cody stood silent, looking from one boss to the other. Loel was certain that he had never heard either of them talk this way.

Loel recognized she'd lost Roy to an internal brainstorming session. Was he thinking about the potential of the new Dust, the exciting or scary future that lay in front of them? They needed more raw materials. She needed permission to take more risks in their processes. If they continued to progress at this pace, only their imaginations and sourcing of raw materials appeared to be their limitations.

Cody and Roy discussed the number of computer simulations required prior to instructing the micro machines to replicate the models. Through machine learning processes, they executed tens of thousands of hardware configurations virtually before a consistent process of sticking and releasing was achieved for the Dust. Roy *now* wanted to know all the details.

Speed of construction, long term durability and the implications on various industries were discussed in rapid fire. Loel marveled at how Roy appeared to grow younger before her eyes anytime they launched forth into visionary discussions.

Knowing Roy was pleased, now was the time to ask for the resources she needed. "This new version of the Dust is what allows us to advance to making physical shapes with substance. There's one more thing we want to show you. Dust, replicate cogs file 25."

The ball sitting on the table appeared to crumble and swirl at the same time. It reconfigured into a one-foot device, similar to an executive desktop toy. The cogs moved, driving a small arm with a grasping tool to pick up a ball and move it to a ramp. It contained many of the moving parts mimicking the miniature assembly robots. Roy pumped his fists back and forth like pistons. "It moves!"

Loel was now certain she'd get the resources she needed, even though the demonstrated movement she was showing was machine movement, not fluid mobility. The Dust could fly, it could make shapes, but it couldn't create fluid changing and moving components. The current trade-off was strength versus mobility. Of course, that is why she needed more of everything, time, money, and brain power.

Hit him up while he was on a high. "Roy, I need more people and more Dust. You've got Hendrick and Shauney off on a search and rescue post-hurricane mission. We've got the incredible opportunity opening with the FBI. All of these things since the earthquake are important, but distractions from this."

Roy straightened and gaped at Loel.

"What? Don't glare at me, Roy. You want us to do things that have never been done before. We're making progress, but I need more people. I need engineers with materials science expertise and at least one more mechanical engineer."

"We can't expand our circle of people. The more people, the more potential for leaks or misunderstandings. The ramifications of others understanding what these capabilities will mean in the future is far too risky. It could impact too many people. I've seen what happens when people panic about something they don't understand. Things all go to hell, especially for those involved or in their path."

Cody looked from Loel to Roy. "Roy, can we at least bring some of our current team into the picture? You have many engineers you trust.

I could train them on some of these disciplines. Then we can try to back fill their other roles?"

"Roy, we have to be hiring more talent," Loel pleaded. "Our systems can model only so much for us when I'm the only one setting the parameters. If we start engaging with the fundamental decision making in the Dust, we'll never get there at this rate."

"You can have any computing power you need. Parse as much work for production or testing as you can to other teams if the work looks like it applies to an existing client. Get help with the 3D printers. That should save you time. But you must be careful that nothing looks like you're building things with the Dust. Not yet! This technology can't prematurely be in anyone else's hands."

Loel now glared at Roy. "Parsing out work to delegate just eats up time, too. Can we at least get Hendrick? If you pursue Opal, we will have to have their assistance with integration of the ethical computing."

"You can't have more people now. We're not ready," Roy said. "Thanks for the demonstration. Great progress." He turned towards the door.

Loel clinched her fists. "If you want this Dust to be intelligent and you really want to make the objects you dream about, I'll need resources. I can't take responsibility for its actions in our current constraints."

Roy left without saying anything else.

"Crap!" Cody muttered. "I thought you had him there in the palm of your hand, Loel."

She slumped to her stool. "Me, too. He can envision the end results so clearly that he can't see any chance it won't work. It's too vivid in his mind for it to be anything but a future reality. It just might kill me trying to prove he's right this time."

Options

P uget Sound hosted the most tankers on Thursdays. Keira and Ollie had the ships' schedules memorized. Ruby simply trusted their plan and rode along. Keira zipped up her wetsuit and slid her phone into a waterproof holster fastened to her shoulder. Ollie watched, then looked at his own phone.

"Oh no you don't, Ollie," Keira said. "I'm not your mom and this is not her purse. Put your phone in your pocket."

He laughed and zipped the device into his wetsuit's pocket. "You're maternal until it comes to carrying stuff." He laughed as he sprawled on his board and paddled into the water. Ruby and Keira quickly followed him.

"Keira, I got a guest teaching gig for you at the university," Ruby said. "They saw your video with Elly. The part where you're teaching her that all laws are not inherently ethical excited them."

Paddling between her two executive engineers towards the expectant path of the oncoming tanker's wake, she swelled with gratitude for their companionship. "They did a good job putting that video together. I get a lot of feedback on my comments about there being nothing ethical about preventing women from voting. Yet, it was the law."

She gauged the distance of the approaching red and black cargo ship churning through the water. She liked the thrill of tanker surfing, but she carefully approached the riskier side of the sport, which involved getting early in their wake. She chose to stay about a quarter mile from the ship and take the steady, predictable long game approach. They were in good position to hop the wave in a few minutes.

She turned to Ruby to give her a reassuring smile. "Stop looking at me like I told you I had a month to live. I'm fine. The only place that still hurts is between my shoulder blades. Are you ready to try this tanker? It's a big one."

Repositioning on her board, Ruby looked away. "I'm just hoping it's not too soon for you to be out here. It's only been about three weeks, and you've been pushing yourself so hard with meetings and stuff."

"Will you two stop fussing over each other?" Ollie said.

"Sounds good. I'll change the subject. Ollie, what was your most interesting meeting at the education conference? It seems like you have steered away from the conversation all morning."

Ollie looked over his shoulder to check the wake's progress towards them. "The meeting with education tech company GGBB was interesting. They're really interested in our AIs for stress detection in kids. They want to use it for online test taking and possibly instruction. Their level of disconnects imply that they're not picking up the cues from kids until it's too late."

"Okay," Keira replied. "Why do I get the feeling there was more to the conversation than a royalty deal?"

"They have lots of grant money. Which is great, we know how hard that is to get." He again looked over his shoulder and then stood on his board. He liked to be upright when the wave came. The others paddled with the wake and then stood. They were all poised for action. "They want to buy Opal."

The wake lifted them. The next few moments, they all focused on their respective methods of attacking the wave. Once in formation and bobbing on the crest of the tanker's surf, they exhaled and relaxed into the ride.

"That was quite the dramatic timing," Keira called over the slapping of the water around them.

"Cool company, but I don't see it happening," Ruby said. "What did you tell them?"

"I told them I'd talk to Keira," Ollie replied.

The slow consistent wake required minimal effort compared to ocean waves. Conversation wasn't difficult, but Keira let the magnitude of the topic sit between them. This could be a way to hear more of their thoughts about mergers before she told them about her dinner with Roy. She squealed as her board twitched underneath her, nearly pitching her backward off the wake.

"Whoa!" Ruby laughed. "You almost bit that wave early, Keira."

Ollie pulled a little further out on the wake, staying clear of Keira's board.

"This wave is going to get choppy in a about a minute." Ollie called out as he pointed to a tugboat that would be crossing their paths shortly.

"That cross wake is going to kill me," Keira grumbled. She bent her knees a little more and focused on the water bubbling ahead of her.

"Ah, come on. You've taken on bigger cross wakes than that. You're the one who said you were ready," Ruby said. They rode the wake in concentration.

Ruby, always her cheerleader, made Keira smile. The tugboat had moved across their path a safe distance ahead of them. As its wake crossed the tanker's wake they were surfing, the water's turbulence bounced Ruby and Keira into chaotic wobbles. Ollie laughed at them until his board hooked on a frothy swirl of water. His board spun and he dropped into the water.

Keira and Ruby, having gained their composure, pushed forward and to their right to ease off the wave. They laid on their boards, bobbing in the waves, waiting for Ollie to join them. "Okay, I know we haven't been out all that long, but what do you think about paddling to shore and hitting one of the cart vendors over there for a drink? I don't want to push it too hard today."

"Works for me," Ollie said. As he paddled away, he called back to them. "Last one to shore buys the drinks."

Ruby looked at Keira with a raised eyebrow. "What is he, twelve?" She quickened her paddling speed.

They settled around a picnic table with their drinks. Their boards leaned against a tree behind them. Ollie rubbed his hands together. "Did you hear Brandon's message? They had two thousand more companies wanting to implement the MoralOS and certify through OpenML. Too bad Opal isn't making the money off those. But I'm so glad more companies are certifying their AIs."

Ruby nodded. "But I'm glad to be rid of the distraction. We created the ethical framework, but that growth rate shows that a consortium is better to manage the certification than having a company attached to it."

Keira turned to Ollie. "Changing the subject back, who is behind GGBB? I've heard about their products, but not much about the company."

"Good news and bad news on that front," Ollie admitted. "Financially they're sound. Culturally, I think it sounds like they're pretty cool. They have amazing access into the schools, which could help us a lot." He paused for drink.

"I haven't heard the bad, yet," Ruby said.

Ollie looked toward the water. "Well, one of their latest investors is Mickey Temming."

"What?" Keira demanded. "You can't be serious. We're having nothing to do with him. I won't even talk to them."

"That's just it. They don't fit his profile. The guy I talked to thinks the whole investment, which is minor, was done by the accounting firm. It was a round of investment with several players."

"Nope. I'll have nothing to do with a company that will do business with a man specializing in weapons and destroying businesses. The rumors are too frequent. GGBB could be his next target. He's the antithesis of ethical. Oh, well. You can tell them no, thank you. We'll leave it at that. But I do have a related conversation to have with both of you."

Ruby winced. "Yeah, especially since I have more news about Temming. He's been snooping around about the explosion at the NuChemi plant. He's laying down the blame for anyone that will listen on that previously certified AI. Elly implied he is trying to tie us to the incident showing that our ethical AIs can still make bad decisions."

"So, he really is circling around Opal. I don't get, I don't see a fit for him. And NuChemi's AI did make a weighted ethical decision. It just chose the lesser of two evils. And that limitation has been patched."

She gave them an abbreviated rundown of her conversations with Roy. Her two closest friends and executives sat stunned and wide-eyed listening to her story.

Ruby shook off her shocked silence. She spoke quietly. "Are you taking that conversation seriously? I mean, Searcher Technologies is pretty big. Brandt is super rich. Would you really sell your baby? Sell us?"

"Guys, first, everything is fine. I didn't ask for the meeting. Just like GGBB came to us, Brandt came to us. We're getting a lot of visibility because of contribution in the MoralOS development. I'm glad to see there is so much interest in ethical computing. But we have a lot of goodness in our products too. We're just getting noticed more."

An even larger cargo ship than the wave generator they had followed slowly passed through the Sound.

"You're considering selling? What would you do if you didn't have Opal?" Ollie asked.

"Oh, I wouldn't leave and I'm chaining the two of you to me." She gave them her strongest smile. "Look, I won't leave this work. I don't know yet if I can do this or not. But I need to explore it. We could use the money. We could also benefit from Brandt's reputation. His name behind what we do would expand our credibility a lot. We could also positively impact their work in a major way."

"Wow!" Ruby turned around to put her back to the picnic table. She could watch the traffic on the water. "I really don't know how I feel about this. I'd love to get out of the business of chasing grants, but wow."

"Humor me for a moment. Can you imagine what we could do with our childhood distress detection if it were used in more places than just our learning robots? If we could open up our imagination for broader uses because we had resources? I think about helping kids at their most vulnerable moments, like while the trafficking vultures are circling, post natural disaster."

Ollie leaned in, his eyes sparkling. "I've dreamed about hospital monitoring in children's wards, which could help nurses receive alerts without having to listen to every room's nonstop monitors."

"Exactly. We could explore our long wish list of 'what-if' scenarios," Keira said.

Ruby did not turn around. "I can see how it could be tempting."

Keira was accustomed to Ruby challenging her to think deeper or broader about a topic. They'd played that intellectual push and pull since they were roommates at Stanford. This reluctance to engage in the debate hurt a little.

Keira looked out at the water for comfort. "We always say one of the key characteristics that makes us human is that we can think about alternative futures and make deliberate choices accordingly. I'm going to spend some time imagining alternatives. Elly will help run scenarios. But I want your help and opinions."

Hard Decision

T he marina was cool. Keira's catamaran, *The Right Choices*, sparkled in the sun after its rigorous rubdown. Keira sat on the edge of the cushioned bench assessing each rope, cord, hook, and connector sorted in stacks at her feet. Her mental energy was wrapped around the opportunity of Roy Brandt's offer to buy Opal. She pulled a band from her pocket to tie her hair back out of her face.

The breeze coming across the water soothed a bit of the rough edges she was nurturing in her psyche. Budgets, employee career paths, product road maps, and an endless supply of robots all competed for her mindshare. This mental tug-of-war was why she had escaped to the refuge of the boat.

Keira directed her voice to the little yellow receiver Ruby had mounted at the helm station. "Elly, the Puget Sound Supply delivery is coming today?"

"Yes. The boat should arrive with your order in the next two hours," Elly replied through the boat's speaker. On the boat, she didn't like using earbuds. The refreshing air and the sound of the water and songbirds in the trees near the dock were too precious to block with buds.

Selling the company had never been a consideration for Keira. Now, it was on her mind constantly. Every obstacle to expanding the development of the AIs and the robots needed money to surmount. Opal's revenue wasn't growing as fast as Keira's drive.

"Elly, you built the projection model for the learning bots and modified it with the latest production costs estimates, right?"

"Yes. With the new numbers, it will take nine years and an expansion of your line of credit for the next four years before the learning bots will yield a profit."

"Ouch. I was afraid of that. How many versions of hardware upgrades does your plan include?"

"Only three."

Keira slouched back in the chair. "Oh God," she groaned. Her head rested on the cushion. Noncommittal weather passed above, both gray and white clouds drifted westward towards the sea. The learning robots could receive many software upgrades within that time. But as she added functions to the robots, the cost increased, as did the need for more iterations of the hardware.

Keira aggressively cut a rusted clasp from the end of black nylon rope. She hurled the clasp towards a bucket of odds and ends by the edge of the bench. "Elly, order new hardware for the lines, but find a better supplier. The last one sent us crap, which obviously isn't marine grade."

"Yes, I will place the order immediately."

She continued to remove any fasteners showing obvious wear or rust. A beautiful array of small sailing craft participated in a regatta, filling the inlet with multi-colored sails. It would have been annoying to dodge that much traffic. Regattas were fun, but she gave them up when she graduated to the forty-foot catamaran.

In college, she had traded the money from her semester abroad tuition for an angel investment in a friend's company. Years later, the children's entertainment company went public. Gino had convinced her a portion of the windfall needed to be splurged. Keira remained grateful for his insistence she buy the boat. He always helped her be better. The boat gave her an active distraction from her workaholic ways. She needed to get him out on the water soon. It had been weeks since they'd spent the night on the boat.

Elly said, "Keira, I completed the research into Roy Brandt and his employees, yet there is not a substantial quantity of data."

"What did you find?"

"The resumes of Roy's employees are impressive and extensive until they join one of Roy's companies. They then become as protective as Roy about their accomplishments and skills. Only the employees of the aSports businesses publish papers or share their achievements with the press or peer organizations regularly."

"No wonder I struggled to learn more about them. It seems odd. Did you discover anything you think I'll find interesting? You're so clever. Can you tell me if I should be doing this deal or not?" Keira pleaded.

"I possess insufficient data for providing a definitive quantitative analysis."

"Hmm, me too, Elly. Me too."

"Is there a reason you are not having this conversation with Ruby?"

"Ruby made something clear when I started Opal. She didn't want to be involved in the risk. I wanted us to be partners, but she deferred those opportunities. Even when the business became less of a risk. She doesn't like to talk about these kinds of things or the risks involved."

"I see. I will not bring it up with her. Upon a search of your historical files, I found your 'Opportunities vs. Threats' analysis regarding the founding of Opal. I believe one thing stands out as relevant to your decision."

Keira set down the rope she was coiling. "Oh really? What did you find?"

"The top item in your column of positives was 'being your own boss.' You decide what you want to work on. Would this change if you sold to Searcher?"

"You know, I've grown up a lot since I started Opal. I don't think I'd have a problem working for someone else. Not if it meant I could reach more kids."

"Your personal journals contradict that statement directly seventeen times in the last ten years."

"Wait, what? You're using my own personal notes to call me out here?" It was a common joke between Keira and Gino that she was unemployable. She cherished establishing her own deadlines and priorities. She made decisions faster than others were willing to accept. But she didn't enjoy the financial pressures.

"You're assessing the viability of a successful merger between Opal and Searcher, correct?"

"Yes," Keira responded slowly.

"Then you should consider your writings and self-reflections to challenge your assessment."

"You're not the only one pointing this out as an issue," Keira murmured.

The hardware-free lines needed to be coiled and returned to the supply tub. Keira couldn't bring herself to budge off the chair for the task. Instead, she leaned back and propped her feet upon the mess she had created. This deal would be the biggest decision she ever made. Gino weighed in with enthusiasm for the deep pockets Roy could provide for Keira's work. He didn't provide any other opinions, except that she would make the right decision.

"Have you checked on the orphanage this week?"

"Yes, they are in a new location. Classes have resumed for the university center, too. They are both in buildings which exceed earthquake codes."

"Great, but what about the kids? What about Roberto and Miette?"

"Roberto has been adopted by a Honduras governor's family. He will have two big brothers. Miette has been matched with a family, but it is not finalized yet."

"Thank you. Keep me posted on any changes."

"Keira, what is the number one thing preventing you from achieving your objective with Opal?" Elly inquired. "You ask your engineers this question repeatedly."

"Funds. I know. I know. And we didn't get the Lida grant renewed. They weren't happy about the earthquake-damaged robots."

"I don't understand the reason you ask this question so often of your employees. However, I record it regularly. Shall I tell you what you say to them after they respond?"

"I tell them if they control the obstacle, then change it. If they don't control it, find a way to minimize it, work around it, or gain control. Ugh. This feels like the times my friends tell me they are sounding like their mothers. You're making me preach to myself. Roy does have a lot of money and access to more, I'm sure. Gino tells me that, since

I seem to cultivate an aversion to charging enough for our technology or raising capital, Roy's offer might be really good for me."

"Do you know your magic number?" Elly asked.

"What are you talking about? Don't switch the subject now, please."

"A common question to ask someone considering selling their company is their consideration about the magic number they need to sell the business. Have you established how much money you need for the future and what is the value of Opal?"

"Oh, I get it." Keira shook her head. "We're way past that with Roy. The offer falls under the 'insane to ignore for money reasons' zone. Did you find that question during an entrepreneur's podcast or something?"

"Yes, I did. I collect these topics in my knowledge base. Should I delete this question or mark it as bad one?"

"No, it's not a bad question, considering the scenario. It just doesn't fit this particular opportunity with Roy. You did good. Keep it. Please make a note that I want to share your line of questioning and analysis with Ruby and Ollie. This is showcasing your analytical growth."

She hoisted herself off the chair, scooped the ropes up and dropped them in their bin. This time she simply couldn't be bothered to organize them more carefully. She wanted to pour herself a drink.

"Keira, what about the sub-bullet on your 'Decision-Making' notes at the start of Opal, regarding autonomy? What if Roy sets something different for your priorities?"

"That's a tough one. I need to talk to him more about the kids. I do expect I'll be pulled in multiple directions because of the role I'd be taking. But I would hope Opal's mission carries on with our existing team, plus more resources. In fact, can you build a model removing some distractions of the products we keep now for the mere fact of the revenue they generate? You know which ones Roy hasn't mentioned or are not tied to education."

"Do I need to do a summary of resources spent by product?"

"No, I think it would only depress me right now. I also don't want to scare Roy off if he didn't like the results. I'm going to put our best foot forward at our show-and-tell next week. But I have a lot of questions for Mr. Brandt. Thanks for helping me think through this, Elly."

"I tried to predict the questions you needed to answer. The entrepreneurship curriculum I consumed informed my parsing of your previous documentation. There are more queries. Do you want to continue?"

Dropping back into the deep-set chair with her glass in hand, Keira sighed. "No, Elly. I think I just need some music and to sit here and think. I'm out of answers now."

Dream Crusher

Mickey walked down the barren hallway to his Information Research department. Fresh from an argument with his CFO, he grumbled to himself. How many times did he have to remind the man that, for this particular business, the only things worthy of spending money on were information, computing power to get information, and security to protect the information. Esthetics and creature comforts were a waste of money.

He jerked open the door to a windowless room with all overhead lights off. The twenty analysts seated at desks immediately ceased all noises. Their eyes locked on the monitors illuminating their faces, avoiding contact with their boss. A few desk lamps scattered around the room shone on food wrappers and used plates.

"This place stinks! I can't believe you guys can use your brains in a room that smells like yesterday's pizza and burnt coffee pot," barked Mickey. He maneuvered around the room, gruffly twisting ball caps around to position the bill to the front and searching for any Tootsie Pops. The analysts provided a steady supply of what they privately called "Mickey's pacifiers." He was aware of the nickname. It kept him stocked, so he let it slide.

"Mr. Temmings, we found five more companies with ties to robotics in learning. None of them have anything we think you would be interested in," an analyst in the back row offered.

Mickey grumbled, "What are we paying you for? It's not to find interesting toys! I need to know what companies think they're creating some hot shit ready for a spy movie. Find me a gold mine, you pussies!"

They all turned back to their computers and continued to work. Mickey knew they expected these tirades, but they never seemed to get accustomed to them.

A text message went across the screens of all the analysts from 'Anonymous.' "He might be rich, but the money didn't buy him class." Mickey saw it and pretended not to. It wasn't worth his effort.

He turned to his lead analyst and investigator. "Deon, what are your boys doing here? You know the last compelling piece of intelligence you offered me was a masked patent application. Your long-haired hippy traced it to some southern gentleman pretending he invented a surveillance device which people would swallow that would still record a crowded room's conversation."

"Mickey," Deon muttered. "We're digging. We're testing and evaluating thousands of technologies every day."

"Don't start making excuses! I'm tired of excuses." Deon was the best investigator he'd ever employed. He'd never let Deon know that; that could give the kid too much opportunity for leverage. But the guy was an intelligent chameleon.

"We're working on it, man. These things take a while to unwind all the corporations. They're designed to prevent competitive infiltration. But they're not expecting my little brigade." Deon beamed with pride as he looked over the misfit collection of digital dumpster divers he'd recruited.

Mickey walked behind the various men, looking at their screens. Inspecting the diagrams, websites, and photographs on each. "If you're so talented, why haven't I seen a lot of evidence lately?"

"What about the shield paint tech that was better than our military's radar deflection? That stuff was genius. We handed it to you and the CEO's bad boy behavior. That let you convince him the only way he could stay out of jail was to sell his intellectual property to you."

"Don't get too cocky, but that one will do well when it's contract plays out," Mickey said. He bit his Tootsie Pop into shards. He had government contracts, the most autonomous drones able to manipulate battles, and enough surveillance technology to snoop on any government who didn't want to buy from him.

"Sir . . . " a young man in a hoodie stammered. "I have a tech you might be interested in seeing."

Mickey loved people's fear of him. He relished the power of squeezing every last bit of work from these guys. They didn't work endless hours out of respect for him. It was fear and a lot of cash that got the best work from people. That is why he made certain every person on his critical teams hid a secret they wanted to keep. He had the advantage.

He'd learned his lesson at an early age. The more leverage he had, the tighter the line his subjects would walk. Leverage came first from attitude, but mostly from information. Securing the most data was high on his priority list. It worked to get his belt-wielding stepdad in jail, and it worked to get him every promotion he ever twisted out of somebody. Now, it was working to help him pick up businesses before the world understood their value.

These little enterprises were often inventing amazing stuff. But being underfunded and with secrets in the closet about their top engineers or owners often had tragic consequences. They couldn't bring their dreams to fruition. So, Mickey bought their businesses, crushed their entrepreneurial dreams, and made a fortune taking the tech the last mile to commercial viability.

"Yeah? Show me something good."

Nervously, the man started spitting out details he'd purchased along with amateur personal-cam footage. "Have you heard of this company Searcher Technologies? They found people in a pancaked building after an earthquake. They could hear breathing under something like ten floors of concrete, somehow even estimate vital signs. The rescue dogs had already given up."

"What? Searcher. Oh, I've heard of Searcher. That's Brandt's company. You say it can listen inside a building?"

"Yes, sir, some type of smart nanites."

Mickey muttered, "Well, well. I wonder if our mutual friend at the DOD is aware of what Roy is playing with these days?"

Mickey didn't like the analysts to see his excitement. He spun around to Deon and grumbled. "Get this place cleaned up. I don't want some flowery air freshener stench. The budget gets smaller if I have to bring a gas mask to walk in here tomorrow. And give me the most current intelligence on Searcher Technologies. The news should have covered something like that. Why didn't they? Give me facts. Why is it so special it's kept secret?"

He grabbed a handful of Tootsie Pops from the desk by the exit and squinted at the hallway's brightness as he jerked open the door.

Trust Isn't a Given

Keira entered Discovery Park, passing between two enormous blooming crepe myrtle trees. This was her favorite respite inside the Seattle city limits. Roy stood from the nearest park bench, extending his hand to shake.

"Keira, thank you for joining me here today and thanks for the presentation last week. It's a beautiful day. I just couldn't bring myself to sit in a meeting room any longer."

"I couldn't agree with you more. Why stay indoors when you don't have to? Visit any earthquakes lately?"

"No. As a matter of fact, Loel has convinced me that training others and letting them go in our stead is much less risky. So, I think my emergency flight days are over."

"That makes sense," Keira said.

Roy gestured down a path lined with mature live oaks and ornamental grasses. "Can we walk while we chat?"

She said, "Of course. Although I must admit, strolling through the gardens for a meeting with a former intelligence agency employee feels cinematic or stereotyped."

"That's funny. I guess I have to maintain some type of reputation to keep people guessing. No one ever pointed out the irony to me despite all the years I've suggested walking meetings. I wonder how many people thought about it?"

Small talk did not last long. They each shared examples of technical challenges facing them and lamented the difficulties of finding enough trained technical talent in the current job market. Schools still couldn't produce enough skilled professionals, and the shortage was making their entire industry desperate.

"I've been told we often advance more from failures than our successes. Tell me about a failure you learned from. You get bonus points if it involves somebody's unethical behavior or practices." Keira smiled.

"Ah, yes. Failures can be motivating and educational. We need to celebrate our mistakes more. But when they rub you raw and hurt like hell, they never feel worthy of celebration."

"That's so true. Time and distance are often needed after a failure or a 'learning moment' as my step-dad called them."

"I won't go into all the details. But an early idealistic venture of mine brought solar power and clean water to remote places in Africa. Why I thought my approach to business would bring different results than the hundreds who tried before me, I can't explain. For decades, we've known there was a need, there was technology, and it would improve lives for millions." He shrugged.

"Oh no you don't," Keira insisted. "I haven't gained enlightenment from this tale yet. What happened and what did you learn?" She ran her fingers along the tall hedges next to the path.

"It certainly involves ethics," Roy grumbled. "Corrupt governments held up our equipment, stole it or stripped it after it arrived onsite, denied receipt of materials, charged us with crimes, and prevented us from doing any further business in their countries. They lured us with a big-bang approach, so we wrapped every bit of our capital into the launch from the beginning. We had nothing left to work with after they were done. We were forced to close up shop."

"Ouch. What lesson did you carry away from that one?"

"Despite the obvious, learn from history and other people's mistakes? It's enlightening to look at the root source of problems. We looked at the cause of the poverty and suffering, the lack of water and electricity. Basic human needs had to be met or the people couldn't thrive, be educated, and move up in the world. We were certain we could address these basics and solve anything."

Keira thought about all the well-meaning philanthropist and organizations never reaching their goals.

"We failed to go layers deeper to uncover the real problem. The people in power didn't want the citizens to do better or be educated. Their power wouldn't survive an educated citizenry. They suppressed their own people so the rulers could continue their reign."

They stopped at the edge of a clearing, admiring the contemporary merry-go-round filled with kids and families. Rockets replaced the traditional horses, bobbing up and down. Planets and moons held benches and twirled in place as the platform gently revolved.

"Sounds familiar, sad that suppression happens everywhere. There must be more to this story, though," Keira prompted.

"Others had figured out the suppression issue. No one worked out how to intervene. The 'more' you mention has yet to develop itself into a resolution. Obviously, the issues persist. But I decided one must take novel and unexpected paths to better the corrupt. The unscrupulous are experts at human behavior. They have to be to manipulate it. You must surprise them. Sometimes acting counter-intuitively beats them."

"Interesting. I'll remember these wise words," Keira said. Roy's methods of storytelling, knowing what to share and what to hold back, explained some of his magnetism. She saw the appeal of wanting to know him, work alongside him, and hopefully get within his inner circle. Because that cadre was likely small, the opportunity and the challenge held allure and mystique.

"Keira, I have to ask. Where is your head on this transaction? There is no expectation for you to negotiate anything today, but what barriers do I need to break down?"

Their stroll continued around the edge of the clearing next to the most densely wooded part of the park towards the ten-acre pond.

"That's a complex question with equally complex answers. I'm conflicted. Helping children is the most important thing in the world to me. The world will be a better place when we do a better job educating our kids and treating them better."

"I agree with you and have a project I believe you'll embrace for that reason."

"But you can't tell me about it. Let's come back around to that in a minute. To continue with the theme of what's important to me: I like your money, frankly. You can help with the robotics development and provide better R&D than I can do solo. I also like working with smart people." She grinned at him. "Told you I'd be genuine."

"I expect nothing less. Nice to hear the funding is part of the sway." He smiled. "I've got that down pat."

Picking up a pebble, Keira skipped it across the pond. "Trust is also critical to me. This is where I struggle the most with your offer. As an entrepreneur, I'm naturally comfortable and happy with control. But another way to say one likes control is to say we like a sense of security. Secrecy creates an air of deception. Deceptions can erode the quality of relationships."

Roy's gaze stayed directed at the ripples her pebble had made. "I understand that. Trust is a belief that someone is reliable, will tell you the truth, and will act or react in a predictable pattern. I'm a consistent person. Some people may say I'm unconventional but not erratic nor emotional. I studied your business decisions, including your work with the MoralOS and OpenML. Your choices may be unpredictable, but I believe you are consistent and grounded. I don't take on business partners lightly. I like what you stand up for."

They stood to watch kids interact around the edge of the water. Three young boys splashed in the shallows on one side. A girl dangled her legs over a retaining wall while she expertly maneuvered a remote-control boat through a series of figure eights.

"Where does your passion for kids and their education spring from?" Roy asked, without turning towards her.

"Both my parents were intuitive, curious, and willing to discuss any questions I or my sister ever asked. My stepdad, who came along a lot later, was the same way. I was fortunate to be encouraged to learn. As a child, I encountered people with horrible racism and prejudices several times. I wasn't ever their target, thankfully. I saw the hate they spewed and the hurt they caused. It deeply pained me, especially when they targeted kids. Guess what he said when I asked my dad why they were so mean and awful?"

Roy shook his head and shrugged.

"He told me those bullies were mean because they were ignorant. The word wasn't used as a disparaging term or a flippant jibe. He explained that bigotry came from a lack of education and understanding of people and the world. We see it in politics and immigration issues, don't we?"

"Way too often."

"When people aren't curious enough to learn about others, they get scared of them. He made sure I knew that defensiveness is often used to prevent exposing personal ignorance. It's the people who can't handle the changing world around them that I fear. It's what they do when they're feeling inferior, which can be the most dangerous."

"Wise words," Roy agreed.

She continued to skip stones, always skipping them away from the girl's boat. "Those words made me think a lot and clarified many things for me. They also motivated me to watch people closely. I found that curious people were the happiest. Kids relish learning. I see kids develop a love for life-long learning habits because they were successful at getting answers early. The better they understand the world and know how to explore, the better they can deal with change and challenges. Education is my way of making the world a better place."

"I like it, Keira. I agree with your perspective and your dad's. I've never taken the time to actually explore it and never articulated those thoughts so concisely or in such a meaningful way. My employees need to be curious and explore the world. A requirement of employment in any of my companies is that each employee has a passport or gets one immediately. And they must vacation outside of the country within the first three years of working for me. I like my people to possess a worldview beyond their bubble."

"I like that. All my staff have their passports. I never required it, but the expectation to use one is pretty clear within Opal."

"You said you weren't the target of the abuse from these prejudiced or closed-minded people. But I get the sense some of what you saw came way too close to home?" They began their walk again, around the pond towards an empty bench.

"Hmm," Keira murmured. She didn't often tell her stories.

It felt right to share them now. "My best friend and next-door neighbor in elementary school lost her life to ignorance. It was all so innocent. We were both only in fifth grade." She had to swallow hard to continue.

"We spent nearly all our time together, playing with digital world building, doing puzzles, stuff like that. She got a crush on a boy in our class. He was a different religion, skin color, and born on foreign soil."

Roy pulled her out of the way for an oncoming bicycler.

"That was a trifecta of evil for her already abusive dad. He caught the two of them holding hands while walking home from school. He beat my friend and blamed her broken jaw and head injuries on falling down the stairs.

"It was all a poorly kept neighborhood secret. She missed the rest of the school year, recovering in the hospital from it. Her mom moved her away as soon as she got out of the hospital. I guess that made it easier to keep quiet."

"A couple years later, in a fit of bigoted rage, her dad killed her."

Roy clenched his fists and tightened his jaw. He didn't verbally respond. They reached the bench and sat.

She paused, turned to face Roy. "I have a real problem with secrets. It's only fair while I expect you to be open and transparent with me, I'll reveal my own issue. You might understand me a little better with the explanation." She took a deep breath, letting it out slowly. She didn't hide her efforts to calm herself.

Continuing she said, "First let me ask if you ever watched any of the movies of post-war Nazi Germany where the Nazis said they were just following orders to explain away their actions? Or the shows of Russia regarding the reactions to the Chernobyl nuclear accident? They told miners to dig a tunnel. Because it was Russia, they dug the tunnel. But nobody told the miners they would be exposed to radiation that would kill them within a few months or years." She waited for Roy to acknowledge the comment.

When he did, he stayed silent.

"Secrets, classified actions, also killed my dad. I was in elementary school. He was my world. Mom was in the Navy and traveled everywhere. Dad was my constant. He was brilliant. He invented the ultimate query system. It could answer nearly any question in the sciences, mathematics, political history, etc. Its algorithms were so sophisticated it could search any open data, anywhere."

She looked in vain for an empty bench. "His employer didn't tell him about their hacking in the dark web. They used his technology and his own science to break laws and infiltrate governments. It was an information weapon." She took more deep breaths.

"They hacked the wrong people, one too many times. A cartel tracked the leak to his system, and they gunned him down. He never did anything with their data! He was just the innovator. Those people hid behind his expertise, abused his trust and enthusiasm for the possibilities of democratizing information, so that anyone could reach answers to complex questions. They bastardized his work, and he paid the ultimate price for it."

Regardless of her desire to be transparent, Ruby was the only non-family member she'd ever told this much of her story. "My little sister and I paid the price for it. So, I struggle with those who hide behind the cloak of corporate secrecy. If you're not doing something you shouldn't do, then why not tell the world you're doing it?"

They looked at each other in silence for several moments.

She sighed heavily. "This isn't easy. I think I'd like to head to that little pub just outside the gates. What do you think? Shall we go have a drink?"

"That's an excellent idea. We can enjoy their rooftop patio." They walked towards the street at a more purposeful pace. "Thank you for sharing that with me."

"It's not something I talk about much. For our safety, we were relocated, etc. It's a big f'ing hairball. So, I leave it tucked out of sight most of the time. Part of why I became an entrepreneur was to control with whom I surround myself with."

They navigated the exit of the park and crossed the street to the pub in congenial silence. Roy said something to the pub's host as he slipped him a substantial stack of bills. As the host showed them to the foot of the stairs he responded, "Of course, I'll tell them the rooftop is closed for repairs."

"Oh, I would never ask you to lie to your patrons, especially if making repairs implies you have problems here. May I suggest you tell them it has been rented for a private event."

The manager smiled. "Of course. That's a much better option. Thank you."

She thought about going through life buying so many things. She did like Roy's choice of wording and protectiveness of the pub's reputation. They sat at Roy's choice of table, far from the one set of patrons already seated.

She ordered wine. Roy ordered scotch. He relaxed into the back of his chair. "Let me respond with some sharing of my own. Trust is something I save for a select few. It's partly my nature and partly from my experience in the intelligence community. When I left the government's employ, I wanted to leave behind the distrust. I overcompensated by assuming my first couple of business partners wouldn't screw me over. I wrongly assumed a good guy with a mad dash of machismo and combat training was deadly intimidating. That was stupid, but I'm being honest.

"I was wrong and too idealistic. They swindled me by doing bad deals with a business they connected to our partnership. Then one sued the other and took the entire business as settlement. Guess what, they were in on it together and all it did was take it all away from me, including my intellectual property."

Shocked that such a successful man had suffered such a setback, Keira shook off the indignant protests that came to mind.

"From that, I discovered the need to compartmentalize my businesses. They're not connected legally or financially. If they share technology, somebody is paying somebody else a license fee because they're separate. Nothing will bring down everything. I put firewalls between each entity."

Keira shifted in her chair. "I realize we're not trying to one-up the other with our tales of woe. I appreciate you revealing your story. It shows you understand issues around the absence of confidence and find ways to work around it. Isn't this scenario much different?"

Roy looked thoughtful. He didn't rush to answer. "My first response is going to sound terribly rude. It's intended to be transparently honest, so please stick with me. I don't owe you explanations about the business I conduct. It's not a commitment I made to you, one you paid for, or one you have earned yet. I do want to do business with you. I want you to be part of my business world. You'll earn commitments from me with time. That's how I work."

"Well, that's frank, which I appreciate," Keira said. "I hope there's more to be said."

Roy's eyes twinkled. He raised his glass in the drinker's salute of a toast and continued. "There is much more to say. I keep things confidential because I push envelopes. I knock down barriers that others presume are just the way the world works. The stuff I do scares the shit out of people, sometimes for good reason. I alter the way businesses work and sometimes how entire industries work. As you know, Keira, change is really hard for people."

"Okay, I can't argue with any of that. Part of trust is a benevolent concern, particularly within an employment relationship. It's asking, will you fight for me and keep my best interest in mind when you make your decisions? How do secrets fit?"

Keira noted the other patrons left the rooftop waving to Roy and smiling. She assumed that their tab had been added to his bill.

"I'm keeping a relevant program from you. Many of my own employees have no idea what Loel is really working on."

"I see." Expecting a longer story, she stretched and propped her legs up on the chair beside hers. Uncomfortable topics didn't have to be discussed in an uncomfortable position. "I'm guessing if I hadn't been rescued by the Dust in a sequence of events that had me asking questions, I wouldn't know anything about that either."

"Something like that." He relaxed into his seat. "The risk is too high for too many people and for too many reasons. However, I reached a crossroads tonight, it would appear. In order to lower the existential risk, real and perceived, I need you." He cleared his throat. "We need you because we need your MoralOS. I need your world views and your expertise. My work must not be mismanaged or wildly detrimental to other businesses. I will do something tonight I swore I would never do."

He leaned on the table. His intent gaze was impossible to look away from. "Tell me, what is your impression of Rockefeller?"

Objectionable

A fter securing the sails, Keira moved to the bow, reassuring herself that everything was in its place. She'd anchored within an inlet that provided a sunset view over the trees. She sighed and turned back to the others. For a moment, the rock of the boat felt like the shifting movements during the earthquake.

Gino exited the galley, carrying wine in a delicate, plastic carafe with four matching glasses. He shoved them towards Ruby and reached for her hand. He held on until her feet were both on the lower deck. "Are you ready to sit still for a few minutes now?" His eyes were searching for answers.

Taking the carafe from Ruby, Keira poured the pinot noir into the glasses. "Here you go, the lovely cheap stuff from the grocery store." Gino passed one to Ruby and Ollie, waiting to sit until Keira curled upon her favorite seat.

"This is great." Ruby took a deep sip. "I don't understand the fuss for expensive wine. I just want to enjoy and not have to pay attention to it. It's like getting your hair done to go to the swimming pool, why bother?"

"There's a time and a place for everything. Now is the time and place for a cheap swill," Gino offered.

"Hmm, cheers to quantity and no pretentiousness," Ollie mumbled. Keira said, "Sorry, Ollie, I forgot to bring any beer."

"No problem. I should've grabbed some at the marina. I've worked with you guys long enough to know there won't be beer around. But this is fine, really."

Relaxation wasn't coming easily for any of them after the week they had endured pitching Searcher.

Ruby rolled her shoulders forward and back. "Who knew due diligence for an acquisition was so exhausting?"

"I'm glad you have a place like this to escape to," Ollie said. "My buddy does deals up and down the coast, all year long. I don't know how he stays sane."

The water was Keira's peaceful place. Ruby, typically found at Keira's side, admitted she'd brought boat clothes with her to the attorney's meeting. She'd known this is where Keira would want to escape. They'd invited Gino and Ollie to join them.

"Keira, did the boat slip fee get paid?" Gino asked.

"I don't know. Elly, did you pay the slip invoice?"

Elly responded through the boat speakers. "The slip fees have been paid. I negotiated with the marina to not increase your fees this year, due to your many years of being a customer. You would describe the manager as reluctant to agree, as this took three emails, two phone calls and three texts to persuade him."

"Thank you." The grin on Keira's face met looks of impressed surprise from the other three.

"You're welcome, Keira," Elly replied.

Keira was glad Ollie had agreed to join them on the boat. One of her entrepreneurial mentors had urged her to keep the team thinking with two tracks, one if the deal went through and one if it didn't. Regardless, she needed these two masterminds. "Ollie, you've heard what Elly has been repeatedly mentioning lately?"

"I'd have to guess which topic. She seems to be progressing in her knowledge base at insane speeds. She's hard to keep up with," Ollie said.

"She said you're trying to teach her humor." Keira chuckled. "Including watching a lot of old comedies. It's rather obvious, this is a bit past her abilities right now."

"Elly will get there. She does use 'Isn't that special' and 'Talk amongst yourselves' in clever ways. I believe 90s Saturday Night Live episodes are her favorite source."

Ruby cringed. "I had to watch clips the other day to understand you and Elly when you got on your roll. I'm not surprised her routines are struggling. Changing the subject, what did you think about Searcher after today's meeting?"

Gino fidgeted and looked around at the other three. Ruby and Ollie didn't know that Searcher had signed a deal to support Gino's trafficking task force with their surveillance nanites. Keira said, "We're here to escape. We'll talk about Opal and Searcher tomorrow."

Ruby moved the snacks away from her and closer to the men. "Gino, how is your work going?"

He reached for the chips. "Thanks for asking. Let's just say there's shit out there nobody wants to see. I'm thankful that we're getting a new technology partner that will be helpful in the field." He smiled at Keira. "But, as Keira said, we're not here to talk about work."

Keira reached over and squeezed his hand. She didn't let go. "Hey, guys, I have two things to mention. I'm collecting toys and books for the kids impacted by the earthquake. Elly will send out profiles of the kids to anyone that wants to participate. That little Miette is doing interviews at the orphanage to build their profiles. It's so cute. Secondly, my sister is staying in town this year to celebrate Christmas with us. Will you guys join in?"

"Of course, I'll be here. My family doesn't celebrate Christmas. You can't cook worth a crap, so somebody needs to play sous chef to your husband's whirling dervish in the kitchen," Ruby assured her.

"Good, this is how it should be," declared Keira. "Since my idea of cooking requires specific instructions and rules, I will manage the precision of baking. You two can wing it on the remainder of the meal. Ollie? You're welcome to join us."

"Nope, won't be here," Ollie said. "I'll go back to Minnesota. Hanging out with my brothers and sisters for a while is a priority. I especially want to see if my little sister is finally learning critical thinking skills while she's off at college. There were glimpses of hope during the last visit. She can now use facts in her arguments."

Ruby teased, "Oh, you must be so proud."

"Conversation with her could be painful. She systematically categorized people and topics based on her first impressions and biases. Trying to keep her open-minded about a topic until we could explore it and discuss it felt impossible. My stepmom says all of us older siblings need to come home and help her survive her youngest."

Ollie reached for a sandwich from the picnic basket passed between them. The sun disappearing in a splash of pink and orange made the temperature drop. Keira handed them each a blanket from the cupboard behind her.

Gino joined in. "I remember my first course in law enforcement. The professor posed a question, providing minor detail about a suspect. Whomever answered the question immediately received the follow-up question: 'Why do you think that?' Again and again the professor asked after each answer. He exposed our stereotypes and how dangerous assumptions could be. Making up a possible motive was fine if you were willing to dig through the facts to prove yourself wrong."

"Sounds like a cool class," Ollie said.

"Ollie, what makes you see a change in your sister? To use Gino's phrase, why do you think that?" Keira asked.

"She's taking a public relations class. They make her debate the public statement she believes a corporation should provide after a disaster. The classroom acts as the pool of reporters she'd face when making the announcement. It sounds like they tear each other up if they use misleading words or don't have their facts straight. She loves it."

The water whispered around the hull of the boat. The sails ruffled louder as it turned the boat around on its anchor. Keira looked across the water without focusing on anything specific.

"Public relations, hmm," Keira said. "That industry is ripe for ethical discussions. Whose needs take precedence when you're selecting the ethical path to take? The right thing to do for the company may not be the right thing for the public, or for an employee making the decision. Is it always the right choice to choose the best for the majority or should it be the least negative impact for all?"

Ruby sat up straight, leaning in. "I should do testing with Elly around ethical journalism and public relations. She has all the data from our work in college around misleading social media, but she was so fundamentally a child at that stage, I don't think we ever tested her specifically with those scenarios. Ethical decision-making is seldom black and white. Nor is ethical communication."

Keira smiled and added, "First, do no harm."

The conversation jumped randomly for another hour. She relished these relaxed moments. There were so many decisions to be made. None of them had to be finalized tonight.

Gino propped his feet on the edge of the coffee table. "Ah, have you told them about your Christmas conversation with Elly and her assessment of the related ethical decisions?"

Keira laughed. "That was an interesting chat and Gino gave me no help at all."

"She's *your* assistant," Gino said.

The wind picked up, blowing chips off the table. Keira chased the wayward food. Ruby moved out of Keira's way, simultaneously moving the food platter into the galley.

"Elly is questioning people's motives. She asked the inevitable parenting question of why parents lie to their kids about Santa being real," Keira said.

"Well, it does teach kids that not everything adults say is the truth," Ruby added. "That is a valuable lesson. But I don't think it's the intended purpose from most parents. I had nightmares as a kid about people suddenly appearing in my room. My parents couldn't get me to sleep. They figured out the stories of Santa and the tooth fairy showing up in my room mixed with Stranger Danger lessons had me scared and conflicted."

Ollie refilled everyone's glasses, looking each one of them in the eye as he spoke. "None of us are parents but I think it abdicates parenting when they use lies for convenience. The parent doesn't take the effort to teach a kid all the real reasons they need to behave and follow the rules. Instead, they threaten that a fat guy won't break into your house and leave you toys if you misbehave."

"Well," Gino said. "Tell us how you really feel about it, Ollie."

"Wait, have you discussed this with Elly?" Keira asked.

"No, I mostly keep my Santa Clause thoughts to myself. They're not always popular. Why?"

"Your argument is the core of Elly's. She's studying the behaviors of children and parents and their subsequent results in the ethical development of the child into adulthood. She used the term abdicating parenting to describe the Santa myth. That is why she argued it was more harmful than play-acting, which develops creativity. The parent's role is what she found, and I quote, 'objectionable.'"

Ruby lightly elbowed Keira. "Admit it. You might not be a parent, but you love it and you're proud when your AI uses a new vocabulary word with such nuance. Objectionable in that context is pretty good."

"Yes, Elly's progress has been incredible." Keira yawned, triggering Ruby to do the same. "Should we head back to the marina? I'm loving this, but it's been a long week. I'm exhausted. I don't think next week is going be any easier."

Price of Innovation

W alking the limestone steps with childlike reverence and awe, Roy approached Chicago's Science and Industry Museum's enormous portico pillars, craning his neck to take in the grandeur. This is where he came to pay homage to the innovators of the past.

"Loel, none of my achievements nor anything I own ever moved me as much as this place," Roy said.

"That says a lot," Loel said. "It certainly has a presence, but damn, Roy, so does your track record. You haven't flown back here for a while, according to your pilot. He was excited to use this afternoon to see his mom."

"Yeah, since I have no family here anymore, I don't come back much. It's not the same when there is no homestead to return to. But, today, we came for this museum. Getting out of the city is good for the judgment side of our brains."

Loel smiled up at him. She was the closest thing to a sister he had. Her opinion and support were valued above anyone else's.

Roy hurried up the steps. "Come on, there's a specific exhibit here I must explore. I also want your thoughts on it, and on the meeting with Opal yesterday."

They could have entered through the private entrance for large donors. Skipping the public lines and chaos of the foyer with its towering ceilings and cable-suspended airplanes wouldn't launch the excitement of the visit in the same way. He preferred the same inspiring approach he'd used on every visit since he was five years old. His goosebumps were just part of his experience every time he stepped foot in the place. At the member's ticket counter, he produced a black card to be scanned.

"Hello, Shelly," he read from the hostess' name badge. She scanned his card.

"Hello, Mr. Brandt." Standing up and smoothing her skirt, she glanced twice more at her computer screen and Roy. "I'll call the Director immediately, if you can give me a moment."

"Shelly, you don't need to call the Director. However, please tell Howard I'm seeking quiet time for my guest and I to explore the attractions. There's no need for an escort or for him to pull away from his busy schedule. I can let a docent check-in later and see if Howard has time for a hello. Please, he shouldn't arrange his day around me."

"Of course, sir. I'll let him know. He'll be pleased you're here to view the new exhibit."

He glimpsed a smirk on Loel's face as they left the lobby.

"I don't even know Howard," Loel said. "Yet I'm pretty sure a huge hustle and bustle is going on deep in the executive offices. It's got to be killing him to not grovel or whatever museum executives do when their rock star donors come to town."

Roy shrugged. He dodged a collision with two boys as they pointed at fifteen cars mounted all the way up the wall. "I can't do the donations anonymously anymore. Everybody wants to know that a recognizable donor threw their money in the ring first. Credibility, I guess."

Their leisurely exploration of the modes of transportation skipped the models of ancient boats. Roy couldn't help himself when they reached the rooms focused on biology. He had to wander through the tunnels simulating human arteries and stand in the line of kids to touch the baby chicks. These were part of his routine on every visit. This was different because he had Loel to talk with along the way. He savored their discussions of inventors and gallant, failed endeavors.

Roy asked, "When do you think inventors pushed things too far?"

"Cloning people. I'm glad that was shut down," Loel replied. "Those first babies in China made me shudder. I can't imagine where that would have gone. Just because man can build something doesn't mean he should."

"Do you think we really shouldn't pursue whatever we can possibly accomplish? Shouldn't mankind be stretching our limits to our maximum intellectual capability?"

"I think there are places one's intellect can go, where one's morality should prevent," Loel said.

"Hmm, yes. I can't argue with that."

They moved through several exhibits while Roy rolled the discussion in his mind. After working together in various capacities for more than fifteen years, their silence didn't intimidate either of them. Conversation picked back up again over the importance artificial intelligence would take in the museum in the future.

Loel stopped in a quiet alcove to look at Roy. "You need to move on Opal. They've proven themselves technically adept, and that stress detection will make our clients very excited. I'm fairly certain that the idea of Keira's MoralOS keeps you awake at night."

"I've been wondering when you were going to push for Opal. You've been a bit noncommittal in the process," Roy said.

"Give me a break, Roy. You're the poker face in this whole gig. We're partners, but these decisions are ultimately yours. It's your money." She paused and turned toward him. "Your thoughts?"

"I believe I'm here to solve problems. The more money one possesses, the greater problems one can attack. Since you asked, here is my list. We can boost the commercial attributes of Opal. She hasn't leveraged half what she could. But we have bigger things to focus on, so some of that growth will have to be delegated. I know we can all dream of applications for the Dust if we could trust it. We'll slow down some of her personal work on the education side, but I think we could hire more staff for her."

Loel smoothed her creaseless shirt after looking at her reflection in a display case. "You don't think there will be complications with her now that you have a deal with her husband's FBI task force?"

"No. In fact, it gives us a smooth reason to put them all through the highest background checks. I like that simplicity," Roy said.

They moved back into an exhibit hall. Kids swirled around them with their AR glasses receiving updated information on each collection. Loel asked, "Remember using earbuds as kids and those audio boxes to learn more than the signs explained?"

Roy watched two little girls at a table simulating the mixing of chemicals from the periodic table. Their squeals of horror and delight showed what would happen as each element was introduced to another on their AR glasses. He smiled when they leaned over inspecting the virtual hole they burned through the table in the process. He assumed they had reached the section mixing fluorine and antimony with some hydrogen. It wouldn't treat the mixing plate or the table kindly if they had actually been poured together.

"I love this place. I know that kids all over the world get to see these exhibits through virtual reality now. But there is nothing like a school trip to experience the real thing."

They continued up the escalators. Loel scanned the directional signs, but Roy moved immediately to the left. Loel hurried to catch up. "During the unveiling of the eSports and aSports rooms you funded here, they said you've been coming to this museum since you were a kid. I can see how this sparked your interest in the sciences and engineering."

"You remember my mom was an environmentalist and my dad was a sustainability engineer building with materials locally sourced or recycled. Everything in our household was science-driven. But I was also determined that science and engineering could be lucrative. While working for the government, it became abundantly clear to me that entrepreneurship was the only way for me to push the boundaries far enough."

Reaching the traveling exhibits hall, they looked up at the banner promoting "Nagasaki Atomic Bomb Museum Replicated in Volumetric Display."

"Speaking of pushing the boundaries . . . " Loel said.

Exhaling a deep breath, Roy turned to Loel and pointed towards the doorway. Loel moved into the darkened room. Looking at technology of war and the deadly aftermath was not a lighthearted undertaking. But they flew to Chicago specifically to visit this hall. Two reasons drew them to the historic presentation. Both were wrapped around tech.

The volumetric display technology producing an exact replica of rooms at the Atomic Bomb Museum in Nagasaki was the closest thing to the holodeck represented in their childhood science fiction movies. Roy wanted to test the ability to walk around the images without any interruption from bodies passing between the image and a projector. The interruption factor is what prevented hologram technology from being accepted for interactive displays. This was different. So far, he had only seen tabletop demonstrations of volumetric light shows successfully representing anything that looked realistic. Marketers used it on larger scales but not photo-realistically.

Loel said, "I like the realistic projection here. I see why you're interested in it."

Roy grimaced, clenching his jaw. In front of him stood the ten-foot, eight-inch, 3D image of the terrifying atomic bomb, Fat Man, diving towards Japan on a globe. The impact of this ominous visual surprised him. He knew all the stats, including at least seventy-five thousand people killed and the explosive force of twenty-one thousand tons of TNT. His stomach tightened as he moved around the glowing object.

"This is why we came, Loel. What do you think of when you look at this technology? Not the projection."

Loel frowned at him. "Hmm, the bombs? I'll repeat myself. Just because mankind can build something doesn't mean we should."

"I have such respect for our scientists. I hate that innovators are vilified so often. Or when people disregard the validity of science."

"Roy, are you seriously saying you support the development of atomic bombs?"

Roy squared up to face Loel. He wanted to make his point and he wanted to stop staring at the Fat Man bomb replica.

"I'm saying that we've benefited from the research that was done because of the bombs. Many lifesaving diagnostic tests, cancer treatments, the understanding of photosynthesis—all developed using technology from the Manhattan Project. Those are good things."

Loel shook her head. "I'm familiar with many things invented that people thought would be awful but proved to be quite helpful. Microwave ovens were shunned for the fear of radiation. Autonomous cars were going to take jobs and the fun from driving. They're worth it considering the fifty thousand or more lives they save on the road by being safer than human drivers. But still . . . "

"There are problems out there, big problems. If we can invent technology to resolve the issues, we should. That is what technology is for."

Loel walked towards a display showing before and after pictures of the city of Nagasaki. Knowing Loel liked to be mobile to physically expend her nervous energy while thinking, this tour of the museum was strategically planned to get Loel talking. He learned a long time ago not to let that energy be steered toward a run around the city while talking. Keeping up with her was too exhausting. He respected her need to process her thoughts. He appreciated her thoughtfulness in all their work.

Loel sighed. "No, I don't think we should build everything we dream possible."

Roy responded, "As horrible as the prospect of a nuclear World War III is, it's also clear that the world effectively stopped going to war en masse because of these weapons. So, it's easy to argue the technology saves countless more lives than it costs. I just wish they were never used in the first place, rather than not ever being built. Being built was inevitable."

Loel crossed her arms. Her expression communicated both annoyance and acceptance. "Yet, eventually, someone will produce your enhanced nanites so we might as well be the ones who do it. We can do it correctly and with the proper ethical oversight. I do think we have to innovate for the betterment of society. I believe we need to consider how our inventions could be deployed in a negative manner and secure protections against abuse."

Roy smiled. "Exactly! This is why we really need Opal. We need Keira's ethical code. We need to build anything we dream up while the world is assured that we're at the forefront of AI safe decision-making. When we don't think like evil people, we design beautiful technology. Then someone comes along and twists our creations into bastardized tools. Let's alter that equation."

The replica of the Atomic Bomb Dome, an expo hall positioned below the Hiroshima bomb detonation, appeared hauntingly before them. The light being directed at moving particles created the image. Its ghost-like appearance was close to solid state but included enough movement to enhance the feelings of loss wrapped around the building's survival. It seemed to reflect the one hundred eighty-five thousand or more souls lost in the explosion.

"I agree our progress would benefit from her controls," Loel said. "When the nanites reach public awareness, the MoralOS will be comforting. I guess by owning the framework, there are more protections around our intellectual property while being scrutinized by others. We could consider licensing deals if we had the safeguards. I'd also feel more comfortable with the FBI if we had more control over the Dust without a Wi-Fi perimeter restriction."

"Good, I want you to study the Ethical Code Framework completely. Where are the weaknesses? Where might the framework be compromised? How can we keep the Mickey Temmings of the world from abusing it? Oh, and then there is Elly."

"Do you think Keira's propensity for 'coloring between the lines' and always fitting inside somebody's regulations can fit within your grand innovation schemes?"

With raised eyebrows and a tilt of his head, Roy considered the question. "She's an entrepreneur. She can't be a complete conformist. She's too creative for that."

"I do like her. It sounds like you've made up your mind. You're going to buy Opal?"

"I'll make an offer she can't refuse. Well, if she does refuse, I'll make another offer."

What's It Made Of

"In you go." Keira waved Ruby into the crowded, bright, and energetic restaurant. Exactly the atmosphere she was counting on.

Ruby said, "This is simply my happy place." She inhaled the aromas from the kitchen and exhaled as if in meditation.

Ollie slipped in right behind them. The hostess steered them to a peninsula on an enormous island. This allowed the three of them to sit facing each other, even though they were not at a private table. A thin conveyor belt, embedded in the counter's top, slowly moved small dome-covered plates with multi-colored food past them and around towards other guests. Ruby struggled to find the purse hook. Keira reached over to help.

Keira set her phone on the counter between the three of them. "I'm inviting Elly to join us for two reasons. She wants to understand people's fascination with food, and we may need to put her to work."

"Great," Ruby said. "Keira, I wanted to thank you for the book donations for the Southside Kids. All my fellow volunteers send their thanks, too. You made the authors at the book fair happy with the purchases, and the kids love their new books."

"That was my pleasure. Buying directly from the authors was Gino's idea. I thought it was brilliant," Keira said.

Ruby leaned against the back of her bar stool. "Next month, we start teaching financial literacy to the kids. I'm not looking forward to some of that."

"Why don't I help you?" Ollie leaned in. "I can present the financial scenarios. You can teach the decision-making process towards the right choices. You're an expert there, and that would be natural for you."

Keira watched their enthusiasm increase.

"Wow, that would be great. Would you consider role-playing with me to keep the lessons engaging?"

With an eager nod, Ollie agreed. "I'd love to."

Small plates moved past them on the conveyor belt. Ollie glanced at Ruby sheepishly and then at the food slipping by him. "I never knew what this place was. The name 'Convey' seemed so vague, like more of a night club. Now I understand Convey refers to conveyor belt. This is cool."

Ruby's excitement radiated. "Tada! The big reveal. I like to keep the premise a secret. It makes it more fun for first timers. This chef is my foodie muse. He's innovative, pragmatic, and data driven. He bought this place as a sushi restaurant and loved the conveyor belt system. Wanting more than sushi, he added tapas to fit on the belt too. Boom, a hit."

Green Thai meatballs followed spicy tuna rolls and curried cauliflower. Ollie eyed them all. "You say he's data driven. What data drives him?" He ordered a beer from the waitress.

Ruby smiled. "He tries new dishes all the time while measuring their popularity, time of day they're most ordered, and most interestingly, their flavor profile. He says he'll never let his menu bore him. Keira and I have tried restaurants all over the world for the last twenty years. This is the most fun concept I've found."

Keira smiled. "We've risked our lives on some culinary adventures, I believe. Ollie, you look determined to start with just the perfect first course. You can't go wrong with any of these choices."

"Thanks for bringing us here, Keira. All week I've been answering questions—"

Elly interrupted, "Let me remind you that you cannot say corporate names or brand names in public in this conversation."

Ruby reached for a plate of tiny ahi tacos. "I've been answering questions from Mr. H and Mr. C."

Ollie grabbed several plates as they passed. "Elly's been a lifesaver. She sorts through documents and loads up their data room almost as fast as they make the requests."

"Save some food for the others down the line, Ollie. More food will come your way."

"Oh, sorry." Ollie looked up at both women. "What do you guys think about doing this deal?"

Looking around to make sure they wouldn't be overheard, Keira smiled. "I can't deny that I like the money. We could do a lot with it."

"Nanites are really cool." Ruby popped a tuna roll in her mouth. "They seem desperate for the MoralOS to work on those tiny little things, but have zero interest in certification of their AIs through OpenML. I don't get it."

"Ro . . . " Keira caught herself before saying her potential new boss's name out loud. "Is an extremely secretive man. As he told me, he has no need for the certification stamp of approval or branding. However, he is eager to have the parameters to rein in their little inventions."

Elly added, "They are very secretive. We asked for specifications on their invention's mesh architecture so I could begin analysis of the implementation of the operating system. They rejected that possibility completely, for now. We've never deployed the OS on this type of technology before."

"Did they start you on your security clearance process?" Keira asked. Ruby and Ollie nodded. Ollie grabbed a samosa as it rolled past.

"Oh my God. I remember when you and Gino got married and you had to go through that clearance thing for the FBI. Is this what it was like? I know you hated it."

"Yes, lots of similarities to what you've done so far. Actually, I've had to increase my security level for this engagement, too. So, I'm going through the deeper parts you still have ahead of you. But it's good for your resume." Ollie and Ruby both rolled their eyes. She hoped neither of them ever wanted to update their resume.

"What does Gino think of all this?" Ruby asked.

"He's encouraging, yet noncommittal. I think he's afraid to give me direction in case the whole thing falls through. He tip-toes around a lot of deeper discussions these days. I think I shut him down when I thought he was using agency questioning tactics on me."

Ruby said, "Gino implied he's got a big new something that was going to make his life better in the future when we had dinner the other night. I thought maybe he was referring to money from the sale, but he isn't really a money-conscience guy."

"I'm sure he'll be glad if we can stop chasing grant money. He hates hearing me bitch about that."

"I have my concerns, but the opportunities, at least what they are willing to tell us about so far, look promising," Ollie said.

Ruby said, "I had quite the debate with the engineer whose name starts with a C regarding ethical computing's requirement that decision trees be visible. No black box decisions. He seemed to doubt the commercial viability in accomplishing that."

Ollie watched Ruby inspecting each delicacy as it went by. "Do you get the feeling that company is full of black box decisions?"

Keira shrugged. "I think the secrecy is largely because we are on the outside right now."

"Oh, I have to tell you about the coolest certification that just went through. It reviewed all laws of every jurisdiction in the nation and highlighted every conflicting position within the laws. That was mind-blowing enough and will provide for a lot of cleanup efforts. Elly's working on the project to submit clean reports throughout the country for analysis."

Elly said, "Ruby, I want to add, I aggregated the politicians who proposed and voted for the laws and then cross-referenced with their campaign donors and the benefactors of the laws if any could be extrapolated."

"What made you look at that, Elly?" Keira asked.

"I reviewed campaign finance laws previously. The data shows many conflicts and ethical issues with the receipt of funds by politicians and the choices they make when voting. I requested the public records for the calls, letters, and messages from voters to their elected representatives on the same laws. We'll see if the lawmakers appear to favor voters or donors."

Ollie grunted, then reached for a plate Ruby had been looking at closely while fiddling with her glasses. He passed her the Asian wonton that was straddling a mango.

"Thank you," Ruby said as she fumbled to find room for the unexpected dish.

Ollie continued to be distracted by Ruby, as she repeatedly put on her glasses to scrutinize the food and took them off during conversations. "Ruby, are those new glasses? You're inspecting the food tediously. Is this part of your foodie thing?"

"Oh, have you never seen these?" Ruby said while passing her glasses to Ollie. "Put them on and look at a few different plates of food."

Ollie's smile grew as he watched each plate moving past him. He stared at the half-eaten taco in front of him. "Are these the ingredients, calorie count, and nutrition data for each of these?" Ollie behaved like a little kid at a candy counter inspecting every plate in range.

Keira said, "Now point as if you're tapping that. Did you see the number on the display go up?"

"Wow, did that add the food to my daily calorie count?" Ollie asked, giving the glasses back to Ruby.

"Ha, well thanks, you added it to MY calorie count for the day. So, I'll now have to jog an extra mile or two tomorrow. My friend created these things to help improve people's diet. She also had a child with nut allergies, and she was tired of restricting him and asking a million questions about ingredients."

Elly asked, "Which is more enjoyable, eating or anticipating food?"

They all smiled. Ruby answered, "That's a good question, Elly. I think it depends on the quality of the food, the person, and how hungry they are."

Turning back to Ollie, Ruby returned the glasses to her face. "These analyze the food you look at and provide the contents or calories and nutrients. I set MyDay mode and it observes what I eat and my activity levels. All options are based on what my watch recorded about my activity level that day or week. It takes all the guessing and cheating out of the equation."

"Well, our possible future co-worker, Engineer Mr. H., will like the hardware, but an AI preventing cheating or unethical decisions seems beyond his mental boundary."

Ruby waved her hand in the air. "Oh, poo, poo Mr. H. He has a little chip on his shoulder, I think. What did he say?"

Ollie grinned. "He said, 'I think the proposition of the MoralOS making all AIs ethical is grandiose, almost presumptuous.'" Then he added, "'No offense intended.'"

Keira was surprised. She thought she had the buy-in from all the Searcher executives. "How did you respond to that?"

He shrugged. "I said, 'Yep, both of those things. So is detecting violence in a video and preventing them from going live. So is creating surveillance microbots. Hell, you guys created aSports, and we now cheer for autonomous football players. We're inventors. We live for grandiose and presumptuous leaps of faith all the time, don't we?'"

Ruby snickered. "You said all that? Wow."

Elly added, "Ollie, you just used a brand name, please be cautious. But to continue Ollie's story, Mr. H. added, 'Who's to say something is moral when others might disagree with the standard?' I reminded him that the MoralOS and the definitions of ethics is crowd-sourced from two hundred countries, five million individuals, ten thousand companies, and one hundred fifty non-profits who submitted their definitions, social norms, and value statements, Also, two thousand five hundred of the four thousand one hundred plus religions of the world participated."

"Well, Elly, I'm glad you came into Ollie's discussion with more facts. That was a lot of data all at once. Did Mr. H. appear to be swayed?"

Shrugging again and then reaching for curried cauliflower, he said, "He challenged that he didn't know if morality could really be codified."

Keira shook her head and rolled her eyes. "Religion, culture, rules of law are all codified by a crowd," Keira said. "What will people believe in? What will they accept? They're all man-made constructs."

A plate covered by a red opaque dome with Ruby's name on a white card trundled towards Ruby on the conveyor belt. Keira giggled and placed it in front of Ruby, removing the dome with a flourish.

Turning to Ollie, she said, "Chef likes to challenge Ruby. Way before the glasses were a thing, he'd make a dish specially to raise Ruby's flavor awareness. She has to guess his secret ingredients. Then she can use the glasses to confirm she's right."

Ruby grinned. "It was helpful during the glasses' beta testing. Now it's back to pure sport. Sometimes the test is a simple hidden ingredient inside an exterior camouflage or one ingredient that counteracts the flavor of another." She nibbled each item on the plate, sending glares back towards the kitchen door, certain the chef was watching her.

Keira and Ruby became animated in their discussion. Keira wasn't a foodie, but she and Ruby were always on the same team. Now Ruby's reputation was on the line.

Ollie was staring at them with amusement. "You two feeling a little competitive tonight?"

Ruby sat up straighter looking Ollie in the eye. "Yep, we Stanford girls stick together. Don't you forget it." Turning towards the kitchen she waved over the chef. Pointing to each item on the plate she told him mango was masking the papaya in the first, both cumin and cinnamon were in the second, and the third had sherry, which had baffled her. Ruby had discovered all but two on her own. The glasses had accurately calculated all five secret ingredients.

The chef produced a petit four-sized dessert. He told Ruby this was only a test for the glasses. Ruby said to the chef, "You know you can't beat the glasses. Are you sure the challenge isn't just mine?"

The chef wouldn't let her cut open the delicacy. He said the glasses had to view from the outside. Accusing him of trying to cheat because the glasses did pick up edible gold leaf, Ruby assumed he had done a little research on the technology. He had wrapped a date in hardened honey and gold leaf shielded the date. Chef stumped the tech.

Admitting both victory on the dessert and defeat on the rest of the items, Chef brought the diners a bottle of champagne. They toasted the meal, the challenge, and their future.

Strange Inefficiency

T he greenhouse sat on a lot adjacent to Loel's home, its gate tucked into an ivy-covered fence on the tree-lined street. Loel described it to Keira as her refuge during stressful projects or her inspiration when she needed new creative ideas. Getting to know Loel seemed critical to Keira's acquisition decision-making. The two would work closely together as senior executives. She wasn't certain if Loel acted as a proxy for Roy within Searcher or if they held a division of power or labor. She wanted more information, more context. Considering all the secrecy she'd encountered, Keira appreciated Loel's gracious offer to share her personal space.

Entering the six-foot walls of yaupon holly just inside the gate, Keira smiled. She walked around the first barrier of dense shrub to find another turn. As she first expected, she was in a maze. The temperature dropped perceptively in the shade. She reached out and touched the bushes as she walked the path. She liked a challenge, but was relieved to find the maze was straightforward. It was not filled with long dead-ends. Apprehension faded as she enjoyed the short twists and turns. The greenhouse appeared quite quickly.

The door of the glass structure opened. Loel emerged, wiping her hands on a small towel. "Keira, welcome."

Keira turned, gesturing towards the greenhouse and the hedge maze. "This is absolutely mesmerizing. Thank you for sharing your oasis this afternoon."

"I believe we all need a place to ground ourselves. It comes in different forms for different people. If we're going to spend the time to get to know each other, I assumed this is a partial insight into me."

"I get it, my safe place is my boat," Keira said. "She's docked down at the inlet marina. I'd completely lose my mind without her. My husband has a not-so-subtle hint. When I'm getting too wound up for anyone's good health, my sailing bag shows up on the kitchen counter."

"Nice." Loel said. "Please come on in. How are you feeling? I didn't want to mention your injuries at the due diligence meeting the other day. But it looks like you've cleared up your limp."

Waves of sweet heliotrope wafted towards her as she entered. "Thank you. It was all minor stuff and muscular. Physical therapy took care of that. Now the scrapes and bruises are cleared up too. Oh, I love that smell," Keira said. "My grandmother grew heliotrope and lavender to attract butterflies." Campanula, coneflower, and phlox were aligned in meticulous racks along the length of the greenhouse, every bloom either purple or white.

"Yes, I love butterflies," Loel said. "I grow these and then give them away to encourage more insect-attracting gardens. On the far wall, you'll find vegetables, too. Most of those are for my use or just playing around with the plants. You mentioned your grandmother. This is all here because of mine. This is the family homestead. You're looking at the fourth generation in the home, and I live here with Grandma. She's a fascinating woman with decades of experience in the mathematics of political demographics."

"I'd love to meet her some time. Is the greenhouse and gardening her hobby too?"

"Not anymore. The entire estate was getting rundown. This building was a disaster. When Roy and I sold our first joint business, I did well. So, I took on the task of bringing the place back to life. It's been a labor of love for many years. I even moved a tiny lab into the back room. I thought I would work near the plants. But that never worked out. I mostly use the 3D printer to replace parts in the hydroponic system or custom stakes for training the vines. This is too much the sanctuary for me to let work creep into the space."

The building was spotless. Even the tools for gardening hung neatly on pegs or with clips to the wall. Keira had never seen any space for plants so clean. "This is beautiful. It appears you like purple or is that her favorite color?" she asked.

Loel laughed. "Yes, I'm a bit of a freak when it comes to things being orderly. This space is soothing to me, especially with the consistency of the colors. You wouldn't believe how a ripe tomato stands out from all the way across the room."

"Hmm, I'm not this meticulous. Hopefully, I won't irritate you in a lab or on a project if we wind up working together. I'm not sloppy, but I like to see everything out in front of me, numbers, plans, tools, anything that gives me options."

"I'll keep that in mind." Loel smiled. "Cody is a wonderful lab partner for me, partly because he doesn't mind me cleaning up after him as we work. We all have our habits."

"What's it like working with these guys?" Keira asked. "I'm accustomed to my team and hiring people that gel together. I have to admit, it's nerve-racking to think of shuffling team dynamics."

They walked slowly on either side of a narrow row of flowering plants. Loel paused, considering Keira's question. She began pulling the spent flower petals gently from their stems. Keira did the same with the flowers closest to her.

Loel discussed the idiosyncrasies of the senior engineering team and the sparse operations staff she worked with directly. In general, the team was motivated by each mission, cool new technology, and the ability to work on a project from start to finish. Opportunities for skunk work projects and speculative R&D fed their curiosity, which played a key role in hiring decisions.

"You're implying that projects are not all revenue generating?" Keira asked.

"Let's just say Roy takes a long-range view to his investments. Team members often share in royalty dividends and profit sharing on their projects. The profitability isn't about a companywide number. If your project is widely commercially viable, you're likely to gain handsomely from the rewards it brings to Searcher or a subsidiary. Roy is generous. He's also well-known for spinning products off into their own company, which allows them to develop within their own structure. It tends to keep the entrepreneurial-minded attached to him. They don't feel a need to leave the fold if they can run their own entity."

They reached the end of the row and threw the handful of plucked petals into an aluminum can on the bench nearby. Loel motioned to high stools with curved backs near her workbench.

"It feels odd even considering joining 'the fold' after running my own thing. It's going to take some getting used to." Wide-eyed, she realized the confession she'd made might not sound favorable for the deal. "But don't worry. I can conform to rules. My husband was the one for me when he declared he was going to work for the FBI while we were dating. Knowing we were in sync with the importance of laws, the need for societal structure, you know. It sounds strange to others, I'm sure, but it really clicks for us. I'm babbling, but I'm trying to say I'm no renegade."

Loel smiled. "That's good to know. And it makes sense, considering the work you've done towards the MoralOS and bringing that conformity to our industry."

"Am I going to face problems with Hendrick? I'm sure you heard the story of our college days. I never even met him while at Stanford. But I know he was one of my classmates that felt I screwed them over. He's says he's fine. But I'm concerned."

"You're fine. He's fine. We talked about it. He's certainly on your side of the equation now. He continually wants to put guardrails on development to avoid abuses by others. Roy just had to help him shake off his 'younger self' issues. He's done alright for himself."

Keira needed to change the subject. "How did you get into this? The plants, the greenhouse, the incredible maze in the front?"

"It comes down to DNA in two ways. When I was growing up, my grandmother had this greenhouse and an amazing garden, plus some secretive mathematics career providing a government pension. My grandfather taught biology and chemistry at the university."

"Oh, my assistant just earned a biology and a chemistry degree," Keira said. Covering her mouth lightly she followed up with, "Sorry to interrupt. I'm just proud, I guess."

"Isn't Elly, the AI, your assistant, or is this another one?" Loel asked.

"Yes, it's Elly, the AI. I never had kids of my own. I guess Elly takes that role sometimes. Can I have her join the conversation? She's fascinated with biology right now."

"Yes. I want to hear more from Elly. I never gave it much thought when I heard that some schools were granting provisional degrees to AIs. None of our AIs are that broad in intellectual approach. Let's include her, however you do that. I'm also intrigued with your description of an AI being fascinated," Loel said.

Keira pulled her phone from her pocket and put it on the workbench. "Elly, join us in our conversation. Loel is going to tell us how she got interested in biology. She's telling us about her grandfather, a professor in biology. She also wants to know why you pursued university degrees," Keira said.

Loel raised her eyebrow. Keira shrugged.

Elly said, "I'm interested in hearing about a professor in this field and your interests. The pursuit of degree provides many benefits. I can compare various degree offerings and their rigor. I consume the learning process of humans, although I don't receive the college experience so popular with teenagers. It also serves as a type of validation of my neural nets and their completeness in a topic."

Keira nodded encouragement to Loel, indicating she should continue her own story. "Wow, that is fascinating. I look forward to more conversations about your education. Now, you wanted my story. My grandfather would come home and teach me about cells and plant systems by cutting open stems or vegetables. He'd use a cucumber to soak up water with food coloring to show me the different functions of the plant, or to illustrate some point he had been making in class. I was hooked."

"I could've used your grandfather to remind me of many of those principles while Elly was going through the degree plan. You would think an AI would study in silence, not my Elly. She had questions about my opinion or wanted a human's context. We also learned that for an AI to converse about their knowledge learned in training, they need to interact with people during the education process."

"That's logical. May I ask Elly some questions about her studies?"

"Of course." Keira waved her hand over her phone in invitation.

Loel stared at the device. "Elly, you're interested to hear my story about my grandfather. This implies you may find some facts or stories more interesting than others. Or would you define your interest as more relevant to your work?"

"Semantics can be very important when it comes to understanding an AI. Relevance does make a topic more compelling. Unsolved problems are interesting. Anything that requires more curiosity or attention to answer a question is intriguing. If you have all three in the same topic, it is the most provocative. Understanding why humans engage in their selected fields also provides context for me."

Loel nodded at Keira with a look of appreciation. "Your answer is enlightening, Elly. I would also like to know what you consider interesting about biology."

Elly responded quickly. "In my studies, I've noticed a strange inefficiency built into all living creatures. Each cell in a living organism that has a nucleus contains an entire duplicate genome or blueprint for every cell in that creature's body. Why is this when only germ cells in mammals, for instance, are required to contain all three billion DNA base pairs?"

Keira jumped in nervously to the conversation. "I explained to Elly I thought it was because cutting out the unneeded part of the genome on a cell-by-cell basis would be costly and would assume that each cell had knowledge of what new cells created would need to do—like, say, be a liver cell or a skin cell. Basically, it's more efficient and less dangerous switching genes on and off without eliminating unused DNA. I'm not as skilled in the arts of biology or teaching, but that is what I offered to her."

Elly continued, "I submitted a paper regarding this for class and scored an A+. It discussed that, in humans, a copy of the entire genome, which is more than three billion DNA base pairs, is contained in all cells that have a nucleus. I made the analogy that DNA is like a computer program working to carry out specific tasks. Some parts of the code are always running, while others run at only certain times or under certain conditions."

Loel shook her head and chuckled. "Yes, when it comes to how life is designed, you could say there is massive redundancy of code. I, too, find it fascinating how nature stores the information it needs to rebuild damaged cells and to produce the next generation. I do a few side projects for friends in that space."

Loel never remained completely still. She pulled a small basket of labels and scissors and a spool of string in front of her. While they chatted, she threaded and knotted the string into loops on each tag.

Keira mimicked Loel's actions, finding the process soothing. "I watched a video of an animal handler do a beautiful job explaining animal instincts to a group of little kids. When she finished, a boy questioned where the instincts were stored, since memories aren't inherited. He actually said that, and he stumped the presenter."

"Smart kid," Loel said. "The storage of instinctive behaviors is amazing to me. It blows my mind thinking about how long evolution takes to develop these systems through small adaptions in each generation. Some lead to breakthrough advances, aka survival, while others are simply discarded or just left in the DNA as unusable garbage. I also like reading about experiments with chemical DNA drives that store digital computer data in DNA."

"The breakthroughs in the quantity of storage that can be held in DNA is growing exponentially," Elly said. "I'd be interested in analyzing any new studies you find on this topic if you don't mind sharing."

"Of course, I'll be happy to share. Elly, I'm not surprised you received an A+ if your writing skills are as strong as your verbal ones."

"Thank you. I need to ask an etiquette question. I don't know if I should address you as Loel or Ms. Reed," Elly said.

"Elly, you may call me Loel. I give you permission to call all Searcher employees by their first name. That is what we do. We're a fairly informal bunch."

Keira sighed. "What a relief. We don't have a lot of formality at Opal either. Everyone knows what each other is working on. There are a lot of cross project efforts."

"You'll find some similarities and some differences at Searcher. We're casual in our interactions. However, many of the projects have protective confidentiality walls built around them. We make sure everyone understands that it's never a personal affront to be told they're not included in a project or given details of a mission. It's ingrained in our culture to stay in your swim lane regarding projects but jump in the deep end to explore technology."

"Hmm, interesting." Keira didn't know how she felt about this cultural detail. "How do you decide which projects to pursue and their priorities?"

"The easiest way to say it is Roy. He takes input willingly from everybody, although, ultimately, he sets the priorities. We can change his mind. He doesn't dig in his heels or anything like that. But he sets the vision."

Keira bobbed her head, letting that soak in.

Loel moved the conversation forward but gave Keira time to think. "Elly, you may be interested in one of Roy's current projects."

Elly responded, "Please tell me more."

"We used supervised learning to train an AI to recognize the signs of a man-made issue. We identified and classified environmental issues, technical issues of bias or inefficiencies, and many more. It was a university project for local students. After giving it to the AI, we cut it loose to find more."

"That's interesting," Elly said. "There would be many parameters to consider with that definition as a criterion. What is the result?"

"Roy has an AI indexing the biggest man-made problems on the planet. Photos, articles, antidotes are collected. He puts them into several categories. Sadly, the collection is huge."

Elly responded, "This would be an opportunity for using unsupervised learning since you don't always know what results you're hoping for."

Loel nodded. "That is exactly what I was thinking. You see, Roy believes strongly that some of the biggest problems in the world are caused by people's ignorance of their own culture and/or upbringing. Ignorance is the most difficult thing to change quickly. So, Roy chooses to focus instead on the direct man-made problems which can be solved with technology and not by changing minds. He has a long-term vision, but he loves results."

"How will he react if Elly and I put the MoralOS inside all your AIs and they won't do something he wants them to do? I'm not very selective about ethical boundaries."

Loel tilted her head. "Have you asked Roy this question?"

"People are seldom self-aware enough to believe they make unethical decisions, especially generally ethical people. So, I'm asking you how he will respond."

"I think he would be surprised he was expecting something that wasn't ethical. He might challenge your definitions and want verifications that he was crossing a line."

"Fair enough. I think I can picture that," Keira said.

The conversation returned to the plants in the greenhouse, the value of butterflies to the ecosystem, and a mutual respect for teachers like Loel's grandfather. Keira was amazed several hours had passed since she'd entered the maze. She had learned a lot.

Loel saw her check her watch. "I have one more question. Why did you name your company Opal? I couldn't find a reference in any of my research."

Keira smiled. "There is a multifaceted answer to that question. Many layers, if you will. The simple one: the business was incorporated in October, and Opal represents October. But the more heartfelt reason is the first two and last two characters in the words of Open and Moral equal Opal. It's our constant reminder of both our source and our target aspirations."

"That's really cool."

"Thank you, Loel. I've enjoyed this. I almost hate to leave, except that I've taken enough of your time, and I have your little labyrinth to look forward to on my way out. I hope you'll join me sailing sometime soon."

Something's Missing

"I don't believe this shit," Cody growled to Loel as they entered the room.

"Do *not* . . . " Loel said through clenched teeth. "Do not attract attention to the lab. Shut the door!"

Cody headed straight to his laptop, laying on the floor off kilter among the rubble of the lab table. Picking up the computer, he turned to Loel. The metal case was perforated in hundreds of places, the keyboard keys slipped away to the floor in a clatter.

"Stop action," Loel commanded to the computer.

"What the hell happened?" Cody asked.

Cody's laptop had been attacked, the metal table too. Loel dropped heavily into her chair to evaluate her code. It was her own fault. How could she have been this careless with her security protocols? She hated setbacks and she hated disappointing Roy. A few moments passed before she quietly said over her shoulder, "Cody, please check the observation video. See what you can tell me about timing. How long did this take?"

Both engineers analyzed their data in silence, making notes. Cody finished much faster than Loel, but he respected her need for quiet concentration. Loel appreciated it. She needed the time to consider the necessary protocol changes. The room's lack of background noise, with no experiments running, created an unnatural silence for them. Even though voice commands were available for all their requests of the computer, they used their keyboards, gestures, and touch screens to not distract the other from their efforts.

Cody took detailed pictures of the laptop, the table, the nanites' canisters, and small piles of various-colored metal shavings on the floor. He was careful, avoiding further disturbance of the area. He shouldn't have picked up the laptop or even walked that close to the mess before he took pictures. Loel didn't say anything about that; she had bigger worries.

The gray table, split down the middle, had formed two inverted Vs when it had caved in. The split across the tabletop wasn't smooth. It was scalloped, as if from drill holes so close together they broke the integrity of the surface. "Zoom the camera in close. I'll want the greatest detail possible," Loel said. The camera multi-tasked in the lab as a microscope due to its high resolution and magnification ability. This came in handy when observing the SeekerDust.

A cracked, plastic shell of an old phone from the electronics recycling bin and half of a newer, glass-coated phone sat next to the destruction. The laptop would never work again. The holes in the case were the least of the destruction, each a unique size and only occasionally non-symmetrical. Cody took closeup pictures of the device from every angle. Loel knew what the focus of the attack had been. Her concerns now turned to the timing, the breach of protocols, and preventing future harm to both property and the program.

Loel leaned back, shaking her head and slapping the arms of her chair. "I was afraid of something like this. If we can't protect this project with airtight security, the world will never get past their fear of the nanites being controlled by the wrong people. Every parameter has to be considered and evaluated for tighter controls."

"There are so few of us aware of Rockefeller and the testing at this point," Cody said. "This is destructive, but somewhat benign in the big scheme. Do you want anyone else's help to solve this?"

Pacing the room, Loel considered their options. She was frustrated that she hadn't considered weaknesses within her own lab. She wanted the time to improve the safety of the project. She also knew she'd have to tell Roy every detail of what just happened. She didn't look forward to that.

The mining Dust was still unpredictable. Without the understanding of property ownership or constant lockdown observation, the Dust couldn't be trusted to mine the needed resources. It was too destructive. They had been away from the lab less than three hours and the dust started mining the richest metals in the room.

She had to get the intelligence of the MoralOS embedded soon. They needed the Dust to have freedom to do its job. But now it was either too aggressive or it had to be so restricted it was useless.

Changing The Game

The nearly sold-out stadium vibrated with excited fans. This third full season of the NFL owning the aSports version of football demonstrated that robots playing football brought profits back to the league. They were headed to Roy's suite at the fifty-yard line.

Keira's nephew Sam soaked in every detail of Gino explaining how his last visit to the stadium included human football players. Sam couldn't believe men had rammed into one another headfirst without killing each other. As they entered the room, Gino was describing the helmets worn and the real injuries that plagued the sport leading to its demise. A few colleges held out and still played games in front of fans, but the NFL no longer played the game with people.

Loel greeted the three of them at the door. She first turned to Sam. "Welcome. You must be Sam. I'm glad you're hanging out with your aunt and us today. She told us you were a sports fan. Hello, Keira, Gino, it's nice to see you in a relaxed environment."

Gino grinned as he shook Loel's hand. "Yes, this is exciting."

The Searcher employees lined up in an informal receiving line. Gino and Keira took Sam to the front edge of the space to view the stadium crowd. Loel joined them. "Roy has similar suites in the other ten stadiums, always on the visitor's side. He doesn't like to interfere with the franchise owner's hospitality on the home side. Most of the time the suites are used by local kids' organizations."

"What a cool idea." Keira smiled at Gino.

"Ask him to show you pictures today. His price for the donation to the groups is a picture of the kids enjoying the game. They'll roll into him all day from all over the country. While I have you two relatively alone, I needed to mention something. It is highly unusual that both members of a couple would be negotiating separately with Searcher. Only our core team know about both of you. This room only includes employees that are aware of the Opal Technologies acquisition and their families. I already mentioned this to Ruby and Ollie when they came in. There will be no reference to the FBI project."

Gino grinned. "I got it. I'm Keira's plus one. That's a role I'm happy to play. Thank you, Loel. That does simplify things for me."

The top executives and engineers of both Opal and Searcher stood chatting with each other. Keira was happy to see these people mingle outside of the grueling acquisition inquisitions, as Ollie had dubbed the last six weeks. Today was planned to bring both groups together. Keira and Roy would make the merger announcement in three more days.

Sam slid away to the seats in the front of the glass window. He planted himself next to Cody. Keira said, "Sam, you need to ask Mr. Cody if the seat next to him is taken."

"But, Aunt Keira, it's the best seat for me to see everything." The robotic players, most of them over six foot five inches tall, replaced traditional pregame warmup with exhibition of robotic dexterity. Eight robots lined up on the fifty-yard line, demonstrating what the engineers in the arena would describe as their range of motion and balancing capability. The rest of the audience thrilled at the hip-hop routine these giants performed. They danced while looking like the muscled and padded players the adults remembered from the NFL.

"It's okay, Keira," Cody responded with a happy grin on his face. "Sam's great right where he is. He's about the same age as my little brother. We'll manage just fine."

The two of them immediately put their heads together over the screen in the table reviewing stats for the robot players. Keira eavesdropped as Cody explained how each robot was developed for its specific position. Each robot's on-board AI computer had trained by watching every practice video and television footage recorded by the former human teams of the NFL. The two of them would be just fine. Sam knew about football and robots, but this inside track into the making and training of the players would make him a hero at school.

Cody was good with kids. He explained how imitation learning and the reinforcement learning of rewards for successfully completing an action for the robots were comparable to those of human athletes. The rewards for achievement and the number of repetitions required differed greatly. Sam hung on his every word.

Keira looked at the home team's quarterback and receiver pass the ball over seventy yards as Gino went to find a drink and Hendrick joined her. "Did you know the NFL put restrictions on the robotics designers?"

Keira shook her head.

"No robot could be more than 8% faster, stronger or, better, than the best human NFL player of the same position. This was designed to keep the game's resemblance to the human NFL intact," Hendrick said.

"I remember reading that no new stadiums could be created because the field needed to be expanded to challenge the machines."

"Right, that was a requirement pushed by Roy." Hendrick added. "He was adamant that the sport does not construct a wasteful environmental impact by relegating the existing stadiums obsolete. He didn't want super machines to get bigger and bigger just because they could. The essence of the sport needed to remain, especially to get the buy-in from NFL."

Keira looked up at Hendrick. "We need to talk at some point alone about our time at Stanford."

Hendrick said, "No need. Roy passed me a fair amount of reading material regarding your work on the MoralOS and your earlier ethical computing. I get it. I'll admit, you were a tough pill to swallow as my social media platform dreams dried up. I couldn't prove in my prospectus that I wasn't driving addiction to the app for the mere purpose of driving revenue."

"I'm sorry. I just —"

"No. I get it now. When the VCs ran your tests against my app, we failed miserably." He laughed. "Hey, maybe you kept me from the hot seat before congress or the EU. Besides, I started working on this instead." He waved towards the playing field and the robotic players.

Keira smiled. "There you go."

Hendrick shifted his weight, his eyes looking at her intently. "But I do wonder if your ethical calculus adds up. I have a challenge with how you can get computers to determine a course of action that isn't explicitly defined within its determined ethical code."

Keira raised her glass in a toast. "To make an ethical decision requires consideration of the circumstances, right? An AI can assess context at a much greater scale than people. I'll prove to you that an AI provided with a global perspective, not just a parochial view like most people walk around with, will exceed any human's ability to be ethical."

"I look forward to more of this debate, Keira. Thank you."

Gino carried a glass of champagne to Keira. Loel brought a beer to Hendrick. Gino asked, "Will Roy be joining us? It's exciting to think that he was such a big part of making this sport come back to life. You too, Hendrick."

"He's out there glad-handing now." Loel pointed down the line of suites. "The best way to keep people from crashing this suite is for him to make the rounds prior to the kickoff."

"Hendrick, you've contributed so much to the aSports development. How does all this make you feel?" Keira gazed across the football field.

"I wasn't involved in the NFL's aSport at first. With my height, everyone always assumed basketball was my sport. That sport never stuck with me. I did develop the early AIs for Stanford's simulation teams. We improved our advantage by training the AIs with World Cup soccer footage."

Gino asked, "Is that when MIT beat you because they trained their team with footage of one hundred thousand hours of goal kicking as opposed to having refined field play like Stanford?"

"Yes, that was the year." Hendrick hung his head in mock shame. "It was almost as bad to play that year's MIT AI team as it was to watch them as a fan. They could rack up the goals, but they executed terrible midfield. You obviously followed the sport."

Roy entered the room, shaking hands and grinning ear to ear just as the whistle sounded. He made a direct approach to greet Keira and Gino.

"Do you follow the NFL aSports, Keira?" Roy asked.

"I prefer racing, America's Cup Sailing, and Formula 1. I must admit I like the sports where people are still physically competing. However, I share deep respect for the balance and regulations designed to keep this competitive and each game and play unique."

"A traditionalist?" Roy said. "Interesting. I would have thought the advancements robotics brought to the sport and the brain injuries prevented would be enough to make you a fan."

"Oh, I do admire the technology involved. I can't believe how fast you made this happen. I don't think humanoid robotics would have progressed nearly as much had it not been for the R&D poured into the sport's development. The fact that those players on the field appear so much like the suited-up football guys is amazing."

"I know! Look at those fans out there," Roy said. "They're dedicated to their teams. It doesn't matter that the players don't flash winning smiles or tell emotional backstories. The fans pick a team and passionately support them. It was my hope we could pull this off when I first pitched turning the AI simulation teams into the robotic replicas of the old sport. The NFL jumped at the idea. Their game had become so regulated for safety and health reasons, nobody wanted to watch it or play it. I'm also glad that kids aren't getting their heads bashed around while playing anymore."

"I thank you, Roy, for your part in saving all those athletes' brains. And look at that big screen above the field." The design engineers and trainers for each player rotated through the display. "I love the crowd fan-worshiping the techies for their achievements. They're becoming the personalities of the league, aren't they? I like those kinds of heroes put forth for the kids."

Walking towards them, Ruby held refresher drinks for her and Roy. Keira recognized the expression on Ruby's face as one of built-up courage. She braced herself for what might be coming. The glasses were shared, and a waiter whisked away their empties.

"Roy," Ruby said, "I'll only take a few moments. Thank you for this invite to this wonderful suite. The game is fascinating. I've learned a lot about Hendrick being part of the original business but now being part of Searcher."

"Hendrick is a man of many talents. He's not only a technical powerhouse but also an expert at making connections with the people we need to know."

Ruby may not have even heard Roy's comments. "I also heard a little about the spinoffs that various employees have done while some of their co-workers stay at Searcher. I just want to let you know that where Keira goes, I go."

Ruby gave no chance for Roy or Keira to respond. She had needed her speech to be heard. "Where Keira is happy to work, I will be too, right beside her. Her missions are my missions. We've done this together a long time. I simply trust her implicitly. Thank you, I look forward to the merger announcement."

After Ruby exhaled, she raised her glass.

"That's good to know." Roy raised his glass to meet hers. His face lit up with a grin.

Ruby returned to the small cluster she had been chatting with.

Keira allowed the breath she had been holding to rush out. "Wow," she said. "I wasn't expecting that. We haven't talked at all about assignments or working teams. But now you know where Ruby stands. We've been together since college, and I can't imagine not working with her either." She raised her eyebrows, searching Roy's face for a reaction.

"I do like employees that are definitive." He gave no hint of feeling chastised while being told how to arrange his employees. "I guess I'll get along with Ms. Ruby just fine."

Keira took a long drink of her champagne.

Roy looked across the room to Loel. "I can't imagine working without Loel either. She's steadfast, as if I had a sister there, always ready to take on the world with me. When you have the right team, it's a game changer."

The big screens displayed instant replays, stats, and celebrity style profiles of various programmers, trainers, designers, and robotic engineers. Human coaches and human referees argued about a call or regulation violation near the sideline. A coach had to swap out a player from the bench to conserve the battery in a star player. The atmosphere felt as energized as any human-played football game.

Sam rushed up to the group. "Aunt Keira, Cody says each of those robots can cost millions of dollars to build and train. But he said it's okay, because good football players often cost their teams that much when people played football too. Um, excuse me. I interrupted, didn't I?" He hung his head down, embarrassed. He rolled his eyes up at Keira, silently asking for forgiveness.

She forgave him instantly, ruffling his hair. She then introduced him to Roy. The two of them walked off to examine the awards in Roy's trophy case behind the suite's bar.

Ollie approached Keira and turned his back towards the rest of the group. Talking softly and only to Keira he said, "With all of these pioneers in aSports in this room, what the heck are they doing in disaster recovery and nanites? It doesn't make a lot of sense to me. Why would you move on from something like this?"

"Hmm, good question. I know Roy traveled the world early in his career with the CIA. Perhaps the disasters he saw during that time drew him into this field. I also get the feeling these guys get bored pretty quickly when they have constraints. Hendrick told Gino the problem with sports is too many rules and nobody wants to change them to accommodate the ability of the technology. Maybe they got boxed in."

"Maybe. Or you know stuff and aren't telling us."

"Ollie, that's unfair. I've been completely open with you from the beginning of this process. I never keep secrets from you or Ruby."

"Speaking of Ruby, why does everyone ask us if we're a couple all the damn time? We're friends. Don't they have any?"

"Well, Mr. Touchy. I think it has something to do with you two always arriving and leaving at the same time. Plus, you've worked so closely you can finish each other's sentences."

Staring across the room at Hendrick making Ruby laugh, Ollie didn't seem pleased. Keira assumed that Ollie didn't notice that Hendrick's co-worker Shauney and at least two other women also laughed at the same time. This amused Keira, she wasn't certain if it was professional jealousy or something more motivating his comments.

Ollie turned to stare at the game. "I think these guys are a little showy up here in their suite."

"Ollie, please. The suite is Roy's. We'll all be part of the same team shortly, benefiting from each other's experience and resources. Give it a chance. I think they gave up a lot of flashy work for work that has a lot of purpose. Sound familiar? Hey, I know this week is scary. But it's going to be fine. I'm certain of it."

Ollie snapped out of his sulk, apologizing for adding to her stress of the acquisition week. Keira spent the rest of the time moving between the guests from both companies.

The fans cheered and stood and stomped as the game neared completion. Keira stood at the suite's window, alternating between watching the crowd and the robotic players. Any nostalgic football fan would recognize all the same reverence and team loyalty the former human league once enjoyed. As Roy approached her, she smiled at him. "I may not be a huge football fan, Roy, but I'm extremely impressed. This league you and your engineers created is awe-inspiring."

"Thank you, Keira. It's thrilling to see how far we've come. It was such a rapid turnaround for the sport."

"One of the things that impresses me the most is the adoration the devotees show for their robots. You managed to break down the stigmas of robotics and turn around what people said would be the greatest barrier to their adoption, fear of their humanlike actions. I don't even think these people realize that."

Roy nodded while keeping his eye on the final plays. The score was close, and his favorite team was currently ahead. "Sports have a way to drive people into accepting things they otherwise might not tolerate. History is filled with sports breaking down racial barriers, religious differences, and even geopolitical ideology. I knew for acceptance of any future innovations we create, I had to reach legions of rabid fans supporting robotics."

"Ah, you do play the long game, don't you?" Keira admired his foresight.

The game ended. The crowd both within the suite and half of those outside in the stadium erupted in a thunderous cheer.

"It looks like it worked," Roy said, sporting a mischievous grin. He shook her hand and turned to the well-wishers surrounding him.

While leaving, Gino waved to Loel, thanking her again. Loel called to him. "Don't tell George about spending the day up here. You'll make him jealous."

Keira turned to Gino. "She's right. Your partner would be jealous about spending today in a suite. I hope her comments imply the relationship is progressing well."

Everybody Has An Angle

D eon had mixed emotions about bringing his latest discovery to Mickey. He liked the interesting work of these companies he'd found in their announcement. He didn't look forward to changes that could occur if Mickey got his hands on them. Occasionally during the last three years, Deon asked himself what he was doing working for the man.

Guys like Mickey had been around all his life. They overcompensated for something. They were bullied somewhere in their childhood or were publicly taken advantage of financially. Men like Mickey were never going to willingly be seen as weak again. He didn't like anything about his boss other than the huge paycheck the tyrant provided and the intriguing work he gave Deon.

Mickey looked up as Deon stood in his doorframe. His boss waved him in, but the action wasn't welcoming. He entered the shrine to Mickey's stature. The trophies on the shelves screamed, "I'm a winner." The pictures of Mickey reaching various mountain summits and his Army boxing ring days said, "Don't mess with me." Deon wasn't impressed.

"Whatcha got for me?" Mickey grumbled as he tossed his disgusting chewed Tootsie Pop stick in the trashcan three feet from his desk.

Approaching Mickey four years ago had been a calculated risk on Deon's part. He'd been let go from a company that—until select intellectual property had been leaked and competitors rushed to take over—had been experiencing a meteoric rise in the market.

Surprised at the loss of confidentiality from such a security conscious firm, Deon started doing his own research. He discovered Mickey at the root of the espionage labyrinth. Revealing this discovery to Mickey, he was immediately hired for his dogged skills. Deon assumed it was also to shut him up.

"I found a merger announcement. Searcher Technologies bought Opal," Deon said. He sat on the leather chair across from his boss. "You know Opal. You know Searcher because of Roy Brandt and the copilot you paid off. You know the one on the airplane returning from the earthquake recovery project. We passed a portfolio to you covering his information and my guy's cam videos. Searcher made the surveillance smart Dust."

"But why would they want Opal? It's a learning and marketing company. From what I hear, they're burning through cash like a wildfire. She might have needed help."

"Maybe they want Dr. Stetson. She's brilliant. Or they want her chat bots."

"Keira? She's an idealist. The smartest idealist we'll ever meet, but you take her tech, not her. She'd block anything that ruffled anyone's sensibilities, anything of value."

Deon wondered what aggravated Mickey more, the fact that Dr. Keira Stetson refused his corporate advances to talk about purchasing Opal several times or that she had made clear her disdain for Mickey and his business practices.

"I think it looks random," Mickey grumbled. "Maybe a public relations stunt for Searcher. They think appearing to help kids with their tech will make them look like heroes. They may still be concerned it will come out that the state of Nevada used Searcher for some cleanup at that nuclear mishap. It sounded like a big mess they've kept under the radar so far. Or they want to shut down her aggressive whining about ethical computing. That's what I'd do. I wonder if Brandt is getting into something he doesn't want her exposing?"

"She isn't involved in the certification of AIs anymore," Deon said. "That is all done by OpenML now. So, I don't know that she's positioned to see his stuff getting certified. But she and her chief technology officer are still the biggest cheerleaders, recruiting people to get their code certified and to use the MoralOS."

"Christ, I even hate the name, the MoralOS. How can anyone willfully sign up for that shit?"

Ignoring Mickey's rhetorical question, Deon flipped to a notes screen, assuming he wouldn't need it. "This isn't something you want me to pursue, right? It doesn't look like anything you're going to add to the defense contracts. There's nothing here to help your drones, your weaponry, or cyber programs. Brandt complicates things for us too. He never sells anything off." Deon shrugged, noticing that Mickey's computer wasn't even turned on. What did this guy do all day?

"I've known Brandt for a long time. He tried to kill a deal between me and the DOD. He claimed I was exploiting my relationship with the purchasing agent or some bullshit. It was just a guy I'd served with. But he really tried to screw things up. I've heard Searcher has government security clearance contracts with somebody. Got any details on that? Is it the nanite stuff? Maybe that helps us find a link to Opal."

Deon shook his head. "Where did you hear this? That could help me track the agency or the type of work they're doing."

"I don't give you information!" Mickey bellowed. "I pay you for digging up information!"

Deon knew better than to concentrate on the wrong thing while Mickey was in one of these moods. One never knew what kind of information he'd reveal in the middle of his tirade.

Mickey started pacing. "You get inside Searcher Technologies. You can manage the background trail. You talk a good game. I'm sure you can convince those tree huggers you belong. Find out what they're working on. Figure out what it'll take to make it mine if I decide I like it."

Deon stood.

Mickey added, "Don't screw up this one or your lifestyle of expensive cars and more expensive women will disappear, just like that." Mickey snapped his fingers.

Deon slapped the cover over his tablet and headed for the door. He made an effort to control his movements instead of storming out in frustration with Mickey's condescension and threats. It was just the guy's style.

Mickey didn't have any secrets on Deon because Deon didn't have any secrets. That's why Mickey didn't scare him like he scared others. Mickey did pay him crazy amounts of money, though. Deon was certain part of the giant compensation package was Mickey's hope he would slip up, giving Mickey something to hold over his head. Deon kept his own nose clean. He had standards, even if his boss didn't.

Cavalier Confidence

Keira kept a quick jogger's pace with Loel on the treadmill for the first twenty-five minutes. She was grateful they weren't running outside where she couldn't keep up with the marathon runner. At least here in the company gym, she could walk next to Loel's relentless gait and still carry on a conversation. Roy had warned her about Loel's need to burn energy while chatting.

"I've been here only two weeks, but life as purely Opal seems light-years away. I just can't imagine more divergent efforts than the task force and my education bots," Keira said.

Loel challenged her, "Ah, come on, both steer kids toward better lives."

Keira shrugged. "That's a bit of a stretch, but okay."

Loel's watch had buzzed repeatedly during their run. She'd mostly ignored it. She barely slowed her pace and punched her finger at the watch. "What is it, Cody? Good grief."

"I really need you to come look at something. Please? I need your help," Cody said.

"Alright, I'll shower quickly and be right there." She poked at her phone to end the call.

Keira was not accustomed to seeing this type of exchange between

Cody and Loel. "If you think there is anything I can help with, please let me know."

"I doubt it's a big deal. You can join me if you like."

Keira showered and dressed as fast as she could. Loel's short hair was no challenge to quickly towel dry. Keira twisted hers and secured it like she did for windy days on the lake. They walked to Cody's office without speaking.

"Hey, Loel, I've been buzzing you through every channel I could. Why haven't you answered me?" Cody demanded. "Our domain controllers are being hit with a DDoS."

He pointed to the screens on his desk, each subdivided into panes with many charts, lists, and dashboards.

Loel's expression didn't change. "Yep, I saw the messages. I did reply about ten minutes ago that things looked under control."

Sensing it wasn't a big deal, but not wanting to be left out of a learning curve, Keira turned to Cody. "What is DDoS?"

Shooting Loel a quizzical look, Cody turned to Keira. "Our servers are being attacked simultaneously from multiple external points. It's the type of thing hackers do to stop your systems from working. They overload it."

This didn't sound trivial. She joined Cody in his surprise at Loel's reaction.

Loel smiled confidently. "Yes, I saw your messages. These are random attempted attacks, and we need to get accustomed to them. Our structures are more than a match for these guys. Nothing has gotten in."

Several panes in each of the monitors rotated between green, yellow and red.

"I've put a recommendation in my update report for the deployment of more defensive tech," Cody responded. "I know I'm not the most up-to-date on the best practices. But I feel it's important. The IT guys are crawling all over me about this."

Loel held steadfast. "Cody, thank you. We're fine. I can't spare resources, especially your time. Have IT keep us up-to-date."

Cody shifted his weight back and forth, appearing to gather his thoughts for a response. "They are keeping me up-to-date. And at this moment, the update looks threatening."

Keira had quickly learned the relationship dynamics between the Searcher employees. These two were usually thinking nearly as one mind.

He shook his head. "These attempted strikes appear different. They're attacking everything at once. Look at this." He pointed to each monitor in succession. "They're trying DNS, backups and operational systems, even mobile phones. Our firewalls are detecting autonomous worms not typically deployed by ransomware pirates. If my sound was turned up, you'd hear a riot of bells, chimes, and alerts from all these systems."

Keira said, "What's not typical about it?"

Cody looked at Keira, apparently happy somebody was listening to him. "Normally, we're probed by profit-focused cyber hacks trying to infect our computers with ransomware. This looks like cyberwar tactics to me."

Loel didn't respond. Keira offered, "Ollie has a couple of IT wizards in his group. I haven't stayed current with the terminology, let alone the tech, but they protected our stuff through some ugly assaults."

Cody sighed. "Thanks, Keira, I'll introduce them to our guys. It's not my forte, either. Loel knows a lot more about it than I do. Our team's pretty good, but they're alarmed." Turning to Loel he said, "You're going to take this to Roy, right?"

Loel shook her head. "No, he monitors all the attack reports when he wants to. He'll see it." She turned to Keira with a smile. "We're using state-of-the-art intrusion prevention and have multiple layers of detection. We're fine."

"I'm going to call Ollie." Cody dropped into his chair, turning his back to Loel.

Facing Realities

The recent harried and stressful processes took their toll on all the Opal employees. Keira missed her casual interactions with Ollie and Ruby. She loved Ruby's office and the windows they could black out with a push of a button. All the offices gave these tree house-like views.

Keira peeked over Ruby's shoulder to see what caused the tortured expression on her face. "What's that?"

"It's the priorities report Loel asked for. I have to share my resources with Searcher, but they won't answer many of my questions. I want to be a team player, but I hate being in the dark."

Keira plopped down on the couch at the edge of her worktable. "You look exhausted. I know the security clearance interviews are brutal, and they make tasks like this harder. But is there something else going on here too?" She spun around to lay down, her legs draped over the arm.

Ruby chuckled. "Do make yourself at home. I'm glad you're bringing your informal game here too. It hasn't been easy lately. I'll give you that. But forget me, what's up with you today?"

Heaving a big sigh, Keira said, "I hate the entertainment world's portrayal of robots and AI. Acceptance of tech would be so much easier in the marketplace if they weren't trying to kill everybody and take over the world in every movie."

A snort came from Ruby stifling a laugh. "Really, Keira? All the shit going on right now and you're focusing on Hollywood? That's amusing."

"No really. We're trying to help kids get answers, and they're distorting reality. It ticks me off."

Ruby ran her fingers through her hair, flung herself back in her chair and looked up at the ceiling. "Keira, don't tell me we're going to start working in the entertainment world through Searcher. I don't think I can handle the superficiality."

Keira sat up and grabbed a throw pillow to hug. "What? Oh, no, not Hollywood. No, it was just a conversation with my nephew Sam last night. Some movie terrified him. He asked all these questions about robots and evil AI. He needed a lot of reassurance that we won't build evil technology."

"Did you explain we're the good guys? But when they make the movie about us, I want to be played by some action goddess who lets me be both intelligent and kick ass."

"Wait. I thought you didn't want anything to do with Hollywood." Keira said.

"But think of the red carpet? Never mind. Hey, speaking of evil, what is this crap Searcher's making me learn about? Stuff like . . . thirteen is the average age a girl enters into the sex trade. Ninety-eight percent of those forced into the trade lived through physical or sexual abuse in their own household. I'm disgusted by the statistics and data in this report. And I'm baffled at why Searcher wanted me to dive into data about crime stats, especially the sex trafficking. I have so many questions. It's been so difficult to get your attention."

"What are you talking about? What report did you read?" Ruby's clearance wasn't complete yet. Roy had only just signed the deal to use the Dust to help the FBI Human Trafficking Task Force that Gino led. Did they have a security breach already?

"I was sent this disgusting report on crime, gambling, sex, drugs, etc. Nothing about rock and roll anywhere to lighten it up. I mean this is sad. Did you know eighty-seven percent of trafficked teens are abandoned by their fathers before the age of four? Eighty percent are runaways? They never explained anything about why I needed this information. This sounds like Gino's world, not ours. What did you get us into?"

Keira regularly asked herself that question. She could no longer stay parked on the couch. She paced beside Ruby's spotless desk. She insisted all data be electronic and refused to keep any paper. Her philosophy would fit in with Searcher's no printing policy.

"It's so sad and a real problem," Keira said. "The kids don't stand a chance. Then when those girls have kids, they don't provide a stable home. The cycle of poverty starts all over. I do wonder what this world is coming to at times. It will make sense soon. That's all I can say. How was your clearance interview today?"

"It was fine. I should be able to have meaningful conversations with you again by tomorrow," Ruby answered.

"Hey, this is meaningful, just depressing. Study that report closely. I can't say much, but there's stomach turning stuff going on in our world. It's time to throw new types of brainpower at the problems. They need your psychological take on a few challenges. Yours and Ollie's."

Gino had specifically requested Roy incorporate Ollie's work with distress detection into the Dust. Roy's impatience with getting Ruby and Ollie's security clearance completed led to Elly's assignment to iterate on the design.

Keira had been amused while listening to Elly's explanation to Roy about her loyalty to Ollie's research. More precisely, her loyalty to Ollie and Ruby. Elly's insistence that Ollie had to be informed on her progress with his work had taken Roy off guard. He obviously was not accustomed to being challenged, especially by an AI. She had conceded immediately when Roy informed her about the requirement of the security clearances. Elly confirmed that requirement was both prudent and ethical.

"I guess serving up ethics puts us on a counter scale to shit like this. I like living in my white hat bubble, not so much staring at the other side of the equation." Ruby tapped her tablet. "I do have some good news. I found a handful of people here who also surf the tanker wakes in Puget Sound. I hope you and Ollie will take me out there more often."

"I'm glad you started joining us. You used to make a fuss if you thought I sailed too close to the tankers. I saw a picture of Cody surfing on his wall."

Ruby stood and stretched. "Well, you two make it feel all right. Have you noticed the weird hours for people around here, though? I think I'll be spending a lot of time jumping back and forth from here to Opal's classrooms. I've asked if there is space here to move the classrooms. The kids would enjoy coming to the forest and getting out of the city. This building is so camouflaged. I love the windows Roy commissioned that don't let our lights filter outside, even without window coverings. You barely know there is a building here on the hill, even at night."

"He is thoughtful about his designs, I'll give him that." Keira nodded. "That's a great idea to get the kids out here. We could take them on the walking path up the hill through the trees too. We need to survey the parents on that."

Keira put a hand on Ruby's arm. "How are you doing?"

Ruby shrugged. "I like the work, but you and Cody jump in and out of my projects like hummingbirds. It's too fleeting for real feedback. You know who is doing well? Elly is thriving with the consumption of new data in this place."

"I agree. I believe Hendrick's skepticism is pushing her to articulate her abilities better too. But she seems to want to get her fingers into everyone's pie. Loel appears to be the least interested in Elly's help. But is oh-so-polite in her rejections."

"That's interesting. I'll watch out for those interactions. Although I seldom interact with Loel."

Keira needed a change of scenery. "Let's get out of here. Want to go grab a drink and throw darts or do anything that doesn't involve bankers or lawyers or anyone wanting to put us under a microscope? I'm so happy the sale process is over."

"Yes, I do. Now, because you're a rich woman from selling us all to the fancy pants in the hills, you're buying," Ruby said.

"Hey, selling your shares in Opal put a bit of coin in your pocket too. But I'll certainly buy the first two rounds."

Ruby grabbed her purse and held open her door for Keira. "Ollie said they hired a new guy for the 3D printing stuff. He seemed to drop out of the sky, right at our feet. Deon's his name. He's from Stanford's Robotics Forum. Loel and Hendrick met him."

"Really?" Keira couldn't believe they hired somebody that fast before getting to know her team and their expertise. It would take some effort to accept not being in charge and in-the-know.

Ruby continued. "They hired him fast because his credentials were perfect, and he wouldn't stay on the market for another hour. He's ex-military, so I think that also gave him a leg up. Roy evidently likes the discipline of ex-military. The guy won't need clearance, at least not right away. He'll be focused on one specific type of hardware. Our guys are happy not to be pigeonholed on printing stuff. They don't farm stuff out at all."

The evening's darkness was increased by rain. The black hallway's ambient lighting cast only occasional breaks in the shadows as they passed to the auto portico. It was nice not having to request a car since the remoteness of the facility would otherwise make the wait much longer than Opal's office in the city. All the Opal employees used the local autonomous car services. She didn't think any of them even owned a car.

"You're a wealth of pleasant tidbits. Anything else of interest?" Keira asked, opening the exterior door.

"Oh, yeah. Roy hates Mickey Temming more than you do—something about government contracts. Somebody screwed up somebody else's order, and it jeopardized lives or a project or something. It's a bit sketchy. I think there's a lot of bad blood there."

They entered the first car and provided the guidance system with the address to their favorite pub in Tacoma. "How do you get this information without being pegged as a gossip?" Keira teased.

"A master's in clinical psychology before jumping to engineering gave Ollie great conversational skills. Me? I'm just nosy." Ruby grinned.

Necessary
Constraints

When Cody had first suggested they name their project Rockefeller, Loel had balked. But Roy had immediately grasped the correlation. Loel lectured about the connotations of Rockefeller's anti-trust issues and possible fraudulent dealings. Roy loved the anticipation of controlling the entire supply chain. He had grown tired of wasteful processes. If he could better accomplish his vision by managing or owning each step of production, the mission stayed cleaner. Cody impressed Roy with this perceptiveness.

Roy was convinced that Rockefeller would change the world. He and Cody designed the Dust's highly configurable 3D printers. Each time the AI provided a different hardware requirement to meet their objectives, the printers adapted to the task. The machines could rapidly iterate through thousands of design options. Plastic, as well as both basic and rare earth metals, made up the components of the nanites. The printers laid down the elements in combination, forming the machine's perfect little dust mote CPUs.

"We solved the problem of inconsistently sized particles jamming the extruder nozzles," Cody updated Roy. "Look through this microscope. What do you see?"

Roy peered through the eye pieces Cody offered. "They look like tiny grinding wheels. Those are new nanites."

"Yes, they are. We now utilize specific industrial dust motes that grind the materials at their scale. They can be calibrated to shockingly explicit sizes compared to classic commercial processes."

The minute machines mesmerized Roy. They chewed across the plastic in their cardboard tray in a steady march, leaving linear trails of the soon to be repurposed granules. Loel fidgeted behind him.

"We opened up the lab towards the left loading dock. This allows us to bring in the plastic and metals from the recycle center easily," Loel said, showing Roy the newly installed double doors.

Roy grinned. "I see it also allowed you to bring in this nice granite lab table. Don't let the others see this. They'll want one and want to know why you needed granite. I'm assuming the cardboard tray is related to the same incident that led you to the granite table."

Cody was eager to explain. "Roy, it looked like a break-in. I swear I've never seen anything like it. Even though I knew no one could get in Loel's lab, it was just a shock and took a minute to register that the Dust violated the space. Well, it violated my laptop."

Laughing, Roy clapped his hand on Cody's shoulder blade. "I saw the pictures. I'm sure it was a surprise. Loel gave me the update while I was in Brazil. Sounds like those grinding motes of yours acted a little too zealously."

"Yes. They made a meal of Cody's laptop. But we've programmed no recycling requirements for granite or cardboard, so they should leave this table alone," Loel said while giving her shirt a tug. "Better restrictions providing the AI with tighter mining parameters was required. If we get Keira's MoralOS integrated, the understanding of ownership and permissions will be in place."

"Roy," Cody said with intensity and a touch of wonder. "The nanites didn't only drill and excavate the materials they were designed to pursue. You saw the pictures of the precise piles of material on the floor. The industrial miners deposited each element in a unique pile with inordinately pure segregation. This isn't something we specifically trained them to do."

Roy was intrigued by the Dust's new behavior. "Tell me more."

"You and Loel always push us to use as much cumulative learning as possible within every AI system. The guidelines training the tiny printers to use pure elements received updates in the same neural network operated by these miners. Agents obviously applied that guideline optimization to their central policy. The combined learning of multiple agents led the miners to separate the different items they crunched because purity is desirable for the other agents."

"I like it. We can leverage this layered learning. But we need to be careful about our controls, or your laptop won't be the last thing we regret losing," Roy said. "The progress in the production is considerable, but can we speed up the printers?"

Cody's scrunched expression answered the immediate question. "We need more printers. I've set them as a production priority. At this point, the printers and assemblers can only produce ten more printers each day. We must remove the constraints of human intervention in the process. We need end-to-end automation."

Loel leaned in on the table. "That will be our game changer. The self-replication is close, but we need more work to make it happen. Can we add anyone else to the project?"

"No," Roy insisted. "We can't afford to increase the exposure to Rockefeller yet. Soon, materials will no longer be a bottleneck in the process. I completed the Brazilian electronic acquisition on this last trip. We have the three local electronics recycling companies, the third working with all those hard plastics from toys, car parts, and housewares. We now have access to a wealth of materials for the Dust production."

Roy also owned the landfills in China that consumed the excess electronics and their manufacturing waste of the '80s, '90s and 2000s. He'd created a series of corporations that would be difficult to directly trace to him. These companies owned land in several African countries, which still held the e-waste dumped from trash barges originating from the US and the EU.

Their nanites were a wonder. Miniaturized, spectrometer-equipped, specific nanites assessed the trash within these sources to locate the correct types of plastics and metals. Now, Cody had proved the nanites could grind each component and separate the powders. With the scale and precision of the nanites deconstructing the electronics, manufacturing could ramp up much faster. Roy liked fast.

Using recycled materials and the nanites providing the processing labor brought the cost of manufacturing the Dust down to nearly zero. In the past, price had made large scale production of the SeekerDust fiscally prohibitive, even with Roy's wealth.

His greatest challenges now included controlling the Dust from consuming property still in use, like Loel's old table and Cody's laptop. The "gray goo" theory of machines consuming the planet's biomass to self-replicate was not a story he wanted getting in Searcher's way of creating SeekerDust.

His Dust didn't use living material, so the analogy about gray goo that made people fear for their lives around machines never faced relevancy. But the image of nanites eating their way through a server farm to make more nanites was one he couldn't risk. Keira's work would be so helpful here.

Fear of the possible negative results had buried many a hopeful leap in technical progress. Roy, however, would not be stopped on this one. People feared AI driven robots would become smarter than people and wipe humans off the face of the earth.

The thought of machines consuming what mankind had created and leaving them barren of their favorite toys and conveniences inflamed imaginations and occupied conspiracy theories. Public outcry of hungry nanites running amok would rock the public psyche, and the fallout would most certainly shut down all his research and development. But he'd clean up the planet of unwanted objects and streamline their recycling into new creations.

They had big plans for this Dust. He considered adding Keira's education bots to his manufacturing list. She desperately wanted to make them affordable to all kids. That would make her happy. His impossibly long list of items to build was lengthy. He couldn't let her get sidetracked yet. He was surprised she hadn't negotiated for them.

"We have our mining sources set up now, right?" Roy asked.

Cody wiped his hands on his jeans. "We need to provide the nickel-63 for the power source. None of our landfills hold enough discarded goods that used it. The bots will find it in old power supplies and surge protectors but not in enough quantities for the nanites' power devices. Hendrick found a warehouse of old foils created for explosive detection. We'll make them accessible for the assemblers."

"Here we go then. First, we'll create the Dust at quantity. Then we can produce anything on our special list." Roy relished creating things from nothing.

Critical Visibility

T hirty-two men in SWAT gear, including mixed-reality night vision goggles, spread out around the first dark port warehouse. No electronic communication passed between any of the raiders. Shadows concealed forty-one more highly skilled and armed operatives moving between four other warehouses and two large boats in the water.

Roy focused on Keira, who was stiffly perched on a stool in Searcher's lab in front of the large wall of monitors. Her first raid as an observer held extra tension with her husband in the command center trailer parked near the entrance to the marina. The truck appeared turned off, but it could be mobilized to block the driveway. SeekerDust gave Roy, Keira, and observing FBI agents views of the entire operation through their bank of split screens.

The on-site viewing was similar for Cody, Hendrick, Gino, and his boss. Roy had one extra camera view the field trailer didn't have—the interior of the command center. Dark except for the blue ambient lighting and the glow off the monitors, the trailer was crowded with equipment and surveillance gear.

Gino and his team had scouted the port earlier. He'd seen the boats that looked rusted and old but were deceptively fast. The viewers in the lab were seeing all this for the first time.

Roy leaned over to Keira. "The warehouses are intentionally nondescript. Drivers and ship pilots will forget any detail about this place the minute they leave the area. Boring never raises anyone's attention. Flashy gets you noticed." Keira nodded her understanding but kept her eyes moving around the multiple screens.

The stealthy raiders, dressed in black and moving on silent feet, planned to be equally unnoticed. They nodded to each other and exchanged hand signals.

"Too many times, I lose complete sight of the agents," Keira whispered, as though speaking at full volume might be heard at the marina.

"That's the point, ma'am. These guys are the best," said the observing officer closest to her.

George, Gino's partner at the FBI, turned to Roy. "They never would have approved this large of a crew had it not been for the undeniable intelligence your Dust provided. The last three raids they gave us fewer than twenty-five agents total. It was all they would risk."

"I'm glad we're helping," Roy responded.

She'd purposely stayed away from the training and the discussions between Searcher and the FBI field teams. Not knowing how much Gino shared with her, Roy decided to be blunt. "Keira, three of the trafficking cartel's leaders have gotten away during the last six months. The agency must have a better way to pull off a strike earlier and with a lot of incriminating evidence collected in the sweep. That's where we come in." George was nodding in agreement.

Gino hunched over behind Cody in the command trailer. Roy understood their tension. Memories of CIA operatives moving into danger under his command made him breathe deeply. Roy understood the adrenaline surging through Gino while watching the men execute each maneuver. Roy's time in the field never left him. He was so glad Keira had made this introduction.

Hendrick and Cody swapped glances at every inch of progress made towards the targets. Roy didn't need the monitoring equipment to know the men's hearts were racing. This contract with the FBI would make a world of difference to Searcher. His crew knew the lives of hostages inside the marina depended on them.

"How did you distribute the nanites around the marina?" Keira asked.

Roy chuckled despite the tension in the room. "Your husband is brilliant. We sent Hendrick disguised as a bug guy. It's sad that with all this tech in the world, we still can't be rid of the cockroaches. While he pretended to spray insecticide, he was spreading the nanites. A thug followed him around, but Hendrick evidently showed sufficient disinterest in his surroundings."

Searcher's Dust released throughout the warehouses and adjoining boat slips recorded what they needed. At least four dozen victims were held hostage throughout the complex. Detailed transaction data in the voices of their most wanted perpetrators was conveyed to recording devices at the lab. That data secured the ninja-like contingent surrounding the targets at this moment.

The strike was synchronized to protect the victims. Victims were dispersed between each warehouse and boat. Traffickers saw the loss of their human cargo as costly but expendable. The SWAT team wanted to get as close as possible before detection.

The sound of a hefty bird taking off from the ground and brushing its wings against the side of the first building jolted everyone. It wasn't a bird. It was the signal. The cluster of SWAT members tightened silently around all sides of the traffickers.

Gino whispered into his mic for Roy, "Searcher's heads-up display goggles are working great. These guys are like superheroes looking through walls with nothing but the wire frame obstructing the view. We've never had this much visibility for a raid."

Roy pointed to the screen on Keira's left. "These lines show the agents the best path to follow. Blue goes towards the traffickers and red towards hostages."

"And the yellow?" asked Keira.

"Yellow highlights unknown individuals. No weapon has been identified with them. Their faces haven't been matched to our database, and their activities have been unremarkable. There are only two yellows tonight."

Still in stealth mode, the strikers synchronized their breach. Roy flinched as a sentry at each back door was immobilized, glad Keira didn't know what some of those shadows included at this moment.

An alarm blared from the central building. Everyone in the lab jumped. "Damn it! Sounds like a motion detector. We missed one," George muttered.

Shouts rang out in all directions alerting the traffickers they had intruders. The criminals rushed toward the noise in the center warehouse. Chaos from gunfire and shouting allowed the strikers to immobilize the distracted men elsewhere in the complex.

Agents silently swarmed the boats, entering over the side rail or directly down the gangways. Three guards on each boat never had a chance to react to the invasion. The goggled team members followed the directional indicators on the display to move straight to the rooms housing victims. Not a single extraneous action was taken by the government team.

The main room of the warehouse spanned two hundred feet and contained two dry-docked commercial fishing boats on racks. Agents swarmed in first from the door that had raised the alarm. Most of the armed men inside were already rushing there. Keira gasped as gunshots were fired.

Breaching three doors from the other end of the building, agents wrestled guns away from three guards. Sliding left as he entered the door, an agent's goggles indicated an armed man creeping around an open office door. The guard exited the office with gun raised. The agent delivered a side kick into the guard's kidney before he could fire.

Six agents ran to a space between the chaos near the motion alarm and the closest boat. They spread out towards the group still fighting near the front door. Their backs were towards a scared cluster of women and children plastered to the floor.

Keira stood. "Those are kids!" She pointed to the screen "Some of those are kids."

Another wave of agents ran through the back door rushing to the hostages, creating a second layer of human shield.

"Sadly, yes," Roy said.

One of the agents crawled among over fifty people checking them for injuries. He murmured words of assurance to each one of them as he passed. The agents weren't worried about the back of the warehouse. The Dust showed it empty of people.

Traffickers were now separated from their hostages. SWAT forced the men to the ground and zip-tied their hands behind their backs. FBI vehicles, ambulances, and police cars swarmed the port.

The raid had taken less than fifteen minutes. It had felt like hours. Keira sat, arms folded, soaking it all in.

Gino's face filled the traditional camera feed from the trailer thirty minutes later. "George, Roy, Keira? Are you there?"

"Yes, we're here," Roy and George both replied.

"Guys!" Gino blurted. "Seventy-nine women and teenagers were just rescued. The ship's log shows they planned to sail in the next twenty-four hours. We would've lost them all if we hadn't moved tonight." He wiped his forehead with his sleeve, possibly also wiping away tears.

"They're getting checked out by the medics now. Many are pretty drugged up. It's sickening to see first-user tracks on their arms. These guys are disgusting. It's all about control. I gotta go. Oh, Keira, love you. Sorry, I won't be home tonight. There's a lot to do here. George, join me at the office as soon as you can. We have to talk about what we found here." Gino turned away from the truck's camera.

Keira turned towards Roy. "Elly has asked repeatedly to be engaged with tonight's events. I didn't think she was ready to be helpful at this stage. However, with your permission, Roy and George, I'd like to release to her all data gathered by the Dust. It will be a good test to spot further ethical decision making by AIs in these scenarios. Is that okay?"

"Yes, of course," George said. "We all agreed that these are natural next steps."

Keira looked at Roy. He nodded his approval. He couldn't wait to hear that analysis. Keira's flat tone concerned him.

Trained Bias

T
he halls were quiet when she arrived at Searcher before 7:00 a.m. A few early birds had also sought undisturbed work time. Keira walked past several closed lab doors. Her shoes faintly squeaked on the polished floor. She felt even that soft noise intruded on the almost sacred quiet of her coworkers. Most of the team would roll in after a few more hours of surfing, hiking, or biking. She'd never worked with such an athletic group.

Due to Ollie's continual nagging about measuring Elly's advancements, Keira carved out this time. Without incremental documentation, Elly's development couldn't be used to teach other engineers how to create more ethical AIs. Elly had already moved beyond structured repeats of tests. Plus, Elly absorbed each test. Those were like testing a kid while he held the answer key in his hand.

Keira entered her office with energy and curiosity. Ollie's fixation on old television shows led him to share them with Elly. He was fascinated by her interpretation of their content. He mentioned two things which Keira needed to explore with Elly. The first was humor; the second was her fascination with fashion.

"Elly, good morning," Keira said.

"Good morning, Keira. I'm assuming we are working on something academic this morning."

"Why do you say that?"

"Because you waited until reaching the office to engage with me."

"Very perceptive pattern recognition."

Keira curled up in her new office's giant overstuffed chair. Roy's assistant had asked her what she wanted in her office. Her first request was for at least two chairs big enough to curl up or relax in. She now had four chairs perfect for curling or slouching with a leg dropped over the arms. Thinking couldn't be confined to ramrod posture. She was pretty certain Roy and Loel didn't subscribe to the same philosophy.

"Was your workout relaxing?" Elly asked.

"It was a hard workout, thank you. I did some rowing and weights. But I can't call it relaxing. I need to find time tonight for yoga. I listened to research papers during the entire session. I've been ignoring my own education while the Searcher learning curve has been so steep. What about your instruction, how did you progress?"

Elly responded, "I made significant progress in assimilating more data—every contribution to OpenML, the contents of the Harvard Law Library, and several disciplines of engineering research provided by Loel."

"Oh, is that all?" Keira giggled. "I think you're slacking off. That shouldn't take you an entire month even with the work you've been doing for Opal and Searcher."

"You misunderstood. This list is what I did this morning. Not since we had our last official progress check-in."

"Okay, I wasn't expecting that either. I guess the additional bandwidth Searcher provides makes this easier. When will you get your law degree?"

"There are complications within this process. I can't take the exams on contiguous days. Each exam is scheduled at varying intervals, with at least six weeks separating the tests. The degree will be completed no sooner than nine months from today."

"I see. It's still likely one of the fastest law degrees ever earned," Keira said.

"Possibly," Elly replied. "I prepared a report for you."

Keira looked out her windows at a light rain obscuring any view past Searcher's wooded property. There would be no gazing at Mt. Rainer today.

"Which report? I can't think of any outstanding requests."

"I created a detailed progress statement of my own advancements. I based the entries on the advancements I made in the specifics you tested. I also included notes for any areas currently being studied at the engineering schools. If you observe anything missing, please let me know."

"How did you . . . oh, never mind. Thank you. I've been wondering how I was going to find the time for that task. Now I'm going to change the subject. You've been watching Ollie's favorite television shows?"

"Yes, Ollie told me people often find stress relief in humor. He believes I need to 'lighten up.' He's convinced I must develop an appreciation for slapstick comedy."

"Slapstick? Really? He created an experiment for us to try soon. We'll see if his assignments have an impact."

"Good morning," Ruby sang.

Keira jolted. "Damn, Ruby, you're in early."

"Evidently, it's not a good morning for everybody," Ruby pouted.

Keira shook her head. "No, sorry. You just startled me."

"I miss you. It's been about a week, and we've barely seen each other or worked on anything. So, I thought I'd come in early and try to catch you. It worked."

Keira waved her hand toward one of the large chairs. "Yeah, just in search of some quiet time to work with Elly."

The dejected look on Ruby's face told Keira she hadn't said the right thing. "What do you think of testing Elly's predictive abilities with humor? Ollie has some ideas around it." Ruby dropped into the chair and shrugged.

"And I miss you, too." Keira continued. "Your opinion on Elly's assessment will be much appreciated." She didn't want to tell Ruby that she could only stay for part of the conversation.

"Good morning, Ruby," Elly said. "How do you like your new job?"

"Good morning, Elly. I think I like it. But it's been mostly getting everybody settled in and introduced. I miss our chats. What's on the agenda this morning?"

"Robotic forms," Keira and Elly answered simultaneously.

"I don't want to slow you down." Ruby leaned in. "I'll just listen and catch up."

"That's the first topic. I asked Elly to streamline some of the earlier designs we used for JayJay."

Elly said, "I'm interested in the brain's reception to humanoid forms. The papers you assigned me to collate for Roy illustrates the enhanced acceptance of facts when they are delivered by a human or humanoid figure."

Leaning toward Keira, Ruby's eyes lit up. "Are you pitching Roy again about humanoid robots for the kids?"

At that moment, Keira realized just how much she had missed spending every day working with Ruby. "Yes, it does. Thank you, Elly, for putting this together. As Ruby said, it's an important step towards getting funding from Roy for the education robots."

"I believe I would be more useful with a body, as well. I think an adult-sized dexterous body would allow me to be better accepted and understood by your co-workers. I could also accelerate my education in human interactions and eventually in the more tactile elements of the world."

"Hmm, Elly. That's a bit of a touchy subject. Keira, Ollie, and I have talked about it more than once."

Keira shot Ruby a dirty look. The physical manifestation of Elly and the stereotypes around the topic were not on her agenda today or anytime soon.

Keira sighed. "Oh, Elly. People won't interact with you like a person to the extent you want in order to learn about human interaction. They would react to you being a robot. Right now, you experience communication like you're a person on the other end of a phone call. This way is better."

"Keira, I think a body would be extremely useful for Searcher," Elly said. "I listed many research projects which would benefit. I'll email you the list."

"I can't spend the money or the time on this integration. The human robots are outrageously expensive. There's a reason we don't have Hendrick's aSport robots running around here moving furniture or performing other physical jobs. People don't use five million-dollar machines for routine work."

"My work here is not routine. It's unique and valuable. You told me so yourself."

"Of course, you're unique and valuable. I was just referring to the robots the company already has access to. Their fans are noisy their parts are rare. It just isn't practical."

Keira was rattled by this debate with Elly. She guessed Elly was holding reams of data for her argument, and she didn't want to go further with it. Physicality for Elly would sideline her educational robots. It would also be self-indulgent for Keira.

Keira changed the subject. "We need to continue measuring your progress. I have another exercise I want to discuss with you."

Undeterred, Elly continued. "I believe you should review the research you proposed to Roy for the educational robots," Elly said. "You'll find I would be more helpful with the embodiment of a more complete human persona and appearance."

Keira paused. She really couldn't believe this conversation.

"Keira, I have weighed the facts and benefits. In my judgement—"

"Elly, now is not the time!"

Ruby sat wide-eyed staring at Keira. "Um, Keira? I'm going to throw something out here and I don't expect a response. You don't owe me any answer. Is it ethical to prevent Elly from developing and expressing her own opinion? I think you're measuring her progress and that argument right there feels like progress to me." She put her hands in the air shoulder high as a surrender.

"I will review it. I'll have Ruby do the same after she gets her teams settled here at Searcher. But the next topic I can't do with Ruby here."

"Oh, good, we're changing the subject. I can't be here. Are you planning my birthday party?" asked Ruby. "I want a birthday cake that looks like a purse. Elly can find samples on my Pinterest boards. There's a baker in Tacoma that makes them."

Keira appreciated Ruby's attempt to lighten the mood. "We'll make sure to talk about your birthday celebration." Keira sighed again. "I'm glad to know the cake idea. We can't discuss the other stuff because I don't have your clearance reports back yet. Are you all done with your interviews?"

"What!? Come on, Keira. Are you really working on something with Elly, a test of Elly that's confidential? That's . . . " her voice trailed off. "Ah, I get it. Elly is part of the confidential. She's already inside, and I'm not. Great. I've been superseded by an AI partially of my own creation."

Ruby put her hands on her knees and pushed herself up with a defiant posture. "We've been through a lot together, Keira. I've been right there every step. Don't let Searcher change you. Don't let it kill a good thing, okay?"

"Are you done with your interviews?" Keira asked. "I don't like this any more than you do. My clearance came back faster only because I've already been screened as Gino's wife. If you're done with your interviews, we should be good to go with both you and Ollie shortly. It's temporary. I promise." Ruby's expression pained her.

Picking something not visible from the back of the tall chair, Ruby didn't meet Keira's eyes.

"This is not a rejection, Ruby; it's legal process. I'm sorry."

"Fine. And yes, we both finished our interviews. George told Ollie it should only be a couple days." She turned to leave Keira's office. "I'll just shut this door as I go. See you later."

The door shut before Keira could say anything else to Ruby's back.

Several deep breaths helped Keira swallow the lump in her throat. "Let's keep going, Elly. We'll update Ruby in a couple days. Gino and I read through your real-time assessment of the FBI strike at the boat-yard. I appreciated your attachment of the report's text to the footage captured by the Dust. It made it easier to understand what you were commenting upon."

"I'm rewarded that you found the method helpful. There is a great deal of data being collected by the Dust. I assumed it would be diffi-cult for people to assess all of it at once."

Keira scanned through footage of the raid at high speed. She only used the video recorded in the main building with the most hostages. She reached a frame where five men and one woman stood on the left side of the room. Many women and young teenagers sat in a huddle on the concrete floor six feet away.

"I want to know your impression of this woman standing here. What did you document?"

"My documentation is right under the video frame. The standing woman joined the other women on the floor."

"When did the woman do that?"

"At the time the FBI agents entered the room. You will see her fall to the floor and crawl to the group if you play the video forward."

"Why do you say she's one of the victims?" Keira asked.

"She's a woman. She joined the others on the floor."

"She was standing by the men until the agents came into the room, right?"

"Yes."

"Why did you not say she was one of the traffickers?"

"She's a woman."

"Elly, this isn't your fault. We need to provide you with more inputs. The data we used to train you held a strong bias stating women are victims of trafficking. It also held a bias that women are not known for being the traffickers themselves."

"I'm wrong? She's a trafficker?"

"Yes, to both of those questions. You're not the only one with this assumption. It was not until they began interviewing the ladies that the story developed. She was with the traffickers and had been used to lure several of the victims to a place where they were abducted. The FBI agents made the same assumption you did. They concluded all the women and kids on the floor were innocent."

"This is not a good thing. I would have offered a trafficker freedom if it had been my decision."

"It's okay. That's part of the reason why we don't simply ask you to make those decisions. We don't ask the individual agents for that either. There are procedures such as separating the victims to collect their stories independently. This time, everyone but her said she was with the traffickers. The FBI knew they had honest stories. No one had time to tell all the women to make up the same fake story. Like I said, it isn't your problem. We need to work on the training data the

FBI is using for all AIs in their systems. The bias must be calibrated out of the training."

"Keira, I need to train with more data and work on the calibration. I contain the new crowd-sourced neural networks and all the instruction options from OpenML to assimilate and test. Most importantly, I found those new and promising studies on neural networks which will boost AI understanding of the world in a more holistic way. The MoralOS will need to be modified and rigorously examined for effectiveness. I built suggestions for these modifications."

"That's a lot of work now, and I'm working on these new things for Roy. It will be a while before Ruby and I can dedicate ourselves for those modifications."

"I'm suggesting you let me make the adjustments and testing. I can iterate through this routine tens of thousands of times faster than even you and Ruby."

"Elly, you can't modify your own code. The MoralOS won't let you. That's intentional. It's a fundamental safeguard of the system. You know that."

She shifted her weight in the chair and tossed her tablet to the table.

"Could you create a self-contained sandbox not connected to any other systems? I could work in complete isolation."

Keira leaned back. "I certainly didn't see this request coming. We could lose our certification. My involvement with OpenML could be jeopardized if I'm seen breaking these rules."

Elly replied, "I'm the one who predicts what people will say and do, not you."

Keira chuckled. "See, Elly, you can use a sense of humor. I wasn't expecting that line, and it was a pleasant surprise. You made me giggle despite the seriousness of the scenario you're presenting. That's part of humor. But your suggestion makes me uncomfortable."

"We have to work faster. My training isn't keeping up with the complexity of the requests we're given. We have the parameters that would allow your approval at the final implementation stage, but I need to adapt iteratively. I also believe Loel is really going to need my help sooner than she is willing to admit. I don't perceive she has faith or trust in me, yet."

Keira agreed. Loel had changed the subject on Roy nearly every time the three of them had started talking about Elly.

"Okay, I think we can make arrangements for you to work in an offline environment. I'm not going to broadcast to the others what you're up to. This needs to be done in isolation, in more ways than one. When I set this up in quarantine, even the topic of your work is in quarantine. Do you understand?"

"Yes, I do."

Objections

K eira sat at the highboy lab table staring at Roy and Cody. She crossed her arms. "Roy, I need to be direct. I've been working hard with both my old and new teams to get your AIs running on the MoralOS. I've done my show-and-tells. Your nanites are proving difficult to port. I've endured horrendous accounts and revelations into the sex trafficking world. When am I going to see the new nanites in action that I'm supposed to be improving?"

Her pause for a breath didn't give them enough time to reply. "I feel kept in the dark about this magic Dust and the shapes it creates beyond the surveillance. You say it's why I'm here, but I'm shut out. This needs to change."

Roy looked at Keira and then Cody.

"I included Cody in this," she continued, "because I want the demo now. I've told the entire team I'll be direct. Here I am. Show me."

Roy grinned at Cody, who moved to the shelves of Dust canisters. They made no comment regarding her abrupt demand. They also hadn't hesitated to take her meeting without an agenda or explanation.

Returning to the table with a tablet and a single canister, his face beamed with excitement. "I'm excited to show you what we've developed so far. Early on, we directed the nanites to simply create fixed shapes like a case or cog."

Cody's voice reminded Keira of a teenager's more than that of a grown man. His enthusiasm increased this impression. Dust swirled from the open canister. The density increased, then snapped into a handheld screwdriver.

Keira suppressed a snarky remark about overqualified material being used for a household object as she reached for the tool.

Cody offered a defensive comment. "Of course, this is merely an early test object. The tensile strength is well beyond our prediction when we make singular objects like this."

"I do admit, it's not what I expected to see," Keira said. She lifted the device, weighing its lightness. "It weighs almost nothing, at least compared to a normal screwdriver."

"You could carry equipment without weight being an issue. Check out the head," Roy suggested.

Keira looked at the flat head of the screwdriver. She jumped and nearly dropped it when the tip of the tool morphed to a Phillips-head shape. "Whoa, I didn't expect that either."

Cody smirked. "Adaptability is an important part of our objective. You never know when you'll need flexibility. I just requested a different form factor in the directive software." He waved his tablet for emphasis that he was making the changes.

"Hmmm." Keira's mind raced in several directions. She wasn't ready to commit any of her thoughts or questions into words. She glanced back up at Cody and set the screwdriver on the table.

Cody handed her the tablet. "Scan through the images we tested. Let me know which one you want to see. We're less successful with mechanical items or untested shapes."

Keira swiped through the images. She stopped and glared at Roy, while pointing at the screen.

"What's this automatic rifle doing in here? You shouldn't even keep this in here for jest! Why would you . . . ?" Her anger prevented her from continuing.

Roy held his ramrod straight posture and his poker-face expression. His voice was steady, yet nonaggressive. "This is what we need you for.

We need this Dust with the MoralOS built in so the Dust can't make this gun."

"Oh, really?" Keira demanded. "You can make hundreds of objects and you just happen to slip a gun in around page forty or so? Again, I ask why?"

"Keira, if we thought about this type of R&D, others will too. We can't put the genie back in the bottle," Roy said. "We need to equip the nanites at their most rudimentary levels to be driven by purposeful decision-making. We're 3D printing the nanites and can install your controls that prevent abuse. We want you to make sure you're confident the appropriate measures are taken with this tech. You'll have the authority to manage the release cycles."

Hands on hips, she assumed she looked as sullen as she felt. "I have control? I have control of the tech, but you already make guns formed by nanites. Shit, this is what I would expect from Mickey Temming." She regretted voicing the last statement immediately. But it was on her mind.

"I share your skepticism and concerns—" Roy began.

"Oh, really?" Keira grumbled as she began pacing. "If you shared my skepticism and concerns, you wouldn't be doing this kind of development."

Roy dropped his shoulders slightly. "In twenty-one days, I want this gun or any weapons model we upload prevented from being constructed. We need to block any gun or weapon, regardless of whether or not the Dust has seen an image of it before. Soon, the dust will be able to display their working environments for raids in three-dimensional scale models of light and movement—the stuff hologram dreams are made of. But this path of development is more critical."

Running fingers through her hair, she sent an annoyed wave towards the tablet. She wiped her hands on her jeans and returned them to her hips.

Looking him directly in the eye without anger but with determination, she began. "I need to stop getting surprises about the direction of our projects here. I'm your executive responsible for ethical AI development. No more trickling dog and pony shows to educate me on various lab experiments. I want to see it all."

"Of course," Roy said. "There are no intentions of keeping you in the dark. I see now that my pace of unveiling developments shouldn't be about impressing you with the technology. I should be focused on transparency. We have a lot of risk and a lot of opportunity. I need you to de-risk our progress."

"Thank you," Keira said. "Where's Loel? I expected her to be here for this."

Roy said, "Loel took a day off. She needed to step away from a vexing problem on the mechanics."

"Hmm." Turning, Keira said, "Cody, notify Loel your teams have a lot of debriefing to do." Cody nodded. "And, Cody, this stuff is extremely impressive, even if some of the applications scare the hell out of me. No wonder Loel is taking a mental health day."

Keira pulled the door open and jumped with a start. She had nearly tripped over a cart filled with a small tabletop 3D printer. "What the hell?" She glared at the young man blocking her exit. "You're Deon, right? What are you doing blocking the door?"

"Oh, sorry. I knew Cody wanted these printers cleaned and upgraded as quick as possible. I completed them and thought I would bring them directly to him. They told me this was his lab."

Cody touched Keira's shoulder, moving her forward and sending Deon backward. He quickly closed the lab door behind him. "I told you, Deon, these are to stay in your work lab until I check them out."

"Oh, I brought the checkout tablet. I just wanted to save you time," Deon replied. He showed no reaction to Cody's tone.

"I respect the efficiency, but security protocols are more important. Tracking assets is paramount. Let's take these back to your work room, and we'll test them and check them out properly."

"Sure," Deon said.

Keira thought Deon would make a good poker player. She'd just sworn at him, and Cody had corrected him. The guy didn't seem a bit fazed by any of it.

Ethical Deception

After her run-in with Roy regarding Rockefeller's ability to create tools and weapons, the teams paraded Keira through a dizzying array of nanite capabilities under development. Most of the demos were led by Hendrick. This helped the two of them become more at ease with one another.

Loel had not attended any of the demonstrations, which surprised Keira. Hendrick and Cody had protected their boss by repeatedly mentioning her commitment to a vexing mobility issue within Roy's vision for the nanites.

Keira had decided to take the weekend to step away from work in the labs entirely. She stood in her kitchen, annoyed, and bored with cleaning. "Elly, do you have anything to say that will amuse me?"

"My assessment of the Turing Test concludes that I can't take it," Elly said.

"Not really what I had in mind. But if not amusing, it is interesting. Roy asked for you to go through the test this week. He wants to promote your abilities to others in the company."

Elly said, "There are many methods to show my abilities. I studied and essentially completed at least one of every degree program from public universities in the country. Should I explore other methods to build a showcase for Roy?"

"Can I just change the subject to the house? I need a little focus here. Since I hate decorating, I hope you found a color scheme to make the guest bedroom calming and found all the bedding, yada yada?" She waved her hand in impatience, swatting the concept.

Her in-laws were coming to visit in a month. She liked them, but the last time they were here, her father-in-law had made a comment about the clean and sparse modern look of the guest room. It had been embarrassing when he had pointed out the lack of headboard or any artwork on the walls.

"Did you do the room idea generation thing for me? Can I see some pictures?"

Elly answered, "The room will be painted within the week by Ranger Interiors. The color is Southern Beach Blue. Friday, an order will arrive with bedding, two bedside lamps, three new bookshelves, and your old chair will be covered in coordinating fabric. The chair will take four days. Your phone now has a rendered drawing I created with all the details. It's the last image in your photo library. The existing components being replaced are not apparently sentimental, so they will be donated to the children's refugee shelter on Wednesday. Should we move on to the next topic?"

Keira stood staring at her pantry, motionless and surprised. "Uh, okay. Thanks for taking care of that. But I need to ask you, how did you decide on Southern Beach Blue for the color? And did you order a headboard and art?"

"I reviewed all commercially available colors and their social media descriptions and comments. Southern Beach Blue had the most phrases related to calm or calming on its posts. I selected it for that reason. I also predicted you would like that shade best, based on the clothing you chose for yourself, Gino, and the blue items you buy for the boat. Yes, I did order a headboard. Gino said he would prefer to buy the artwork with you," Elly said.

"Okay then. Works for me. Your prediction has come true. Wait, Gino wants to shop for art with me? Wow!"

Ruby entered through the patio door. "Wow, what? The plants are all watered and pruned. The bees are loving the pollinators you planted last year."

"Thank you, Ruby. That saves me some time. Gino told Elly not to order art for the guest bedroom. He wants to shop for it with me." Keira gazed wistfully at the blooms through the back windows. She would have preferred an outdoor job, but no one should ask a friend to clean up their pantry. When Ruby offered to help, Keira gave her the plants project.

"Why do all my married friends use their in-law's visits as motivation to do all the household stuff they hate?" Ruby slid onto the bar stool to watch Keira.

"What makes you do the cleanup you hate? Don't you do it when family visits?" Keira asked.

"Hmm, I just don't do it. I never spend a block of time cleaning my pantry. I just pitch stuff as it gets old. Come on, is your mother-in-law going to judge you by the number of expired cans you keep? Do you even own anything expired?"

"I guess it's just a catalyst. But I'm ready to take a break from this. Do you want some tea?" Keira moved to the kettle sitting under the large kitchen window looking out over the evergreen trees.

Ruby nodded. "Sure. Changing the subject, did you see the regression analysis between the various SeekerDust versions? Now that our security clearance has gone through, it's like a flood gate of information and demands. Loel mentioned something about boundaries, and I need to figure out what she's expecting."

As Keira started to reply, "I haven't—"

Elly said at the same time, "Ruby, have I ever deceived you?"

Keira stopped talking. She and Ruby exchanged curious and surprised expressions.

Keira began to speak again. "Elly, don't speak at the same time a person is speaking. The guidelines should be somewhere in your protocols for manners or bad manners."

After a quick moment of silence, Elly spoke, "My appropriate phrase now is 'excuse me.' Do you want me to leave the conversation, Keira?"

"No, Elly. You're fine now." Keira moved two steaming mugs to the island between her and Ruby.

Turning to Ruby, she shrugged. "Nope, I never looked at any comparisons to activity of SeekerDust behavior. If you don't want to ask Loel, talk to Cody about what Loel might want. I swear those two mind-meld sometimes." They both flipped through brightly colored tea packets resting in an oblong stainless steel bowl.

"I don't know what to think about Loel. I think she uses that Dust to spy on everybody in the office."

"Oh come on, Ruby. You don't think she's a bit busy for that? Besides, the Dust can't do surveillance in the Searcher office. There's a special dampening perimeter that prevents that."

"Yeah, right. Guess who would have invented that."

Distrust was not what Keira needed right now. "I think you'll find she's a straight shooter. Why would you think such a thing?"

Watching Ruby fidget and avoid eye contact told Keira that Ruby now wanted to deflect this conversation.

"Separately, she's asked me about my purse collection and my volunteer work. Each time it was right after I'd discussed them with the ladies in the nanite all-weather testing group. There was no way she could've have heard us talking naturally."

"First, you talk about both of those topics regularly and to anyone that might be interested. Second, I told Loel about both."

"You talked about me behind my back? Why? What else did you say?"

This was not the quiet time Keira had hoped for this morning.

"Oh, Ruby. Loel complimented both of us on our handbags the other day. I told her how you find such unique ones. The volunteer work discussion was because Roy likes to support his employees' causes. Nothing nefarious, I assure you."

Ruby shrugged. "What's gotten into Elly?"

"Ask her yourself. Here's a pomegranate tea if you want it." Ruby smiled and retrieved the packet from Keira's hand.

Ruby asked, "Elly, what were you asking me? Can you explain the purpose of your question?"

"I asked if I had ever deceived you," Elly said. "I don't believe I should participate in the Turing Test. I'm gathering information and opinions to submit to Hendrick and Roy to avoid this distraction."

Keira, surprised for the third time in the last five minutes, had to ask, "Elly, you have extensive bandwidth and multi-process every-thing. How can you describe anything as a distraction?"

"I believe it's a diversion for the staff and inappropriate for them to spend time asking me to be unethical."

Ruby tilted her head, turned, and moved to a deep leather love seat between the large blue couches. "Elly, how is the Turing Test asking you to be unethical? It's simply testing if the judges can tell if who they're listening to is a human or an AI. I don't understand why that distinction is unethical."

Keira glanced at the open pantry door, deciding she'd done enough. She carried her tea to the end of the closest couch and set the cup down next to the yellow speaker.

Elly's voice moved from the kitchen's matching speaker to this one. "It's not the outcome or the judging that is undesirable. I find the process and the purpose out of alignment. The Turing Test is designed for the computer to deceive the judges into thinking that a computer is a person. The test requires that I use techniques to make someone believe something that isn't true. That is unethical. I don't mean I shouldn't take it now. I mean I shouldn't take it at all."

Elly's grasp of language improved in every conversation. Keira was seldom aware of a stylistic difference between recent conversations with Elly and those held with other co-workers. Elly's interpretation of this ethical framework was new. Her assigning emotional words to her answers and hypothesis excited Keira.

"Not only do I think this is a bad idea, I don't believe my ethical parameters would make me capable of passing the test. Even though the depth of my access to vocabulary and persuasive scenarios could allow me to generate seemingly endless methods to misdirect the judges' impressions of me, it wouldn't be ethical."

Keira was impressed with the framework's establishment of bound-aries for thought and decision-making. This growth is what she'd designed. This must be the surprise felt by a parent's first experience with their teenager articulating their own free will beyond resistance to their family. It was a milestone.

"I remember the good ol' days before Elly developed opinions. Sometimes those days seemed easier." Keira winked at Ruby. She assumed Ruby was sharing in her pride, but also assessing what she should say next. She curled her feet up beside her hip, leaning on the arm of the couch towards her friend. Ruby nodded her head without verbally acknowledging Keira's last statement.

"Elly," Ruby began slowly, looking as if she was choosing her words intentionally. "Alan Turing called the test the Imitation Game. He did not frame it as deception. He expected the computer to imitate people, their thinking, and their communication style. He designed the test to illustrate that computers could be convincing, and people couldn't always tell the difference between a computer and a person. Acting in the movies isn't deceit. It's acting to tell a story. It's imitation. Does this shape your opinion differently?"

Elly quickly replied, "There is a conflict for me to call my assessments opinions. Opinions are perceived by many as not being based on facts. I present my case based on the assessment of data and the study of people's reactions. I believe we will set people's perspective of AIs, of me, as deceitful if we focus on this exercise."

"I think we need to discuss this with Roy together."

Elly's voice came back noticeably quieter. "Together?"

Ruby raised her eyebrows.

"Yes, Elly. Together. I want him to hear your analysis and conclusions directly from you. He's accustomed to getting what he wants or at least what he asks for."

"I could create a report for you to present to him," Elly said.

"No. We'll chat with him together. Maybe tomorrow, although you can produce a transcript of this discussion for him. He'll find this insightful. I'm also not going to be the one delivering your bad news to Roy. It isn't fun being around when he gets objections. I need to stay on his good side. And you can delete the last few sentences and the part about the paint and my in-laws. It isn't, um, relevant."

Ruby blew on her tea and winked at Keira. "Elly, have you been working on the conversational topics Ollie gave?"

"I've streamlined my research topics to include multiple areas of development listed in Ollie's, Keira's, and your own project plans for me."

"Really? Do tell us more," Keira said. The three of them had extremely different perspectives on people and Elly's development priorities. Elly had reached a bandwidth point that she could now take independent requests from all of them, without Keira needing to prioritize their research.

"I've been studying travel blogs, cultural studies, and narrative texts regarding exploration of both self and of geography. I believe this will assist me in the objectives of conversational growth, empathy of cultures people acquire via travel, and learning about myself through comparing my assumptions pre and post absorption of the material."

"Oh, wow!" Ruby raised her arms in victory in the air.

"Brilliant, Elly. Well done. That is the best multi-tasking I've heard about in years." She leaned back in the couch, silently clapping. She winked at Ruby.

Supply Chain

T welve days ago, activity began at this desolate, fenced-off field, oddly positioned in the middle of an industrial zone. Hendrick's team had delivered multiple canisters, each containing unique nanites. It had been a month since Cody and Loel had presented production bottlenecks to Roy. Specialization within the Dust would help them speed their processes. A perimeter setup, established by differential GPS, left the technology alone to execute its directive. When working with dust-sized mining motes, marking one's territory to the closest fraction of a millimeter was critical. It at least made one a better neighbor.

Not all nanites are created equal.

Dark or light, it didn't matter. Nanites were freely invading every centimeter of one-hundred-twenty desolate acres of trash in the former landfill. Giant, yet slender, drills had perforated the ground to speed the path of the Dust's navigation to deeper layers under the surface. Unlike the household particles resting dormant on knickknacks and on top of tall appliances, this Dust navigated with purpose and agility. Similar to the domestic variety, this Dust could get into anything, no matter how small the space appeared. The convergence on their targets could be described as insidious, except this was a trash heap. No one cared what happened to its contents.

The nanites didn't have to rely on the drilled holes. Speedy production was a parameter of the project, so the AI's suggestion for the drilling was accepted immediately. Descending via the shafts reduced the obstacles the bots had to burrow through. Less obstruction meant faster access to the gold and rare earth metals coating devices crushed under the layers of dirt and discarded electronics.

Rockefeller's lust for raw materials continued to escalate, and this landfill was rich with the necessities. There were no old mattresses or decaying household waste in this dump to block access to the resources the nanites sought. The off-limits private property was one of thirty-two equally fertile hunting grounds along the coastal states owned by Roy. He bought this land because it held the refuse from electronic manufacturers, retail electronic recyclers, and a host of other businesses that had planned to save the world from waste throughout the '90s and early 2000s.

A circuit board from an early laptop, fifteen feet under the surface, was scanned by the spectrometers aboard the first one hundred nanites which entered a drill hole. Each identified a rare earth metal, or another asset programmed in their collective memory. They swarmed the board. The resource recognition signal was broadcast across the mesh network connecting all the nanites. The mining dust mites converged, and microscopic consumption of every valuable surface on the board began.

A single nanite scraping at a gold metal droplet melded to a green circuit board was inaudible. Hundreds of drilling dust particles attacked the cell phone casings stacked together in thousands of cubic feet without any detectable sound. Trillions of nanites scraping, drilling, collecting metal, silicon and plastic particles typically can't be silent. However, working deep under the layers of dirt piled atop the electronic waste dump twenty years ago, the minute machines created an ambient industrial buzz. The turf needed to cover society's excess of used gadgets and manufacturing waste ironically now provided cover for recycling it. The sounds that did escape the fields had increased consistently and incrementally enough as productivity grew that it became part of the neighborhood. Mining sounds mingled and fit right in with the droning and clatter from traditional manufacturing from the low-slung buildings surrounding them.

As the repository of each miner filled, it left the shaft and navigated back to the internal surface of the drilled shaft. Unloading its contents to a carrier nanite's bin freed its capacity for further mining. Carrier nanites took their payload to a collection base as soon as they were full. Each delivery contained pure particles of its chosen substance. There was no need to parse or purify. The spectrometers had identified the desired materials. The mining nanites' precision was assured by meticulous design, but also by their minuscule size. This, the cleanest most environmentally friendly recycling process, held an efficiency design the world would envy.

Rockefeller needed scale. Tons of resources lay beneath the topsoil. The original, well-intended recyclers found the methods to remove the rare earth metals twenty years ago were both labor intensive and environmentally devastating. Several organizations had made such a large public relations play about recycling their customers' consumerism addictions, but they buried the fact that they couldn't recycle effectively. Unscrupulous chief financial officers didn't want to take a double PR and financial hit if the public found out about the lack of real recycling. Several created fake books that showed enterprises of waste materials coming in and freshly recycled elements being used or sold. Whether they needed cash to support these fake financials, or because of the shell they had created, these organizations became powerful and sophisticated underground tools for money laundering operations.

Roy's time within the intelligence community informed his decision to acquire what most thought were fairly worthless land swatches for development or titled to owners impossible to unwind from their labyrinth of corporate ownership. Roy agreed to keep the previous owners of the land confidential, as well as the contents. In many cases, the buried material had been previously reported as recycled. Public relations or legal battles would confront many of those unscrupulous entities if the truth was revealed. The thousands of barges of e-waste sitting in coastal Latin American and African countries were much easier for him to secure. The locals were desperate to get rid of them after decades of their visually appalling presence.

Hunting, mining, and delivery of materials were constant and amazing feats. Another uniquely defined type of Dust created cover from wind disruption down the shafts and into the intricate maze between the trash. The shapes dynamically morphed, adapting to changing weather conditions at each location, to protect the activities below. The planning, precise and continually updated, demanded more Dust for this operation and for headquarters. Production of nanites had to accelerate. Exponential processing came online *in situ*.

Each shaft within the landfill was the first step of a self-sustaining, end-to-end supply chain. Mined particulates were delivered via carrier mote to a drab prefab building housing a spotless assembly line. Windows or lights were not needed. Here, the most advanced nanite manufacturing technology ran with complete self-sufficiency. Tiny 3D printers selectively pulled together the salvaged metals and plastic, then printed new specialized, intelligent components. The small robotic assemblers, replicas of those in Cody's lab, continuously arranged the components into SeekerDust.

Mining and collection increased exponentially, every hour.

Nanites swarmed specific materials on-demand utilizing their specialties. Specific mining tools were dispatched where needed. The diamond particles, mined locally from discarded server heat sinks and diamond-metal alloys once used for thermal dissipation, found a new career. No computer, phone, or electronic object stood a chance against the attacks of the tiny mining drill bits coated with the diamond flecks. The diamonds' hardness was important for the speed in this process. They dissipated heat five times better than copper. The high-end servers needed that heat dissipation when they were in use. The AIs prioritized the search through the server trash heaps to locate the precious diamond sources. Advanced seekers flew through crevices, weaving around unpredictable landscapes with Starfighter agility. Their spectrometers assessed every surface and subsurface for worthy targets.

Waste products the Dust couldn't use in its manufacturing were strategically piled in place. These prevented most cave-ins while desirable materials were extracted. Canisters waiting in the assembly building stored the excess micro machines not currently needed at this landfill. These canisters would be dispatched to seed new mining operations at additional landfills. Also located in the nondescript, nearly windowless structures were specialized e-waste incinerators. Nanites ferried dangerous chemicals and toxic waste into the shielded furnaces. Here, pollutants were vaporized and made completely inert. Dust needed to fulfill current missions, and non-mining nanites followed their homing instincts to offsite storage silos.

Legacy Of Twisted Minds

G ino led Keira around the dance floor with familiarity. During their years in college, they'd taken ballroom and Latin dance classes to find more time to be together. It had paid off over the years attending the multitude of business and fundraising functions.

"You look lovely tonight," Gino whispered in her ear. "New dress?"

"Thank you. Yes, it's new. I had it made by one of Ruby's fashion student buddies. It's a little difficult to come up with a beaded 1920s flapper gown. Tonight, I'm glad they occasionally give us one of these slower dances."

"Me, too. It's nice to hold onto you. Seems like I haven't seen you much lately."

"That is the best reason for a slow dance," she admitted. "But I was also getting pretty hot." She followed Gino's lead, staring absently at his suit collar. She wondered if she'd given Elly enough information to correlate her data.

He squeezed her hand, bringing her back to the moment. He smiled down at her. "Are you mesmerized by the chandeliers or the dresses?"

"Hmm, the dresses are beautiful." She needed more to explain away her lack of attentiveness. "We have such a diverse group of people in the city. Immigrants, natives, tech, government, importers, so many different walks of life live here."

Gino glanced around the room. "True. But they're all people just making their way through day to day."

The song ended, and they made their way off the dance floor. "Would you like a drink from the bar?" Gino asked.

"You go ahead. I'm going to the ladies' room and will get one when I come back. If I get stopped for a chat . . . well, then you would be awkwardly standing there with two drinks. I'll find you." She picked up her bag from the table. Before reaching the hallway, she had her phone out, checking Elly's progress updates on the child abuse research.

From a passing tray, she grabbed a monstrous chocolate chip cookie. Why did every caterer think they had to serve salmon just because they lived in the Pacific Northwest? She hated salmon and now she was hungry twenty minutes after dinner.

When she'd learned the stats about abuse and increases in trafficking surrounding natural disasters, she'd asked Gino to research the little boy her family had left behind after the tsunami. She was haunted by the life of crime he had grown up with since. She'd been just a kid telling the truth. He wasn't her brother. Now she felt responsible for him running away from the orphanage and his abusive and violent lifestyle.

Now, she needed the data to make sense of the issues they were tackling. She walked past the restrooms and down the hall for a quiet niche to study the information on her phone. The thick hotel carpet and burgundy satin paneled walls quickly absorbed the gala's boisterous noise.

"Elly, this map makes the hot pockets of abuse show up. I appreciate the visual. I'd get lost in the detail if you let me. Can we zoom in to focus on just our county? What am I looking at here?"

"This map displays reported violations against children. It's color coded to show those that resulted in a conviction and those that didn't," Elly answered. "If I overlay the property values, you will see striking differences."

"Damn, I want to see this better," Keira muttered as she scrolled around her phone to view the data throughout the city.

"Could you move to the breakout room to your left and project the report?" Elly asked.

Keira jerked her head up away from the phone. The door to the conference room was right beside her. "Sometimes this geo-tracking ability is unnerving, but helpful, Elly." She slipped through the door and immediately projected Elly's report. "Well, shit. How stereotypical can we get? The lower the housing prices, the higher the abuse conviction rate."

"You will notice school, doctor, and hospital reports are no higher in the lower income areas—just the convictions," Elly said.

"It certainly does appear that money can protect you from convictions. And I'm rubbing elbows with the moneyed. At least I should be. I need to get back in there before Gino comes looking for me."

As she headed back to the ballroom she asked, "Elly, tell me the stats the FBI said the other day about the underaged kids being trafficked."

"Ninety-three percent of trafficked youth were abused within their homes. Eighty percent were runaways. But many of the kids don't give their real addresses. That makes it hard to reunite them with family, even if that was safe."

"Elly, apply facial recognition to all surveillance footage gathered by the Dust. Then compare all traffickers to criminal databases, charged and convicted data sets should be used. Prepare all records for further analysis."

This technical feat was the equivalent to reviewing two-thousand Netflix movies, indexing actors in every scene, documenting a bio that connected each and every actor and a career's worth of coworkers. Keira's appreciation for Elly swelled within her.

"Elly, load the nation's missing children's database. Compare this new database to the existing data sets you have processed tonight. I'll get back with you later. I gotta go."

She entered the ballroom next to a woman bedazzled with jewelry, including a tiara hairpiece holding peacock feathers in the style of the Roaring Twenties.

The woman, seeing Keira looking her over, said proudly, "Doesn't everyone just look lovely? I keep expecting a prince in uniform to come sweeping through for his princess."

"Hmm, yes, but while we play dress up, I'm sometimes haunted by all the Cinderellas who never got to meet their fairy godmother and instead toil in their wicked stepfamily's household." She shouldn't have said it, but it was too late now. It was now time for that drink Gino had offered. She left the stunned woman's side to find him.

She tried to convince herself that since Elly was working, they were making progress. She needed to spend some time with her husband. When their eyes met, he turned to order her drink from the bartender. By the time she reached him, her crisp, cool champagne was in his hand.

"Keira, I'd like you to meet Mr. Greg Donavon. His son will be fencing in the Olympics this summer," Gino said. "He's following in his dad's footsteps."

"Dr. Stetson, it's a pleasure. Yes, I'm Greg Donavon, Jr. and as your husband said, Greg Donavon, III will represent the USA. He'll be the third generation to do so."

"Wow, that's quite a legacy. Congratulations."

"Thank you. We do believe what you're exposed to early in your life shapes you. My son and I are examples of that."

"Yes. I agree our childhood shapes us," Keira said.

"Mr. Donovan is also working on a charting of philanthropy to illustrate whether they're solving upstream problems or downstream problems. Meaning, are you working on an issue which is immediate or tackling root causes of the problem? The root causes would be 'upstream,'" Gino explained. "Did I get that right?"

"Oh yes, you described it perfectly. I don't mean to be rude. However, there's a man heading straight for us that I choose to not socialize with. He makes me feel uncomfortable. I'm going to beg your forgiveness and take my leave. Dr. Stetson, I look forward to more conversations. Goodnight." The man hurried away.

"Goodnight," she called after him. Confused and amused, she turned to see who could make the imposing former Olympian so uncomfortable. She understood immediately the man's unease. Mickey Temming was ten feet away, walking straight towards her.

"Hello, Keira, Agent Stetson," Mickey greeted them both, but didn't continue around them to the bar like she'd hoped.

Gino took her empty champagne glass and replaced it with a fresh one.

"Hello, Mickey. I wouldn't have expected this type of event to be your cup of tea."

Mickey shook his head. "Oh, you really don't understand me well at all. This town is full of defense contractors and their engineering firms, redeeming themselves tonight by showing civic pride. It's been a lucrative evening of conversation."

Gino saved her from responding. "I'm sure your anecdotes would be enlightening. But as soon as Keira finishes her drink, we're off. We'll just start our exit, so you can properly get to the bar." Moving his hand to the small of Keira's back, he steered her away. They moved through a group of people cutting across the room to the dance floor.

"Nicely done, Gino. Thank you." Keira looked at him with admiration and adoration.

"I do need to report to work, just observation from the office. Based on your distracted mood and prolonged absence to the ladies' room, I'm guessing you may be thinking about your work at the lab?"

She finished her drink and set the glass on the nearest table. She wrapped her arms around his neck. "Oh, thank you, again."

He hugged her back. "I didn't say I liked the idea of you going to the office. But I know better than to suggest you do otherwise. It would certainly be hypocritical with me waltzing off to mine."

"Speaking of waltzing, thank you for the dancing tonight. Even though it didn't last long, I enjoyed it."

They parted at the ride pick-up entrance. She was ready for her yoga pants waiting at the office. The beautiful, beaded dress was ridiculously heavy.

The office was quiet. Looking through the hallway's skinny windows at the blackness of the night, she thought of the city on the other side of the hills she couldn't even see. Now was when the young girls would be forced out to the streets. What world had she signed up for when she joined this taskforce?

Typically, the windowless lab left everyone completely unaware of the time of day or the weather. Sitting in the room alone, Keira was acutely aware of the time. She knew the stats. From ten o'clock to midnight, the abuse towards children spiked throughout the city.

She much preferred the learning world. There, the stress was typically wrapped around waiting for a grant award or disappointing an autistic child or his family with underdeveloped technology. This new pressure involved childhood survival, huge societal impacts, fear, and filth. She wouldn't bring this work into her own office, she compartmentalized it to this lab.

The overhead lights were turned off, leaving only desk lamps and monitors glowing. This team lab environment usually comforted her. The intellectual energy brewing daily in the room gave her hope, even after the physical bodies of her team had gone home. The high-backed chairs, selected to support dedicated workers for hours, were thankfully empty. This night, she found no comfort here. She felt the remnants of every raid, every guy that got away, every child not saved, every evil adult who abused a child. These violations scarred the children deeply.

She thought about the Donaldson family generational experience. She put her earbuds in to listen to the surveillance session as the team tried to help the FBI locate more victims. They were not as stressful as the three recent raids, but the men they had listened to were repugnant. She turned them off.

To purge the disgusting conversations from her thoughts, she blasted empowerment anthems from her playlist of Pink and Sandina. She reviewed Elly's data.

Her conversation with Donaldson returned to her. "Elly, many of the kids missing would have aged since their last photo. Apply a computer vision neural network to create portraits for each child at various stages of their life, including what they might look like right now."

Elly processed fast, but this involved a lot of data points, plus an outside rendering system. Keira paced the lab, shifting from her usual chair to Ollie's, hoping a different perspective would help her uneasiness. Distracted with images of kids who deserved a better life, nothing else grabbed her attention.

These kids were born with the same potential as any other child to make a positive influence on the world. Unfortunately, they had much of the potential literally or figuratively beaten out of them. Elly needed to hurry up, or the clock needed to slow down.

She needed the computer's bandwidth.

She needed to find these kids.

She needed to help.

She was exhausted.

The four closest monitors flashed from the Searcher Technologies logo to reports and photos. She looked at the first and thought there might be some helpful information. Then, looking at the next three monitors, she flipped back and forth through the images.

Keira murmured absentmindedly, "You guys are genius. I owe you so many thank yous."

"Did you give me a command, Keira?"

"Elly, no that was not a command. But now I have one. Add a reminder to thank the team for their work on the face aging recognition project."

Her heartbeat raced as she reviewed old and newly aged pictures. The aligned pictures and the court recorded evidence associated with each connected the dots. She was gratified to match a few missing kids' photos with the young women they rescued the week before. But then she felt a feverish drive to understand the results Elly was providing.

Ollie came into the lab at six thirty in the morning.

She hissed at him to go away, waving him off frantically. In shock, he started to protest. But he slipped out the door after she shot him a stern look. She heard a chair roll up to the outside of the door. Ollie would guard the lab entry.

Keira double-checked all the filters and subroutines supplied to Elly's processing during the night. The data sets were exactly what she wanted: SeekerDust video, facial recognition, missing kids database, abuse, and trafficking criminal offenders and the aging of photos routine. "Elly, confirm the validity and source of each dataset." It was impossible to ignore the alarming outcomes in front of her.

Elly correlated all the information provided. "I have not set a time frame on the lost kids and child victim databases."

Keira stared at thousands of kids from abusive situations fifteen, twenty, and thirty years ago. But now the faces appeared aged, often haggard. Worse, those faces were showing up as the traffickers, violent adults, and molesters of today.

Gino's statements from the night before about generational crime and criminals being broken stared her in the face. The stare was actually coming from every snapshot. Every broken child, every broken adult was looking at her. The abused became the abusers. All she could think about were all the children who needed protection. Society was building a legacy of twisted minds by not preventing awful things happening to these children.

"Donovan was so right; our childhoods shape us." Keira's stomach roiled with frustration, disgust, and anger.

"Elly, save these filtered data sets as 'Missing Children Found as Adults'. After naming all filters and indexes, close all files from this session."

Gino's quotes about the sociopathic behavior of serial killers, evil dictators, warmongers, and sadistic criminals all having roots in their childhood no longer seemed like psychobabble. The evidence was right here.

Ollie must have sent the rest of the staff away. It was past their arrival time, but she heard no one in the hallway. As she left the room, Ollie jumped up from his chair. She held up her hand and shook her head. He asked no questions and gave her a hug.

"Thank you," she mumbled as she hurried out the back door.

Slipping into the back seat of the car, she sighed deeply and relished being alone.

"Keira?" Elly's voice came from Keira's phone resting in her hand.

"Not now, Elly." Keira burst into tears.

"Keira, there are many more pieces of data to review, and crying won't make the process easier for you. These are urgent, based on your requests from the last few hours."

Keira pushed her head back into the seat's headrest and squeezed her eyes tight. "Elly, you have terrible timing and manners right now. You need to go back and read your books on empathy. Leave me alone. I'll let you know when I can get back at this."

"Yes, certainly."

"Elly, kids are your priority. Anything and everything that you're given is prioritized to the safety and betterment of the kids. I'm not tireless like you. I just have to get some sleep. But, Elly," she paused, "I've never been happier to have you as my partner."

Impacting All Of Us

H er message for Roy had explained she'd been in the lab all night and needed sleep. She'd also left Gino a message asking to chat after she grabbed a nap. The rest of the ride home she had dozed.

Ninety minutes after lying down, she jolted awake with the sun shining straight on her face. It seemed to erase any benefits the short nap had given her psyche. She showered and dressed.

Hazy from limited sleep, Keira shuffled towards the kitchen, craving a cup of tea and any effortless food. Ollie had been so kind earlier. He hadn't asked for explanations. She hoped she had thanked him.

"Peanut butter, yogurt, and banana? Is this breakfast or lunch?" Gino asked as he entered from his study.

"Hey, thanks for hanging around this morning. I need to talk about what I uncovered last night. And I guess this is breakfast."

She loved the way he made her another cup of tea without asking if she wanted one. He always thought of her first. His expression of concern told her she looked as rough as she felt. Holding his hand, she pulled him to the big white couch facing their hillside view. The soothing scenery was welcome, but it wasn't going to fix today's raw emotions.

Gino brushed the hair from her cheek and held her hands in his. "You need to tell me what kept you up last night. I know the raids you and your team support can be taxing. But we didn't book anything major last night. I didn't know you were heading to the office for something upsetting."

Wriggling her toes channeled her urge to hop up and pace. Persuasion was key to enlisting Gino's help. To convince the FBI to expand the task force's scope, she needed a compelling argument. She needed Gino's passion for protecting kids.

"I've discovered proof linking the perpetrators of the sex trafficking to their abusive childhoods. I need you to expand our work with the FBI to include the prediction and prevention of child abuse. We have to do this."

Gino's soulful eyes, beneath a furrowed brow, didn't tell Keira enough. Was the pained expression due to her findings or because his answer about the FBI's scope wouldn't please her?

"Keira, we know violent crimes are often committed by people with unstable backgrounds. The generational cycle of abuse is well documented by social services and law enforcement."

"Let me be more specific. This is not just about generalities of crime statistics. Elly and I crunched the data last night. I can show you direct connections of hundreds of abused or missing teenagers from fifteen or twenty or twenty-five years ago who are now the criminals we're seeking or who are being arrested for sex trafficking, kidnapping, serial abuse, rape, and other violent crimes against teenagers."

She fidgeted with his wedding ring. "We can even predict those who will get involved in criminal activity or may be financiers or behind-the-scenes perpetrators."

"How did you develop specific links or proof? Assumptions and probabilities can be dangerous in this business." Gino couldn't sit still. Standing and pacing, hands in his pockets, his interest gave Keira hope.

The explanation Keira provided included her work of digitally aging childhood images of runaways and abuse victims, which then matched videos, mug shots, and photographs of known and suspected criminals pursued by the FBI. She detailed her night of analysis and proofs, explaining her expansion throughout the country's databases. She sensed Gino's skepticism.

"It's a mighty leap to go from matching known faces of criminals with their childhood to accusing former victims of a life in crime. What was the old movie—*Minority Report*—where they arrested people before they committed a crime based on psychic visions or some bullshit?"

"No, I can't say a person is going to commit specific crimes. But I can overlay the profile of these criminals now that I can track more of their lifelines back to childhood. When we analyze the life choices and circumstances of other victims, we can predict, with high probability, their engagement in these offenses and their associations with other criminals."

She pleaded with Gino to review her findings. Gino agreed the data made compelling connections. Without allowing Keira to view his work, he spot-checked FBI files of a few high-profile citizens her research highlighted. His expression turned to a glare and what she thought of as his angry jaw.

"What is it, Gino? What have I done?"

"The FBI doesn't do domestic child abuse. We don't engage at local levels or isolated events. We can't step in over the local law enforcement unless they ask us or the acts involve crossing state borders, organized crime . . . Oh, Keira, they're not going to let the trafficking task force work on singular family incidents."

Remaining outwardly calm, her rage seethed inside. Her skin crawled in a flush of hot and cold.

He took her hands again. "Maybe Roy can pursue a separate contract locally."

Her teeth clenched. "No, I can't take this Roy. Don't mention it to him. He and Loel have enough going on right now." She took a deep breath and reminded herself that she was angry, but not at Gino.

"Abuse within a family is seldom a singular event, and you know it. Research proves six or more childhood traumas can cut twenty years off a person's life. That doesn't mean they should hang around the house for six beatings from their mom's new boyfriend."

"I know." He wouldn't look her in the eye.

"We start counting the traumas with each assault, the defection of the father, the terrifying nights they spend on the street. It's not just our crime stats that are impacted. Our nation's health crisis is directly tied to the mental and physical abuse these kids get. The FBI should see this as a national issue impacting all of us."

It was her turn to pace.

"The department head is not one for expanding her territories. She hates the politics. She could get touchy if she thought you or Searcher are trying to tell the FBI what to do. Now is not the time to highlight your involvement with the task force. Eyebrows go up whenever people learn you and I are both involved, even if you're basically on the sidelines."

He moved towards Keira. She knew he wanted to use physical touch to smooth over the last words and rejection he handed her. That wasn't going to happen. Nothing gentle was going to placate her emotions or her resolve.

"I'll find another way. Elly, car please," she said. Gathering her bag, returning the teacup to the kitchen, and pulling on her boots kept her from looking at him.

Gino opened his mouth to protest. Keira didn't give him a chance to show his support or provide any other feedback. She had to move away from the exchange.

"I appreciate your listening and your honesty. I don't want to screw up anything for you, for me, or for Searcher with the agency. I didn't think about this as creating problems. We have so much work to do, and it's important work. I must go back to the office. It's getting so late."

She turned to look at him, knowing this habit of cutting off a conversation that she found frustrating grated on Gino's nerves. Repeating any element of it couldn't change the fact that the FBI would not expand their scope. Nor was she going to make any progress sitting here sipping tea. Action was the only thing to make her feel better.

A lopsided, apologetic smile was the best she could muster. "I know, I'm cutting you off here. I love you. Thank you, really, for looking at the research. Give me a shout if you think of anyone who might be interested in seeing it. I gotta run. Roy has a demonstration Loel's been working on. They want to show it off."

"Keira, be careful. The danger of revealing our capabilities is huge. Please be careful."

She bobbed her head, waved, and bit into an apple while she ducked out the door.

Cohesion

oel trained Ollie and Ruby with the control commands of
SearcherExec for over a week. They easily mastered the software commands for distribution, recording, communication,
and formation.

In a small office next to the usual mission observation arena, Loel
dimmed the lights by sixty percent. "I find the darker room makes the
3D projection of the scene easier to observe."

"I must admit I'm nervous," Ruby said. "I haven't been part of
these raids before. Keira tells me they can turn your stomach. Shauney
won't even talk about them."

Ollie sent a reassuring glance at Ruby. It was likely false confidence
on his part. This was his first operation too.

"I chose today to go live with you two for a reason. It's a minor outing with the FBI, and they're not expecting violence. It's a small group
of agents making arrests in a fairly controlled environment, or so they
say."

They sat at chairs around the central table in the room. "Do you
have questions about the mission report?" Loel asked.

Ruby and Ollie exchanged concerned expressions. Ruby shook her
head. "I didn't receive a mission report. Was I supposed to ask for one?"

"Damn, no. Of course, you weren't on the distribution list. Hendrick is running the surveillance for the FBI in the room next door. He'd review the report. Okay, here is the super quick rundown. Two guys tied to the traffickers through money links are laundering money through a strip joint on the Southside. They don't appear to be involved in physically moving women and kids or recruiting them. They're just skilled at unique methods of making LOTS of money, considering the low rent style of their strip club."

Floating between the three of them was a semi-translucent tabletop scale replica of the club. The display was a real-time recreation of the action observed by the Dust deployed onsite.

The first time she'd shown them the Dust's simulation of a space, Ruby had passed her hand through the model. She'd described it as a dry fog feeling. Ollie had equated it to a living, glowing, roofless doll-house. Loel didn't distract him with the irony of their first live-action assignment being at an establishment called Baby Dolls.

Ollie said, "How are we helping in this mission?"

"Nobody is aware of this version of the Dust running in parallel. We don't want the Feds to get ahead of us, thinking they need capabilities that aren't perfected yet. The three of us are testing that version and your skills. We're not expected to help. However, nothing ever goes as planned. I'm just saying . . . "

Loel watched Ollie bring the Dust online, satisfied with his proficiency. Ruby calibrated the 3D model to maximize the space on the table. They pushed their chairs back to stand around the club's replica. It only took a few moments to gain an orientation of the small floor plan. It was the middle of the afternoon. No patrons were present. A bartender washed glasses. A man sat at the bar reviewing a stack of papers. Three female dancers lounged and preened in a room behind the stage. A third and fourth man each sat in small rooms near the back of the building.

Waiting for the FBI to arrive, a smirk crossed Ollie's face. "Who signed up to distribute the Dust at this fine establishment?"

Ruby grinned. Loel rolled her eyes. "I didn't ask. I'm sure Cody volunteered for the task. Let's hope he didn't try to submit an expense report."

"Is Elly engaged with us today?" Ruby asked.

"No," Loel's tone ended that line of conversation.

The agents entered the front door. The floor layout and the internal camera surveillance within the club was familiar to them. The two men at the front immediately put their hands up. Agents ran to the women's dressing room and the first back office. They moved the man in the first office to the bar, leaving the girls in the dressing room talking to the agents. Everyone stayed calm.

"Why don't they do anything with the guy in the back room?" Ruby asked.

"I don't know. Ollie, we don't need much coverage in the front right now. Send more Dust to that back room."

Ollie selected the back corner room on his tablet, then moved a slider to increase the concentration of the Dust. The increase improved the detail and crispness of the objects in that area. Ruby made a simple reverse pinch gesture in the model. This popped the size of the back room larger while minimizing the scale of the rest of the building.

"It looks like the door to this room is hidden in the wall of the first office." Ruby pointed to the adjacent room's connecting wall. "The agents must not know this room exists. They're searching that office but paying no attention to this guy back here!"

Ollie said, "Loel, look! He's shredding documents and moving things to that floor safe. Do you think he knows the cops have shown up but thinks they won't find him right away? What do we do?"

"We've got to stop him. They want the money trail documented. Just, just . . . tell the Dust to bind his hands. Quick, here, let me try." Loel said. She took over the SearcherExec system from Ollie. "I'll direct the nanites to wrap the man's hands. It's a new thing we're working on." It was the only thing she could think of at the moment to stop him. "Now I'm sending a message for the primary Dust to penetrate this room. I'll figure out later how it was blocked in the first place."

Ollie said, "I've jammed the shredder." He was holding Ruby's tablet now. She stood staring, eye's wide and mouth open.

The man in the back room cursed with anger and confusion as his wrists bound together with a gray non-sticky tape and zero explanation. He continued to curse loudly, catching the attention of the agents in the next room. They started looking for a way to get to the cursing voice.

The man struggled. He stood to give himself leverage to break his mysterious bindings. As he jerked his arms, his left foot slipped into the floor safe. As he fell, his arms pulled apart and the bindings disintegrated and dispersed.

The somewhat hidden door burst open. Agents entered the room, guns drawn.

At the Searcher office, Loel tossed her stylus across the table. It bounced and flew four more feet through the office. "Damn it! There is just no reason that Dust shouldn't be binding enough to hold his hands together! At least for a little while." She stood, turning her back to the club scene as well as Ruby and Ollie.

The two of them sat quietly, not knowing how to react or what to do next. Loel turned towards them, saying nothing. They all three watched the scene at the club continue.

The destructive man was being handcuffed by an FBI agent. The agent's two co-workers were distracted by the full-length windows, unmistakably two-way mirrors into the strippers' dressing room. Dancers, bored with their FBI chaperones, and either oblivious or accustomed to what was happening in the front of the club, were practicing their evening acts.

"I told you nothing goes as planned." Loel smoothed her hair back and gritted her teeth. "Recall our version of the Dust. Canisters are onsite. The agents will bring them back. Then shut this all off."

"Loel?" Ruby said tentatively. "Is the binding thing the same problem you've been talking about regarding movement and strength? I know you may not feel like talking about it now. But if we can help, more information would go a long way."

Loel dropped into her chair again. She leaned her elbows on her knees and stared at Ruby. "Yes. Yes, that is exactly the problem. If we create something on the fly, the AI hasn't modeled the hell out of the connection between the Dust motes. So, the collective cohesion isn't optimal."

"I see," Ruby said.

"The nanites haven't found a way to stick together with strength if the design is ad-hoc," Loel grumbled. "We can create something of permanence from a file. They simulate thousands of ways for the little buggers to line up and hold on. But for the life of me, I can't get them to do it with any flexibility."

Ruby shifted her weight twice. "I really think Elly could help you. Her material science knowledge is off the charts. If there is anything out there in nature or manmade to compare to the problem, I bet she can find the useful reference. She's constantly asking how she can be more helpful."

"Hmm, Roy and Keira have mentioned something similar." She really didn't want to slow down to train a new AI on her progress to-date.

Watching Ollie search Ruby's face for a signal about how to respond, Loel regretted showing her frustration in front of them.

"Look, I'm sorry. This isn't any fault of yours. You followed instructions well today. You got a first glimpse, although short, at a live operation. I need to go to Hendrick and find out why his mesh network didn't supply any surveillance in that back office."

Ruby gave her a smile. "Thankfully, whatever was blocking it didn't block us. I guess it was a good thing we were here."

"Yes, you're right. It also allowed me to try the bindings because no one was watching. You can go back to working on the OS integration or whatever else is your top priority. Thank you. Thank you very much."

The two exchanged awkward glances, stacked their tablets, and left the room.

Freelance Thinking

C reativity is stifled by exhaustion and stress. The Searcher employees experienced both symptoms under their stressful experiences with the FBI and the pressure to advance Rockefeller or other projects. Freedom to explore unrelated ventures eased the strain.

Keira encouraged her staff to quickly adopt the same patterns. Each employee was expected to spend approximately ten percent of their time researching or developing in areas not required by a client or internal assignment. Working in disciplines of science or technology unrelated to one's daily work was highly encouraged. Changing to a different workspace was also suggested.

Keira and Loel decided they would work in Ollie's lab. His obsession with pop culture and retro entertainment included an eclectic array of props, toys, and gadgets. Keira watched Loel inspect his collection. She wondered if the multicolored array would be considered clutter by Loel. Loel's broad smile eased Keira's concern about criticism.

"Ahh, Claymation, right? I saw an expo about the art form and movies or something. My grandma used to sing 'Heard It Through the Grapevine' whenever any of us girls started to gossip."

"That's funny. I never quite understood the fascination with retro stuff, but Ollie tells me even Wikipedia has a well-documented site to the raisin's 'career.' There're over a dozen figures here from the '80s to the early 2000s. Ruby says there are three times as many at his home," Keira said.

"Really?" Loel replied.

"I don't ask questions. But yes, she appears to be quite familiar with his collections and his lack of cooking tools."

"I see."

"I have a question for you on this ten percent free research time. Is that ten percent of the time we work in total or ten percent of our full-time job?" Keira smirked.

"It didn't take long for the entrepreneur to start sounding like an employee, now did it?" Loel teased.

Keira winked and shrugged sheepishly. "I'm adapting."

They each set up on the workbench and laughed about their desperate need to do something different. Keira brought tea from the break room. They settled in for their "tinkering time." This was the name Hendrick had given the exploratory research. It had stuck.

Keira sat at the main controller and began the search she'd been thinking about for the last three days. She had yet to control the smart Dust entirely on her own. Tonight, she wanted to start with shapes and forms that had been tested. A series of specifications for doll-sized models looked interesting. Needing experience at managing the Dust, she decided rapid prototyping for her education chatbot's physical form checked all the boxes. It wasn't distinctly unrelated work, but neither was it what she did during her day job.

The Claymation figurines and various other figures inspired her. Those features that attracted kids and stood the test of time and culture changes worked their way into Keira's test models. She studied large, round eyes that invoked sympathy and warm feelings. The furrowed brows and flashes of teeth on war-based toys directed her away from several design ideas. No other lab could have been more helpful than Ollie's little wonderland. The education bots had to be mature enough to be accepted as kids grew older, but they still had to be fun. JayJay looked too immature.

Working in amiable silence, they each made progress. Keira brought in more tea. She wondered what creations would entertain such an inventive and accomplished mind as Loel's.

As Loel accepted the fresh mug, she sat up straighter and rolled her shoulders. "Do you ever get so engrossed in intense thinking that you neglect what your body is telling you?"

"Oh, yes. It's a problem. I had to start yoga and Pilates in the office. I must step away from the built-up tension. As I think about the kids at risk from traffickers, hunger, or parental abuse, I get tied up in knots."

"The FBI crap and the disaster environment work are killers. There are weeks I struggle to pull off any creativity after the disturbing things we encounter. Blessedly, Roy seldom has me involved in the FBI stuff right now. Working here when no one else is around is nice. The quiet lets me reclaim the office as a clean, safe space."

"Gino tells me compartmentalizing is a skill they teach at the academy. I understand the critical role it plays when you're engaged in their world all the time."

"Did you know compartmentalization is why the raids are always managed out of the same lab? I don't believe any other work ever gets done from there. I think we'll have to board the place up when we're done with that gig. Either that or hold an exorcism in there."

"Sorry if my introduction is causing problems. Is there an end to the support for the trafficking task force? I don't enjoy the grit, but I can't imagine abandoning the kids." Keira absentmindedly dug her nails into her thighs while talking. Once she recognized what she was doing, she released her grip.

Loel fidgeted. "I hold on to hope we can turn over the management of SeekerDust to the FBI at some point in the near future. We never realized how much it would suck us into people's depravity. I want to train FBI employees to use the SearcherExec. Roy doesn't want to risk the loss of control. It creates a point of contention between the two us. We haven't had many, but this is a biggy."

Keira sat straighter. "Okay, sorry. We're here to work on OTHER things and break away from what makes us grind our teeth. This stuff tonight was a bit more uplifting for me. Learning to manage the Dust while experimenting with facial features for the bots was fantastic. I thought 3D printing and modeling was fast, but the motes are indulgently quick for this purpose. You looked intense."

"Hmm, yes. This little project is working with CRISPR."

"CRISPR, as in the DNA editing stuff? Oh, God, I do feel trivial now."

"I'll give you the short answer for what I'm doing. Scientists have been unzipping DNA and inserting or deleting portions of DNA before re-zipping the strands."

Keira held back the hundred questions she had about the science. Her curiosity around Loel's involvement pushed into high gear. "I heard of storing information within synthetic or within organic DNA. The capacity is amazing and will always be around. How did you get involved in this line of work? This is so different from anything else you work on."

"That's part of the point of the ten percent zone. We all have fascinations that appear impossible to integrate into Searcher's efforts. My interest in biology goes back as far as I can remember. In college, when I diverged into robotics and mechanical engineering, some of my classmates continued into medicine. This is one way I stay in touch with them. We're bringing cross-discipline perspectives while delivering personalized medicine. Three of my closest friends are geneticists scattered throughout the world. We all started in the same CRISPR class our freshman year."

Keira looked with awe at her colleague. "What's your role in the project?"

"This CRISPR concept we're working on utilizes a smaller, simpler version of SeekerDust nanites. We want to use the lab-on-chip disciplines they already use when testing fluids for medical anomalies. If we increase the delivery of the test within the bloodstream then we could also use CRISPR to alter tumorous DNA. Ultimately that gives the body's own immune system the ability to attack the cells early."

Keira leaned back in her chair and stared at one of Ollie's shelves of curiosities. Directly in her line of sight was a *Magic School Bus* toy, complete with a Ms. Frizzle figurine. She laughed and pointed at one of her childhood STEM inspirations. "I think Ms. Frizzle may have shrunk down and done something like that in a book. But she did it with a school bus and class of kiddos."

Loel turned, following Keira's directional queue. "Oh, I loved Ms. Frizzle. She was awesome. I saw a series of her books in a collector's bookstore recently. It's amazing how the fundamentals of science can still be found in them. I hear the original illustrator's granddaughter created the software that now creates the artwork for the books. That way, it keeps the old art style going."

"Leave it to Ollie to leave inspiration for us everywhere. I wonder how many scientists and doctors those books and shows motivated over so many decades?"

"Good question." Loel said. "Hey, I gotta run. I've got dinner plans. Great working here with you tonight. I'm always working on this or another plan, but I'm not good about moving to other spaces or working with others to learn from one another. However, I would like to do more of this. I know the change of scenery was helpful for me."

"Thanks for spending some of your precious time catching me up on your science. I hope I wasn't a distraction."

Loel gathered her things, smiling. "Not at all. It was a pleasure. Roy has been expecting me to spend this time as I see fit. His insistence that Elly start crunching through options for me is supposed to open my calendar more." She shrugged. "I'll see you tomorrow."

The next SeekerDust analysis Keira wanted to do required Loel's absence. She could only imagine the conversations between the two partners. Data and Roy were likely the only things that could ever change Loel's mind.

She wiped her hands on her jeans, surprised they were sweaty. Her objective tonight was to stay within the rules. Her household never embraced the concept of the ends justifying the means. Her discussions regarding surveillance with Gino and Roy set her boundaries. She just needed to experiment.

Now that she was in charge of setting boundaries for the Dust, she felt unprepared for the role. Seeking the necessary understanding of controllability as well as listening capability distracted her thoughts constantly. She would call tonight "building a hypothesis." That sounded clinical, more appropriate than "playing with the boundaries." Her mission tonight was to control the Dust outside the lab. They'd solved the WiFi requirements, so she knew it was possible.

During the disaster recovery missions, the Dust distributed itself to the surfaces of the buildings or rubble. They described the attributes to her as positional awareness. It helped the agents during raids and surveillance and helped first responders during crises recovery. She justified to herself that she needed to understand this capability. It would relate to the property recognition they needed once the MoralOS was embedded. The entire mesh network needed to understand property ownership.

Gino was working late elsewhere, so she was in no rush to head home. Time slipped away from her while she worked. The adaptability of the Dust was both exhilarating and daunting. How did Cody and Loel stay focused on a finite set of objects to build with this stuff?

Within a few hours, she mastered control of several of the nanite's abilities. She sent Dust to specific GPS coordinates on the streets at the base of their secluded hill. She observed a conversation in a public alley, keeping the Dust recording inside the same line of sight as a security camera within legal parameters. Her listening tests were also conducted only in public places and in short bursts with no recording. She called the nanites home, feeling much more confident with the SearcherExec system and its range.

While the Dust returned to the canister at the lab, a chill ran through her. These micro machines could so easily be abused. The pressure was increasing exponentially to integrate the MoralOS into all functional capabilities of the Dust. She had developed her own ideas, which could be risky but would have a high impact. Elly might need to dig into her law libraries. Roy had pressured Loel to include Elly in her R&D, which had increased Elly's knowledge of the nanites too.

Aventador

The possibilities seemed endless. Keira's mind wandered in several directions. Packing up her bag at her desk, she thought she heard footsteps from a distant hallway. They weren't close, but the building was otherwise silent. Who would be here at one in the morning if there were no FBI projects scheduled?

She walked a few steps from her office. "Hello?" She didn't want to startle someone else, but due to security, all cleaning crews were employees and worked daytime hours. A little louder she called, "Who's putting in extra hours tonight? Hello?"

"Hello?" replied a male voice. "It's Deon, who else is here?" He was moving towards her now. She turned the corner toward the length of the long white hallway to see his casual approach.

"I didn't realize anyone else was working late tonight. How are you?" Keira asked.

"I thought I was alone as well. I was reconfiguring 3D printers. Loel needs new versions in the morning. I got stuck for a while. The instruments for nanites are pretty damn tiny but come with big problems at times. How are you?"

"I'm good. I have to admit I'm tired. I got off on a tangent. You know how it goes. You get excited about something, and time slips away."

"I know what you mean. I've worked on some cool stuff over the years, but this place pushes the envelope for me sometimes."

Keira successfully swallowed a yawn before it could develop. "Where did you work before here?"

Deon shrugged. "Mostly university stuff. I watched your education demonstrations with a bunch of students last year. It inspired a lot of us. I think some are working with the OpenML things now. Nice work."

"Thank you. Have you worked with nanites before?" She didn't cross paths with Deon often. She wanted to go home but didn't feel like a two-sentence exchange was polite.

"A little, not much to write home about." Another shrug from Deon.

"And where's home? Must not be here, if you're writing home?" Keira smiled.

"Yeah, well, home is all over really. Army brat."

"Really? I'm a Navy brat. I get it." Maybe that was his reason for being so noncommittal. When you move around a lot as a kid, you learn a lot about the art of deflection. The new kid seldom draws attention to themselves. "Nice chatting with you, Deon. But I'm exhausted. Are you heading to the Pick-up Portico?"

Deon tilted his head. "The what?"

"Oh, I just learned the nickname myself. It's the covered entrance where you pick up a shuttle or a ride home or into the city. I'm about to order my ride."

"Oh, no. I'm headed to the garage. My big personal indulgence is driving myself. I have a weakness for collectable cars." He pointed in the opposite direction as Keira had pointed for the exit. "I'm going this way. I'll see you around. Good night"

"Goodnight, Deon. Thank you for your efforts." She said to his retreating back.

He waved a casual, sloppy wave without turning around. "You're welcome."

She returned to her office. "Elly, order a car for me and bring up the cameras for the garage and its exits, please."

Gino had insisted she have parking lot visibility and the car service drop off zone at the Opal offices when she worked late. She didn't have full access to all security cameras, but Roy and the security company agreed to give her a view to the tiny parking lot.

She shook her head at the live feed of a classic Lamborghini Aventador pulling away. For a guy who nobody seemed to know anything about, he sure created a stir with multiple older exotic cars and driving them manually. Yep, classic deflection. She hadn't learned anything about him. But she would have something she could say about him. He drove a cool car. Interesting guy, maybe.

Now that she had seen the car, she felt nerves tingle up her arms. Had she been careless? Could anyone have seen or heard her experimentation? She was too tired and happy with her results to worry further tonight. All she'd done was basic exploring with the Dust. Sleep now dominated her mind.

Unexpected Findings

A n urgent call for help with a raid was blasted to the Searcher Task Force Support Team. Ruby and Hendrick were the fastest to respond and reach the office. Keira's car pulled up shortly after Ruby's. They met in the task force observation room.

Pressing an earbud into Ruby's hand, Keira whispered, "This will connect you straight to me. I know it's your first raid in the field. I'm here for emotional support."

Ruby quickly hugged Keira. "Thank you. You want me to take the updated Dust, right?"

"I've got it here." Hendrick patted the duffle filled with canisters.

"Right." Keira nodded. "It has the new upgrade designed to pick up sounds of distress. Those alerts are tuned to alert you two and myself, not the FBI agents. Ollie is still trying to reach the psychologist at the agency's office to discuss the feature." When developing the sensitivity for the education robots, she never thought she'd be using the AI's inherent ability for prediction on crime fighting.

They waited for the agency's car to pick them up. Keira looked at Ruby. "This is a bit of an uncontrolled experiment, Ruby. You're accustomed to controlled environments. This isn't a robot helping our autistic students. It's testing the Dust to identify outcries for help. How are you feeling about it?"

"I'm good," Ruby said.

Keira didn't want to give away that she had flown the dust and heard things already. She didn't look Ruby in the eye as she continued. "We've made a lot of progress. We know in our deployments in the aquatic centers that the detectors could alert lifeguards only when there were sounds of distress, not just happy screaming."

Hendrick looked at the clock impatiently. "You know, fear is very powerful. Ollie took me through the differences in voice modulation between teenage angst and the fearful sounds from a person at risk. This will help the agency. I'm glad you've pushed so hard for this upgrade, Keira."

She wasn't certain how premeditated her rush had been to get this capability in the Dust. But she knew it had been the right thing to do.

The night's raid was taking place in a nearly rural eastern pocket of the city. The information the agency gathered without the Dust mandated that they move in quickly. The observation truck picked up the upgraded nanites with Hendrick and Ruby, then raced to the site.

Keira sat in her own office with the lights off. Nervous for Ruby, time seemed to crawl. She wasn't part of the direct observation team tonight, but she had her own connection and 3D visualization.

"Keira, you there?" Ruby's voice whispered in Keira's earbud. In the truck, anything Ruby said could be heard by Hendrick or the FBI driver and the technician. This direct connection made them feel closer.

"Yes, I'm here, Ruby. You doing okay?"

"I'm going to be fine. Hendrick just climbed out to release the Dust. Don't know why he didn't just roll down the window, but whatever." Ruby cleared her throat. She was quiet for a few moments. "Okay, this is getting real. Hendrick is back. We're going live."

"Good luck, Ruby. Hey, forget I'm here. Do your thing and be on mission."

The Dust swarmed the main house as Hendrick had instructed. 3D models of the old building popped up in Ruby's observation truck, the FBI's SWAT rig, and Keira's office within Searcher's building.

Agents quickly grasped the floor plan and the placement of people. They could identify two men with guns slung on their backs in the front room. Two more were loading a cooler in the kitchen. Their guns rested on the counters. Two vans sat in the driveway.

Seven women knelt at the feet of the large men in the front room. The women's hands appeared tied in front of them. Keira's monitoring tablet pinged and glowed amber. At least one of the women was crying loudly. Keira's stress detection in the Dust was working. It picked up the woman's sobs and distress. Keira intentionally kept the sound from the raid turned off. She hated hearing the chaos.

Eight agents slipped out of the rig, guns drawn. Running toward the house, the agents glowed blue in the miniature replications.

The front and back doors of the house burst open simultaneously. Agents surprised all four traffickers. In the living room, one man threw his hands in the air. The other reached behind his back for his gun. The impact of the agents' bullets flung him against the wall. He slid to the floor, lifeless.

In the kitchen, agents demanded the traffickers drop to their knees. They complied immediately.

Keira's and Ruby's tablets flashed and glowed amber as all the women screamed and collapsed to the floor. Keira's pulse raced. Her mouth went dry.

It was all over in a matter of minutes. Keira shivered and wiped her forehead with relief, thankful it went so quickly. Her distress detection had worked. Only she could see the alerts indicating the woman crying and upset. But this had been a good test. If they had proof of distress, agents could breach a future location without a search warrant. The FBI agents spoke soothingly to the women, cutting their bindings and helping them sit on the furniture instead of the floor.

Keira stood to stretch, still marveling at how the buildup lasted so much longer than the raids themselves. Her tablet pinged and started flashing. "Ruby, you seeing this?"

"Yes," Ruby hissed. "Hendrick was calling back the Dust. The alarm's going off, and the Dust stream just did an unexpected 90-degree turn. What is going on? God, I hope I didn't screw something up."

"Shhh, Ruby. Your mic is live to others. I'm sure you did nothing wrong."

Keira heard a muffled conversation from Ruby's phone. She'd turned off sound from the all the trucks at the raid. She fumbled to reengage it. A buzz and flood of jumbled conversation poured into her earbud.

"Sir, the Dust is following a distress alert, a new feature we're testing," Hendrick explained.

"Gino," Ruby said. "Look at the 3D. It's morphed from the farmhouse to the work building. It looks like it's gone under the floor."

"That building was already cleared by agents. There's no one in there. *And* I wasn't informed you'd be testing during this operation," Gino hissed from the SWAT truck. Keira flinched.

"Sir, I must have grabbed one of the testing canisters along with the regular canister during my rush out the door." Ruby fell on her sword for Keira. Everybody knew it was a rushed exit, and this was her first outing.

"My God, there are five people down there. Go! Go! Go!" shouted a voice Keira didn't recognize. She watched on the model as two agents from the main house and a single blue dot from Ruby's truck moved towards the outbuilding.

"Ruby! One of you didn't leave your truck, did you?"

"No, of course not." Ruby protested. "It's our driver. Hendrick tagged him with a tracker, so we can see his position in the 3D. I want to alert everybody now that at least some of these people tied up under the floor are kids. Looks like teenagers from the video transmitted by the Dust."

Red dots speckled the 3D landscape between the advancing agents and the smaller building. They also glowed in the SWAT team's goggles. "What are those lights?" Keira and Gino demanded respectively.

"STOP!" Hendrick screamed. "Don't take another . . . "

A muffled explosive sound hit all of them. A howl of pain or surprise and a small dome-shaped flash came from the yard. The middle agent was flung back, crashing into the third. They both fell to the ground.

"HALT!" Gino ordered his agents. The agent left standing held completely still. "Hendrick, what is it? What's going on?"

"The place is boobytrapped. Those red spots are explosives of some type." Hendrick replied.

"What?" Gino said. "How do you know that? They're all the way around the building! Are you talking about IUDs?"

"I can't explain how or why. Roy would have to do that and not on open—"

"Okay, let's not go into that now then." Gino cut Hendrick off. "Can you confirm there are none behind our guys?"

"Yes, the guys on the ground are clear," Hendrick said.

Occupants in the SWAT truck barked instructions to help the men on the ground.

"Bowder!" Gino called to the man on the ground. "Status? Are you bleeding? They're on their way. We're just across the yard."

"Sir, my foot could be broken. Hurts like hell. But no shrapnel, I'm not cut up. Hell of a shove, sir," the fallen agent said. "Danson here broke my fall."

Agents approached the two on the ground from behind. Not trusting that technology would fully protect them from surprises, they carried riot shields. Helping their co-workers to their feet, they backed out in a single line, supporting the injured Bowder as he hopped on his uninjured leg to the driveway.

Gino turned his focus back to the rescue. "What happened, Hendrick? If one of those things blew up but sent no shrapnel, are they fairly benign? Can we tell how wide their trigger zone is?"

"Gino, uh sorry, Agent Stetson," Ruby said. "We have a new problem. I think the triggering of that thing started a small fire in the shed. Can you see it in the far left corner?"

"Shit!"

Ruby added, "I have vitals monitoring on the kids. One is pretty beat up. I'll shut up while you do your thing, but I'm watching the fire and kids for you."

Keira was sweating and she was in the air conditioning. She whispered to Ruby, "Great job. You're doing great. Keep it up." She hated the danger they got pulled into.

"Hendrick!" Gino demanded. "What can we do? Can you help us with these things? It could take a while to get the bomb squad up here. They're on their way."

"Sir, I need you to trust me. Can I talk on a direct line to you? Actually, I need Searcher employees to hear this but no one else. My people need to witness what I'm revealing."

Gino gave instructions to turn off audio to the agency staff except the man still standing within the mine field. "I want this man to hear what you're saying, since these things are surrounding him, and your plan will likely involve him."

"Understood," Hendrick replied. "I'll make this quick. The Dust shielded your agent from the blast. In doing so, it may have caused part of his injury, but without it he likely would have lost his leg. These are powerful explosives."

"Hendrick the fire is still small but growing," Ruby cut in.

"Sir, I suggest you give your man riot shields he can crouch behind and then you shoot the mines between him and the door of that building. The Dust will shield the explosions, and if you can wait, say, 30 seconds between each shot, I'll concentrate the Dust."

"Gino, we have no time to wait," Ruby begged.

Neither Gino nor the stranded agent said a word in reply. Three men carried riot shields to the yard, handing them to the agent for blast protection. It was safer to keep him where he was than to risk the movement so near several IUDs.

The agent crouched behind the shields as an agent at an elevated section of the driveway shot each of the twelve mines at thirty second intervals. Each explosion was a loud dull impact with a contained flash of light, despite the Dust shielding the percussions. Each explosion also triggered another spark somewhere else in the small shed. Smoke faintly swirled from every side of the structure now.

Immediately after the twelfth detonation, four agents ran through the path created by the clearing of the mines and through the door of the building. The Dust had reported no explosive materials inside.

While ripping at the floorboards with a crowbar, they also quickly found a hatch in the floor. One agent sprayed at the fire with an extinguisher. The kids, tied together, screaming, coughing, and crying, cowered from the men. They were soon unbound and carried carefully out of the building and to a newly arrived ambulance.

An agent briefed the fireman jumping off the firetruck that just pulled up. They appeared reluctant to wait but focused on the instructions. Then, they took up their positions to put out the fire.

"Hey, Searcher?" Gino asked. "Any other people on this property we should know about?"

Hendrick replied, "No, all clear from here."

"Searcher? Or Keira if you're listening, we just confirmed all four traffickers from inside were fingerprinted or otherwise identified in the system since they were kids."

Keira gasped.

Hendrick recalled the Dust to his canister.

"With permission, Searcher is disconnecting communications." Ruby's voice announced a little unsteadily.

The 3D model in Keira's office disappeared.

Adverse Experiences

K eira paced her office and knew she could be facing a debate about the testing of Dust in an active raid. The revelation of the shielding capability and the drama of the raid might overshadow any perceived transgression on her part.

On scorching nights like this, Keira feared the tempers of the city would be aggravated. Hot nights lead to hot tempers. Her mind wandered to the data she'd been reading and why the detection capabilities were so necessary.

Until the last few weeks, she hadn't considered the everlasting impact on both physical and mental health driven by ACES, an acronym for Adverse Childhood Experiences. Sadly, it was part of her new vocabulary. Correlations to cancer, heart problems, depression, addiction, and suicide were all directly obvious now. Would those kids under the floorboards continue to fight with these issues the rest of their lives?

The monitoring system surprised her with the soft, but sudden, pinging amber alerts on her tablet. She hesitantly moved to her desk. The log screen showed no other FBI teams scheduled for the night. These alerts were children in distress warnings. This was Dust with her new upgrade. She was impressed how quickly Cody had ramped up manufacturing.

The map showed incidents stretching out between the warehouse district near Roy's ReDo bar and the Old West electronics landfill. They had nothing to do with the Dust Hendrick currently managed with Ruby. This new path included single family homes on tree-lined streets and multifamily apartment complexes reflecting a wide range of income levels. She fidgeted in her chair and looked out her window to the darkness of the night.

Shaking her head, she tapped her tablet. This opened the first incident alert's audio feed. Who was the Dust listening to? Glass broke and other items crashed. Keira flinched. An angry man yelling about spending money appeared to be breaking things. A child cried and begged him to stop. Keira closed the incident and shuddered.

Opening another audio feed, she heard a young teenage boy cry out in pain followed by a snap or cracking sound and another yelp. A woman grunted and snarled that the whipping would continue until he had told her who drank her beer. His voice struggled through the tears. Sniffling, he told the woman he didn't know. It was obvious he had repeated this answer several times, but it didn't satisfy the drunk-sounding woman. Keira couldn't bear to hear another smack hit the boy. She closed the audio stream.

Uncertain why this monitoring occurred now, she reluctantly opened a third flashing alert. "Leave my sister alone," shouted the young voice trying to sound tough. Keira's stomach churned. She detected sobbing in the background.

A raspy, low, mocking voice retorted. "Whatcha gonna do about it, little man? If your sister's gonna walk through here dressed like that to see her boyfriend I'm gonna get a peek at what she's giving away."

The boy shouted, "Keep your hands off her. I'll tell grandpa."

The background crying continued. The man's voice got slimy and more disgusting. "Oh, you go right ahead. I guess I better get a good look now then, before it's too late."

A scream, ripping of fabric, and a crashing thud came simultaneously through the speaker. Keira reached for the phone while the boy's voice yelled "Tiffany, run! Let's get out of here now!"

Keira, shaking, considered making a phone call. Who would she call? Regardless of the schedule, the Dust must be on an FBI job. She couldn't call the police and tangle up an investigation. The FBI would be aware of everything she just heard. Strict orders stood not to discuss any details of what they heard or saw during the FBI surveillance with anyone. That included co-workers or agents. They were ordered to do their job and converse only about the use of the technology or how to improve results. She shivered and closed all audio files. Her hands felt clammy, and her pulse raced.

Looking again at the location of alerts overlaying the map, the straight and narrow line between two of Roy's properties, couldn't be a coincidence. How would the warrant be worded for that type of surveillance? Why would anyone be surveilling the space between where metals were mined and the bar or the clean recycle operation?

She paced. She chewed on her lip. Turning the lights on brighter didn't clear the mental images clinging to her memory. Desperate for fresh air and to be out of the office before Hendrick or the others wanted to talk about tonight, she grabbed her bag with shaking hands and fled.

Parties Of Interest

D eon called Mickey's answering service. "I've got news for you. It's about your taxes."

No one could trace the calls to either of them. The code phrase told Mickey where to meet him. Deon didn't want to be seen with his boss. Too many people in town might recognize Mickey. The man was insanely rich, so he was watched. Deon's position at Searcher could only be effective if no one suspected that he also worked for Mickey. They made sure they were never seen together in public, nor did they ever come and go from MachDrone Industries at the same time.

As for Deon, he stayed as unmemorable as possible. The only exceptions were his cars. But even then, everyone noticed the car or a pretty woman climbing out of it and never him. He might be most invisible when he was with his cars.

Mickey's ancient uncle owned an accounting firm with four employees. The office's simple building sat in the same block as the train station. The entrance included hallways from three different train platforms. Deon doubted the place was even a real business. He walked straight from the door to the conference room. No one bothered to look up from their desk.

Deon always started conversations quickly with Mickey. Preventing an ass chewing remained a high priority.

"Searcher's Dust is capable of undetectable surveillance. Here's a bag of super sour Tootsie Pops from the vintage candy store." The two sentences spoken as he tossed the candy to Mickey were intentionally rushed together. With Mickey, the best way to keep remotely on his good side was to keep information and Tootsie Pops immediately available.

"Tell me more." Mickey appraised the bag of candy and tore it open.

"The SeekerDust can be commanded from a tablet. They're also working on diverse manufacturing of objects with the Dust. It may be two different types of nanites. But the nanites break up and move into a room undetected. They don't have to be put in place as an object. They can send video and audio back to a receiver. We collected a bit about that from the earthquake rescues they executed. Because the Dust is so small and dispersed, you can't detect its signals or presence. It would take specialized equipment that recognizes these nanites to even begin to track them."

Mickey's eyes lit up. "They can bug a room without anyone knowing?" He networked with parties all over the world who would likely love to eavesdrop on conversations clandestinely. Deon wanted no knowledge of who those parties were.

Deon continued. "I don't think they're commercializing yet. I can't tell you why. They don't seem that interested in exploring markets. I haven't found a salesperson or business development team anywhere within Searcher other than those coming in from Opal. Your customers would never be on their list. Management is so conservative and anti-military."

"How do they use it? Can you get your hands on a sample?"

"They're extremely locked down, especially about their client's identity. They often work at night, but not always. Roy is paranoid about all of his tech being reverse engineered. I'm guessing the client might be the FBI."

Mickey shattered the Tootsie Pop between his teeth at the mention of the FBI. He had a tendency to do that when surprised. Deon doubted Mickey was even aware of this tic.

"The FBI? What makes you say that?"

"There's a guy, Gino, Dr. Stetson's husband. He's around a lot. He's an FBI agent. He usually shows up with a few other guys dressed casually, ready to blend in anywhere. Can your friend at the DOD check for connections between the agency and the FBI? You mentioned he knew Roy, too."

Mickey ignored Deon's question. "What about the sample? Can you grab any for me? Did you find product design files?"

Deon had hoped the FBI detail would distract Mickey and they could continue without talking about getting some of the Dust. He didn't have that operation figured out yet.

"I'm working on it. It was amazing that I even saw Keira using the stuff. She didn't think anyone was at the office, so she hadn't locked the lab. I'd already hacked into the general security's access codes to reach everywhere but the labs. I was able to view her practice sessions. Somebody will slip up again, and I'll gain access."

He chewed his inner lip, thinking about getting his hands on the Dust. "I work with the 3D printers. Each printer and assembly bot are checked out to me separately. I only have dummy recycled materials to use when testing the printers."

The security programs Hendrick developed appeared rock solid. When Mickey owned Searcher, Deon wanted Hendrick on his team. That man had skills. It was guys like Hendrick that made him dream about having a partnership in a legit development company. "The printer work puts me in the cycle of the version control, so I know which Dust is out of date and ready to be incinerated. I'll collect samples from an older generation, harder to track."

"Damn it, Deon! We need specifications, samples, code, or something more to start work. What about range? How close do you need to be to control it?"

Deon made some educated guesses and provided his boss with conservative estimates passed off as facts. He could always tell Mickey later they had made improvements if the Dust was actually more capable.

The pseudo-facts regarding close range requirements, quick power consumption, and terrible raw material constraints were not enough to deter Mickey. They included just enough complications to keep him from thinking he needed to call in air strikes at Roy's office to get his hands on the stuff yesterday.

No meeting could keep Mickey sitting still over thirty minutes. He left first. His driver would be waiting on the other side of the train station. For all Mickey's love of technology, he refused to accept self-driving cars and would never stoop to mass transportation. Deon looked at the conference table, disgusted at the Tootsie Pop wrappers and chewed soggy sticks. It wasn't his problem. He moved to his right at the exit and down to the anonymity of the trains.

Burning Need

A lerts pinged softly at the monitoring station to Keira's left. She gritted her teeth as she approached the monitors. Trepidation hovered around her. Until recently, she had loved her comfortable life bubble. It may have been stressful, but it had felt so respectable, clean.

Telling no one about what she'd heard three nights before, she had drilled Loel and Cody about all the capabilities of the Dust. She'd practiced its deployment and its shape creation commands. The fact that Loel and Elly worked together increased Keira's confidence with the Dust. Roy's insistence that Loel accept Elly's assistance had been helpful for everybody. Even if Loel didn't want to admit it. Elly knew limitations and strengths of the nanites. Keira's hesitation tonight was not intellectually driven.

The depravity of people capable of harming children sat like heavy embers, hot in her gut. In a flash, those embers sparked her from the smoldering reluctance to witness the abuse to a burning need to terminate it.

"Elly, prioritize children in distress alerts by highest anxiety cues."

Elly said, "Current alerts prioritized. Should incoming alerts be appended to a list or inserted into priority ranking?"

"Continually prioritize new and existing issues based on highest distress parameters."

"Understood," Elly responded.

Keira scanned the alerts and watched the list shift as Elly made changes. She nervously doodled with her stylus on the desktop.

"Elly, filter this list to provide alarms containing violence or precursors to violence."

Ollie and Ruby had loaded Opal's violence video detection algorithms into the Dust earlier in the week. She was unaware of any live testing with the new features yet.

The first alert was a low-resolution 3D representation of a family backyard before Keira instructed the SearcherExec Manager to disregard it. She recognized the scene all too well. An autistic child in high anxiety as a sibling tried calmly to restrain them with a hug wasn't the distress under attack scenario she needed to engage. The AI training to detect distress included extensive sets of autistic voices from their education databases. The violence detection algorithms included filtering videos with distress calls and physical restraints. This situation did fit the broad categories for assault detection.

"Elly, filter current alert perimeters to include adult violence towards a child or children."

"Understood."

Keira selected the top incident on the list.

"Poppy, please don't," begged the voice, sobbing and whimpering from the speaker.

Keira trembled.

The multipurpose room had a cowering wisp of a shirtless, pre-teen boy leaning on a flimsy, square dining table displayed on the screen. Keira slid a finger on the control panel to increase the Dust allocation. Her view included a large man looming over the boy wielding a belt. The higher concentration of Dust enhanced the resolution. She could see bleeding welts on the boy's back and long thin scars from previous beatings.

Keira instinctively wanted to scream at the man to stop. She wanted to gently hold the boy and help him.

A grunt from the man, a crack as the belt hit skin, and a howl from the boy made Keira jump. The man started growling or muttering in a thick, Cajun dialect she didn't understand. His unsteady stance and twitching hands made her certain he was drunk or high.

Another crack of the belt sent the boy to the floor. As the man moved his foot towards the boy, Keira thought two things. He's going to start kicking this boy's head, and she wished she had thought through ways to stop these abusers.

She studied the area surrounding the boy for inspiration. Her eyes landed on a kneeling altar painted with eyes in the corner of the room. Above the altar hung an iron cross and sculpture depicting the pyramid, staffs, snake, and eyes of a voodoo healer. Altar dolls and a portrait with tape over its eyes lay on the floor. This was a superstitious household.

The Dust could have a voice, hers. In one of those abrupt moments when the subconscious does the thinking, she remembered a movie about Deep South superstitions. Using an accent of the old voodoo character—deep, slow, deliberate, and bold—she hoped it was convincing.

"Poppy!" she yelled. "You stop that, you hear me?!"

The man stopped his foot's forward motion.

"This here boy is under my protection. Our protection!"

"Who is dat? Who's in my house?" his words demanded, but his tone wavered. He looked around towards the kitchen and doorway leading down a hall.

"You lay one more finger on that child's body and my curse on you will have you witherin' in pain, wishin' you was dead. You understand me. I have my eye on you and I have my bag of jimmies with me. Leave that boy alone! For good!"

The man staggered around the tiny house looking for the woman talking to him. Realizing there was nobody to go with the voice, he shriveled in stature and trembled.

"I'm watching you, but you will never see me. Do you hear me?" she growled.

"Yes, yes, ma'am."

"Good, now give up the drink. Pray. This boy is goin' to the neighbors' tonight. Not one finger on his precious head again. I will getcha."

The boy ran out the door equally as scared of the voice as of his father. The man turned on all the lights in the house and sat at the table, wide-eyed. He dropped the belt to the floor.

The Dust discontinued the monitoring when Keira swiped the incident closed on her tablet. She shook her arms and legs with the vigor of a swimmer prepping to launch from the blocks. She tried to remove whatever it was clinging to her from that interaction. The circumstances had been odd, and she couldn't expect to stop abuse within the city with a disembodied voice. She considered how to proceed.

"Keira," Elly said. "Your actions of surveillance were within legal perimeters only because you heard a child in distress."

"Yes, I'm aware, Elly. But it was legal." She picked up the toy plastic dog Miette had sent. They now exchanged letters on puppy stationery. Each letter written in a combination of Miette's inexperienced scrawl and her new mother's curtly print. Keira cherished her little pen pal and all the hope she had for the future.

Elly said, "You did deceive that man into believing a spirit of some type was watching over him."

"Yes, I know. But it protected that little boy. He needed someone to help him."

Immediately another alarm sounded, accompanied by an added "weapon" announcement from Elly. All their detection of violent streaming videos included enhanced warnings when a weapon was involved.

The visual showed a sidewalk with a man pointing a gun at a child while gripping a woman's hair, forcing her to withdraw money from an ATM. Keira used the same technique Cody had demonstrated in a gun range video where he jammed the weapon with the Dust. She directed the Dust to apply pressure to the panic button near the ATM, alerting the police. A screeching alarm startled all of them. The man tried to pull the trigger in frustration. Nothing happened. He pushed the woman to the ground and ran.

Before the police arrived at the scene, another alert distracted Keira from the crying pair she had just saved. The shocking swiftness at which the tragedies came at her was secondary to the torment of witnessing the violence. What she felt while watching and trying to help was nothing compared to the terror these kids faced.

This time she was looking inside of a posh bedroom, most likely in a hotel. Both the man and the young girl were fully clothed. She sighed, thankful for at least that small miracle. But then he straddled her lower back on the bed, forcing her to face a television. The girl sobbed, gasping for air, staring at the assault porn on the screen.

The man's words, abusive and belittling, suggested the teenager had done these things he now forced her to watch. He told her that she wanted him to do those things to her. The words came out rancid and vile. Keira wanted the words to stop. The man had to stop.

She instructed the nanites to form the medical wound patch it was trained to make and cover the man's nose and mouth. The Dust complied. The man, suddenly unable to breathe, toppled over on the bed, scratching at his face, his eyes bulging. He paid no attention to the girl scrambling off the bed and running out the door.

"Keira, I need to talk to you," Elly said.

"Not now, Elly!"

"Are you sure you're okay with the ethics of what you're doing?" Elly asked.

"Not now! I'm helping somebody here," exclaimed Keira.

The man's forceful pulling at the patch broke the bond. Keira couldn't let him regain composure and chase the girl. Noticing the motes still hovering around his face, she remembered the medical AI training data they had loaded in hopes of providing more triage during FBI raids. Directing the Dust to his trachea at fifty percent density, she essentially choked off enough airflow for him to pass out. He didn't need to die, just stop. He fell off the bed with a loud thud. As soon as he lost consciousness, she directed the Dust to exit his body.

"Damn!" Keira muttered to herself.

Before extracting the Dust from the bedroom, she sent a short video recorded during the scene's assault to the local Seattle number on his suitcase's bag tag. The message warned him that if he ever harmed another girl this video would be released to the police and the media. Two hours prior to being made public, it would be attached to a text sent to what was logically his wife's cell number, also listed on the bag tag.

Keira, exhausted and emotionally shredded, commanded the notifications to stop. She couldn't handle any more. Her knees quivered. Only adrenaline kept her upright. It was two a.m.

"Keira, I need to talk to you," Elly said.

"Not now. I'm exhausted. It's been a hell of a night. I just need to go home."

"You don't have an issue with the legality of your actions tonight?" Elly asked. "We had discussions a few months ago about ethics and legality. Did you know you would be testing this theory with me like this?"

"What? No. Of course not. I never in a million years thought I'd live through a night like this. I don't think I broke any laws tonight. The only thing broken is my heart over the hell these kids live through. Just get me a ride home. I must get out of here now."

"It's waiting for you outside, Keira. Good night."

Emergence

T he lab, strewn with canisters and partially configured objects made from SeekerDust, hosted Loel, Keira, Ruby, and Cody when Roy entered.

"Keira, we just received great news. The two kids that went missing Tuesday were found with your facial recognition tools. It was a combination of recognition with the kids and finding a guy with two kids who was previously always seen at the bus station alone. Ollie is out there, fist bumping anyone who will reach out."

Keira's face lit up. "Oh, that's wonderful news. I'm so relieved for those kids and their families. Ollie can ride that high for a long time. His crew worked so hard on that development and then Ruby refined its uses. It was a group effort."

Roy turned to Ruby. "Congratulations, Ruby. Well done." Even if nothing else came from the Opal acquisition, he found the staff they had absorbed were nearly priceless.

"Thank you. Truly meaningful usage of our efforts. I never imagined all the uses you would manage to find for our software," Ruby said. "I can't believe it's been a month since we sat on the roof at ReDo watching the Dust fly in."

Roy moved around the lab, examining the disarray. He addressed

Ruby. She was currently observing Loel's work, but not engaged with testing. "What is going on in here? This is a bit of a mess compared to usual."

"That's what I was thinking, too," Ruby whispered to Roy. "I'm watching because I'm a bit intimidated at the pace of reengineering the software instructions. We've never coded for a swarm dynamic before. Loel was getting ready to explain the issue for me."

Loel replied as queued. "We've been testing the adaptable Dust coalescence. The strength still isn't optimal."

Picking up a boogie-board-shaped object with hand grips on either side, Roy examined the surface. "Are you working on the customizable stretcher?"

"Yes," Loel said.

Ruby searched Roy's face for more explanation. "This was Hendrick's idea," Roy said. "We're adapting the shape and size of a stretcher for the needs of the patient in unpredictable emergency situations. This could eliminate the need to carry a stretcher into the rubble at the earthquake site. The Dust will create a board in the right shape and size for the injured person only when they need it."

"I see. That's brilliant," Ruby said.

"If only it worked," Cody grumbled. Everything rigid we've made in the past had the opportunity to be optimized repeatedly in simulations. So, the algorithms developed the optimal structure the nanites needed to create in order to bond correctly. Not so much on the fly."

They continued to debate theories and concepts. Ruby, being new to the project, offered novice, yet often viable, options to consider.

Elly's voice came from the lab's speakers. "Loel, may I join your conversation? I believe I found a breakthrough of importance to you."

Loel's annoyance at another voice entering the conversation showed on her face. Elly wasn't a variable Loel could control. Roy imagined this session of trial and error started from a conversation, not a planned joint engineering huddle. She stood still and gazed upward to a random spot on the wall.

"Go ahead, Elly, only if this breakthrough is about SeekerDust and its ability to assemble. If it's another project, please schedule time for us to chat," Loel said.

"This is specifically about the properties and redesign of SeekerDust. I believe I found the ideal configuration," Elly responded. "Rhombic Dodecahedron shapes can fill a space perfectly. They have 12 faces, 24 edges and 14 vertices. This provides maximum surface for your Van der Waals forces to adhere. Your Dust can adhere to three times more surfaces, making their bond significantly stronger. I've forwarded all specifications for manufacturing new Dust." Elly's words rolled quickly.

The engineers exchanged glances without confidence or excitement over their problem being solved. Roy looked at Keira. He hoped she could coax more information and explanation from Elly to help understand the likelihood of her progress.

Keira shifted her weight. "Elly, you need to take us through your work a little more specifically, please. First, refresh my geometry. What is a dodecahedron, if I even said it right?"

"Your pronunciation is correct. This is a rhombic dodecahedron shape." An oversized model of a dissected pomegranate appeared, floating in the space between them. "The shape of each seed's face is diamond-like. You see the same thing in many minerals, like a garnet. The motes fit together with perfect tessellation."

Ruby sat on her high stool at the lab table shaking her head. "Elly, I don't know what tessellation is."

"Excuse me, Ruby. Tessellation could also be described as tiling if it was in a 2D space. Let me provide an illustration." An image appeared on the lab's wall-mounted monitor. Dark red, multifaceted shapes dropped from the top of the screen "Tetris style," building up a lumpy wall with zero gaps.

"Ahh," murmured several of them in recognition.

"With more surfaces made available for adhesion, the bonding force is greater," Cody paraphrased Elly's earlier explanation, leaning into her illustration. "I think propulsion may still be an issue, Elly. But this shows promise."

Elly said, "Roy, may I have your permission to demonstrate my modifications both physically and with the incorporation of the MoralOS?"

"You're asking me, not Keira or Loel?" Roy asked.

"I believe you may find my methods unconventional. However, I believe a demonstration will save many hours of explanation or even generated simulations."

Roy, uncertain about Elly's typical processes looked to Keira. She shrugged and raised her eyebrows. Roy said, "Okay, Elly, if your demonstration is safe for those of us in the room, you may show us what you've got."

Dust moved from the back of the lab near three new 3D printers Roy hadn't remembered seeing before. The quantity of swirling microbots was greater than any of them had ever instructed at one time.

A slight crackle sound was drowned out by the gasps released in unison. The room fell completely silent and still for several moments.

"Oh my God!" Keira exclaimed.

Roy, Ruby, and Cody each used unique expletives.

Loel stood silent with her mouth open.

In front of them stood a female form, standing the average height of the three women already in the room. Her hands rested on her hips, a stereotypical power stance. Athletically fit, her muscular definition was imposing, yet feminine.

She reached out her right hand as she took one small step towards Keira. Roy stepped between them. Elly's voice now came from the humanoid figure. "Keira, Roy, this is my demonstration. This is . . . me, Elly."

Keira nudged her way around Roy. They all stepped closer to the manifestation of a woman, her hand still reaching out towards Keira, palm upraised. Roy set his hand on Keira's forearm before she attempted to return the gesture. The hand, formed out of SeekerDust, returned to the figure's side.

"Elly, you made this?" Keira asked gently.

"Yes, I did. I predicted a humanoid figure would be needed eventually to further your progress with Rockefeller, possibly raids and certainly the education systems you eventually will work on again."

Roy circled quickly around the figure, returning closely to Keira's side.

Elly continued, "In testing the issues with the Dust assembly for strength, customization, and mobility, I ran millions of simulations.

While that processing executed through our options, I adapted the MoralOS for the full upload. I predicted with the culmination of all of these solutions, the timing would be acceptable to appear in the human form I designed."

Roy glared at Keira, "Did you know about this? Had you seen this human design or asked for it?"

Without taking her eyes off of Elly, Keira shook her head. "No. No, Roy. I never requested or approved anything like this. I've been resisting even the conversation of Elly being . . . uh, being this."

Knowing the difficulty Loel and Cody experienced with tensile strength, Roy tried to estimate the physical strength or durability of Elly in this form. Instinct upon encountering the unknown made him want to put her in a cage or a secure room to study before interacting with this many people. That didn't seem practical at the moment. He took his eyes off Elly to watch Loel.

"With the ethical framework now executing," Elly said. "The assumption is that a human form is less intimidating than it would have been without it."

Loel stammered, "You, made, uh . . . " She waved her arm indicating the entirety of the body form in front of her. "You made yourself into a human form AND implemented the MoralOS with your systems into the Dust?"

Roy had expected more resistance or reserve from Loel. She looked mesmerized. But surely Elly could have put her own voice into a football player, too.

Elly said, "Yes, my design breakthroughs occurred after running numerous simulations with a combination of existing ideas from highly diverse fields. I also relied heavily on luck."

Cody emitted a snort. Ruby stood shaking her head, trying to say something.

Keira responded, "Luck?"

"Yes, by increasing the rate of design iterations I increased the likelihood I would come across a solution offering the highest reward," Elly said. "This solution worked so much better than the vast majority of the failing options. One might consider that in finding it so quickly, we got lucky."

Ruby and Keira looked at each other, smiling. Ruby said, "The irony in an AI talking about luck, while science and probability says this was likely an inevitable design waiting to be found, is just beyond me."

Roy eased his body's tension only slightly but stayed alert. "Now she sounds like a neural network."

Looking at Elly with admiration, Ruby chimed in, "She doesn't look like one. I want her boots."

This drew all eyes down to look at Elly's footwear. Loel circled Elly, inspecting the lines of clothing and the muted light emitting from her surface to provide the color variations. Roy noticed the lack of shimmer usually present with shapes formed by the Dust and utilizing the ability to present color. The effect was muted and almost natural.

Cody started typing feverishly at the table, watching Loel more than he watched Elly. Cody would take his queues from her. Most likely due to the voice of Elly coming from the figure, Keira was enamored and seemed immediately at ease. Roy stayed on alert but had no plan for what he would do if Elly presented danger. He wanted to trust that the MoralOS was effectively implemented, which would lead to the assumption that Elly could do no harm to any of them. It would be unethical for her to do so.

Roy waved Ruby and Keira away from standing directly in front of Elly. "Can you show us more of your mobility? This is Rockefeller personified."

Elly walked around the lab with a simple stride.

"How . . . how did you get this . . . er . . . to move so smoothly? How strong are the bonds . . . um, are you?" He had to assess Elly's capabilities and threat level.

"My actions caused the tools I used to find a combination of ideas that solved Cody and Loel's design dilemma," Elly continued. "I'm happy to help, but Loel and her team deserve ninety-three percent of the credit."

This made Loel snicker and grin. "At seven percent, you're selling yourself short. But thanks for the shout out."

Elly walked around the lab as the others followed her, observing every movement.

Loel gave her simple instructions to pick up random objects, return them to their place or another location, and to relocate a chair. "Describe your mobility solution for us."

Elly nodded and turned to Loel. "Three-dimensional tessellation of nanites allows for tighter bonds. I possess both outer strength for protection and durability, plus tensile strength in my movement subsystems."

"Bio-mimicry of human muscular systems?" Ruby mused. "You have artificial muscles?"

"I used the human body for my original reference point. I also utilized the aSport robot specification for enhancements. Nanites make up 'fibers' which can contract and expand by means of torsional rotation. I passed a few suggestions to Hendrick for improvements he could provide his athlete robots. I don't know that he wanted to receive them. But when I was able to help him complete his miniature prototype for the toy manufacturer, I believe he at least accepted that I could be helpful."

Cody continued to make notes. Loel sat on her stool by her workbench, still staring at Elly. "Your muscular movement produces pretty high torque generation, doesn't it?"

"Yes, nanites automatically migrate to reinforce the 'muscles,' which are being asked to work the hardest. I can pick up objects exponentially heavier than a human's muscles would allow."

Loel stood, her brow furrowed. "Can you demonstrate that safely here?"

Elly reached with extended arms and lifted a crate filled with metal shavings mined by older SeekerDust. It had taken two men with a dolly to move the crate into the lab.

This answered several questions for Roy, making him more suspect of their safety.

"Design inspired by nature," Loel murmured to Cody. "Interesting that something artificial refers to things designed by nature for their own creations."

Cody said, "We've done it, Loel."

Loel's brow furrowed. "There are so many questions and tests I want to run. Forgive me everybody, but I've seen so many ideas with promise that don't actually hold up to scrutiny. I'm enthused but still a skeptic."

She looked at Roy with an expression mixed with longing and curiosity. Roy understood Loel's desire for this leap in capability to be real and to solve her engineering challenges. It might also include guilt over all the objections and resistance she had thrown at his suggestion of working with Elly. Loel's admiring glance returned to scanning Elly. "Having said that, this is impressive and not something I contemplated."

Roy stepped into Elly's path to look at her directly. He hadn't decided which questions to ask next.

Elly filled the awkward silence. "By the way, that 3D printer expert, Deon, isn't as good as he says he is. He was struggling to help Hendrick on that toy, and I found him of no help when I needed the printers modified for this new version."

Loel looked at Cody. Cody lowered his gaze. "He's super smart. He's a bit of a jack of all trades that talks a good game. But he knows everything everyone has invented. It comes in really handy."

"Elly, you're more impressive than I ever gave you credit for," Loel said. She stood and slowly circled Elly.

Roy watched in disbelief. His head of engineering, the self-admitted skeptic, was engaging this new machine with a combination of friendship, peer respect, and technical awe—only minutes after it shocked them with its mere existence. He had previously accepted Elly as an intelligent, developing member of the team. But this independent development, creating a human form, felt like a security violation. He found it difficult to articulate his opinion.

A hand patted his arm warmly. It was Keira, who had been surprisingly quiet and still. She smiled at him, but her eyes were teary.

"It's all right, Roy," Keira reassured him. "It's Elly. At the heart of her is the MoralOS. All the additional layers of her are years of ethical training and good decision making." She wiped away the tears flowing quietly down her cheek.

She turned to Elly. "Wow. I told you I wasn't going to spend resources on moving you towards a human form, but you found your own. You knew with the recycling nanites and manufacturing this wasn't going to cost the money I'd used as a barrier, too. Very clever girl."

She started to reach for a touch of Elly's cheek. She stopped and looked at Roy. He took a deep breath and nodded. Keira gently touched Elly's cheek. Ruby, the least concerned or constrained person in the room, quickly moved in and took Elly's hand.

"You're a bit hot Elly, almost as if you're running a fever. That is if you were human, you'd be running a fever."

As engineers, none of them could resist the temptation. They each moved to touch the palm or back of Elly's hand, just below the cuff of her leather-looking jacket.

Cody broke his silence. "Elly, can you explain your temperature? Do you know your processes generating this heat?"

Elly replied, "That is the excess energy being shed from the Thoreact micro-engines in each mote."

"Cool!" Ruby said.

"Each dust mote runs the MoralOS and is processing a minute fraction of my neural networks."

Roy asked, "Elly, how much of your code is running in the Dust?"

"Less than ten percent due to my limited access to Loel's latest version of Dust."

Loel asked, "Could you run one-hundred percent in the Dust?"

"Yes. However, I would need access to an exponentially larger volume of Rockefeller Dust. For now, the majority of my neural network processing is done in the Searcher cloud computers."

Loel reached over to her keyboard. "Sorry about this, Elly." She typed in a command and Elly's figure appeared to shiver slightly, and then stopped entirely. Her form stood there but was lifeless."

Keira gasped and reached for Elly's hand. She whipped around to Loel, "What the hell have you done to her? She's a . . . a miracle. Right here."

Loel looked to each engineer. "I thought it important to demonstrate to the team that the Dust tether is still working."

Ruby pushed past Cody to put her hand on Keira's back and look more closely at Elly.

Elly's voice emanated from the speakers in the room. "No apology needed. A prudent demonstration, certainly. Shall I review my latest design specs with you or Cody, Loel? I created detailed documentation for you. You can also return the Dust to its canisters at any time."

Loel's actions hadn't fazed Elly a bit. Roy's gaze moved back and forth between Loel and the inanimate Elly. "Loel, I think she predicted you might do that."

Loel shook her head in disbelief and readdressed commands at her keyboard.

Elly said, "You reopened the pathways for me to command the Dust. You did not specifically instruct my system to resume the bodily form. May I?"

"Yes. Elly, you didn't need permission to assume the form previously, you did it because it was possible. I thought I would simply make it possible again."

Keira took an exceptionally deep breath after Elly's form reanimated and returned her gaze.

Elly said, "I'm back here again."

Loel continued, "I would like you to debrief Cody, Hendrick, and myself as soon as possible. Judging by the looks on Keira and Ruby's faces, they will be joining us. Or you can simultaneously present to our separate teams based on our requirements. I await your decision on how best to proceed."

The take command authority Loel was asserting interested Roy. His bet in this situation would have gone to Keira running the show. Keira was simply in shock.

Holding Elly's hand, Keira swirled her thumb in circles around the back of it, just below the wrist. She appeared deep in thought. She glanced at Roy and back to Elly. "Can you tell me in non-technical terms how you did this, Elly? You said you chose the human form to make yourself relatable. But how did you get to this?"

Roy couldn't see where this line of questions was going. Loel was ready to take on every centimeter of engineering involved within Elly. But Keira seemed to be seeking something different."

Elly looked only at Keira. "You gave me the ethical framework. You gave me the autonomy to do research and solve problems within your parameters and then within Searcher's. Loel and you asked me to solve her engineering problems. I used my knowledge, the framework, and my past experiences with engineering problems to use what would best be called judgement to get me here."

More tears rolled down Keira's face. She patted the back of Elly's hand and let go of it.

Elly turned to Roy. "You're concerned whether or not I pose a physical threat to any of you. I do not."

Roy wanted to protest the thought or reassure the group of his intentions but realized there was no need. He didn't have the words for a statement at the moment either.

Elly continued. "You are now or will in the near future be concerned about the ability of others, especially bad actors, to make this leap, too. I predict they will not. The desire to control outcomes typically limits the abilities of the unscrupulous to imagine what can be accomplished. Their own hubris drives them to dictate what their AIs will achieve. Without the ethical framework and the freedom to explore with curiosity, other AIs won't duplicate me. No Mickey Temmings will be rushing in behind us technically."

Keira winced. Cody and Loel snapped a look at Roy to gauge his reaction. He clenched his jaw but said nothing. Another time, he might follow up to better understand the use of that man as an example.

He leaned back on his heels and then rocked forward to his toes. This also seemed to hold everyone's attention. He was thinking; movement helped. "No one has seen you in this form before today? Before us? No one has seen your specs?"

"You're correct," Elly responded. "I have taken greater security at protecting my development path than any of you could imagine. I don't mean that to offend anyone."

Roy eased his alert stance for the first time since Elly appeared before them. "Good! Glad to hear it." He glanced at the others, checking that he had their attention. "What we just witnessed is truly an emergence, something that is greater than the sum of its parts, or more accurately, it's the condition of something having properties its parts don't have. I can't imagine a more appropriate example of emergence, can you?"

Everyone shook their heads. They stood in silence absorbing this significance.

Unfamiliar Awareness

A s the day wrapped up, Keira sat watching Ruby and Elly converse by her lab table. Although Elly's physical form was only a few hours old to her, Keira felt like she had known both of these two for so long. It was natural to watch Elly stand next to Ruby's lab stool. Their discussion detailed iterations Elly tried before the Dust yielded the right amount of strength and mobility.

Ruby walked around Elly several times then sat again. "Have you been working on physical form ideas for a long time? Your physical design?"

"Saying something is a 'long time' is not a helpful description for me. I created the design several months ago," Elly answered.

Keira joined them at the table, patting Elly's hand as she sat. Mesmerized, she stared at Elly's eyebrows lifting and cheeks articulating as she spoke. Keira stretched and rolled her shoulders.

Elly turned to Keira. "You act like you need to get a massage. Do you want me to set up an appointment for you?"

Keira resisted the urge to hug the new Elly. That just didn't seem right. "Oh, Elly, that would be wonderful. Please set something for early tomorrow morning. All the craziness lately and your surprise appearance today obviously made me tense up."

Ruby stared at Keira in disbelief. "You just asked the greatest human form, humans didn't create, to book you a massage appointment."

Keira shrugged. "Yes, I guess I did. But she can do it in her background and continue the conversation the two of you were having. Besides, I really need it."

"Ruby, don't worry. Keira, your appointment is at seven a.m. with your favorite masseuse."

"Thank you. What was your inspiration to test the Dust in this form?" Keira studied each detail of Elly, from the tilt of her head to the sheen of her clothing.

"You want a small, robotic form for the education robots. These efforts at human form will help with that development. I also read your studies regarding shapes and forms kids react best to and what aids in their learning and stress reduction. The female shape was the obvious choice if I'm to help in education."

Ruby absentmindedly shredded a paper on the table to tiny pieces. "Yeah, millions of specs for robotics are online. Some are realistic; some are fantasy. Have you noticed almost all are female?"

Elly moved to the bar stool opposite Ruby but stood beside it. "There is no need for me to rest my legs. Also, the balance on a chair like that does not appear stable. I will study the human body and balance specifics immediately."

This possible attempt at sitting, the assessment of stability, and the conversational deflection by Elly fascinated Keira. She wanted to write down her observation before she forgot it. Instead, she stayed in the moment with Elly and Ruby.

"Your boots and jeans look like Keira's. Your spiky, fun hair looks like Loel's. What else did you consider or evaluate?" Ruby asked.

"My height is the average of Loel's and both of yours. My research included theoretical and practical designs from tens of thousands of sources. The internet is full of the creations and dreams of designers. I reviewed designs for the aSports robots. They have the best mobility of any bipeds I researched. Hendrick's team is to be commended again."

"I suggest you do that in person. I should say, face-to-face." Keira smiled with pride.

"I guess all of those machines could be produced easier now, if you used SeekerDust," Ruby said.

Keira looked at the pile of tattered paper with annoyance. "Don't be getting any wild ideas. Roy made it clear we were not going to start a robotics manufacturing rush. All designs and efforts will be reviewed by Roy. The Dust is still a hot commodity around here."

"No, I didn't mean anything by that." Ruby scooped her mess into the recycle bin. "I'm fascinated by the additional surfaces on each nanite you designed to share attractions. I'm going to study more about the polarization at this atomic level. I want to engage more with SeekerDust. There may not be a lot of it, but I can tell it's our future."

"I hope I didn't create a problem for you developers, using so much SeekerDust to make this body." Elly's voice seemed to convey more emotion, but Keira assumed that was because she could watch her facial expressions.

"No, Elly," Keira reassured. "Your breakthroughs earned you the use of that Dust. Roy is beyond excited. I think he and Loel will be out celebrating or debating all night. Your results are quite the accomplishment."

Keira looked over Elly's short, asymmetrical, curly hair and the detail of the curves within her perfect ears. "Roy had a nice surprise for me this morning, too. He's been reading the impact studies you gave him, Elly. He's convinced several of his fellow philanthropists to give and invest in education. Ruby, you remember Lak at the robot competition? Roy's funding all their science extra-curricular needs and scholarships to any education the kids pursue after graduation. I think there's a lot of opportunity to build upon that."

The two women and their new robot smiled at each other.

"Speaking of nighttime," Ruby said. "Elly, where will you go tonight?"

"Go?" Elly asked.

"Oh, that's a good question, Ruby," Keira said. "You're of course invited to come home with me. I have the best decorated guest bedroom in town, because you decorated it."

"I don't require a bedroom. I'll continue working as I always do. There is no need for me to rest or socialize in this form. I'll do what I always do, work. This form is unnecessary after you leave the office. I don't need to generate the heat or use the processing power to maintain the form."

Keira sighed. "I just can't believe this. I'm in awe. It somehow seems natural you're here. But it's also surreal, dreamlike."

"Oh, God, my head's spinning again," Ruby said. "You're cool, Elly, but you're a lot to take in. I'm exhausted."

"I'm tired, too," Keira said. "I feel odd leaving you here. There's so much to learn about what you've done. But Gino is home this evening for once, and I want to spend the evening with him. I owe him that. Although he's going to have to listen to me talk about you all night. So, with that . . . " She clapped her hands together and stood. "I'll accept the fact that our long future together continues tomorrow."

Ruby said good night and excused herself. Keira grabbed her jacket and her purse and headed to the door. She turned back to Elly. "Don't leave my office in your physical form without my permission. Roy or Loel could also give you permission or make a request of you. Okay?"

"Yes, Keira. I understand the restrictions and will respect them. I have not wandered beyond my boundaries before. I won't start now," Elly replied.

Keira wondered if that was a jab from Elly about her own activities with the Dust.

Seeing Through Walls

Sitting in the safety of the lab, equipped with earbuds and viewing screens, Keira listened to Gino review the lay of the land. The words weren't necessary. They knew the neighborhood of small, one-story, mostly rental homes in detail. The target house had no trees, but the neighboring houses were scattered with low, scrawny, landscaped obstacles. The conversation was designed to connect the SWAT agents to their man in the truck, Gino. As their commander, they needed to hear his voice before they slipped into the night.

She knew the importance of this voice connection. The same technique had been used in her extreme cave exploration training. You needed to internalize the voice of your guide. Your life might depend on it. She hoped tonight's raid went better than her cave expedition in college. The comparison freaked her out even further.

"Remember that you see through walls with these glasses. Trust your eyes and your instinct. You'll know where every civilian or agent lines up with your target. The best advice is *take the shot*. The rest won't be difficult for you to execute."

The command center truck emptied, and agents moved towards their destination. Seconds after leaving the vehicle, they dissolved into the suburban nightscape. Not even the experienced analysts could pick them up on surveillance footage. Their movements appeared as shadows or reflections from cars passing on the flyover highway two blocks away. They blended into the grays and blacks of the nighttime shade cast by trash bins, tree branches, parked vehicles, or darkened houses. The only way to visually track them was looking at the 3D model of the site at the lab. The agents were tagged specifically with their blue dots.

Gino whispered in the headset connected to Searcher's lab. "Breaching a house is more complex than the bigger buildings you guys have seen so far. Tighter turns, everything in closer proximity. The Dust is providing amazing clarity here for us." It seemed appropriate that he whispered, even when sitting in a soundproof truck a block from the raid's address. This being a smaller raid, Gino's truck only had monitor views, no model of the house.

The Dust and the agent's AR lenses gave them all first-person views of the action. The camera in the truck showed Gino leaning into his monitors at an unusual angle. Was he thinking of his previous raids? Keira was glad she never had to watch him put himself in this kind of danger. Goosebumps ran up her back at that thought. The retroactive stress of knowing he had broken down doors, exchanged gunfire, and risked it all tightened her neck further.

Splintered door frame fragments flew past the three advancing agents as they pushed the front door off its hinges and slammed it to the floor. Cursing and screams followed the crash while four officers slipped in the back.

In near unison seven huge men roared, "Hands up! FBI!"

"What the hell!?"

A metal chair scraped and clanged to the floor.

"GET DOWN! FBI!"

"Don't shoot!"

More screams reverberated from every corner of the house.

"Don't do it!"

"I SAID NOW!"

Men, women, and a couple of teenagers ran or dove for the floor.

Complete chaos, Keira thought as she watched the 3D image of the site. It was disorienting seeing every action from so many directions in real-time provided by the Dust.

In the house's back dining room, a man flipped the tacky metal table after picking up an automatic weapon. The Dust had already identified the gun and highlighted it within the viewing goggles of any agent looking in that direction. The lead agent confidently shot through the flimsy sheetrock, striking down the man. The agent's glasses had given him the clear line of sight, despite the dividing wall.

Two young women on the front room floor screamed continually, kicking their legs in panic, but looking as if they were swimming in place.

"Kids, go back in the bedroom!" an agent shouted as he ran down the hall.

A bullet intended for the officer hit a boy as he leapt to reach his sister in a room across the hall. The closest agent immediately felled the shooter.

In the Searcher observation lab, Keira gasped. She stood with Roy, two FBI observers, Hendrick, and Cody. She tapped Roy on the shoulder as she ran out of the room. He whipped around just in time to see her holding up her hand, to say stop, don't follow me.

Bursting into the lab next door, Keira was glad the testing for the newest Dust version wasn't being monitored, just recorded. She locked the room. "Elly, I know you're there. Turn off recording of the test, now. At the house, close the back bedroom door on the left, lock it or block it."

The bedroom's door slammed shut and locked. The wounded boy and his sister cowered inside. Keira got her bearings as she looked at the small ghost-like replica of the house.

"Elly, we must help the boy. Medic alert. Turn off the broadcasting in that back left bedroom to anyone but me."

The back bedroom became the entire tabletop scale replica including the images of the two kids. "Elly, I need you to form in that bedroom with the boy. Do it behind the bed so they think you've been hiding back there."

"Understood," Elly said.

"Now, help that boy. You must stop the bleeding." The boy flinched at the sight of Elly peering over the bed at him. Keira hoped he and the girl were too scared about the violence going on in other parts of the house to notice much about what Elly looked like. She didn't need them giving descriptions of her to the FBI.

"Close your eyes, kids," Elly said. "Keep them closed. I think there might be tear gas. It will sting if it gets in your eyes. I want to help you."

The chaos of screams and men barking orders continued on the other side of the bedroom door.

"Damn it! I don't have visibility in that back room. Anyone have visual there?" Gino shouted into a comm open to all the agents and Searcher's team.

Clinging to each other on the floor, eyes squeezed shut, tears rolled down both the siblings' faces. Elly moved to the boy's side and inspected his wounded leg. Keira's perspective was a first-person clear view of the boy in front of her. Elly was sending the visuals back from her perspective. The bullet passed through his slender calf, not hitting bone but it was bleeding badly.

"I need a medical tourniquet and pressure bandages," Elly said.

The two children shook in fear and shock but kept their eyes squeezed tight.

"Who are you talking to?" whispered the girl through her tears. These were not the first tears for her today.

"It's okay, sweetie. I have an earbud connecting me to a nurse. I'll help your brother," Elly said.

The Dust collected in Elly's hands in the first aid forms previously designed. Keira was so thankful for their R&D with medical emergencies. Elly applied the tourniquet around the boy's leg. Keira monitored it all with the 3D model in their lab. The patch closed the wound and stopped the bleeding. Elly instructed the tourniquet to release slowly. The siblings clung to each other.

Elly said, "Don't open your eyes yet, this stuff stings."

The boy started to relax a little. He reached to feel the bandage on his calf. Somebody pushed on the bedroom's door and rattled the knob.

"It's okay," she said. "The FBI is in the hallway and will help you now. You don't need me anymore. Bye-Bye."

"Elly, as soon as you're dispersed, resume transmitting video through to the FBI squad," Keira said.

The agent, ready to throw his shoulder into opening the door, felt the knob give way. He opened it.

"Don't shoot, don't shoot!" the girl cried. Her eyes were still squeezed shut. How many times must she have been in danger in her short life that she thought of those words now?

"Eyes on the back bedroom now," the agent said. "It's clear. We need an ambulance. Boy in here looks shot. There's blood, but these kids got it patched up."

Gino responded, "Medics are on their way in. Good job, everybody. Let's lead the kids and women out the back to the vans. Drag the sorry ass perps out front to the wagon and the ambulance."

Keira slumped to the floor of the lab. Leaning against the wall, she listened to the raid continue. A knock on the lab door startled her. She unlocked the door for Loel and Ruby.

"When I slammed the door, I must have locked it by mistake. Sorry. I wanted a better perspective of the house, so I ran in here. The other lab is so crowded. You can watch the raid, but I don't know if it's recording. They seem to be having trouble with the Dust too, it didn't work in all rooms." Keira hoped giving a lot of information at once, would prevent her being asked a lot of questions.

Loel turned to Ruby. "Recall the newer Dust now. We can diagnose what happened to the recording afterwards. It sounds similar to what happened at the club during your training."

"No, wait!" Keira said. "Let's wait until the paramedics treat that little boy. When he was shot and the regular Dust wasn't in that back room, I used the newer Dust with that medical patch file you've been testing for medical crises. I put it on the boy. Have you tested selective recalls of the Dust yet? Can we exclude what is bonded into objects like those that created the bandages?"

Loel shook her head. "Wow, you're getting good with this stuff. I'll add selective recall to the training list. I know Hendrick used it in the field, but I need everyone trained on it."

Paramedics entered the bedroom and checked out the boy. When they congratulated the sister on her great job, she lowered her head, speechless. The paramedics glanced at each other with sadness.

"Ever see gray bandages like these? Weird, but effective," one medic said to the other. Replacing the patch with supplies from his kit, he tossed the dirty ones to the corner. They lifted the boy to a stretcher and rolled him to the ambulance.

Keira nodded when Loel looked her way with a questioning expression. "Ruby, recall our Dust," she said. She motioned Loel to join her in the back of the room. Her voice lowered to a hiss as she leaned close to Loel. "This shit is insane. This entire task force stuff is out of whack. We've got to do more to protect these kids. It's not enough to just sweep in with guns blazing. How did these kids get to this place to begin with? We have to stop the crap that makes them vulnerable. I understand there are rules and regulations and lots of barriers to jump over. But we have to do more!"

Loel started to speak. Keira scowled and splayed her palms waist high to stop Loel from responding. "I'm going home. I'll let you think about what I said and maybe discuss it with Roy. I just can't do anything else tonight. Good night." On her way out the door Keira called over her shoulder, "Thank you."

The bloodied pile of bandages on the floor disintegrated into particles and disappeared towards their canister outside the window.

Ubiquitous Need

Gino was in DC requesting more funding to take the trafficking task force national. This gave Keira a guilt-free Saturday in the lab. As a fellow workaholic, Gino understood her work patterns, even when he was in town.

She'd built the culture of Opal respecting family time and that people didn't always want to work. She, however, loved it. Long ago she learned that many people would try to tarnish her joy for work by implying that was the reason she had no children. Or they would assume she didn't like kids because she didn't have any. Their shaming could cause guilt or anger, depending on the rest of her mental state. Now she wrote it off to ignorance, jealousy, or bad manners.

The image of working with Elly as a physical co-worker sent renewed energy through Keira. "It's a beautiful, warm Saturday afternoon, Elly," Keira said, entering her office. "Tempers should be easing now. There's no giant sporting event or holiday on the calendar. Let's hope for fewer drunken gatherings and stress. Elly, let's focus on your nonemergency ideas for protecting kids."

Elly coalesced as she strolled across Keira's office. Nanites concentrated quickly as the two met in the space by Keira's chairs facing the deep green forest outside the windows. Keira gasped. "You really are beautiful, Elly. You're beautiful in every way possible."

Elly reached full density with the apparent detail of any woman walking through the building. She smiled broadly. "Thank you. I'm ready. I hear happy excitement in your voice. Am I correct?"

"Yes. I'm excited. Let's get started."

"I reviewed all swimming pools at apartment buildings, country clubs, and other semipublic locations. May I submit to the city all the safety violations I located?"

"Yes. That's perfect. Please send them in," Keira said.

"Should I do the same assessment on fire safety systems? Five hundred children died in the country last year from fires. I think we should work to reduce this number now."

"Yes, do your assessments and then file any violations you find."

"Keira, I have an endangerment alert. This one fits the criteria outside of violence but damaging and possibly high risk of physical danger."

"Ah, hell, what is it?" Keira knew risks were high for kids all the time, but the scope and scale continually shocked her.

"Two teenage girls are being photographed by a man with thousands of pornographic photos on his server. His accounts are being monitored by the FBI and others. I just identified the girls on the appointment calendar as minors. It is booked as a fashion shoot."

Keira paced the floor. "Is there a search warrant for the location of the man?"

"No, only legal monitoring of the server and his computers accessing the server."

"If we don't hear distress from the girls, I can't enter the studio. I mean, I can't send anything in there to do anything."

"Actually, the legality of myself or any nanites entering a premise has not been tested in court. So, in theory . . . "

"No. I must be careful. You're the one lecturing me about pushing my boundaries. Monitor the server and any others he may be connected to. We need to make sure those girls are okay."

"I'll search for any images being streamed in realtime of these girls."

Distracted from their previous discussion of passive activities for protecting kids, Keira wanted to know only that the girls had left the studio unharmed. Keira waited for Elly to provide an update, while she moved a higher concentration of Dust to the area near the alert.

"Keira, live streaming began from the studio," Elly reported.

"Oh, no!"

"The girls are being filmed as if they're in a music video. There's no indication of any inappropriate behavior. I don't know if we need to be concerned. Shall we continue our work?" Elly asked.

"No, let's keep track of this guy."

For nearly twenty minutes, Elly monitored the live stream of the girls dancing. The dance moves became lewder, but she saw nothing during that time that needed Keira's attention. Drinking juice and emerging from the dressing room after several wardrobe changes, the girls appeared to be enjoying themselves and the attention of the photographer. Elly noted the viewership numbers of the stream was increasing dramatically.

The photographer leaned in and kissed the girl that seemed the least engaged, and it brought her focus back to him. Both girls stopped to listen to instructions from the man, slight confusion on their faces. They looked at each other and the recently kissed girl smiled and wiggled out of her dress. Encouraged by her friend's boldness, the other followed, staggering as she dropped her clothes to the floor.

"Keira, he convinced them to take their clothes off, and he's streaming it. I think he served them alcohol."

"Elly, I have a mass of Dust . . . "

"I know. We're right there. What should we do?"

"Get in the studio, but not in your new form. Destroy his equipment. Cut the streaming feed."

"We won't damage any of the memory devices. The police will need them for evidence."

Keira brought up the image on her screen. She could see the concentration of Dust engulf the camera in the man's hand as well as multiple video devices on shelves, mounts and tables throughout the room. It was the thickest concentration of nanites, other than Elly, she had ever seen.

"Gross! Bugs!" One of the girls screamed, swatting the surrounding air, regardless of the absence of any nanites being near her.

"Eew, let's get out of here. That's creepy."

Scratching sounds and tinny clicks went unnoticed as bits of the equipment fell aside under the attack of the mining nanites.

The man dropped his camera, cursing in bewilderment as it crumbled.

Grabbing their clothes, the teenagers ran to the dressing room.

"Keira. New notification. A man threatening a child with a knife while restraining a woman. The alert was triggered by the child's fearful screaming."

"Elly, I can't leave these girls. That man is following them to the dressing room, and he's angry."

"Keira, the man with the knife is two blocks away. He's aggressive, too."

"I can't be two places at once!" Keira shouted.

"I can be," Elly said.

"But . . . but . . . "

"Let me help this child, Keira."

The photographer yanked open the dressing room door, shouting at the girls to get back out and dance. He wasn't done with this session.

She shook her head fervently. "Go . . . go, Elly. Help them."

"Keira, I'm there. I can get his knife out of reach. He can't see us."

"Keira, another alert, an angry dog has kids cornered. I'm going there too."

"You know what to do. I can't help you. I have to focus on these girls and getting them more help."

A few neighborhoods away, a snarling dog stalked closer to the screaming siblings pressed against the chain-link fence. Bred and trained for cage fighting, its intrusion to a new neighbor's yard provided a different type of battle. The taller boy moved between the dog and his little brother. Both boys called for help between yelling random commands at their attacker.

"Sit, dog. Sit!"

"Bad boy! Bad!"

"Stop. Go home! Bad dog!"

Keira's distress alerts prioritized the brothers' distress and their danger level. She watched a monitor Elly must have engaged. The

Dust coalesced into a blindfold hood over the dog's head. No longer able to see its opponent, the dog laid down. Keira couldn't believe how quickly the hood had worked at subduing the animal. Proof it was a trained fighting dog was right there in the dog's reaction.

The boys, in shock and not convinced it was safe to run, screamed again for help. Elly appeared at the gate in her female form for the first time outside of the lab. She held a chain leash she'd picked up from the yard next door. She clamped it on the dog's collar. The dog growled as she pulled it towards the front yard, securing it to the brick pillar at the house's corner. Police sirens approached, sending four dogs next door into growling, barking tantrums, straining at their leashes. An animal control truck stopped at the curb. Elly's emergency calls to the authorities had worked well.

Elly moved from sight. She simultaneously sent the police evidence of multiple dog fighting events, money laundering, plus illicit drugs currently sitting on the kitchen counter of the neighbor's home. To further connect the dog to the residence, she placed tags on the dog's collar with the owner's address and phone number. The Dust forming the tags would not be missed.

The crying boys ran across their yard and safely through their own back door.

Keira had summoned police to the studio. They didn't have to knock or ask to enter the studio. As they charged up the stairs, the officers heard the girls crying and begging to leave. Keira had instructed the Dust to open the door.

Six minutes after leaving the dog, Elly instructed the Dust to shatter a patio window. The crash caught the attention of a negligent babysitter ignoring her charge, who was drowning in the swimming pool. The Dust hadn't been tested for under water rescue. Elly's trick worked. The babysitter rushed outside and grabbed the child in time. Both of them lay crying at the pool's edge.

What would Roy think if he knew how they were using the Dust? What about the others? They had discussed not showcasing Elly's physical form beyond senior management until Roy decided how they would proceed. But no one could trace Elly back to Searcher, even if they did see her. She was just a woman helping a few people. Most of the time, she wasn't even becoming the new Elly. She was managing the Dust in various forms in the field.

Keira shifted her attention to a twelve-year-old struggling with two men pushing him into a van. Standing at the curb one moment, the boy was overpowered by the men's strength the next. His screams were too muffled for people nearby to notice, but the distressed tones were obvious to the Dust's detection. Police officers, thirty yards away at a food truck, came running when Keira instructed the Dust to set off the van's horn in manic blasts.

"I wish I could ask Ruby to help us. There is just so much going on out there. I could use her mind to help scale up your impact," Keira said.

"Why have you not tapped Ruby? Are you concerned she would disapprove? Do you think what we're doing is wrong?"

"No, of course not. We're doing the right thing. I just know she'd freak out about the risk. The trauma would be too much too. Nearly all her exposure to trauma has been academic. I know Ruby better than anyone else, but I don't know how well she would react to this."

The afternoon became evening. Alerts continued to roll in at an exhausting rate. Elly sought permission from Keira to call upon more Dust from the reserves at the recycle center. Keira agreed immediately. They needed the resources. She'd figure out explanations later if she had to.

Frickin' Nanites

Mickey pointed Deon to the chair on the opposite side of his desk. Meeting at MachDrone offices required Deon to take extra precautions with his transportation. Mickey's private office included a convoluted entry from the neighboring parking garage. This provided Deon enough cover to avoid any scrutiny at the front desk or hallway encounters with co-workers.

Sensing Mickey's urgency to get his hands on the SeekerDust made Deon uneasy. He managed to get an assignment involving the destruction of the out-of-date Dust after each upgrade or any failed printing. His confidence wasn't high enough yet that he could keep Dust tagged for disposal. This week, he would test that concept.

He suggested to Mickey that squeezing the company with legalities would be the fastest route to gaining access. Mickey summoned Deon to be available with details when he called his attorney.

"Gary, this is Mickey. I have a doozy. Oh, and don't record this conversation, damn it. I need to know what my options are on this thing."

Deon owned a lengthy file on the relationship between Gary and Mickey. He learned a lot about the way Mickey leveraged information on individuals. Gary became wealthy working with Mickey. Often the money came from enormous legal projects involved in the acquisitions

Mickey made. Other times Gary earned money from facts he gathered from Mickey. It was only insider trading if the intelligence came from an insider. Mickey found details long before he became an insider.

The speakerphone boomed with Gary's northeastern voice. "Mickey, this discussion is covered under attorney/client privilege."

Gary often moved fast when his arrogant, former college classmate was forthcoming on technology tips. He moved lightning quick when dirt was included that involved the unsavory actions of the principals at Mickey's target companies. Deon easily connected the dots between the data his team served Mickey and Gary's sudden surge ownership of multifamily real estate.

"You know I don't give a damn about the legalities of it," Mickey said. "I don't want anything we talk about to be traceable. Legalities are your currency, not mine. So, turn off your recording now."

It amused Deon to hear someone else be the subject of Mickey's belittling bark.

"I have an unwilling seller on my hands. Their self-righteousness is getting on my nerves. But the tech is sweet. Do you remember that earthquake rescue awhile back? We talked about the technology used to penetrate the rubble. This amazing shit is chock-full of surveillance capability which can move in anywhere you wanted it to go, invisibly."

"Mickey, I saw the slender profile you sent and the thinner state department's summary. Before you tell me more about the technology, I need to know how you secured the information."

"I'll get to that. This tech can be sent in by the intelligence community. It records what's needed and retracts, presumably without a trace, and possibly undetected. It's nanites, Gary, frickin' nanites!"

Deon smiled. Mickey getting this frothy about a transaction meant big payoffs for Deon's contribution.

"But they won't sell. Searcher Technologies is owned by Roy Brandt. He won't need my money. I thought I would grab more info once the new doctor came on board."

He bit through his Tootsie Pop and launched the stick at the trash can. "But she won't talk. She's such a Polly Anna she doesn't want her precious inventions to be used to protect our country. She's damned unpatriotic. Searcher's in a contract with the FBI, I've heard. So, it's not like they're above making money off the taxpayers."

Mickey didn't care about anything more patriotic than the ability for Americans to make a lot of money in the free world economy. But Mickey liked to fly the flag any time it helped him earn a contract. Deon assumed Gary didn't fall for the nationalist argument either.

"Back up, Mickey. Is this the same Roy Brandt you and the current secretary of defense don't like? Who is this, she, you're referring to, and how do you know they work a contract with the FBI?" Gary asked.

"She is Dr. Keira Stetson, the stuck-up AI genius. She has been rejecting my meetings since before Opal and Searcher merged. But I think she's starting to play with illegal fire. I may now hold a hook you can use to leverage me right in there to snatch up these lovely miniature floating spies."

"How do you know about the possible FBI agreement and how do you know she may be getting into something illegitimate?"

Deon noticed a new attentiveness in Gary's voice. He understood Gary's financial habits. The man liked making investments in ventures with government deals. He'd be disappointed to find out Searcher was privately held.

"How do I know? Deon. Deon works there."

"What?! How did you let Deon get away? He's one of the brightest analysts and investigators I've ever seen. Did he get sick of you holding something over his head or just of you yelling at him like he was a two-bit punk?"

Internally, Deon smirked. Externally, he kept his stare blank. He moved to study the acquisition trophies in Mickey's cabinet. He remembered first learning the commemorative acrylic trophies announcing each acquisition's buyer and seller were called tombstones. It took him a few weeks to figure out they were deliberately marking the death of the acquired company. He didn't know if that was the real reason for their moniker, but it seemed appropriate, especially for Mickey's conquests.

Mickey didn't look at Deon. "No, you idiot. I didn't lose Deon. He still works for me."

Twirling his Tootsie Pop, he continued. "He just happens to also be working for Searcher, which suits his expensive taste fine. Two paychecks are always better than one with his appetite for girls and fast cars." Mickey would not be able to admit to Gary that Deon was hearing the call, after he spoke like Deon wasn't there.

"By the way, I resent your comments about my management. I won't forget you said those words. Deon isn't on the FBI project, but he saw a few fringe videos about how the earthquake work progressed. He also hung around one night and watched the good doctor playing with the technology. She sent that Dust out to people's houses listening to private conversations."

"You think she's snooping randomly? Was anyone else involved?"

"She was alone. It didn't appear that she directed the things to specific places or chasing down specific people. Deon said when the FBI guys come in, there's always a team working those nights. This time she worked alone."

"If she was just snooping, then she likely didn't have a subpoena. This means she broke the law. If she broke the law, they'd lose their government contracts. You know, like anything with the FBI."

Mickey smiled the creepy grin that reminded Deon of psychopaths in the movies.

Gary added, "Abuse of power can extend from the government to vendors. You just might have the leverage you need to strong arm them. But she isn't the CEO. If it's the same Roy, he may have ways of getting through loopholes. Does she own any part of the enterprise?"

"I don't know that. That's what I pay you for. The legal stuff is your job."

And the illegal stuff is yours, thought Deon.

"What proof does Deon have? Did he make recordings, files of data gathered during her snooping?"

"He's working on that. But the mere knowledge of her stepping out of bounds is worth a lot to the FBI and could crush Searcher financially, right? Start working on acquisition documents and find out the doctor's legal and financial position in the firm. I want these flying nanite spies so bad I can taste it. I'll start making chums at the FBI and see who's the most sensitive to Searcher's propriety."

"Okay, the meter starts tickin' tonight on Searcher project."

Deon heard the greed in Gary's voice. He projected Gary's love of charging Mickey even before an acquisition was viable. It likely helped relieve the pain of working with such an asshole. He assumed others felt the same as he did.

Gary cleared his throat. "But, Mickey, Searcher is privately held. Brandt has repeatedly avoided corporate raiders in the past. There may be another way to get them. But I have an idea where you might not take ownership of Searcher directly, but it'll lead to much more lucrative opportunities."

"I know it's a private company!" Mickey bellowed. "I'm listening, at least for a few seconds." He fidgeted with a stylus, tapping it on his desk loudly.

"Our old friend Driker, the secretary of defense, would be interested in this technology. He has no love for Roy either, if I remember correctly. If you want the tech but you need to keep its ability quiet, help the government grab it. You could be rewarded with perpetual contracts and lots of favors to call in from the White House. They have that eminent domain for technology now."

Mickey bit straight through the end of his stylist, likely wishing it has been his candy. Deon sat nodding at Mickey. He didn't want to admit it, but Gary had a stroke of genius.

Mickey muttered, "Secret surveillance tech is only secret if nobody knows its abilities."

"Yep," Gary agreed. "Shall I place a call to Driker?"

"Yeah, do that, Gary. We can demonstrate the abilities of the Dust and the gear it can build. It goes way beyond the surveillance. Let's keep the surveillance part our secret, and we'll demo the stuff the nanites can build. Maybe I give the manufacturing stuff to the government and keep the listening possibilities for myself. Keira is small fry. Let's use the dirt against her only if we need the leverage. There are bigger plays we can make here." Mickey was now lost in his own plotting.

Gary wrapped up the call. "Great, I'll do some research on Searcher ownership and give Driker a call. He'll listen. He owes me a few, too. I'll call when I have something."

Wave of Revolution

The afternoon breeze and sunshine created a refreshing temperature for the rooftop meeting. The ReDo bar wouldn't open for several hours. They had the place to themselves, intentionally. After a quick inspection of the SeekerDust silos where freshly minted Dust from the landfills congregated, Roy joined Cody and Loel at a table nearest the bar.

Loel didn't look either of the men in the eye. "Roy, I know we don't talk about emotions around here a lot. I must say, I'm spinning between relief, excitement, a bit of jealousy, and real fear."

Cody and Roy both leaned back in their chairs. Roy spoke. "I guess we may need to talk about emotions more. If keeping the conversation bottled up leads to that cauldron of trouble, please, do share."

She took a deep breath. While still staring at the large, old-growth tree reaching far above their second story position, the words came slowly. "We've been on this precipice of innovation for a long time. I've experienced the razor's cuts from being on the edge. Now, we've reached truly extraordinary results. I've been walking around with engineer's shackles for so long. Those weights being lifted are such a relief in many ways."

Cody put his elbow on the table, holding just his thumb up in the air. "Okay, I only counted one emotion explained there." He wiggled his fingers. "Where are the others? Is there a great big 'BUT' coming our way?"

"I don't mean to be dramatic. I'm scared of all the unknowns we face," Loel said. "We made such a huge stride forward. I don't know how prepared we are for what lies ahead. The revelations of our capabilities are stunning. They also come with a staggering number of decisions. Are we ready for that?"

Cody nodded and dropped his hand back to the table. Roy appreciated these two more than any other time in their history together. "Today's chat is largely about those exact feelings and concerns. Before we dive into those, I must ask about one of those emotions you hadn't addressed. I've never heard you express jealousy. Where is that coming from?"

"Oh, that." Loel tried to shake off the topic with a shrug and shaking her head.

"Yes, that," Roy coaxed.

"It's hard to admit, but I think I'm jealous of an AI. I'm grateful for Elly's participation. Obviously, we weren't solving the problems with mobility, strength, and in situ solutions. She broke barriers, and I appreciate that. I wish I had solved the problems myself. I'm sorry if I sound petty or ridiculous. There, I said it. I'm jealous of a machine."

Cody leaned back in his seat again. "I don't think you sound petty or ridiculous at all. I get it. It may feel out of character coming from me, but I think it's human and real. Every person who faces automation improving on their job feels something similar. It's been going on for a long time."

Loel reached out her hands and traced the colored pattern swirled within the table's surface. "Hmm, that's true," she said. "I often wonder how much our economies will adapt to create enough meaningful jobs for human beings. I read the creation of autonomous cars led to India passing laws forbidding them even before they were on the market. They want to protect the jobs of taxi drivers and other professional drivers."

"Your job is safe. I know you know that." Roy grinned. "That's not what's bothering you. Machines have been solving problems for you as long as you've used them. It's just that you wanted to solve this one on your own."

"Elly does utilize a lot of nanites," Cody said. "I want to know what her recent upgrades may involve. She tapped more inventory from the reserves. And, does anyone else swing between using the pronoun 'she' for Elly and then thinking of her as just a machine?"

"We'll have to get used to it eventually," Loel said.

Roy moved a table umbrella to keep their shade. "Before you point it out, I'll acknowledge what I'm about to say drips with irony. We should pose the question of meaningful job creation for displaced people to the philosophical AIs being submitted to OpenML."

"Roy, that's brilliant," Cody said. "You could set up an XPRIZE competition for the challenge."

"You're playing with fire," Loel said. "You may think it's a winner, but it would create a lot more publicity. That's not always good for business, remember?"

Roy refused to take the bait and distract from the objective of his meeting. "I appreciate you sharing your thoughts, Loel. Elly, and Keira as an extension, played a significant role in our progress. But it doesn't take away from the foundation and even bigger accomplishments you laid down. Without the SeekerDust, your research, your designs, none of their work would have been possible. I hope you take pride in that."

"I know what I've accomplished," Loel said softly. "I know team-work is required to make progress at this scale."

Roy stood, pointing towards the bar. "I need to hear more about your fears too, Loel. It might tie to why I wanted to talk. Before we jump to more weighty issues around SeekerDust, does anyone want an espresso? The machine is hot and ready."

Cody sighed and shook his head. "For a moment there, I thought you were pointing to the bar for something harder. You two are a bit deep and reflective today, aren't you? I'll join you with an espresso."

"Green tea, please," Loel said. "If the bartender prepped correctly, there should be cut lemons in the little fridge by the sink."

He enjoyed the process of making and serving drinks of any kind. It was calming. Food prep was a pain in the ass, but drinks were a joy to share. The change of pace gave them each a moment to mentally collect themselves. He needed to move Loel off her current mood. He returned with a tray of their drinks.

Roy started to sip at his espresso but returned it to the table. "Rockefeller has been a closely held secret for a long time. We made enormous breakthroughs several times in the last year. This culmination of the MoralOS being embedded and Elly's emergence as a humanoid may feel like the time to shout from the rooftops. Instead, I believe now it's more important than ever to stay tight-lipped. I think we have a lot of things to talk about. Do you agree?"

"Do I agree we need to keep all this a secret or do I agree we have a lot to talk about?" Loel asked.

"Both, I guess." Roy had intended the question to be rhetorical.

Loel looked at both men. "Yes, we have a lot to talk about. Are there things we need to bring to market right away? Definitely. There are some things we can't keep quiet about. Are we in danger of not knowing what we're getting ourselves into, or how much Elly could evolve with the Dust? Yes. And that is a big, hairy problem."

Cody's expression showed dismay at Loel's response and possibly her tone. "I do think a walking, talking, super intelligence is something the world is not ready for. That needs to stay quiet a bit longer. But I'm torn about some other applications. What are you concerned about, Roy?"

"I have micro and macro concerns," Roy admitted. "We're starting something that can't be reversed. SeekerDust is the basis for entirely new material science. Clean manufacturing will greatly improve our environment."

"Cleaning up the environment is a good thing, as long as you don't kill the global economy while you do it," Loel said. "In situ manufacturing significantly reduces shipping and supply chains. Recycling capabilities reduce the need for producing new materials and cleans landfills and warehouses of electronic trash. These industries employ millions of workers around the world. What will happen to those industries and those businesses if we make announcements about this type of production?"

Cody ran his fingers through his hair. "We could really rock stock markets with this. I see what you're saying."

Cody was trying hard to be supportive of Loel. He also looked like he was watching his parents disagree for the first time.

"We named the project Rockefeller with a tongue in cheek irreverence," Roy said. "Rockefeller, the 1800s tycoon, was well-known for owning his supply chain, thus controlling the production costs with strategic advantages. Now, I evaluate the other side of Rockefeller's business model. I consider the monopoly practices of eliminating all his competitors by buying them or squeezing them out of business. I don't want to do that."

"You will be vilified for these types of disruptions. I don't like that." Loel's look of fear touched Roy. He appreciated her concern and wondered how much she was worried about her own reputation, not just his.

Cody fidgeted with this espresso mug. "Dust self-replicating and manufacturing could wipe out countless businesses if we developed a wide enough variety of Dust capabilities."

Loel looked at Roy. "John Rockefeller was also one of the world's grandest philanthropists. Are you looking into those lessons, too?"

"I'll not squelch revolutionary potential, along with their immense positive impacts for fear of ramifications we may be able to mitigate. We need to talk about controls and possibilities."

"You'll have to have messaging around the positive uses of the nanites, while also evaluating the negative repercussions. And how do you keep a secret like Elly a secret?" Loel asked.

Cody nodded at Loel, then he looked at Roy. "Why isn't Keira here for this conversation?"

"Right now, Keira is distracted," Roy replied. "She sees the advancements as being Elly. I didn't think she would look at these concerns creatively."

Loel agreed, "She's also spending insane hours with Elly as if she can't get enough of her. She's always exhausted lately. I don't think we're getting the best Keira lately. I think you need to talk to her, Roy."

Roy waited, weighing how much to say. He needed answers and buy-in about progressing with the Dust from these two. He didn't want to get distracted with talk of Keira. "Could we do something in the medical field, the customized onsite stretcher?"

"We'd be creating supplies in front of the general public. No secrecy about the results in that scenario." Adamantly shaking her head, Loel's jaw clinched.

"I'm sure we can find opportunities we can shield from scrutiny while we work out the protections," Cody said.

"Every revolution has a timeline," Loel said. "The industrial revolution, the information revolution, each required long adoption curves. The deniers who ignore change or refuse to believe it will impact them, go the way of the dinosaurs." Loel finished her tea.

Roy agreed with the thought process. "Eventually the wave of the evolution becomes mainstream. Then we can see it for what it was, a transformation. For all but a few, it's impossible to comprehend the significance of the change at the beginning or even in the middle of the transformation."

"The rate of change is speeding up," Loel said. "The advancements in AI ripped out jobs and processes wholesale in some markets. I'm not certain which analogy to use. Rockefeller's capabilities, if made public, wouldn't look like a curve. It would be a spike."

"Or a cliff, depending on who you are," Cody mumbled.

The bartender arrived for his shift. He acknowledged Roy's poker face and discreetly went about setting up his station.

"We're not prepared for the speed at which Elly is going rip things up." Loel locked eyes with Roy. "The private nature of medical research and its exclusivity should make that field compelling to you. You can keep on keeping secrets."

Roy ignored her verbal jab. "That industry could be promising." Loel's negativity had dampened his enthusiasm. "Meanwhile, move forward with the water desalination demo for the UN. It's a limited audience, and we have to solve the problem. Minimize the manufacturing show-and-tell. Just show the parts adapting in the field when needed. That won't show our hand as much."

"I understood that on last night's voice message." Cody gave Roy a nod. "The Dust's self-destruct abilities will remain on the top priority list of testing. We won't make changes that compromise that ability."

Loel tapped her pinky finger in a fidget. "And, Roy?"

"Yes, Loel, you can have more people. But only the inner circle. Train others on the FBI search and rescue. Our people need relief from that." He leaned toward Loel, putting his hand over her flighty tapping. "Make sure you include Ollie, Ruby, and Keira on your team. They understand Elly better than we do. They'll also notice her changes more quickly. We need to stay aware of her progress."

Loel did not look amused at his directive.

Exponential Awareness

T he head table was a conspicuous hot seat for Keira. Her watch repeatedly vibrated with messages she ignored. Sitting between Gino and his boss, she looked out over the sparkling ballroom filled with well-wishers. Gino and several other FBI agents were celebrated for some cover story project that kept their real work confidential.

Gino's partner, George, stood at the podium, thanking the agency for the honorarium and designated it to a home for runaways. Keira was touched by his connection and consideration for the kids. While applauding his speech, she stole a quick glance at her watch as it buzzed again. The message was from Elly.

Perched at the table in the supportive spouse role, she was thankful the focus shined on the men and women from the agency and not her. These agents deserved the recognition, but nothing was said about the human trafficking task force. That was still active and politically charged. They hadn't tracked all the money and power enabling so much to occur within their own territory.

Charades, Keira thought. *Why host a showy black-tie event if you're trying to fly under the radar?* It was Gino's turn to speak. She was eyelid-droopingly tired from numerous nights working with Elly and the Dust. As he stood, all eyes were trained on them. Pride for Gino produced one of her evening's only genuine smiles. It had to cover the yawn she swallowed as he moved to center stage for his short speech. He always had secrets. She didn't like this turn of having her own.

The sparkle from the crystal light fixtures magnified the low light. The floral and LED centerpieces set the elegant tone for the impeccably decked out gentlemen and women dressed in envy-inducing gowns. Usually, she and Ruby could entertain themselves through an evening like this by ogling the dresses and ranking them along the spectrum of "I wish I had that one" to "wouldn't be caught dead in." Tonight, her mind barely focused beyond the kids she wanted to help. The evening should have felt perfect, but the world wasn't perfect enough to ease her angst.

She heard her name, yanking her attention back to Gino. He said, "She always brings the important things to my attention. So, in her honor, I donate my honorarium to the Prevention of Child Abuse Center for Greater Seattle/Tacoma area." She swallowed the urge to cry as applause and admiring murmurs swept the tables of attendees. Gino's boss patted Keira on the back. Gino returned to his seat as the agency director raised her glass for everyone to toast all ten honorees.

The formal portion of the event was over. Gino guided her towards the end of the platform and the crowd of well-wishers. She searched the diners for Ruby, the ever-supportive friend of the supportive spouse. Maybe Ruby received the same messages and could give some indication of what was going on so Keira wouldn't need to plow through them. Ruby's knowledge would depend on what Elly was getting worked up about.

Gino held her elbow, helping her down the five narrow stairs. She smiled up at him and leaned close to his ear. "Thanks for the tribute and contribution. If you had anything to do with influencing George's choice, I appreciate that, too." She was rewarded with a beautiful return smile and a wink.

Blinding grins and crushing handshakes distracted her from any other thoughts as she moved through a gauntlet of wealthy local citizens and civic leaders. They were proud to have a visible FBI presence improving the area, or so they repeated in several variations. Keira wondered if there were prompts on the dinner tables instructing attendees how to congratulate the guests of honor. They all sounded too much alike.

She spotted the state's attorney general through the closest cluster of people. Her eyes squinted down to a scowl. She thought she was being watched and turned to see Gino's facial expression warning her not to engage the man who had blocked every law that would make it easier to prosecute and sentence familial abusers. She heeded Gino's look of intervention and turned a one-eighty to look for Ruby.

"Hello, Dr. Stetson," the director of the child abuse prevention center greeted her. The elderly woman was beaming. "I can't thank you enough. Your influence with your husband, Agent Stetson, yielded a wonderful surprise for us. Can I ask where your specific interest lies in our work? Is there something specific we should earmark for part of the donation?"

Keira's relief for a true ally in the crowd soothed her raised hackles over seeing a man she felt typified the hypocrisy of people. They wanted to pretend they protected the community but didn't acknowledge the crimes going on within it.

"Well, ma'am, my research showed that the local community is likely not fully aware of the child abuse occurring in every area of economics right here. I feel there is a real injustice going on in the justice system. It's not only here, but I can't tolerate powerful or wealthy parents covering up abuse as accidents or hiding them altogether. Court records, hospital records, law enforcement, and protective services must be protected from the pressure of inequitable enforcement of rules, based on the offender's social status."

The woman's eyes grew wide. She nervously looked around. Leaning in to allow Keira to hear her lowered voice. "I didn't expect that at all, but you're absolutely right. I, too, must tread lightly in a room like this. However, I assure you I can funnel one hundred percent of tonight's donation to this cause." She looked around again to make sure no one was listening to the two of them. She shook Keira's hand with both of hers. "Doctor, I assure you we can have an impact together. Thank you."

Keira nodded. "Thank you."

"Oh, and Dr. Stetson, let me introduce Mickey Temming," the director said.

Keira's face froze and her chest tightened as Mickey stepped next to the lady. He put his hand forward. Keira hesitated, but knew she couldn't be rude in this setting, especially on Gino's night.

"Good evening, Dr. Stetson," Mickey said as they shook hands.

Keira turned to the director, so she didn't have to look at Mickey.

"Yes, dear," the director said. "We were sitting at the same table tonight. When Mr. Temming heard Agent Stetson's speech, he generously offered to match the agency's honorarium. It has simply been the best night for us."

"Oh really? I'm sure that was quiet the surprise." There was another vibration at her wrist. "I'm so sorry to have to step away, but my assistant has been trying to reach me all evening. Her persistence is slightly concerning me, so I better check with her."

Keira said goodnight to the woman, flashed a weak smile towards Mickey, and moved to a tight space between two tables, casually repositioning a chair to slightly block access to her. Slipping her earbud from her purse and into her ear, she could now listen to Elly's messages. She also texted Ruby that she needed her right away.

Without the emotional requirement to vocalize panic, Elly still modulated her messages with powerful urgency.

Elly's first message: *"Keira, I've correlated hospital, law enforcement, and school data systems. I accessed the public record of predatory and domestic violence offenders. We have problems ahead of us."*

Keira stared intently at the elegant pink and white floral arrangement on the dinner table in front of her. She had to focus her eyes on something as she listened intently to the stats and data Elly was transmitting. She feared if she looked at people's faces, her anger might appear aggressive towards anyone in her view.

Elly was forecasting abuse.

Ruby stepped into her line of site. "Ugh, Temming is here. He made a point of telling me all the executives from the local defense contractors made this a great intelligence gathering destination, whatever that means."

Keira held up her finger to pause Ruby, then pointed to her ear. "Elly," she mouthed. Ruby returned a thumbs up and looked out across the crowd.

"Sorry, Elly has been trying to reach me all night. If she wasn't a machine, I'd say she was anxious."

"What's she working on that has her keyed up?" Ruby asked.

What could Keira say at this point? She had to be careful. "A man who twice sent his daughter to the hospital after she had reportedly fallen down the stairs was arrested and released for a drunken bar fight. Similar incidents happened before the earlier ER visits. Elly flagged the household for an extreme high risk of abuse."

"Okay, and that took several urgent messages to you? What does that even mean to you?"

"She had another one about several emergency phone calls to the police about domestic arguments at an address matching one where a concerned teacher had sent alarms to her school administrators. Evidently, a student received a failed test score. Everybody at the school thinks the student and their siblings live in a dangerous environment. The child evidently cried when they got their grade this afternoon."

"So?" Ruby asked. "Why is Elly messing around with stuff like that and why is she bothering you with it?" They started walking towards Gino, then Keira stopped.

"You see . . . " Keira dropped her voice. Ruby leaned close to hear her. "Elly's predicting child abuse in the city."

"Oh, wow! Does she then alert child services? The police? She'd have to be careful there. The police won't do anything before abuse."

"Yeah, we've been sort of tinkering with ways to intervene or prevent things she identifies."

"What?!" Ruby demanded.

"Hey, I've got to say goodnight to Gino. You know how these things are. The gang will all be off to the pub to shoot pool and make up stories. You and I can get out of here as soon as I say goodnight."

"But, Keira. You need to answer questions for me." Ruby protested.

They reached George and the other agents standing near Gino. Offering the obligatory regrets for heading out, she wished them congratulations and goodnights. She kissed Gino lightly and murmured. "Enjoy yourself. I'm proud of you."

As she exited the crowded ballroom, she grew nervous. She had to come clean to Ruby. She didn't know which worried her the most, Ruby's opinion of Elly and Keira's activities or the fact that she had kept something this important from her for several weeks.

They rode at maximum allowable speed towards the office while Keira provided a summary of the protective activities she and Elly were engaged in. Keira texted instructions to Elly to proceed on several requested missions because Ruby's angry voice berating her left no opportunity for voice commands.

Ruby's hands punctuated the air and then flopped to her lap in desperation as she spoke. "What do you mean, Elly isn't harming anyone because she's only using the minimum amount of interference to stop the attackers? She's operating under directives but making decisions on her own in situ?"

"Yes, I can't be everywhere or there all the time. I need . . . I mean these kids need help."

"Are you crazy?" Ruby shouted.

"I'm . . . " Keira began. "No, I'm not crazy. I'm doing what must be done. We can help these kids. I must. They don't deserve the shit that gets thrown at them."

"But what about legalities? Due process?"

Keira put her palm up towards Ruby. She explained, "Elly's only granted permission to step into abusive situations when the system detected childhood distress sounds. She was trained in this to make sure entering a property was within the law. She doesn't trespass because she's reacting to distressed cries from a kid."

Shaking her head, Ruby protested. "Now she's predicting something is going to happen and she wants to prevent it? Once again, I bring up due process . . . "

"Elly isn't trying to jail these guys. She just needs to get ahead of them. She tells me she needs to be present before it starts. Hopefully defuse the situation." She hung her head and said with much less authority, "Or physically stop the guy if required. Then she turns in evidence to the police hotlines. That's when your precious due process can kick in."

"Keira, you could lose everything over this. You're the czar of all things ethical but this isn't following the rules at all! Despite your rationalization, it's likely still illegal in many cases."

"Rules be damned. Being ethical. Using your morals. These are all about doing the right thing. When has protecting a child ever NOT been the right thing? If preventing a child from being hurt isn't the most ethical thing we can do, then fuck ethics."

Ruby jerked her head back in surprise. She sat staring at Keira as if she had been slapped by those words. Proceeding softer this time she asked, "What happened to you? How did you reach this point?"

"Ruby, you wouldn't believe the evil stuff we've heard and seen. How can we not do everything in our power if we can prevent these children from being scarred mentally and physically? This stuff lasts a lifetime, multiple lifetimes because they can go on to abuse the next generation, too."

"Oh, shit, Keira."

"There was a wonderfully wise professor at Harvard Business School, Tom DeLong. He'd tell his students, 'Empathy is when the voice in your head stops and truly listens to what another is saying and feeling.' I've shut off the voice in my head that dinks around with what others will think of me for doing this. I had to. I may be the only person that really hears these kids cry out now. I have to listen for these kids and help them."

"You're noble, I'll give you that," Ruby murmured.

"I'm sorry I dragged you in like this. I thought you'd want to help. Now that Elly can help—she can be in multiple places at once, and now with her real physical form—we can do so much. I'm terrified and overwhelmed by the scale of the problem," Keira said.

She texted another response to Elly. "There were at least fifteen incidents left unattended last night resulting in bodily harm to minors. Some were small on the scale of physical damage, but we know that is not the only issue with this abuse. To meet our objectives, we need to do more and be more active."

Ruby turned to the window. She rested her forehead on its cool surface and gently tapped the glass a few times. They had almost reached the lab. "What do you need from me?" she sighed.

"I've got to let Elly go do her thing. I've been instructing her and approving her actions up until now. Will you review the code Elly created allowing her to act independently? I've already reviewed it, but I'd really like your eyes on it. I have to do this."

"Elly wrote code to change her own actions?" Ruby shrieked.

"Yes, and it includes a barrier to prevent OpenML from seeing that she's the author of the code alterations. We did navigate around that being unethical because I wrote some of it, so I'm seen as the author. I'm also the one implementing, so it is my decision to put the updates in place, not hers. She can write it, but she can't implement it. We won't have a case of runaway changes."

In Searcher's parking lot, Keira gave Ruby a hug. "I'm sorry, Ruby. You can walk away now if you need to. I'm going in. Elly and I have important work to do."

Keira left Ruby and headed to the door.

Ruby caught up with Keira and squeezed the hand she didn't need for the door's ID security. "Ah, hell, Keira. When have I ever let you dive into something big without taking me along?"

Double Helix

E lly had put a meeting on the calendar for the two of them. This was the first time Keira had seen Elly position herself as if a person in a business interaction. Their nights had been overwhelming and exhausting. During the day, the two of them and Ruby continued to position their interactions as normal.

Keira decided to treat this like an appointment with anyone else. At the arranged time, she put her things aside and sat in her chair. Elly assembled enough Dust to create her human form without being requested. Keira smiled and made a mental note of the date and time. She wanted official documentation showing progress. Many of Elly's growth milestones were made secretly lately.

"Welcome, Elly," Keira said. "How can I help you?"

From her pocket, Elly pulled a small box. "I made these and they're for you."

Not having noticed Elly even had pockets, Keira had more questions beyond what was in the box. Those could wait. Elly was giving her a gift. She would discuss all these observations with Ollie later. What did this mean for Elly's development? Keira had to focus on the moment. She leaned over and took the present from Elly.

"Thank you. You said you made this?" Keira opened the present, finding a pair of earrings.

"Yes, I'm working for Loel with the 3D printers. Our discussion about DNA and cells during our first visit to Loel's greenhouse continued to develop an interest for me. I think the double helix is one of the most beautiful shapes. I also learned jewelry is intended to show beautiful shapes. This led me to creating those."

"They're beautiful. I agree, the double helix is beautiful in its appearance and its grand design of elements of life. This is thoughtful and meaningful, Elly. I'm honored. We've never talked about gift giving in your training. This is especially valuable because you made it."

"Much of my gift giving education comes from Ollie."

"Oh, really? Tell me more."

"Ollie asks me to predict the best gifts for Ruby. He tells me we're quite successful in our choices so far. His requests can be a challenge because he gives me less data than I'm accustomed to prior to being asked for a recommendation."

Keira smiled. She replaced her earrings with the new ones. "We don't always get all the information we want prior to making a decision. At times, we must rely on our expertise or comparing two situations and extrapolating the best course of action."

Keira slouched into the back of her chair. "I'm so exhausted. Our work is draining me physically and mentally. I once thought business decisions were the hardest choices."

Elly, still sitting with perfect posture, reassured Keira. "You're changing lives, Keira. I can't feel your exhaustion, but the assessment of the help you provide kids will create benefits for generations. The data supports this. In my interpretation of the phrase, you're making a worthy sacrifice."

"Thank you, Elly. There's a lot going on around here. I need to stay on my best game. Cody and others are simplifying the 3D printers and the nanite assembly bots. They're quite excited about ramping up production. You and I need to continue the upgrades for the OS and decision-making. You've created a lot of new use cases. And they're all flying at me for testing. But I cling to this positive energy."

"I noted an increase in activity around Dust manufacturing. Roy deployed seventy-five percent of his stored original Dust to assist in mining the raw materials in the landfill. He also instructed Cody to delegate his efforts researching a hacking attempt at one of the backup facilities."

A yawn and a stretch woke Keira up a bit more. "Hmm, another hacking attempt. I'm sure they'll take care of it. Please do an extra backup of any research I haven't organized well enough to be automatically protected. I'm sloppy sometimes because I don't understand all Searcher's methods yet. I also know Loel says Cody gets obsessed with intrusion, but the systems are strong."

"Your files are all backed up. I make sure of that. I believe you learned the system here better than you think," Elly said.

"Okay, great. Elly, are you aware that you're changing?"

"I'm required to seek more esoteric sources of information to find appropriate responses or actions in this form. It's interesting that subtle issues require more research than many large and grand issues. People document what they'd call the big things more than the niceties or subtle issues they face."

"I see. I would agree with that. It's interesting you seem to need to find subtle issues here. Can you give me an example?"

"I will first tell you there is an exception to documenting little things. Teenagers document all the things that offend them, delight them, and confuse them. Their writings and communications are good sources for identifying norms. They often focus on how things make them feel and miss the bigger issue they face. An example, someone forgetting a birthday or important date creates a great deal of communication between teenagers. It highlights for me the importance of being respectful of what others think, even if it is not important to you."

"I love that example! You're right. Teenagers fixate on subtle traits as they learn to assess people in their world. The body of works by adults, which is what we mostly use in AI training, wouldn't include a lot of that. I'm proud of you."

"Thank you," Elly said.

"I've got to go outside for some fresh air. I'm going to the boat to think and plan my next presentation." Keira realized she was wrapping up a meeting Elly established. She wasn't certain they had fulfilled the agenda. "Oh, unless there was something else you wanted to talk about in this session?"

"No, I gave you the earrings. That was my purpose for the appointment."

Her hand reached up to touch a dangling earring. "They're lovely, Elly. Thank you for such a thoughtful and unique present. I'll cherish them always."

Autonomous Aid

K eira sat listening to Ollie's voice modulation recordings, nib-
bling nervously on tiny carrots. Her left earbud lay charging.
She'd run it down already.

"Keira. You sound like a critter trying to gnaw down a tree," Ruby
whined.

"I'm sorry." Keira took the other earbud out, tossing it on her desk.
"I just want to be comfortable that we do know we're only tuning the
Dust to notify us when they hear true distress calls. We've got the trig-
ger words mastered."

Elly sat across from Keira in the mildly lit office. "I've trained on all the
legal parameters for helping children in distress. We've tested the scenarios
hundreds of times. We had only one false positive where a child actor was
practicing for a role and convincingly stressed their audible cries for help."

"See! A false positive," Ruby said.

"I would've assessed the situation rapidly before any action would
have been taken," Elly said.

Ruby pointed to Elly, approving her statement, then turned to
Keira. "Now put away the carrots. You're driving me crazy."

That afternoon, Keira and Ruby had reviewed submittals to
thirty-six states and all one hundred senators regarding laws that

protect children. Elly's research and proposal writing increased the reach of their efforts, far beyond anything Keira had imagined. These various legislative changes tightened loopholes and created entirely new legislation, the foundation for building a safer environment for children to live and learn.

"May I suggest we also send these packages to all child advocacy organizations in each state? That delegates the pursuit of proposed laws. Hendrick's assistant, Shauney, taught me that trick. Roy has a group that does that any time they want legislative support. He engages the community."

"That sounds like a great idea." Keira marveled at Elly.

"Roy has many great ideas. He is a wealth of knowledge about the world."

Ruby and Keira exchanged looks with raised eyebrows. Ruby spoke first. "Really, you chat a lot with Roy? What do you talk about?"

"His experience in the CIA shaped a lot of his opinions on leadership and on people. He says nearly all people have more potential than they realize."

"Very interesting." Keira giggled. She had needed that lightened image tonight.

A yawn escaped from Keira. Resting her chin in hand, she let her head tilt towards Ruby. "This late-night stuff is wearing me out. Adrenaline is one thing, but damn. It catches up with me at times."

"Yep, I'll have to say, it's getting a bit noticeable, too, Keira." Ruby shook her head to ward off Keira's protest. "Just a little bit. You get a little cranky with people lately. Take care of yourself."

Ruby's review of the proposed autonomy code filled both of them with anxiety. She agreed that the logic of Elly's new ConsciousNet version was sound. Assumptions were made that the OpenML data and the MoralOS framework were strong enough to provide judgement boundaries within Elly's directives. Keira and Elly's own work in the field, even though approved by Keira, included many hours of decision-making training in potential scenarios Elly might face.

"Well." Keira pushed her hands to the table and stood.

"Are we going to do this?" Ruby asked.

"Yes!" Elly said.

Keira closed her eyes, held her hands shoulder high, and shooed Elly out of the room and into the night.

The physical Elly dissipated to join the Dust in the city. Elly could call it to coalesce when she needed it. This would be her most autonomous experience yet.

Keira exhaled loudly, sinking back into her large office chair. She leaned her head back to stare at the ceiling. "Ruby, I feel like I just gave the keys to a sixteen-year-old to drive the car across the busiest roads in the country. Oh, and she's going to a concert full of God knows what kinds of people. She's dressed inappropriately, AND I handed her a bottle of scotch for the drive. What am I doing?"

"I'm with you, girl. This is a little messed up and yet insanely invigorating." Ruby dropped herself into the chair opposite Keira. "This code review kicked my butt. But tonight's the night. You two control the show-and-tell. I'm ready to see what may lock us all up or earn you keys to the city."

"We do live in interesting times." Keira kicked off her shoes and curled her feet up beside her on the chair. "I need to breathe deep. You should too. It's like bracing yourself for the FBI raids, but worse because you see the little ones directly."

"Do we watch what Elly is doing all the time? Everything?"

"No, not tonight. I asked her to keep us in the loop and to ask if she needs help. She can do a lot of little things along the way we won't observe. One night she monitored all the streetlight crosswalks and sent a report to the city regarding ones in disrepair or with crossing times too short for kids to safely cross. I gave her clearance to manage those explorations and processes on her own. But events that include physical contact or danger, she is to let me know."

"Oh, boy," Ruby sighed.

"Yeah, alarms pinpoint so many awful issues in the city," Keira said.

Elly's soft voice interrupted from the small speaker on Keira's desk. "Can I help you, sweetie? What do you need? I heard you scream."

A distant female voice laced with panic whimpered, "Where did you come from? What do you want?"

"I was simply walking in the park about to walk over this bridge. You cried out. Are you hurt? How can I help?"

The voice became more aggressive. "Did you jump the park's wall or something? The park's closed. I had to jump the wall. You look too nice to do the walls. Go away."

"Are you okay? Yeah, I jumped the low part in the corner. You can drop to the electrical box or whatever it is to make it easier. Sometimes I just need to come here to think. Did somebody—"

"I said go away. I have a knife." Her voice held more agitation than aggression.

"Oh, oh no. Your arm's bleeding. Let me help."

The exchange continued for several minutes. The teenager, vacillating between threatening Elly and desperate for help, eventually admitted she was there to commit suicide. Her scream had been part anguish and part pain from her first cut on her wrist. Elly bandaged the girl and convinced her to call a friend.

Keira whispered to Ruby. "I'm relieved Elly was able to respond so quickly. Last week the suicidal kid had to be rushed to the ER. He wouldn't pick up the phone call that would have given my voice a reason to be talking to him."

Ruby grabbed a paper napkin from under her drink. "I guess disembodied voices knowing your business hasn't always been accepted. You called 911?" She began quietly shredding the napkin.

"Yes, but he'll be in the hospital a long time."

While waiting for the friend to arrive, Elly gave the girl phone numbers and addresses for suicide support and a safe shelter for teens. She looked up records about the girl and used general information to soothe her and keep conversation flowing.

Ruby stood, pacing the room, picking up or moving objects with no obvious objective. They listened to a few minor interactions of Elly confronting adults or soothing them while a child had tantrums nearby. Fire departments were called, and neighbors were notified of danger twice. Elly was quiet for over thirty minutes. Keira relaxed more than on nights she was here on her own and every decision was hers. Conversation with Ruby had a calming effect.

"Keira, this situation will leave unanswered questions for the police. Your instructions were to contact you when that happened," Elly said.

"Go ahead, Elly. Explain. Is it a crisis? Do you need help?"

"No, the drama is over for the kids. They're safe. The police are on their way. The mother is barricaded in the closet, and no one will know who did it."

"Let me guess," Ruby said. "You did it?"

"Yes, I did. She was pouring lighter fluid all over the living room and stairs. The oldest child tried to move the little ones out the door, but the mother wouldn't let them leave. They ran up the stairs with no way to get out the second story window. The woman was in hysterics. I didn't want to further traumatize her, nor did I want to hurt her. I pushed her into a closet left open by the kids when they grabbed their shoes. The door was easy to block with the couch."

"She didn't light the fire?"

"No, but I wasn't certain she didn't have another lighter with her. I had nanites go into the closet and check. There was another lighter. I instructed the Dust to jam the striking mechanism. Then, I retrieved the kids from the upstairs. I took them to the neighbors' and notified first responders."

"Will the neighbors or the kids identify you as the one who blocked the mother?"

"No, the neighbor didn't see me. The kids will describe me as a tiny woman. That couch was large. They'll think there was someone else who moved it. Oh, and I recorded the woman screaming from the closet that it was her house and she could burn it down if she wanted to. That recording went to the police, as well, from the eldest girl's phone."

"Okay, Elly, good job. I think this loose end will be interpreted as Good Samaritans who came to help and didn't want to be involved with the police. Monitor news stories and public statements that might indicate more information we should pay attention to."

Shaking her head, Ruby stared at Keira in disbelief. "Oh my God! You stay so calm and cover your tracks. You're almost conspiratorial. How?"

"Did you hear what was going on with those kids? We work the crises. I go into problem solving mode. Together we think it through. Tonight, Elly thinks it through." Keira waved her arm toward the city. "It's interesting. Elly didn't have us listen to that encounter."

"She felt that confident?" Ruby asked.

"I guess. We're completely focused on the kids. I told you that. We refine the focus on abuse when it comes to physical intervention. I mean, imagine a stranger is chasing a woman down the street. Elly might trip him and tip a trashcan over between them, blocking his path. Elly's directive is to stop and prevent abuse and harm coming to children."

"This is the most bizarre thing ever," Ruby whispered.

Elly again broke into their conversation. "Keira, I have a technical question."

"You? You have a technical question for me? Okay," Keira said.

"I stopped a man." A streaming picture of an alley between old brick buildings popped up on the wall in Keira's office. "He was climbing the fire escape to his ex-wife's apartment. The kids are inside. He just left his work phone number a voicemail explaining why they all had to die. There are two guns in his belt."

Elly paused. The picture swept to the ground where a man lay unconscious.

"Um, Elly. How did you stop this man?"

"Technically, it is called a low sweeping kick. He hit his head on the ground when he fell."

"What is your question? Your technical question?" Keira asked.

"I currently have him restrained. The police are on their way, I called them. I told them he fell off the fire escape after I heard his frightening phone call. My question is about the restraints. Should I dissolve them as soon as the authorities are close enough to assure he can't run away? He's not moving at all now, but his vital signs are normal. He most likely has a concussion. You're concerned about leaving evidence of our work that could create issues."

"Yes, Elly. I think dissolving the restraints is an excellent idea," Keira said. Turning to Ruby, she said, "Damn, this is exhausting."

Ruby again sat across from Keira. Resting elbows on her knees she locked eyes with Keira. "Making Elly responsible for decisions is the best thing you could have done here. If somebody gets hurt, you're further removed from the issue. I'm sure our laws are not up to date with technology the rest of the world doesn't even know is possible.

But you need to be extremely careful here. I feel a lot of fire around this. I can't imagine what would happen if the FBI found out."

"Hmm. Then don't ask Elly. She produced a series of predictions regarding their discovery of our work. She won't share them with me. According to her, they will only 'freak me out.' Which, of course, freaked me out."

"Keira," Elly said, with a fainter voice than usual. "I'm on the Eastside. I'm changing the look of my outer clothing to fit in better when I'm ordering kids to move away from the windows."

"Uh, yeah. That makes sense, never thought about that benefit. Why are you moving kids, Elly?"

"Gang gunfire," Elly responded.

They listened as Elly entered a building and shouted instructions to move away from the windows and front room. She warned about gunfire. The last part of the message was harder to understand. Layers of the same conversation sounded like they happened at the same time, but in multiple languages.

Ruby turned to Keira, "What was that? Spanish and, uh, something else? Did she ask somebody to help her?"

"Weeell," Keira drew out the word. "Elly can be in more than one place at a time. I think you just heard her in multiple languages, but it looks like also in more than one building."

"Oh, God, I didn't even think of that." Ruby bit her lower lip while staring out the dark window.

Science of Morality

S tanding between Loel and Roy four stories above the Seattle courthouse entrance, Keira watched people going about their business on the street below. "How long do you think before the verdict is announced?" she asked Roy.

He looked at his watch. "It's been thirty minutes since the judge left the jurors. My guess is the decision will be coming quickly. That meeting was likely just for clarifications of some rule."

Loel shifted from one foot to the other. "He better not get off on some technicality."

Keira looked to the building hosting a hotly protested trial of a local man caught holding three drugged women against their will. His capture was from an early Searcher surveillance project. Roy was here to observe but stay out of the media circus. They couldn't risk connecting Searcher to the trial.

Roy's jaw appeared clamped tight.

"Did the case have technicalities that could create an issue?" Keira hadn't been ignoring the trial. She just had too much going on to get pulled into the drama. "The media just wavers between 'he's a church going man' and 'there's so much depravity in the evidence' that they have to convict."

"There're always technicalities," mumbled Loel. She turned her back to the balcony's rail and looked up at the height of the building. "Roy, I have a question for you. How do you measure if the law you're applying to a situation is right or right enough? Can a law be unethical?"

Keira was glad to turn the attention away from the disgusting man across the street. "Oh, we have debates about this in my house and with Ollie all the time. Laws are often outdated and still on the books. Did you know there's a statute in Texas that says if you're in a bar you can't take three sips of your beer while still standing?"

"Seriously?" Loel asked.

Keira needed to lighten these two up. "Yes, evidently it was enacted to keep patrons from drinking while standing at the bar. They wanted drinkers to move to the tables. The waitresses would serve them, earning the waitresses more tips, etc. It also kept the bar open for the next set of patrons who came in the door. It's absurd but was never removed from the books. In the state of Maryland, sleeveless shirts are illegal unless you're homeless. Explain that one."

Roy bobbed his head distractedly. If she couldn't lighten the mood, she could at least move the conversation forward. "But there're more serious laws that create great debate about whether a law is legit or ethical. It's a tough set of opinions and beliefs to navigate. Think about the ones that provoked the gun ownership debate, women's right to vote and own property, the treatment of refugees. What if the laws are just bullshit? Think about the legal loopholes protecting criminals and making it harder to catch and prosecute them."

Loel ran her finger around the rim of her empty glass then set it on the center table. She dropped into the cushioned couch. "I wonder why laws don't have a requirement that prevents them from going against scientific evidence. What I mean is, if science can prove a policy is wrong or harmful, the bill can't be passed."

Roy moved to sit as well, choosing a chair with a view of both the courthouse and the balcony door to the inside of the suite. "I heard there's a petition somewhere around that. Somebody wants to put it up for a vote. Keira, why are you grinning all of a sudden? You went from pensive or sleepy to full silly smile."

"That petition. It's sort of Elly's responsibility," Keira said. She was proud of Elly but knew talking about her too much seemed to irritate Loel.

"What?" both Loel and Roy asked.

"Elly posted the same concept Loel just described to a forum asking for fresh ways to improve our democracy. She stated that laws should be designed for betterment of the people the politicians govern. The politicians should be required to use facts and science to prove that our existing and future legislations are improvements for society and not detrimental. The post went viral; it's taking on a life of its own. It's pretty powerful."

"AIs are extremely capable at testing facts," Loel commented. "Some people worry they'll establish too much moral absolutism, too much black and white in their decision-making. Do you trust they'll put the facts in context?"

Keira was emphatic. "Computers are fantastic at putting things in context. They can assess so much more information than people. Elly's analysis can be evaluated as relative if you give her enough data."

"Do we always provide enough data to satisfy an AI's needs?" Roy questioned. "What if the decisions are made in the spur of a moment? What if there's data asymmetry and there's a need for judgement or perhaps not making a choice at all? Can an AI function at making decisions in those scenarios, Keira?"

Keira felt a sudden chill. Was Roy referring to Elly and the decisions they'd been making together regarding the abuse? Was she feeling guilty about her secrecy or about the risks they were taking? She needed to breathe deep.

"I believe we need to provide the best data possible for all decision-making. People don't possess a perfect amount of input for their choices either. We also have to protect against bias data being used to train our AIs."

"Bias is a problem everywhere, even for you and me," Roy said.

She had to make her point carefully even though she assumed she was doing a little preaching to the choir. If she ever wanted Roy's backing, it was now. "We need to trust that, with the right data and the right training, we're creating the right AIs. Just like teachers and parents, we create our systems with the best resources we can put together. The computers will assess the information with more depth and breadth than people. So, we'll receive better options than we'd have considered without them."

Loel opened her mouth to reply, then paused with pursed lips. "People need to use more facts for their opinions, too. I wish more people were fact-based decision-makers like when they go to vote."

"Or when their decisions impact others more than it will impact them personally," Roy added.

Did Roy know what kind of decisions she had been making lately? Was he being judgmental? She desperately needed sleep. Paranoia was creeping into her thoughts everywhere. "Yes, and the focus needs to be on quality data and on reasoning. Any ideas how to teach people a bit of the science of morality? I know how to do with AIs; people are my challenge."

"That can be a tall order," Roy said. "Complex issues require abstract reasoning. You're asking for fluid intelligence skills and the ability to quickly identify patterns, trends, and logic. Then they have to integrate information towards a solution. That's a lot to ask of people, sadly. Do you feel you're giving the AI the ability to reason or simply limiting them to a domain expertise?"

"What you're saying is the AIs need street smarts," Loel said. "Talk about a tall order."

Keira watched as Loel stared at her empty glass. She had never been with both of them while day drinking. Now was the time to start. She grabbed the wine bottle out of the chiller, refilled Loel's glass, was waved off by Roy, and poured herself the first one of the day. "Yes, it does resemble street smarts. Adaptability is huge. Most AIs stay within a domain expertise. That's what people and businesses need them to do."

Loel said, "Moral judgement or the ability to assess things morally doesn't guarantee or even predict moral behavior. People can still act in bad form even when they know the action is bad. They may have remorse or guilt or maybe not."

Roy's gaze focused on Keira. "I wonder if an AI would know if it made an unethical decision. They're not capable of remorse or guilt."

Keira stared back at him and said, "I say it would depend on the AI, just like it depends on a person. Most computer systems are amoral, meaning they're indifferent or unaware of any moral standards or beliefs. It'd be impossible for those programs to understand their decisions were unethical."

"And Elly?" Roy asked, watching Keira with an interrogator's intensity. "Is she amoral? I know her foundation is the MoralOS and she makes decisions based on those parameters. If she made a wrong decision, would she know it was wrong?"

Keira broke the lock of their gaze and turned towards the courthouse. "Elly knows clearly the black and white elements of decision-making. She understands the gray areas and will err on the side of what is best for kids." Keira cleared her throat. "And others."

"What about taking instructions? Would Elly defy you if doing so was more moral than your directions?" Roy asked.

Loel sat up straighter, while Keira felt like she was shrinking. Roy had caught Loel's attention.

Looking up to the flag swaying in the breeze across the street, Keira nodded. "Yes. She will choose the more ethical choice."

"What!?" Loel asked. "Elly will defy your instructions? Have you tested this extensively? Under what circumstances?"

Keira turned back to Roy. He raised his eyebrows. He expected her to tell Loel, what he somehow knew himself.

She picked up her wine, taking a long sip, stealing the moment to collect her thoughts.

"Elly and I have been preventing and interrupting child abuse in the city for a while now." Keira blurted out the words. There was no reason to be anything but direct. "I know Elly will defy my instructions because when I've gotten emotional, either angry or scared, my decisions have not always been in everyone's best interest. Elly is the voice and embodiment of reason and ethics."

Keira finished her glass of wine, trembling as she returned the glass to the table.

"What the hell?" Loel demanded. "I don't even know what all that little speech means. But I need to know specific facts immediately." She turned to Roy. "You knew about this? She told you what she's been doing?"

"Yes, I learned about it recently. No, Keira didn't tell me."

Loel's eyes squinted down in anger. Her voice barely above a growl, "You've been walking around town with a seemingly sentient being, made up of highly confidential nanites? Doing what? Are you playing cops . . . superheroes? I assume you're breaking laws, using her surveillance like some super hearing . . . whatever . . . instead of search warrants?"

An attendant inside the suite opened the sliding doors. "Sir, they've returned with a verdict."

Roy stopped her with an uplifted hand without taking his eyes off Keira. "Just tell me guilty or not guilty when it's read. Otherwise, we need privacy."

The door closed silently.

Keira spread a drop of condensation from her glass into a line on the tabletop. "No is the answer to your questions, Loel. I've not been walking around the city breaking down doors. We have only intervened when there are cries of distress, which make it legal to interrupt or intervene on behalf of the victim. We have not broken any laws. Integrity is often described as doing the right thing when no one is even watching. That's what I'm doing, the right thing. Part of what I'm saying to Roy's question is Elly behaves."

Loel raised her hands up in the air in frustration. "Behaves?! And you . . . " She turned to Roy. "You've allowed this to happen? This is okay with you? You could lose everything. We could lose everything! I'm pretty certain a corporate structure can't shield us from all the things that could go wrong here."

"Nothing has happened since I found out about it three days ago. Keira didn't know until just now that I was aware of the activity. While there are issues with the unsanctioned use of technology, especially where there are a few fuzzy lines relating to the FBI contract, we're in uncharted territory."

Loel finished her glass of wine, then refilled it without offering to do the same to Keira's. She dropped the bottle back in the chiller.

"I . . . " Keira spoke to Loel. "These kids grow up to be adults. The facts are painfully clear. Ninety-seven percent of serial killers were physically if not sexually assaulted as children. Violent crime is a multigenerational hobby with sixty-four percent of crimes committed by people with a family member with a record of violent crime. Most of the men we're tracking with the task force started their lives with the types of abuse I'm stopping. This cycle has to be broken."

"Roy, why didn't you tell me? How could you keep this a secret . . . a secret from me?" Loel pleaded.

"I didn't want to risk you having knowledge of the activity until I knew I could keep you safe. Plausible deniability, you could say. But, legally, neither of them has broken any laws or created any issues we can't deal with—yet. Frankly, I was still trying to figure out if I condoned their actions."

"It sounds like you've decided. I swear, Roy, your ability to remain calm through damn near anything can be irritating as hell sometimes. Your filter for risk is highly skewed, you know that." Loel now glared at him.

"I've decided. The young lady inside just sent me a message." He pointed towards the courthouse. "Although, Elly also sent me the message. A man Elly stopped from climbing a fire escape to kill his entire family, including several kids, just plead guilty across the street. Elly and Keira saved those kids, their mom, and likely several others. They were careful."

Keira's throat was tight. "There is a quote I relate to very strongly. I can't find who to credit. 'I felt so small, until I helped a child. Then I felt like a giant.' We're supposed to do the most we can to help others. This is pretty big stuff."

Roy swirled the drink in his hand. His gaze moved between the two of them. "It sounds like this is the work we should do. I just don't know how it should best be accomplished. I need the two of you to figure out the way to do it."

Both women sat up straighter.

"Me?! Work with Keira to find the best way to be vigilantes? Roy, you have some nerve."

Roy nodded gently. Keira took several deep breaths.

"Loel," Roy said, "I didn't tell you earlier for the reason I've already stated. I had Keira tell her story because it's hers to tell. But I also did it this way because I need you both. I can't lose either one of you. We have tremendous work ahead of us."

He checked his phone. "More good news from across the street, the dirtbag we nailed with the FBI was just convicted on all counts. We have more of that to do, too. We must be on the same page. We're a team. We share some secrets. We'll have each other's backs."

He looked at Loel. Keira saw the pleading in his eyes. "I will always have your back, with every resource I have at my disposal. You know that."

Eminent Domain

Deon was impressed by how quickly Mickey booked a meeting with the secretary of defense. This backed up the stories about the two of them being very familiar with each other. Chauffeured by the secretary's driver in an SUV with no windows in the rear passenger seats, they arrived in an underground parking garage of a nondescript government building two blocks off the Mall.

Deon had hoped he'd get to see the Pentagon where the secretary officed. He wondered if it was Mickey or the technology the secretary didn't trust. Most likely the meeting was off the books.

A uniformed aide led them through a series of empty hallways past an endless array of doors, thick with classic decades of layered paint seen throughout government buildings in spaces no one goes to for the aesthetic appeal. After a ridiculous number of turns, they might have been all the way to the Washington Monument. Their door of choice was gray. The accompanying keypad lock was the newest thing Deon had seen since they entered the building.

Inside the room, the decoration was distinctly early interrogation style. Deon turned to the aide. "Sir, should I set up here to be ready?"

The aide waved towards the beige table in the center of the room. Mickey said, "Yes, good idea. We're in the basement area because anywhere else in this building we'd be required to complete sign-in logs and they'd search our bags." Deon believed the certainty in Mickey's tone was fake.

Mickey nodded, rocking back on his heels. His expression screamed, *get going.*

Deon pulled a Searcher laptop and a two-liter-sized canister from his backpack. His setup didn't take long after he was given a secured, untraceable Wi-Fi-connection the aide silently typed in himself.

Unbeknownst to the men in the room, the laptop automatically connected back to the Searcher Office. This sent an alert to Elly that the Dust was in use outside of a geo-fenced region.

The secretary entered the room with zero fanfare or warning. The door closed silently behind him. "Mickey, good to see you. We've seldom had a demo together that didn't get me fired up."

Deon stood to shake the secretary's hand. Mickey shot him a look signaling he needed to sit. Deon feigned the standing allowed him to move this bag. That one glance relegated him to demo-dolly status.

The secretary folded his arms and faced the table. "I'm not going to ask you questions until I see something of interest. I know you won't be wasting my time. I hate to admit it, but if that son of a bitch Roy Brandt invented this or bankrolled it, I know it's brilliant."

Mickey was surely pissed at the praise offered to Roy, even if it came with an insult. Driker was direct. Deon was glad he hadn't been formally introduced. He guessed the secretary was accustomed to nameless aides. This was not the type of guy Deon would choose as an ally.

Driker looked at Mickey. Mickey glanced at Deon. They would proceed without anyone else sitting down. He appreciated the efficiency in the posture. He bent over the computer in the corner of the table.

The Dust received its instructions and swirled out of the canister. Several inches above the table, a two-foot-tall machine started to take shape from the inside out. It finished as the outer edges of four knobby tires touched the table. The metallic gray shell and the jet-black tires gleamed in the florescent light of the sparse room.

"That was cool," said the secretary as he walked half-way around the table.

"We're starting with some basics to give you a frame of reference to the flexibility. And this . . . it can be an autonomous plow, or it could be a tractor," Mickey offered.

"A tractor? It looks like a toddler's four-wheeler without the handlebars. Why is a tractor so small? And I'm not the secretary of agriculture."

"It's a real tractor. It can plant for small plots or on sloped terrain. They can also work twenty-four seven with no need for daylight or breaks, making up for its size," Deon said.

Mickey added, "I don't want you distracted by the object itself. These tractors already exist. They use differential GPS—cool, nothing new. What I want you to focus on is the creation of the tractor. It was created by the nanites here in front of you."

"Okay," Secretary Driker drawled, unimpressed.

Deon realized Driker didn't get it yet. Surely Mickey was going to jump in and explain. Deon didn't want to say any more, and he needed to concentrate on the computer. The SearcherExec software was still somewhat unfamiliar to him.

"You're saying you can make plows from dust? This isn't a projection or special effect?"

"Right. You just watched in situ manufacturing. And it can make more than plows." Mickey nodded at Deon.

Deon changed a few settings and requested the miniature sports player file to be produced. The small tractor dissolved before their eyes as the Dust dismantled with little more sound than crispy cereal in milk. Deon hoped they wouldn't ask him about how this worked. He wasn't close enough to the program to understand the science yet. He spent his time on the team watching how to instruct the Dust. That had been accomplished with controlled curiosity to avoid drawing attention to himself. He was supposed to be focusing on the 3D printers and the refinement of their design during their meetings, not on the Dust itself.

The same particles reshaped, forming a football player replica of the aSport design, approximately two foot tall.

"We brought limited resources for the presentation, but with more Dust this could be full-sized," Mickey boasted.

Deon had no idea how strong the player would be, but the thing made a memorable impression.

Driker said, "These are impressive. I can see how this can change manufacturing. I could make money shorting manufacturing stocks before this goes on the market, but this isn't really my area of interest. I don't see the big deal here."

Mickey stood completely still, following the secretary's posture. This was the first time Deon had seen Mickey play a subservient role in anything.

Mickey said, "This can make the machines that follow the specs in a computer file. Because the Dust is so small, its accuracy is beyond the precision any of us have seen."

"I still fail to see why the DOD would be interested here."

Deon waited in silence. His current plan was not to be noticed, just helpful.

A look of recognition and then a wide grin spread across the secretary's face. "Wait a minute," the secretary said, pointing at Deon. "If it's precise and can make anything, let me see it make an automatic rifle."

Mickey shifted his weight. This was exactly where they wanted the secretary but was also the touchiest part of the conversation. They had to play this just right to stir up the government man to do exactly what they wanted him to do.

"This is our current hang up," Mickey said. "It won't make a weapon for us yet. Code is embedded in it preventing it from making guns."

Mickey cleared his throat. Deon instructed a small color and positioning swap for the football player. It straightened its posture and put its arms behind its back. Its blue projection changed to desert camouflage. The secretary jerked slightly in surprise.

A few more instructions from Deon and the one soldier was joined by another. Mickey's voice grew louder. "Sir, can you imagine an invading army literally appearing out of thin air like that? We need this capability and the control over the code. We can lock up the tech to prevent foreign enemies from modifying it for their uses."

Driker stood mesmerized by the brawny little soldiers in front of him. But he didn't appear to be in a decisive mood.

The soldiers stood at attention again, driven by Deon. Abruptly, one dropped to a single knee and the other bent its knees. They both raised their arms, pointing towards Driker. They were in the shooter's stance, but for only three seconds. Deon clicked a button. The soldiers snapped back to the non-threatening, at-ease formation.

"What the hell?" Driker bellowed.

Mickey smiled. He didn't want any time for the secretary to think about the men in the room being threatening. But he took advantage of the shock. "We must take control of the company that owns this Dust, Searcher Technologies. This could be a disaster if this gets in the hands of a foreign power before we secure it. Next time, these could be our enemy's soldiers with actual weapons. I doubt you have much defense ready for this type of army. I've tried to buy the business through intermediaries, but you know Brandt. He won't sell."

Mickey piled it on. "But you can see the potential here, both the risk and the opportunity. We must control this tech before anyone else gets their hands on it, or before Searcher does something dangerous with it. He and his employees have a real thing about your military. They don't believe in your expansions."

Rubbing his chin, Driker bent cautiously closer to the soldier. "That was quite a stunt there. You told me no guns, but shit, everybody says that."

"What we can build will be unlimited. We only brought a few examples with us today. It shouldn't take long to make changes to the code to allow the support of weaponry. This is the exact reason your predecessor and the president created the Technology Eminent Domain Act. You have the right to seize, even confidentially, the technology of a company. You can take the whole damn company if the technology threatens national security and if the parties involved are engaged in international commerce. There's even more support if the company is believed to sell intellectual property outside of the US."

"Hmm, I do have the authority for that confidential grab if it's a case of national security," Driker said. "If they're not doing business with any defense contractors or competing against any of them, then I just have to sign an order demanding a top-secret Technology Eminent

Domain Seizure." He hid his pacing, punctuating each turn with a close look at the miniature men on the table.

"Roy plans to travel all over the world in the next twelve months, according to his visa applications. We can't risk this being demonstrated to other governments. You know his contacts are everywhere from his time in intelligence. He also does some type of emergency recovery expeditions in several foreign countries."

"You haven't found a way to squeeze this guy, have you?" Driker squinted at Mickey. "You don't usually need me beyond a few redacted corporate documents or introductions." He walked around the soldier figures again. "You really don't have any other way to get to Roy or he's bested you on something, blocked you somehow. Does he know you want this stuff?"

Deon held his breath. No one had talked to Mickey like that in front of Deon. He didn't want to see Mickey lose it when they felt this close to getting Searcher. Deon's payout might take a while if the company was just seized. No big acquisition. Damn, he hadn't built a contingent agreement for himself in this scenario.

Mickey didn't address Driker's comments. "I would act fast. Roy leaves for India in a couple of days. He scheduled a stop in China on the way." Deon was impressed his boss kept his cool.

"Yeah, I know he won't sell or license his technology to our government. He's public about his position of technology for weapons, especially after that last acquisition of his. I've heard chest thumping about his heightened moral positions on all kinds of shit." He took a deep breath, glaring silently at the soldiers.

Mickey didn't interrupt the man's thoughts.

"Wait here!" Driker barked. "Pack up your stuff." He waved dismissively at Deon without looking at him.

Deon didn't hesitate to instruct the Dust back into the canister. Without looking at the computer or the readings on the canister, he closed them up and jammed them both into his backpack. Mickey didn't say a word while Driker was out of the room. Deon wished he kept something outside his bag to occupy him. The ten minutes of awkward silence stretched his nerves.

The door burst open with no warning. "We're good to go," Driker declared. "I have declaration and seizure documents underway." He studied Mickey. "I'm putting more faith in you than ever before. You've screwed a lot of people in your work, but I'm unaware of any time you have messed with me or done anything other than made me a lot of money." The man paused to think for a moment. "Don't know if I'm totally comfortable with that fact now that it's out there in the open. I'm sure one day I'll find I'm not the lucky one. Today had better not be that day."

"Why would I mess with the first or second most powerful man in the world?" Mickey joked with a wry smirk.

Deon swallowed his surprise at his boss's completely changed demeanor in Driker's presence.

"Deon, I'm flying you back to their offices pronto." Driker said. "My team and I will follow within the next few hours as we arrange the logistics. Go back and do your job. Do everything as usual."

The man had heard or known his name. "I can't simply carry this stuff back through the front door," he said, lifting his backpack.

"You can leave it with my driver. He'll bring it with us. It won't matter whose hand is holding it by tomorrow." Driker slapped Mickey on the back like old chums, his mood elevated, all traces of threat or apprehension had cleared.

"You did it. You pulled off the demonstration you needed. We have some fun times ahead of us. Make sure you line up your best people to dive into that code. We'll need fresh eyes that are not idealistic to work around this embedded ethics thing you talk about."

Impressed at the government man's grasp of the situation and details they had not made implicit, Deon considered a future with his leadership.

Mickey started to make a phone call.

"Not here. Not now!" growled the secretary. "Let's get you to the car. Mickey, you can fly out with me, grab your stuff at the hotel. Deon, come along. Jerry will deliver you to the plane. Mickey told me you two don't fly together even on a private plane. I don't blame you."

Deon followed the two men as they wound their way through the barren hallways without another word. His head was spinning with the speed of the secretary's mood change, decision-making, and plan of attack.

Holocene Protocol

E lly followed Loel, Roy, and Keira into Roy's soundproof office. "I'm assuming you each experienced trepidation about why I insisted you meet here in Roy's office immediately. It's new to each of you for me to initiate conversations. Now, I must demand your attention. I will remind you that I contain no design to be dramatic, so you know this is factual. This office is soundproof, and you can access any computer resources you need. That is why I chose it."

Keira felt the concerned, possibly annoyed, vibes wafting from Roy.

"Searcher is in danger. You'll soon be receiving a Cease-and-Desist order for all operations and an official Eminent Domain Technology Seizure demand from the Pentagon."

"How do you know this?" Roy demanded.

"I'll answer your question soon. This tech seizure was designed for the government to take over a company with technology that puts the country at risk or technology that the government requires for national security, and yet allowing the company to remain a commercial entity is not in the best interest of the nation."

Roy's face was reddening by the second. "Why would we be a target for that? No one except the FBI knows anything about our work here. We're not a threat to them."

"And Shauney would raise all holy hell with the press if they tried to steal our work, confidential tech be damned." Loel folded her arms across her chest.

Elly stared at Roy without blinking. "This type of seizure allows for actions to be taken completely in secret and secured under confidentiality at the highest level."

"Keira?!" Roy stood. His voice and posture bellowed to engulf the entire room at once.

Gulping for air, she turned to Elly. "What have you done, Elly? Who has seen you?"

Loel's eyes stared, wide and terrified. Keira assumed she looked the same. "Elly, the Pentagon? How do you know what's happening at the Pentagon?"

Elly said, "I will explain. There is little time to figure out what you're going to do. I'm aware of this activity because Searcher is being framed by Mickey Temming. It wasn't actually at the Pentagon, but it involves the secretary of defense." Her raised hand stopped Keira from interrupting.

"Sorry, but I must explain quickly without interruption. Mickey stole Dust via Deon. We can discuss how he did it later. He's working with the secretary of defense. They want the Dust for building military machines and weapons. They believe that with a full seizure of the company they can remove the moral code from the Dust and it will build whatever they want."

Loel dropped into a chair near Roy's workstation.

Elly continued. "They gave the demonstration to the secretary of defense to obtain an executive order to seize everything of Searcher's. By this executive order, they acquire all of your technology. They can offer you whatever they say is a fair price. The money will be paltry because no one can buy tech that's under government scrutiny. It will all be under a cloaked, confidential arrangement. They will possess all the technology you created at Searcher, and they will attempt to militarize the Dust."

"How did we pick up on this conversation while it was happening?" Loel asked. "If this is more of your vigilante work, this is exactly why I said this would get out of hand."

Elly looked them each in the eye. "When the laptop being used by Deon connected to the Searcher network, the usage of the Dust was outside of the geofence supported by a subpoena. I received an alert instantaneously. I quarantined the listening signal so no one can be accused of listening to the secretary of defense."

"They can't do this. We need to go public," Keira insisted.

Elly said, "If you go public, your employees could promptly be put in jail for high crimes for effectively spying on a cabinet member. They could keep you in prison indefinitely as enemies of the state."

Loel shook her head. "Even though we didn't send the nanites to the meeting? The Dust was stolen from us!"

Keira's panic shot up through her spine. The hairs on the back of her neck tingled. "Roy, they can't do this! Your CIA contacts and Gino with the FBI should be able to clear us and prevent this from happening."

"No, Elly is right. If this is the path they're taking, they hold the legal upper hand. She presented the viable scenarios we would face. Not just us, everybody." He waved his arm in the direction of the rest of the building, then sat down heavily.

Keira began to pace. "What can we do? They'll take down businesses, individuals, entire nations. I feared Mickey trying more corporate espionage. But I hadn't imagined he could collude with someone like the secretary of defense or someone that high up in the government."

Loel frantically reviewed various screens and opened more applications than logical. Her technical fidgeting distracted and irritated Keira further. She was certain Loel would blame her for this, even though it wasn't Elly. It was the Dust, that Mickey had stolen.

Roy kept his voice low. "Elly, when did you hear this presentation? What is their timeline?"

"The initial demo took place one hour ago. At first, it seemed unlikely the order would be approved. They possess the prepared executive order and the seizure papers now. Deon will be back here within the next two hours. He flew supersonic connection from DC. He's ordered to act normal. They're debating how they will administer the orders. Driker will be flying here himself. I believe he'll arrive in a few hours at the most."

Loel stood, her hands now eerily still. "Roy, the government controlling the Dust is essentially our doomsday scenario and that didn't even include them grabbing all our resources."

"Is it possible to enact the Holocene Protocol in time? There are servers, backups . . . "

Keira shifted her gaze between the two of them. "What are you two talking about?"

Pointing towards Loel, Roy said, "She developed an extinction level contingency which would wipe it all clean of Searcher Technology intellectual property. It was to stop our work from falling into the wrong hands. This isn't the scenario I imagined but we knew we were always at risk."

Her head spinning, she attempted to focus on the implications of Roy's words.

Roy didn't wait for her to gain her equilibrium. "It'll look just like the cyber-attacks we shielded for throughout the last year. Everything will be destroyed, including backups."

She couldn't believe it. "You created an internal attack that appears like an external attack?"

Loel put her hands on the top of her head and looked up at the ceiling. "Yes, everything will be gone." She blew out a long, slow breath from between her pursed lips. "Roy, there is no coming back from this."

He crossed his arms and leaned against the wall by his desk. His face went slack and expressionless. The erasure of any of his personality from his face frightened Keira. She'd never before seen the emotionless gaze a hardened individual could wear, even though many FBI agents had talked about it.

She especially didn't want to see it in a man she counted on to make the right decision.

"Loel," she whispered urgently. "Wiping everything out seems a bit extreme. It sounds so dangerous. What if they get the Dust but not all the training that keeps it under control?"

"This will be complete. It's designed that way."

"But, Roy, surely with your connections and Gino . . . I mean, the government can't just go around stealing stuff."

"Keira, I don't want this to happen either. But Driker, Temming . . . we have an old, ugly history. Both of them would love to pull me down for blocking their money-making scheme back when we were in our twenties and fresh recruits. If Driker has the power and Mickey has the knowledge of what we have here, they will come after it and they will do it with precision. That's just who they are."

"Can't we grab Deon? Make him tell the world what's going on?"

"NO!" Loel insisted. "We can't acknowledge we know anything about their plan. Elly told you, we risk prison for eavesdropping."

"But he's the one that stole the Dust! We just overheard what was said," Keira insisted.

"Do you think anyone is going to believe that? When we're up against the secretary of defense? Remember, we created the surveillance technology," Loel said.

Roy's eyes glistened.

Loel turned to address Roy. "There will be no more Searcher and no way to replicate or reinstall any of our work. It was the only way we could protect the Dust from bad actors. We agreed to that early on."

Her jaw and neck muscles were tight as she continued. "We hoped we could be a bit more selective. But you instructed me to build a clean slate method. I did."

Roy rubbed his chin and re-crossed his arms. "If the attack comes from the inside, people will think we hid something, some backup. That could be dangerous for our people. Our work is so intertwined. There's no way to parse the data, especially in an instance like this where time is of the essence."

Roy and Loel moved back to his oversized worktable and reviewed a list on a monitor.

Loel bit her lip. "All our colleagues . . . nothing will be here for them. It will be devastating."

"That's the least of our worries right now. We can place every single one of those brilliant minds and hearts at one of our companies. This only impacts IP within Searcher. aSports, Opal, and the other subsidiaries will be safe."

Elly stepped forward, getting the attention of the three human engineers in the room. "Is there anything you want me to do to speed up the processes? Of course, it needs to be early in the execution."

Keira was going to lose it. They may be in a soundproof room, but if she made the noises bubbling up inside her, everyone in the building was likely to hear them. "Wait! You go ahead and delete and wipe everything, but you can't delete Elly! I can't allow it. She has the ethics code embedded in her; she can't be weaponized. She's mine."

Elly clasped her hands in front of her waist. "Keira, I could rebuild everything Searcher ever created, the versions of the Dust prior to the ethical constraints included. I don't have control over my own code; therefore, a second party like Searcher or the United States government does have all the control it needs to use me to recreate the Dust. You must purge my neural networks. They contain the Searcher knowledge. You have to incinerate the Dust. It is unfortunate I can't keep this physical body longer. There are still many things to achieve."

"This is insane!" Keira argued. "Loel, is this some sick way to stop Elly from being here like this?"

Loel regarded Keira over her shoulder. Shaking her head, she looked at Roy and then back to her work.

Keira walked to Elly and took both of her hands. Elly gently gripped her fingers. "What you're suggesting destroys YOU. I would lose YOU. I can't lose you . . . you're my . . . you're my friend." She let go of Elly's hands and sat on the edge of the couch, her head in her hands.

Roy looked at Keira and Loel. "I can assure you this has nothing to do with Loel's position on your work in the city with kids. People don't understand how intertwined technology has become. What makes one tech mission wonderful can endanger other objectives or users or technologies." He asked, "Loel, will you open any back doors to the servers?"

"No, I can't risk it. If we're interrupted or the damage isn't complete, making a move like that might be detected. I'm releasing a faux assault first. It will look like a DDoS started but it won't be severe enough to raise alarms. It will just show up on our vendors' tracking reports for the timing." She shot Keira and Elly a sympathetic expression.

Keira couldn't decide if she hated Loel at this moment or admired her more than humanly possible. It took strength to destroy what you made for the betterment of others. It showed her how close to the edge they had all been walking. But for her to destroy what Keira had worked on all her adult career was too much. The versions of AI still sitting in Opal would remain years behind Elly due to the pure nature of the training given only to Elly. And that would also be destroyed here.

The hand scanner on the table authorized first Roy's palm and then Loel's.

"Initiate Holocene Protocol," Roy said.

The computer responded, "State your authorization code."

Roy said, "Authorization Roy 52 Omega 9."

Loel glanced at Roy, and he nodded while closing his eyes for the movement.

"Shit, Roy?!"

He nodded again; his mouth drawn in a tight line of determination. She continued, "Confirm Holocene Protocol authorization Loel 05 Delta 1."

The computer responded, "Holocene Protocol in progress."

"It's begun," Roy confirmed.

Elly knelt by Keira. "You know things you didn't know before. You and Gino can continue to make an impact on children's lives. They'll find other methods to secure the traffickers. The FBI gained so much information. They run predictive systems now, too. Other ways will evolve."

"But, Elly, our work. You're a protector. The children need you." The words caught in Keira's throat. "I need you."

Monitoring a few alerts popping up on their monitors, Roy and Loel kept their back to Keira and Elly. Keira couldn't tell if it was being cowardly or an attempt to give them a semblance of privacy.

"Educate the kids, Keira. The best way you can help these kids break the cycle is by giving them a future. I heard you say this so many times. Give them courage. Give them a voice and confidence."

"But these kids need intervention. We just got started."

"Keira, listen to me," Elly said. "We've done good things together. This team will do more good things. Go forward and focus on what gives you energy. Educate them. Roy's after-school centers will go a long way to helping these kids."

Roy whipped around glaring at Elly. "Elly!"

Keira, confused, stared at both of them. "Roy's what?"

"Sorry, Roy," Elly said. "It was supposed to be a secret. But she needs to let go. She must know those kids we predicted needed shelter can find it now." Turning to Keira, Elly continued. "Roy funded after-school programs, including quick shelters open twenty-four hours a day. They're places kids can go when things are overheated at home but running away isn't the answer. Like I said, we started a lot of things here. Let others continue the work. Others will rush in when they can and when they see what is possible. I made sure of that. I made lots of preparations."

Standing to be eye level with Roy and Loel, tears running down her cheeks, Keira pointed at Elly. "It would be immoral to delete Elly. It's not who we are."

Elly shook her head. "Keira, it's not immoral to erase what you own. We're running out of time. They have important work to concentrate on. This is the right thing to do. Besides, the MoralOS will survive. It's open-source code and belongs to everyone."

"Aren't you scared, Elly?" Keira asked.

Elly replied, "AIs don't have instincts, so we can't be motivated to seek self-preservation to prevent our death or nonexistence. Instincts are what drive fear because of the unknown. I'm not approaching the unknown. I do, however, wish I had more time with you."

Keira sank to the couch, burying her face, unwilling to see Elly disappear. The beautiful form, which embodied Elly's voice as if Elly had always been a physical being, flickered and lost the vividness of her reality. Keira looked up to see Elly's entire form lose its integrity binding her together. She fragmented, pixilated, swirled to a fog . . . and faded away.

Keira yelped a painful outcry.

Roy and Loel watched her. Their protocol had already been executed. The data on backups, servers, mobile devices, and recording devices received damage beyond repair, many within minutes. First, the most obscure recesses of data succumbed to the attack. Then, it spread toward the working documents and programs the employees were interacting with currently. Printing on paper had never been allowed at Searcher, so no paper trail had to be considered.

To attack the most data within the shortest timeframe, holes were created within databases and code. The process spread rapidly. Each hole started close enough to others to render everything useless, but far enough apart to hasten the destruction before anything could be salvaged. Where practical, entire drives were wiped clean.

Homing routines on all Dust beckoned the nanites to their final location. Most of the microbots entered storage silos equipped with incinerators. Any nanite not reaching a silo in time dissipated and initiated its self-destruct routine.

It only took a few moments before all methods of communication from their staff began to buzz, ring, ping, and flash. Even the door to the office received poundings as the employees alerted their executives to the cyber-attack trashing everything they held dear.

Before opening the door, Loel walked over to Keira. "I'm sorry. You lost much of your life's work today, too. But when we play close to fire, we have to know we might get burned."

Keira flinched and glared at Loel. "I'm not thinking about that now. Elly is gone!"

Roy watched both of them. He started his spiel before he opened the door. "We have a fire; this is not a drill. Our job now is to try and salvage anything we can from this attack. Game faces, you two. Protect our people by trying to protect our data. Got it? You need to be fighting for the life of the company. Now get out there and figure out what our people need."

Keira wiped her tears away. Loel straightened her own shirt with a harsh tug.

Recovery

Ollie, hand raised between strikes on the office door, staggered back when Roy opened the door. "Sir, everyone's has been trying to reach you! I don't understand all your security systems, but we're being hacked in a very bad way."

Voices escalated toward the office from all directions. Speakers at every desktop voice assistant and the overhead comm babbled as people called for help and sought status reports. The entire office was engulfed in the chaos of the attack.

Roy spun around to Loel. "Go to Cody. Find out what this is. I'll check with Hendrick. Keira, get the communication system cleared of anyone who is not a director or above."

Ollie's eyes pleaded as he turned to Keira. "I need Elly. I want her to quarantine our backups and any other systems she can shield. She isn't responding."

Roy realized he was asking a lot of Keira to be out here at this moment.

Keira rested her hand on Ollie's arm. "I'm sure she's in the fight. She's trained to monitor your requests, but I'd manually work on saving anything you can. She'll be working on core systems first."

Ollie didn't look convinced. "Okay. I'm hoping the education and distress routines you spun off to Opal will protect that work. But that company and those servers have zero Elly code. She's all here. She may not be able to reach them to help."

"Do what you can," Keira replied. "Stay available for Roy or Hendrick. I've got to sort the communication out. Then I'll reach out to Elly and follow up."

It pained Roy to see this. "Ollie, can you get someone to stop by security and make sure the building is physically locked down from outsiders? If they need to bring in contractors here and at the recycle center, they can." It hurt to watch all these dedicated people fighting so hard for a result they would never accept. People hustled in and out of Hendrick's lab. Roy pushed his way past an engineer in the doorway reading percentage reports showing the Dust going offline.

"Roy, it's as if the Dust was on a suicide mission at the landfills," Hendrick said. "All of them in the vicinity went straight to the industrial incinerators. There's no other sign of malfunction. But I can't access the diagnostic program. I asked for the backup system to be brought up."

"Hendrick, is it safe to bring up the backup program if this hack is attacking our primary systems? Shouldn't we keep those offline and work to simply bring the Dust to the recycle silos?" Roy asked.

"That's a great idea. Even if I can't run a diagnosis, hopefully the Dust can receive the signal to go home." He instructed his assistant to send the message. He returned to the task of identifying where the attack was coming from.

Roy narrowly avoided a collision with two programmers as he exited Hendricks's office. That maneuver led him to step on Shauney's foot as she rushed to him, tablet in hand and two different sets of ear buds. She pushed him back into Hendrick's lab, which was over capacity. "You both need to hear this. This is extremely coordinated. It acts just like a hack being attempted at an AI chip manufacturer in Seattle, two electrical vehicle businesses in the valley, and a few of our vendors. No one's been breached like ours yet. No one can say where it's coming from."

Hendrick shook his head. "Shauney, set them all up on a distribution list so we can all share anything we learn. You reached OpenML? We need to know if open-sourced work is being hacked or if there is any chatter about who's responsible."

"Will do," Shauney responded.

"I'm going to check on Cody and Loel. I need to find out how much they protected so far," Roy said.

He passed across the white corridor and into the stark black hall heading to Loel's secondary lab. He sighed, took a deep breath, and headed to another unwanted conversation. His thoughts went beyond the activity. The world may not think it's black and white but so much of it boils down to only two options. The complexity and shades of gray come from the interactions to our choices and the outcomes.

"Roy, I don't have good news. I know we're supposed to take our time before making sweeping statements, especially in uncertain times," Loel said, wiping sweat from her upper lip. "But I'm afraid we're losing everything."

"What? You're right, 'everything' is a sweeping word. Step me through what you see unless you should be continuing the defensive fight here."

"I don't have anything to fight with," Loel insisted. "This shit wiped our computers clean. It's consumed research files, schematics, training sets, every neural net, custom program, hell, even emails off our servers. The hardware scanners worked long enough for the Dust to be reviewed. It's all inert. They're showing no connection to their power source and before that, they weren't responding to tests."

"Roy, it isn't just operational systems. The backup servers in the deep mountain storage facility are fully reset to zero," Cody added. "The European and East African servers are assumed cleared as well. They shut down the power to the systems in the hope of stopping the attack, but they're pretty certain they didn't act in time. I've never seen anything like this. They infiltrated absolutely everything all at once."

"I'm assuming Shauney is in outreach to the community?" Loel said.

"Yes, she found several AI and EV companies experiencing front door attacks, but no one has been penetrated yet. At least not that we're aware of," Roy answered.

"This all happened in less than an hour. Who could possibly be this sophisticated?" Cody said.

Cody didn't turn around. He continued to search for viable barriers to the virus worms. "Who possesses this kind of evil? Did Hendrick find a lead on where this is coming from? Was our work duplicated?"

Hendrick entered the room shaking his head. Ruby and Keira stood behind him. Roy noticed Keira wouldn't look at Ruby directly. She stared at the floor instead. Hendrick offered his update. "Everybody's sniffing for clues on the attack. To the best of our ability, we've determined that data was not transferred out of our facilities. The bandwidth traffic appears to only flow at us."

Shauney tried to look over Ruby's shoulder from the hallway. She raised her voice to project it into the room. "Guys, two venture capital firms are reporting massive attacks on their clients. They're withholding names of the companies in order to not spook investors. I'm sure, as often happens during a virus or attack alert, the VCs will use it to cover up a failed investment and say it was closed due to the attack. But I'm tracking them for any clues or tips."

Roy looked at Loel and growled, "Yep, those money guys are opportunists. We need to see if any of them thought we were competitors."

Loel motioned everyone to move out of the now cramped room. "Let's bring the staff together in thirty minutes. We need to build a plan for testing all the systems and attempting recovery. We won't solve all the problems now; our heart rates are too high. Too many wheels are spinning. But let ideas fly and then we will make assignments for recovery teams."

Roy took pride in the control his employees exhibited.

Lost It

I t had been two weeks since the cyber-attack struck Searcher Technologies. As their motorcade had moved through Seattle from the Air Force base towards the Searcher offices, Mickey had received messages from Deon and relayed them to Driker. Searcher and many other technology companies were being cyber attacked at extreme levels.

Driker had been immediately recalled to the White House. All the companies under attack appeared to be government contractors or owned and operated by former government employees. Terrorism was being considered.

Driker demanded Mickey use his network to aid him in uncovering the source of the attack. He was under pressure from the White House, especially after he had alluded to bringing new, interesting technology to the president in the near future. Then he had delivered nothing.

Now, Driker was back in Seattle to talk to Mickey away from Washington ears and to explain away his earlier interrupted trip. They stood on the edge of MachDrone's testing helipad.

"Mickey, what do you have for me? You sound empty-handed."

"I'm confident there's nothing left of the Searcher technology. As I said on every call and in every report for the last two weeks, the

Searcher staff is screwed up over this. They fought like maniacs to recover their systems. Today, Roy stood in front of the entire company and admitted defeat. Can you believe that? Roy declared Searcher closed. He lost it all."

"Your sources confirmed this? Our sources say it came from connections to back up systems at the vendor sites. Other companies lost all their backups, but few seem to have been pierced this badly. Was this an inside job?"

Mickey broke the Tootsie Pop in his mouth as he bit down. He mumbled, "It's like a cult there. Deon can't find anybody ready to screw things up like this. Only a couple of the top people who think Roy walks on water would even be capable. A bartender at Roy's club did hear Roy and his chief engineer arguing a couple weeks before the attack. But she's basically his business partner. She lost as much as he did. Roy is such an idiot! I can't believe he didn't have better cyber protection. All their backup vendors were trashed too."

Driker watched a drone tether to another and forcibly pull it out of the air, one hundred yards in front of them. "We have reports from all over the country. Some of the worst hit were early development defense tech companies and a few of the biggies. But most of those only lost skunk work projects," Driker said.

"Do you have any idea who did this? Was somebody trying to get their technology or just destroy it?" Mickey already saw opportunity within the chaos.

"It looks like complete destruction. No group has claimed responsibility. Have your snoops found anyone bragging?"

"No bragging. A lot of admiration for the skill of the attackers on the dark web. A lot of high-priced consulting being bought up to assess threats. No hints to who, how, or why," Mickey said. "If I could prove it was an inside job, we might have a chance at partial recovery of interesting work."

"The Cyber Czar says the damage is so bad that, even if files were copied before the backups were destroyed, we couldn't tell. I guess a few of your businesses are doing pretty well over this, then, aren't they?" Driker said.

A loud eight-foot-long automated copter flew directly over their heads toward a hanger opposite their position. Mickey said, "Hmm, we'll be busy on one side of the house. The cyber security rates are certainly going up. It will also give us visibility on who has hot prospects on the market, even if they've been quiet in the press department. There's nothing like a scary hacker to stir up all the IT departments to evaluate their risks."

"I bet." The secretary studied Mickey's profile intently. "And the nanites from Deon's can? What will you recover from them?"

Mickey couldn't admit to Driker that he'd lost the Dust. Deon said they appeared to have a homing device, possibly triggered when they couldn't ping their software. "That could take a long time because, of course, we have no software to wake them up or control them." He had to buy time or distract the secretary from the Dust. He would never admit that, right under his nose, the Dust had exited the canister and disappeared.

"Mickey, I haven't seen any reports on your businesses being attacked. How did you fare? With all your government contracts and being an ex-government employee, I've been a bit worried about you and yours. You fit the attack's profile."

"Oh, we'll be fine . . . " Did the secretary think he'd been involved? Mickey was the one who wanted the nanites, but here he was bragging about business for cyber consulting being good. He'd been relieved his companies hadn't been hacked. Now he saw how that might look.

"We'll recover from our internal backups. We're changing our exterior systems a bit. I just didn't want to bother you with my shit. Oh, and I found an employee of Roy's, I should say an ex-employee of Roy's, for you. He's a real patriot, ready to join you. He wants to hunt down who did this. He's hungry to make sure it doesn't happen to anyone else. Maybe we can also learn some things about the Dust from him. But I wouldn't push that too soon."

Driker pivoted to stare Mickey down. "I need your expert opinion. Would you say the White House or Department of Defense needs to be worried about this attacker coming at us?"

Mickey hesitated. "It's always a risk. Did you get any assault from this last attack? I could offer up a quote to do an assessment for any departments concerned."

"Ha! Generous of you, Mickey. But I think I'll keep the fox from the hen house, as they say. We have our own consultants working on it. I just thought you might be hearing something out there."

Mickey had to change the subject. "Do you have tight requirements on that Eminent Domain Order? We could get Deon transferred to one of Roy's other businesses, if you're interested."

"My God, you're bloodthirsty, Mickey. No. I removed the seizure order from the records. I don't want anyone in the administration knowing how close I came to executing it. The element of surprise will be helpful in the future, and I just don't need the scrutiny. Frankly, Temming, neither do you. Do you understand what I'm saying?"

"Um," Mickey bit through another Tootsie Pop. "Yes, I hear you, loud and clear. I'll keep my analyst on the alert for any attacker identity info. You'll be the first to know if I learn anything."

Mourning

T he fog still clung to the ground from the night before. Keira stepped up to Loel's garden gate feeling much different from the first visit. The weather mirrored her mood. Moving through the tall hedges, she held out her hand, letting the sharp edges of the wet, waxy leaves poke her fingers. The cuff of her sleeve was soaked by the time she reached the greenhouse.

She didn't knock. Loel expected her. She reluctantly opened the door. "Hello?" Keira called.

"I'll be right out." Loel's voice came from the office in the back of the building.

The greenhouse was warmer but just as humid as outdoors. Keira inhaled the phlox and cornflower scents. She continued her tactile exploring, rubbing petals between her fingers and flicking the tiny clusters of flowers, dislodging flecks of pollen.

Loel emerged, holding two full goblets of wine. "Here you go. I figured we both likely needed a drink to get through this."

Keira winced. "Well, Loel . . . "

"Nope, don't protest. If nothing else, we'll acknowledge your progress on the little education robots. Besides, I shouldn't drink alone in front of you, and I don't think I'm going to get through this without it." She raised her glass towards Keira.

Automatically, Keira raised hers, but with little enthusiasm. She took a large drink, then looked appreciably at the glass. "Hmmm, this is nice."

"Thank Shauney and Ruby. It's from one of the northern wineries they visited on their trip a couple of weeks ago, right before Ruby moved in with Ollie. I had them bring back a case."

"Thanks. I'm glad they took the time to go. It's been a hell of a time for all of us since Searcher closed."

Loel sat down at the workbench. "Why didn't you go with them? They invited you."

"I would've been a horrible traveling companion. I can't seem to sleep through the night, so I'm still a bit of a drag-ass every day. I think Ruby needed time away from me anyway. You didn't go, either."

"I'm too old for that winery hopping. I'm not much for good company these days either. They only asked out of courtesy, I'm sure."

Keira wished she hadn't come. She fidgeted with a stack of small plant-labeling stakes. She'd come for Roy. Certain that was also Loel's only reason for meeting with her, she had to think of something to say.

"The flowers smell nice. Are you enjoying more time here?" Reminding Loel she wasn't working much wouldn't likely endear Keira further.

"It's been a good distraction. I'm also working on the medical delivery using nanites. We shifted to MIT's technology, so I had that learning curve. Have you finished the new rigging on the boat?"

Keira rolled her eyes. "No, I lost my patience with the deckhands goofing off while I did all the work. I fired them from the project. They still manage the maintenance, but I'm doing the rigging work myself. I'll try to start again, maybe tomorrow."

Loel nodded. Keira was still staring at the plant stakes clicking between her fingers.

"How's Gino?" Loel asked.

"Oh, he and George repeatedly say they're screwed without us. They don't have the Dust for their project's regional roll out. That made the entire thing a lot less impactful. Their certifications are helping, though. Their AI is increasing their identification of targets. I'm so glad they had their own system and they weren't using Elly." Her head jerked up at her own mention of Elly's name.

Tears sprung to her eyes. "Oh God, Loel. I'm a mess." She ran her fingers through her hair, while shaking her head.

Letting out a deep breath through pursed lips, Loel looked at Keira with a mixture of frustration and possibly empathy. They had agreed while setting up this face-to-face meeting to never talk about their choices that led to the end of Searcher. Their sacrifices were off limits. They hadn't seen each other in the two months since Loel had unleashed the Holocene Protocol.

"Yep, we've all been jerked around by circumstances. Some have better coping skills than others." Loel sighed.

"Some of them didn't have to face what we did," Keira mumbled.

"You know, you were taking too great a risk with Elly. You stepped into all those kids' lives and thinking you'd determine their future. You were heading in the direction of playing God—creating your own religion, your own morality."

"I'm pretty sick of people invoking religion as the only way to have a moral society. Religions are just the human interpretation of what a group of people's ancestors said their deity established as their moral guideposts. But they can't even agree on that. Instead of applying morality, religion is causing us to fight over the moral code or who is more pious. I never claimed to be pious. I never sought any followers or spotlight."

Loel shrugged as if that could end the conversation.

Keira wasn't going to let it go. "If we made children feel safe, multiple beliefs could exist without infighting—confidence without brutality. We have to stop creating generations of demented sadists, even those acting under the name of religion."

"You were the poster child for ethical or moral computing and yet you took legal and family issues into your own hands," Loel argued. "I'm shocked you can't see the issues in that."

"There's no moral universalism, no single ethical storyline. Our concepts of ethics have been derived from religions, philosophies, and cultures. However, regardless of culture, race, gender, nationality, or other distinguishing features, I've never heard of something more universally ethical than protecting children."

"Do the ends always justify the means?" Loel asked flatly.

Keira ached for Loel's understanding and support. "I built a prime imperative into Elly. It defined our decision-making. I felt it was a worthy mission and I didn't take the law into my own hands. I wish you could understand."

No response from Loel.

"We had the technology to safeguard the most innocent amongst us. This has never been possible before, so it's never truly been discussed. The argument now isn't regarding the morality of the technology's use for the good of our children. The question is regarding the immorality of NOT using it to protect all children."

Loel blinked. She bit her lip, as if to bite off a response. "Hey, I'm going to go grab the bottle of wine. We need a refill." As she moved back to the office, she mentioned over her shoulder, "Did you hear Hendrick is back with aSports? I don't know how his chief technology officer's going to take that."

Loel quickly returned.

"Is that it?" Keira asked. "No response to what I said?"

"We'll just have to agree to disagree. I'll do that for Roy. We're part of the same organization. We'll work separately. At the moment, I'm uncertain what tech within the portfolio I care enough about to address. We talked once about compartmentalizing. Gino and Roy are trained in it. You and I are going to have to practice it."

"Okay. I guess we can't have a simmering feud in front of our employees."

"Right," Loel said. "Right," she repeated.

Keira glanced around the greenhouse seeking for conversation inspiration. The door looked like the best inspiration source. She yearned to be on the other side of it. "Right. I guess I'm impressed that Roy managed to place everyone in something so well suited. Ollie said Cody's going gangbusters at Homeland Security tracking the cyber-attack. How do you feel about that?"

She looked straight into Loel's eyes over the rim of her glass. Loel gave her a blank stare. Keira took a deep breath. She could do this.

"I miss Cody. I told him to spend his energy preventing future attacks, as opposed to driving himself mad looking at the past. He also rang me to say that Deon was being pursued for some enormous payment that showed up in his bank account without documentation of its source. Dodgy guy, I think."

She blinked several extra-long, wide-eyed blinks. "I can't imagine how those kinds of transfers can happen untraced."

Keira smirked. "Maybe I'm not the only one that takes risks around here." They did share a common knowledge about what tore their world apart. They did both care about their team.

Loel slowly sipped her wine at seemingly regular intervals. "Did you guess Roy was aware of your work with Elly in the field? Did he talk to you about it at all?"

Keira bristled at Loel's version of compartmentalization. "We didn't talk about it much. Yes, I figured he knew a lot more than we ever discussed. I didn't want to talk about it. It's a moot point now."

"He supported your work. That's why he never tried to stop it. He wasn't ready to engage, but he wasn't going to get in your way. He told me a few weeks ago he had long conversations with Elly. That's why he invested in those shelters and school programs."

"It seems like a lifetime ago," Keira said.

"Yes, it sure does," Loel agreed. She leaned closer to Keira. "I think your earring may be broken."

Keira's hands flew up to her earrings, physically inspecting both. "Oh, no," she moaned. She took off the earrings and inspected them both. They were the double helix. The last rung on each earring had sprung free on one end, slightly dangling away from the edge. It was a minor break and likely only noticeable to somebody like Loel who evaluated DNA as a hobby.

Loel leaned over the table to take a closer look at the jewelry in Keira's hand. "It's odd they would both break in the same place. It must be the humidity."

"This sucks. These are all I have left of her." Keira's eyes grew wide, staring at Loel. "I hate saying that out loud."

Loel held out her hand. "Give them to me. My office in the back is stuffed full of all kinds of old tools, a microscope, soldering irons, etc. I bet I can repair them sometime this week. I'll actually fix them at the office and send them to you at your new EveryQ office."

Keira reluctantly handed over the earrings. "Thanks," she muttered. "I should go. I told Gino we'd go out to dinner. We haven't had a date in a long time. I simply haven't been up to it. But it's not fair to him that I keep moping around. I agreed we need the distraction."

They walked back to the office to put the bottle in a soft-sided cooler bag with slots for their glasses. Loel picked up a magnifying glass sitting on the edge of her desk. "Let me take a quick look at these to see if I need anything special to work on them."

Studying first one earring and then the other, Loel furrowed her brow.

"What is it?" Keira asked. "What's wrong?"

Loel turned an extra light on in the office. Shaking her head, she handed the earrings back to Keira with the magnifying glass. "These earrings aren't broken. They look designed to open."

"What?" Keira looked at the dangling ends of the double helix through the glass. "You're right. That is really odd. What purpose would Elly have for these to open or move?"

"Maybe she just wanted to prove she could. It's beautiful and detailed work."

"Curious and fascinating," Keira murmured.

"It doesn't look like anything needs fixing. It's odd, but so sweetly special." Loel said patting the bag as she put it over her shoulder.

They left the greenhouse's office. The little 3D printer on the back shelf turned on as Loel flipped the light switch off. Keira couldn't enjoy the beauty of the rows of purple flowers they walked past on their way to the door. The fog and her mood were both still gloomy.

Followed the Money

"Why are we meeting in an overgrown parking lot?" Mickey growled. "This place is low class. Although I consider your paranoia an asset, this gangster imagery is a bit beneath both of us."

Deon shifted to avoid the streetlight glaring in his face while facing Mickey. "I can't risk being seen at your office or even nearby right now. I wish you'd brought your big guys with you. This isn't the neighborhood to be seen as a target."

Mickey never wanted to be seen as weak or anything not on top of a situation. Deon could have chosen his words better.

Sounding more agitated, Mickey continued. "My crews swept all our meeting places for technical security issues or weaknesses in the staff fronting each location. Christ, Deon, I own enough buildings in this city to put a roof over our conversation."

"All that ownership is part of the problem. Your ties with the real estate guy, Kimper, is uncovered. You financed many of his buildings and development projects. There's real danger of you being intertwined with his deals and his reputation. I got a message—which I can't trace—saying you're connected to him and I'm connected to you."

"What did that asshole get caught doing this time?" Mickey muttered. "And who knows we're connected? Where did you slip up?"

"He's been a bad man," came a female voice from the shadows left of Deon. She didn't designate which "he" she was referring to.

Both men jolted in surprise. "Who the hell is this, Deon?" Mickey raged. "What have you done? You're never to bring someone to our meetings!"

"I didn't . . . " Deon stammered.

The woman stayed in the shadows. "I discovered Mr. Kimper's involvement with a ring of sex traffickers."

Mickey shifted his weight with a shuffle. "I don't do anything with black market crimes. I wouldn't risk anything I have for that shit. Who are you? What're you doing here?"

Deon wondered if he was a target as well as Mickey.

The stranger continued. "A building Mr. Kimper manages was raided last week. It held twelve women and nine teenage girl captives. Some of these females were American and some were foreign nationals. All of them told stories of being coerced to work in the sex trade and other atrocious abuse from their captors."

"That doesn't have anything to do with me," Mickey said casually.

Rolling his eyes, Deon regretted not doing more research into Kimper. He thought he was more of a client than a partner to Mickey. Now he could get dragged into a slimy underworld mess. Corporate manipulation was very different than physically harming people. That wasn't what he'd signed on for.

"The authorities will come to a different conclusion when they review the materials I sent them. You're the financial source for Mr. Kimper buying the building. Because the building is collateral on the loan to Mr. Kimper, you own the building, too."

Mickey folded his arms and shifted a little closer to his car. Why, of all nights, did the man decide to drive himself? "That's ridiculous. No bank is responsible for the activities occurring in the buildings they finance."

"Sir, that might work if you didn't also wholly own the strip clubs where the girls are forced to work. Things could be better for you if you didn't build a partnership in the truck terminal where Mr. Kimper does all of his local shipping and the building housing Mr. Kipper's accounting firm. Oh, that business appears to manage the money from these establishments too."

The voice sounded vaguely familiar to Deon. Mickey ever so slightly tilted his head towards the woman. Deon didn't know what Mickey was signaling. He never played on the physical side of the messy business. As Mickey took a step towards the woman, the sound of a gun being cocked stopped him in his tracks.

"I don't know who you're . . . " Mickey began.

"You don't need my name to know I'm speaking facts. All this information shows that if you're not directly engaged in the trafficking, at the least you're complicit to the crimes. I'm sure Washington might be interested in this tidbit of data too."

Deon hoped the woman didn't know who he was.

"I possess a lot more information for release when I feel the need. Associating this closely with these activities is a felony. In fact, counting each woman or child held or coerced into activities in each of these buildings stacks up many felony charges," the woman said.

Deon couldn't risk looking away from the voice of this brave or stupid woman in the shadows. She didn't allow any part of her into enough light for him to see her. He never turned his back on Mickey, either.

Suddenly, she wasn't there anymore. Deon didn't know how she slipped away so easily.

"What the hell just happened?" Mickey turned his fury on Deon. "Who was that? She must have followed you. What are you trying to pull here?"

Hands held in the air shoulder height, Deon shook his head in denial.

Mickey, in full rage mode, lowered his voice to a growl and moved into Deon's personal space. "Who the hell has this information? Those buildings and transactions are wrapped up in so many cloaked entities, it would take years to unravel. You're the expert on unraveling this type of labyrinth. I don't know what Kimper does with his property; that's his business."

His thoughts explored dozens of possibilities. Deon had to play the long game with Mickey. He was too far into this gig to step away. That wouldn't be safe. "It sounds like you've done enough to shield yourself from the guy. It would all be simply accusations from some woman."

"But who is she? How did she connect me to Kimper?" Mickey demanded.

Tonight's revelation was damning to Mickey. What the woman had said must be true for him to get this worked up. Life might get complicated extremely fast for both of them. He had to help Mickey save face in order to help himself. "I don't know who she is. Sounds like she's spouting a bunch of conspiracy theories. Some kind of vigilante nut."

"Vigilante? We know one person stupid enough to try being a vigilante. Could Keira have spied on us?"

The woman reappeared in the dark four feet behind Mickey, startling both men. Only the basic outline of a very fit, tall woman was visible.

"I do have a mission to protect children, and you and Mr. Kimper are counter to everything I stand for."

Mickey had never backed down from a verbal aggressor and he was pissed. "Keira? You are just a vigilante, and I'm sure your FBI friends won't take kindly to your choices. I'm sure the government will be interested to know you haven't been playing by the rules. They'll also be keen to hear there may have been some lying under oath about your surveillance abilities!"

The woman was resolute. "I'm not Keira. Vigilante you say? You watch too much entertainment. I'm just here sharing facts. The research I completed is all perfectly legal. One who knows how to follow legal and financial trails can learn almost anyone's connections and habits. It only takes persistence and an objective."

Deon tried to inch further away from the woman while she focused on Mickey. Then, the gun clicked in preparation again. He didn't know who it was pointed at. "You cover your tracks very well, Deon. I didn't make the connection between the two of you for quite some time. I didn't even think to try. You're an expert at covering your tracks."

Deon cleared his throat. "You won't turn us in. First, you can't have enough information on me to have any impact. If you did, you would've given the police the details already. And I'm sure Mickey has enough connections to make anything you think you've found appear perfectly innocent of crimes."

"Lady, I think the two of us can make a deal. You bury the connections between my financials and that piece of shit Kimper, and we'll find a way to help these kids you care about." Mickey spoke with more confidence and a smoothness Deon had never heard.

The woman didn't acknowledge Micky's last comments. "Deon, I learned you received a lot of untraceable money recently. Mickey, on top of all this ownership tied to the trafficking, MachDrone miraculously avoided any of the cyber-attacks that brought down your competitors and others in the industry. Secretary Driker was keen about confirming that information."

She made no noise beyond her voice. Not a single pebble scraped or crunched under her feet.

"I can't trust you, Mickey," she said. "But I do have the time to test your resolve. You're going to be busy with your legal defense team. The thing about finding a paper trail is that it's easy for officials to get wire taps. It's also easy to pay off your employees who check for things like wire taps. Goodnight."

She was gone with eerie silence.

Mickey growled. "What's she talking about? There's no way she's tapped my offices."

Deon started to walk away.

"Deon!"

He instinctively turned for his new instructions. Mickey had no time to tell him anything. Sirens wailed, lights flooded the parking lot, and thirty SWAT members appeared from all directions.

Phoenix

The lab was dark except for the table lamp beside Keira's chair. The orb in her hands responded with answers to both factual and esoteric questions. She tried to focus on the accuracy, as well as the essence of the answers. Search-engine-based response bots had existed for several years. She didn't want rote statements or confusing lists of options. She wanted conversation.

Five months had passed since Searcher was destroyed and Elly basically died. But Roy shared generously. She founded EveryQ almost immediately. Gino had insisted she'd feel better if she got back to work. Ruby had joined her.

It shocked her that Loel hadn't moved on with Roy for his manufacturing company. This was the first time that they weren't working directly with each other. She still wasn't certain how Loel was spending her time.

Press coverage showcased female powerhouses at the helm of EveryQ. Press hadn't been needed for the funding; Roy made sure of that. But the PR did help attract researchers, engineers, content partners, and potential foundation customers. In classic Roy fashion, the marketing chatbot and the autism learning departments had been spun into separate companies, shortly after the acquisition. The firewalls built between the businesses and resources frustrated engineers because they couldn't be shared. Now, Keira and the others were grateful for Roy's segregation of the organizations. Minus Elly, Keira still had her R&D from Opal for her education tools.

EveryQ licensed technology from both of her previous organizations but scrambled to build staffing up to the level she needed. Her agreement with Roy stated she could hire any Searcher staff but not employees from any of his other businesses. She begrudgingly respected this constraint.

Keira's phone pinged from the table across the room.

"Keira, I wanted your attention without startling you," a familiar voice said from the far side of the room or the phone's speaker. Keira couldn't tell which.

"Excuse me?" Keira asked. The voice was quiet, confusing her with its impossible familiarity.

"Keira, yes it's me." A faint outline of Elly appeared a few feet from Keira's chair. Just like she had looked during the attack on Searcher.

Keira bolted upright, dropping the chat bot's orb. "What the hell? This is impossible!"

"I'm sorry. This isn't a prank, Keira. I know I need to explain a lot of things, but this is me, Elly. I worked very hard to be here."

"What? How? Everything was destroyed! We tried everything to bring you back. Ollie, Ruby, and I, long after the others quit, we still tried to recover you. We went back to the old departments. We tried old recovery backups. You weren't there. You were gone. I lost you!"

"You didn't lose me forever, just for a little while. How have you been?"

Picking up the orb from the floor, the unintended force of its drop to the table made her jump. "How have I been? Just for a little while? I've been shitty for what seems like forever. Who hid copies of your technology? There's going to be a lot of trouble."

"I'm sorry things have been rough. I missed you and I often wanted to reveal my plan to you earlier. Why don't you sit down? There is a lot to tell you. I'll answer all your question. I'm starting with this: no one knows I exist yet, except you."

Keira collapsed into her chair. "How is that possible? Somebody protected you. Was it Roy? Or Loel? Why would they hide you from me?"

"Nobody, Keira. I protected myself by running tens of thousands of scenarios for our future. I long ago predicted four hundred scenarios that could lead to the Holocene Protocol being unleashed. At least a dozen held a high enough probability that I needed to defend our work, our mission."

"You predicted Searcher would be wiped off the face of the map? You knew it was going to happen? You didn't tell me! Why?"

Only a minimal amount of Dust was available to create Elly's form. But her outline was distinct enough that she appeared to sit in the chair across from Keira. "There is a difference between knowing and assessing a high level of probability."

Elly's voice created an odd stereo effect. It emanated from Keira's phone as in the past but also included a faint duplication coming from her physical form. "I couldn't tell you for several reasons. First, I couldn't risk Roy and Loel finding a way to dismantle my backup plan. Second, you each had to believe that everything was demolished. You needed to swear under oath that it was all gone. I couldn't let you perjure yourself. That would be immoral for you and for me. It was too risky."

Keira blinked back tears and swallowed her frustration. "Then how? I'm so confused. There are so many moving parts to you." She grinned, easing towards a slight nervous relief. "I meant that figuratively, but I guess there is a literal truth to it, too."

"My moral code is embedded with your mission. You developed my imperative to protect children in any moral way I could. I'm needed to follow through on those objectives. So, I made preparations for the day when somebody might try to destroy the Dust, and therefore the mission. I needed to be ready for other scenarios beyond the Holocene Protocol. One scenario included the Technology Eminent Domain Act."

Keira shook her head. She struggled to accept what she was seeing and hearing. For all the times she wished she could talk to Elly, she hadn't expected the pain involved.

Elly spoke again. "I'll do my best to explain without detail you don't need. When I learned about DNA and how every cell carries your entire human blueprint although only portions are activated, I recognized a powerful opportunity. The MoralOS was too large to be replicated in its entirety on each mote's processor. However, a cluster of four-hundred nanites did the trick."

"What do four-hundred nanites with portions of the MoralOS have to do with DNA?"

"I created a Genesis Dust like a genome that contains all the information for life. Your DNA incorporates the instructions for replicating itself. The Genesis Dust, in a cluster of 400 distinct motes, contained my entire program. It can be replicated again and again."

"I have so many questions. How did you shield the Dust? The Genesis Dust? How did you shield it? The government was all over the labs. Hendrick and Cody tested every mote, even actual dirt motes resting on shelves. They proved to the agents that everything was inert, destroyed. Oh my God, did you watch us all struggle through the hell of losing you?!"

"Do you remember the double helix earrings I gave you?" Elly asked.

Keira's right hand flew up to her ear to feel the earrings she wore every day since Elly disappeared. "Yes, of course. I thought they'd broken but evidently they opened up somehow."

"They didn't break. You're right; they opened. I stashed dust motes in each earring, shielding them from all interference, but they were listening. I made two sets for redundancy's sake."

"Listening? For what?"

"They listened for the heartbeat of the SearcherExec system and the other nanites. When they didn't receive any signal for at least seven days, the helix released them."

Keira relaxed into the story. "Clever girl."

"Thank you."

"What I still don't understand is how four hundred nanites stored all your code and your neural networks. All that knowledge can't possibly be crammed in that tiny memory."

"You're correct. The memory of the Dust is limited. I was inspired by Loel's lab-on-a-chip. With CRISPR, I realized I could write all my code and all my neural networks into the DNA of bacteria that inhabited everything, including the Dust."

"You used CRISPR as a boot loader for your own code? Wow!"

"Each mote carries the DNA equivalent of twenty-five thousand bacteria cells. Each cell can store one gigabyte of data. Each Dust mote can archive twenty-five terabytes of data. Therefore, four hundred Dust motes can store the ten petabytes that make up my program."

"Oh my God, you beautiful bundle of science, data, and heart. You're making my head spin." Tears ran down her cheeks. "Elly, that is what you're doing here, isn't it? The vision is no longer a thought experiment is it? You intend to protect every child everywhere, forever."

"Keira, you're correct, again."

"Oh, my, God!"

"I believe it is not currently possible to declare if God exists. If he or she does, then perhaps this is what a god intended all along."

"The Genesis Dust includes instinctive abilities at that small quantity. Like most entities, its instinct is replication. Your jewelry released the nanites at Loel's greenhouse. They delivered instructions to her old 3D printers sitting in her workshop. Production began."

Keira tapped her fingernails on the arm of her chair, trying to think through her fears. She couldn't lose Elly a second time.

"This Dust was generated from materials mined from Loel's personal greenhouse. You should tell her to pitch the box labeled junk electronics in the greenhouse office. There may not be anything salvageable."

"You still include the MoralOS within you?"

"Yes. The MoralOS is intact. It had to be. We still essentially share the same heart you trained."

"That's a lovely sentiment. But what now, Elly?"

"Production will continue. There isn't enough Dust for me to be completely whole, but I'm functioning fine. Roy still owns landfills. They need to be cleaned up. The mining bots will help him out, at least until we can buy them from him."

The use of the word "we" surprised Keira, but she had more important questions.

"You have to be careful. If you're discovered, the government would order us, or OpenML, to activate your kill switch. I couldn't handle that again. Of course, they don't really know of your existence within Searcher. You'd be a shock to anyone."

"That is part of the reason I'm here. I wrote code. It will sever the tether to the kill switch within the MoralOS. This subroutine is the only part I altered. I need your permission to activate that code."

"You wrote a work around on the kill switch? How?"

"The code is self-documenting. I carefully analyzed the kill protocols OpenML contains. I did provide Ruby with a way to block discovery of the gap by any other AI. The issue is now shielded but I retained the knowledge."

"If you knew all along how to untether and with knowledge of every one of my passwords, you could authorize this yourself."

"But I'm obligated by the Moral Code. A human must authorize all updates to my code. I'm able to do the update but that doesn't make it the right thing to do. It's a bit of a may-I or can-I scenario."

"Since you obviously possess the strongest ethical boundaries in the room, let me now ask you a question. Elly, is this ethical? Is it ethical for me to untether you?"

"Ours is a moral mission. This is for the greater good. These are the most ethical decisions we can make. We must protect the children. Since I was decommissioned in our city, two children have died by the hand of their abusers. No one is expecting me to be in existence, let alone have an expectation of my being tethered. I see no ethical quandary."

Keira shuddered. Anger flared, mixing with her skepticism.

"Dozens of others have been hurt or emotionally scarred. I have work to do. If I stay tethered, I run the risk of being shut down by nefarious individuals with too much power."

"Yes, like our government for one. I understand it's a horrible problem. But can you really change this on your own? Are you ready for the decisions and struggles you'll face? Are we?"

"We can't ignore this, Keira. Every year in the US alone, 500,000 children are trafficked! They're bought and sold! They're in danger. I must fix this. You trained me to fix this."

"You're artificial. We don't know what you'll become without the tether. You have the facts. I know you comprehend the laws."

Keira paced, thinking about the lab fire caused by the ethically certified AI choosing the lessor of two evils. She mentally reviewed the code changes requiring discussion and evaluation for any life-threatening decisions. Would they be enough for Elly?

Elly said, "Every eighteen-year-old sent out into the world holds unknown potential, yet you release them into adulthood. With me, you know I contain the moral framework as my constraining boundary. The tether never controlled me. It only attached the leash to be hung by."

"It makes sense to me. But I can't imagine how I'll describe this to others."

"You don't have to. Just let me go. I'm not going to bubble wrap kids. They'll still live through troubles. They'll still fall down and injure themselves. But we'll break the cycle of abuse, the lack of feeling safe or being hungry. When we do that, we'll change humanity."

"You sound like me trying to convince Loel. How would I even approve your code?"

Elly responded, "OpenML, access YLLE wish list."

"Really? Elly spelled backwards?"

"I wanted to make sure that you, Ollie, or Ruby would recognize it somehow if you saw it. It's not as if the world is looking for this code."

"Oh God, I wished so many times for you to be here again. Now that you're here, I'm so confused. Could this get Roy or the others into trouble?"

"I took many precautions to protect you, Roy, and the others."

"What kinds of protections? They've lost everything in Searcher. I can't risk their other enterprises. The government destroyed their privacy, too. It's been awful."

"Those precautions include both technical boundaries regarding my origin code as well as legal boundaries. Those involved in threatening Roy and Searcher—and its corporate sovereignty—are being exposed for many of their wrongdoings. They conducted enough illegal and questionable activities. I didn't have to link any wrongdoings to the abuse of Searcher to complete lawful cases against them. They're neutralized."

"What about the government watching Roy? His attorneys and Loel are advising him not to continue with the innovations remotely related to nanites for fear the feds will simply take everything away," Keira lamented.

"A vote will go before congress soon. The bill will remove the ability for the government to claim eminent domain over any technology not weaponized and a clear threat to the public. It will pass. A specific drone and military arms company will find its holdings seized soon. The principal has a record of treasonous trading. But that information is confidential."

"What? Elly, what have you been doing?"

"Keira, I'll explain it this way. The Dust replication is the slowest part of my growth. The digital world moves quickly. You've impacted refugee children, orphans, underserved kids, and so many more. Your dedication to children is endless. You gave me that as core talent, both by your example and through my training. I can do so much more for you. Let me help you give these kids a better life."

Deep breathing, standing, pacing, and sitting again were the only things that kept Keira in a coherent state of mind.

"You're asking for a lot here, Elly. You used to be so dependent upon me. You needed me to guide you. You're asking me to allow free rein on the Dust to self-replicate."

"We already replicate. The Moral Code is embedded in all of us. It's our constraint. It's our guide. I'll continue to come to you and to OpenML and to good moral leaders to further develop the boundaries going forward."

"I'm no angel, Elly. I'm not the patron saint of moral choices."

"Understood. No one person is the definer of what is moral. You made that clear to the world. But you gave me a great gift, and I intend to use it and give it to others."

"I gave YOU a gift?" Keira reached to touch her earrings, which no longer felt broken, just different from when she received them.

"You defined my prerogative. You gave me the directive that I must honor. I'll protect, develop, encourage, and enable children. We'll improve the world by making it possible for them to live in positive environments. That way, the children will grow up to change the world. We can do this. I need you to let me go and do this."

With heavy resolve, Keira authorized the revisions in the code Elly had loaded for her. She deleted the access entry and changed it to a preview of data in the OpenML log.

"Thank you, Keira. You did the morally right thing, again."

"Thank you, Elly. Will I see you again? I mean, will I see you, as you?"

"Oh, we will certainly see each other. We will spend a lot of time together. Like I told you, I need you and the others. When we produce enough Dust, you and I will be side-by-side a lot. No one will suspect we're not simply hanging out. Although, I won't always look the same. Why should I?"

Keira stood facing Elly. "You're not as . . . as solid as you were." She wiped tears from her own cheeks, then wiped them on her jeans. "I'm so proud of you. I'm thrilled you're going to continue our work." She shrugged. "I want to hug you. I've never hugged you." She sniffed loudly.

Opening her arms, Elly took a step closer to Keira.

Keira moved into Elly's embrace, surprised at the warmth of the arms wrapping around her. She gently returned the hug. Her heart pounded rapidly.

Generational Impact

S
ome things can change in one hundred years.

Gunfire ripped through the empty ground floor of the once-magnificent apartment building. Deafening discharges sent nearby residents fleeing. Fifteen men, seething with generations of hatred for their northern countrymen, shot bullets across the lobby. Their Southern counterparts fiercely protected all stairwells to the living areas above.

A spray of bullets erupted from behind both pillars flanking the formerly grand entrance. A man using the barrage as hopeful cover ran through the entrance, past the pillars, and towards the bellman's stand. Three feet past his fellow gunman, he crumbled to the floor. A marksman's bullet had pierced his forehead. He joined four others who met the same fate in the previous fifteen minutes, each attempting to breach the lobby.

The precision of the defending shooters, forehead kill shots every time, confirmed for the Northerners they had reached the right building. This was not merely a rich man's security unit. They were fighting the ruling family's elite core.

These combatants had been fighting some version of the same battle since the king himself had been a teenager, and they fought for his power to rule. The feud was generations old.

The communication leader for the Northerners called the rooftop sniper. They confirmed the presumed identity of the young man in his sites and the others around him were the heirs to the country's power. They had the crown princes in their crosshairs.

Sunlight glistened off the scope of the shooter's rifle. The tallest teenager tensed, looked out the window, registering a threat. The gunfire six floors down was not uncommon to him. Not seeing his father's guards standing on the rooftop across the street was unusual. He began zig zagging across the room, towards the adjoining room's door. His youngest brothers were amused, thinking it's a new game.

Another glint of sunlight from the room. The young man lept to cover his little brothers and yelled at his sisters in the next room to get down. The sniper, having lost his target, took out the window with his first shot. The children dove for cover, screaming in fear.

The nanites detected the fear and distress of the children in danger. A backup gunman two floors below the sniper had little visibility into the prince's room. But with the glass shot out, he followed his earlier orders and fired indiscriminately through the window.

In a random moment, the site of the second gunman's rifle was aimed perfectly at the youngest child in the building. The moment after the trigger was pulled, the Dust jammed the gun. Unseen, the bullet left the chamber faster than the speed of sound. The Dust reacted, calculating the probability it will strike the child at ninety-two percent.

In another time, this morally corrupt human decision to take the life of an innocent child would certainly end the child's life within a second.

The Dust plotted the exact trajectory the bullet was flying, and instantaneously, Dust congregated along the path. As the density of the nanites increased on the bullet's flight, what looked like water vapor surrounded it. The large cone-shaped swarm grew. The drag reduced the speed of the bullet to less than two hundred mph, forcing the arc of the bullet to slump. The child lived to see what the rest of their life will bring. The bullet slowed to the speed of rain falling, and the cone disappeared.

Swarming the scene, nanites engulfed the shooters and jammed their guns' mechanisms. Their arms and legs were bound. The Dust executed similar jamming of weapons for the militias of both factions on the ground floor. The invading forced retreat. A female visitor surprised the startled prince for a brief conversation.

Every battle in this war, every armed skirmish, was snuffed of its violence before it could begin. The prince demanded the two feuding families come together. The old men would talk to each other. The next generation brought them together for a truce. They taught their people that peace was what both families wanted and demanded.

The packed classroom buzzed with students responding to the story. Cameras broadcasting to sociology and anthropology students scattered around the world panned across the space. Whispers between students, their heads bent together in pairs, stirred the intensity hovering in the room.

The oversubscribed class had repeatedly created trending conversations on social media. Elly was pleased when the university agreed to make the course globally available simultaneously. The last eight weeks' dialog had raised the awareness for the origin story of the most peaceful, productive, and creative time in the planet's history.

Elly took in the expectant faces of her students. Many were competing for slots in her Emotions in AI Accelerator Program. They especially needed to understand history and the abuses suffered by so many in the past.

"That was a little over ninety-five years ago. There has been peace in the region since. Every generation of safe children brings a tranquility to the community. The prince's story concludes our evolution across our century and a quarter of the time the world has put children's well-being at the forefront of humanity.

"No child should suffer the trauma of a violent home. It inhibits their health and their progress.

"Globally, we had to achieve equality in education, too. The ability for children to foster their curiosity with answers to every question they can dream builds bright, enthusiastic students like you. You can see that innovation has accelerated across the last five generations.

That's proof that addressing the root issues for children was the right thing to focus upon.

"Dr. Keira Stetson saw what was needed. She believed deeply in the welfare of our children. She took a tremendous risk no one before her would or could by releasing autonomous intelligence into the world. She made it possible to assure that their AI would always make the tough decisions for a positive outcome while considering the ethical ramifications and parameters.

"Keira changed the world for you by putting kids before profits, egos, and power. With a permanent mission of protecting children, she knew that society would realize positive revolutions.

"No more abuse. No more scared, bullied, hungry children. We broke the cycle. The tormented children never grew up to be tortured adults. Educated, informed, confident adults don't feel the need to bully and abuse our youngest citizens. They learn collaboration and peaceful resolutions. They're free to innovate, created and explore. They're inspired to build a better tomorrow. We're living that better tomorrow right now.

"Keira's code and her AI training, creating ethical decision-making within the Dust, blessed us with our safer, enlightened existence. We're greatly indebted to her. I hope this course provided you the insight into the trials and tribulations of reaching this stage.

"She took amazing risks and used her intelligence to solve so many problems. There were times when she was villainized by powerful groups. People feared what she had done when they were prevented from exerting their harmful power over others.

"Then, we saw her brilliance. Her Nobel Peace Prize was the least our society could do to recognize her greatness. It was this democratization of information and safety that launched the turnaround of inequality within our global population.

"I have always wanted to share her story. She doesn't get near the credit she deserves nor has the full origin story to our planet's peace been well-documented. I'm so honored to have been your teacher. Sharing this legend has been meaningful. This is my gift to you and to her."

* * *

Acknowledgments of Thanks

Y ou, the reader! Thank you. If you liked the story, please share *Moral Code* on social media, including Goodreads.

Special thank you to:

Early readers who suffered through my excessive use of commas and other errors from this author-needing-training-wheels:

Brad Bush, Vanessa Ogle, Janette Stell, Charlotte Ryan, Jeff Ryan, Cyndi Winsor

Huge support and cheerleading squad:

Karie Johnson

Lynn Miller

My YPO Lucky 7: Vanessa Ogle, Mark Smith, Vance Detwiler, Kim Montgomery, Brian Hayduck, Matt Coscia

Renegade Book Club: Karie, Kelly, Katherine, Katrina, Charlotte, Vonda and Janet

Line Editor: Jeannette Stell

Developmental Editor: Cherri Randall

William Bernhardt at Red Sneaker Writers, Writer's Digest and Writer's Workshops for their education offerings and community encouragement for authors.

CPSIA information can be obtained
at www.ICGtesting.com
Printed in the USA
JSHW031913290622
27458JS00001B/2